HEROES IN THE EVENING MIST

WILLIAM ASH

Like a dim dream recalled, I curse the long-fled past –
My native soil two and thirty years gone by.
The red flag roused the serf, halberd in hand,
While the despot's black talons held his whip aloft.
Bitter sacrifice strengthens bold resolve
Which dares to make sun and moon shine in new skies.
Happy, I see wave upon wave of paddy and beans,
And all around heroes homebound in the evening mist.

MAO ZEDONG

From the poem Shaoshan Revisited (June 1959)

HEROES IN THE EVENING MIST

WILLIAM ASH

WORKABLE

Heroes In the Evening Mist

First published in 2018 by Workable Books, an imprint of New Internationalist and the General Federation of Trade Unions (GFTU)

New Internationalist
The Old Music Hall
106-108 Cowley Road
Oxford
OX4 1JE
UK
newint.org

GFTU
84 Wood Lane
Quorn
Leicestershire
LE12 8DB
UK
gftu.org.uk

Designed by New Internationalist
Cover design by Juha Sorsa
Cover image by banjongseal324/Thinkstock

Printed by TJ International Ltd, Cornwall, UK, who hold environmental accreditation ISO 14001

British Library Cataloguing-in-Publication Data
A catalogue record for this book is available from the British Library.

Library of Congress Cataloging-in-Publication Data
A catalog record for this book is available from Library of Congress.

ISBN 978-1-78026-473-8
ISBN ebook 978-1-78026-474-5

Foreword

John Callow

Bill Ash crammed the work and the adventures of several lifetimes into a single existence. He was, as he once wrote 'the same age as socialism in the world, having been born a few weeks after the October Revolution' of 1917. He could tell you tales of his childhood friendship, in New Mexico, with an old gunslinger who had fought alongside Billy 'the Kid' in the Lincoln County War. He had been a witness to the Great Depression in Texas; ridden boxcars across the dust bowl; and given up his US passport in order to fight against fascism in Europe, in 1940. Though he denigrated his own talents as a public speaker, he could hold a packed room spellbound with his account of the moment when, as the clouds parted in the midst of a fierce aerial combat above the Channel in February 1942, he suddenly found himself looking straight down the funnels of the Nazi battle cruiser, the *Scharnhorst*. While attention has, quite understandably, focused upon his daring wartime escapes from German prison camps and debate has raged – and will continue to rage – about whether or not he was the model for Steve McQueen's charismatic portrayal of the 'Cooler King' in the 1963 movie of *The Great Escape*, there was much more to him than that.[1] The same sense of anger in the face of injustice, and the almost total disregard for authority, that had marked him out during wartime as an irreconcilable enemy of fascism and equipped him with the grit, determination and guile to be able to survive the Gestapo as well as escapes through the mud of Poland and ruins of Germany, also hallmarked his subsequent career as author, broadcaster and political activist.

The struggle and suffering of the war years; the 60 million deaths and the extermination camps of Auschwitz, Belsen and Dachau, should – he firmly believed – have taught people that they deserved better 'than fear, stupidity and greed' and that, collectively, they could work to re-forge the world and hope to 'soar as well' and as high 'as any Spitfire'[2]. In his own case, an assignment as the BBC's representative in Delhi from 1950 to 1953 familiarised him with the politics of a newly independent India, and also introduced him to 'an entirely different civilization than the Euro-American one I was born into'. Indeed, his BBC office in Connaught Place began to feel like 'a base camp in a strange land from which I could make forays in all directions, discovering the treasures of the written word stemming from the most ancient times and spreading out into some fifteen contemporary languages, each with its own highly developed literature; becoming acquainted with philosophical schools and logical systems quite distinct from anything I had studied in an American or British university; and getting to know something of the rich art of India – [the] marvellous sculpture and frescoes'.[3] At the same time, his cultural discoveries were mirrored by equally significant, and long-lasting, political and personal developments. He met and married a young and extremely gifted academic, Ranjana Sidhanta, and, largely through her example and contacts, discovered Marxism, as embedded in workers' study circles, agrarian co-operatives and characterised by practical, militant, application.

The rooting of Marxism in the praxis of the struggle of colonial peoples for independence, and for economic as well as political justice, appealed to both Ash's intellect and his instincts. It appeared as both the logical extension of the fight for freedom that he had seen waged in Europe from 1939-45 and as a direct and highly effective course of action, calculated to end exploitation at a single stroke. Such experiences and insights, drawn predominantly from Asia, but also informed by the struggles for recognition and dignity of African workers in London, were – if not quite unique – then certainly exceptional within a British labour movement that had tended to think of communism in terms of purely European and, overwhelmingly, Soviet forms of expression. Ash's militancy, preparedness to countenance revolutionary action and his focus upon an agrarian form of communism, rooted in the experiences of the Southern hemisphere, as opposed to the corridors of Moscow, seemed – and, in all probability, was – wholly incomprehensible, iconoclastic and dangerous for the officials of the London district Communist Party of Great Britain. After a cordial, if lengthy, exchange at the offices of the *Daily Worker* on Farringdon Road, he was informed that his application for membership had been declined. True to his wry, puckish sense of humour, Bill recalled that: 'It must be as difficult to get rejected by the CPGB as it is to get sacked by the BBC and I, in a relatively short space of time, had managed both'.[4] Undaunted, he went off and helped to found a rival Communist Party with explicitly revolutionary aims, which eschewed a parliamentary road to Socialism and looked towards the anti-colonial struggles of the developing world for its inspiration[5]. 'Socialist goals,' he noted, 'aren't something we realise under capitalism: they are the fruits of the Socialism we replace capitalism with.'[6]

Despite his marginalisation at – and eventual departure from – the BBC, as the Cold War hardened attitudes and froze many creative arteries, Ash was able to hone his craft as a dramatiser of plays and novels for afternoon slots on the radio, re-working staples from the Brontës and Dickens, but also nurturing, encouraging and commissioning work from a rising new generation of writers like John Arden, Rose Tremain and Faye Weldon. 'There is a sense,' he wrote, 'in which an editor who handles something produced... out of another human being's life experience ought to be as delicate and careful as a heart surgeon. He has to be aware of the influence he is inevitably having on other people just where they are most exposed and vulnerable,'[7] A man of his word, his approach to the texts and the visions of others was always supportive, thoughtful and constructive.

This was in marked contrast to the treatment that his own novels often suffered at the hands of critics. Though Anthony Burgess and Terry Eagleton championed his growing literary output – which would eventually stretch to some ten works of fiction, besides his political writings and adaptations – he was first excoriated and, latterly, ignored by a literary establishment that found both his subject matter and his staccato style of prose difficult, unpalatable or often just simply unfathomable. By the early 1990s, workplace struggles, discussions of the dispossessed and of the distortions wrought, among both peoples and emergent nations, by neoliberalism and the apparent triumph of globalized capital, were hardly fashionable topics for the publishing industry. After all, if the news corporations and even much of academia had stopped defining the nature of imperialism (whether in its cultural, economic or military forms) and were increasingly shy of acknowledging its existence at all, then novelists who insisted upon examining its pathology were scarcely likely to be the flavour of the month. 'If you don't mind me saying so,' opined one commissioning editor – adding to Bill's increasingly large number of rejection letters from the major publishing houses – 'I find some of the issues and themes of the book [*But My Fist is Free*] a trifle dated, and the characters a little bit stereotypical.'[8] Bill's response appears to have been a shrug: 'If your ideas don't cost you something,' he wrote, 'they can't be worth much.'[9]

Ideas mattered to him. They ran through all of his writings, from the first to the last. Indeed, his novels – as one of his most perceptive reviewers thought – were intended 'to be an imaginative testing by fire' of theoretical propositions, that would, in Bill's own words, signify 'the working out in fictional terms of all the political implications of identifying oneself' with a particular cause, a set of choices or a topical debate,[10] His final novel, *Heroes in the Evening Mist* – published here for the first time – was particularly dear to his heart. It reprised some of the themes and characters from his *A Choice of Arms,* published in 1962, but this time his mythical Asian country, Malia – a true 'utopia', or no place, where dreams can be dreamed and human possibilities explored – has shifted, like Michael Moorcock's *Tanelorn,* from an approximation of Malaya to a composite, that – while owing something to his experience of China – is largely rooted in the recent history of Vietnam.

Shortly after returning from India, Bill had stayed in lodgings above a café run, and frequented by, the nascent Vietnamese community in London. He got to know them, 'used to watch films in the basement there of the struggle against the French whom the British had re-installed in Indo-China', and celebrated alongside them as the news of the victory at Dien Bien Phu filtered in through the news wires. He was at the demonstration outside the US embassy in Grosvenor Square, in October 1968, when the police ran amok with their teargas, horses and batons; he chaperoned the delegations sent by Ho Chi Minh's (as yet) unrecognised government to London; organised solidarity campaigns and the first appeal for medical aid to war-torn areas. 'Of all the causes I became identified with,' he wrote, 'Vietnam claimed my most consistent and committed sympathy.' Throughout the 1980s and on into the 1990s, he and Ranjana were conspicuous and honoured guests (she in her colourful saris, he still bolt upright and with his flying officer's silk cravat wrapped about his neck) at the embassy's Tet, or lunar new year, celebrations.

Yet, while old friends remain – systems of government often change. Gradually the veterans of the anti-war campaign, of medical aid for Vietnam, and of the left-wing inspired friendship societies dropped away – through old age or disenchantment – to be replaced by a younger, slicker, more acquisitive breed, in search of contracts, influence and personal advancement from a rapidly liberalising economy. Bill could not have helped but notice the incremental change, or the manner in which – after all the years of sacrifice and bloodshed – the offices of the multinational corporations (including some who bore the guilt of prosecuting the war in Vietnam) began to steal back into the land, disfiguring the skylines of Hanoi and Ho Chi Minh City, through the raising of skyscrapers and vulgar office blocks that signified their resurgent power and presence, as the modern heirs of the old East India Company.[11] The gulf that separated rich and poor began to grow again, the political slogans on the street corners emptied of meaning, and the capitalist worm began to grow fat within the socialist bud.

In essence, therefore, *Heroes in the Evening Mist* is a novel about happens when a revolution 'goes wrong'; when inspiration and idealism atrophy; when the revolutionary impulse dissipates under the deadening hand of bureaucracy; and when the party machine, itself, becomes corrupted by personal greed and petty jealousy. It is certainly a novel about loss: the squandering of a victory, the debasing of a revolution, and the human cost entailed, not least in the wrench of separation felt between a father parted from his young son. However, it is also – perhaps more significantly – a story of love: a love for a people and a love of ideals that are worth fighting for, however much they might be (temporarily) laid low by grubby political realities and expedients. It is, consequently, a novel of renewed hope rather than despair.

Bill was acutely aware of this and may even have been rehearsing the themes that define *Heroes in the Evening Mist* when he composed a circular letter to friends and comrades to welcome in the year 2000. He considered that it was:

> 'very tiresome having to end the year, the century and the millennium to the sound of so much global capitalist triumphalism... We don't need them to tell us that communism, which is true democracy, unlike bourgeois "democracy" which is all they know, cannot be imposed on working people from above. It's something the working class have to be organised to win for themselves. There's plenty we have to go on telling those stooges of the profiteers – not that they'll learn anything from it; but the young people listening in to the debate undoubtedly will... That's rather a lot to expect of us (particularly those as long in the tooth as I am); but there it is – something to unite us in struggle as a new era dawns. Since we can't be bought off, we're bound to get our message through to the right people.'[12]

This book is part of that process – of getting the message of socialism 'through' in the end. For, as Bill knew, ideas are tricky, elusive and thoroughly unpredictable things. They do not respect borders, or authority; they are more durable than gold and worldly fame. They can bring down empires and cause peoples to rise up. They can even remain, hidden away in the pages of an unpublished manuscript until they can have their time again, and emerge, though tested by fire and flame, fully fledged and capable of transforming the world. Rather than being a museum piece, *Heroes in the Evening Mist* is a novel whose time is yet to come.

1 W Ash, *A Red Square: The Autobiography of an Unconventional Revolutionary*, (Howard Baker Press, London, 1978), p 234; W Ash & B Foley, *Under the Wire: The Wartime Memoir of a Spitfire Pilot, legendary escape artist and 'Cooler King'*, (Bantam Press, London, 2005), pp 6-7, 10-20; P Bishop, *The Cooler King: The True Story of William Ash: Spitfire Pilot, POW and WWII's Greatest Escaper*, (Atlantic Books, London, 2015), pp 279-280.

2 W Ash, *Under the Wire*, p 281.

3 Bishopsgate Institute, William Ash Archive, ASH/17, (W Ash, interview with the *Indo-British Review*, 'A Time for Friends', c1991-93).

4 W Ash, *A Red Square*, p 203.

5 Professor George Thomson, who had written two landmark studies of Classical Greece from a Marxist perspective, was a particularly strong intellectual influence upon Bill and Ranjana Ash. See: G Thomson, *From Marx to Mao Tse-Tung: A Study in Revolutionary Dialectics*, (China Policy Study Group, London, 1971), pp 140-141, 150-160.

6 Bishopsgate Institute, William Ash Archive, ASH/17, (W Ash, 'The End of Socialism?' typescript c1990).

7 W Ash, *A Red Square*, pp 225-226.

8 Bishopsgate Institute, William Ash Archive, ASH/17, (letter from Robert McCrum of Faber & Faber to Bill Ash, 6 September 1991).

9 Bishopsgate Institute, William Ash Archive, ASH/17, (scrap note by Bill Ash, c1991-93, later worked into the text of his novel).

10 S Sedley, 'William Ash as a Marxist Novelist', *Marxism Today*, (October 1962), p 317; W Ash, *A Red Square*, p 179.

11 G Kolko, *Vietnam. Anatomy of a Peace*, (Routledge, London, 1977), pp 11, 110-118, 132-143, 154-160; R. Templer, *Shadows and Wind. A View of Modern Vietnam*, (Penguin Books, London, 1998), 286-289, 292-293, 313, 317, 344-346, 354-355.

12 Bishopsgate Institute, William Ash Archive, ASH/29, (circular letter, December 1999).

PART ONE

1

The Dakota dipped in a wide curve below the level of the surrounding hills and straightened for the descent to the single runway. Off to the right, Colin Frere could see the capital city, Rani Kalpur, with the high-domed Government Palace and several newly constructed high office buildings at the centre of town and on the outskirts, shining in the afternoon sun, the magnificent gold-plated spire of the Great Pagoda.

The tyres screeched, the plane bounced once and settled, the application of brakes threw Frere forward against the seat belt. At the end of the runway the Dakota pivoted right around and taxied back to stop on the paved apron in front of the small airport administration building.

The Indian flight steward opened the door and the dozen or so passengers collected their accompanying luggage and began to file out of the plane – a merchant and his family, a government official and his aide, several Europeans who either worked in an international company or held posts in one or other of the embassies, an American woman in her early thirties whom Frere suspected of being, like himself, a journalist. He remained seated until the last of the other passengers had ducked through the door and then, pulling his own bag from the overhead storage bay, climbed down the steps, went inside and tagged on to the end of the queue going through passport control.

He presented his passport to the policeman on duty, who stared intently at the photograph, shot a quick look at Frere, checked the name on the passport against a list of names on a sheet of paper held down by his elbow and then handed the passport to another policeman standing beside the control booth.

This policeman said to Frere, 'Please to follow', and led the way to a door marked Airport Control. The American woman who was waiting with the others turned to watch him as he disappeared through the door.

Inside the room the policeman placed Frere's passport on the desk before a very senior police officer who had two rows of Second World

War ribbons on his tunic. He was about fifty with a spruce, clipped moustache and a distinctly military bearing. He riffled through the passport, pausing over the pages stamped with entry and exit notices, the last being a rather florid visa for Malia dated May 1968 and valid for one month only.

When the officer spoke it was with a spruce, clipped Sandhurst accent purged of any trace of Indomalian: 'You do a lot of travelling, Mr Frere.'

'I'm a foreign correspondent.'

'Do you know why you've been brought into my office?'

'I can guess. But I thought everything had been settled at the High Commission in London when I finally got my visa.'

'That is so; but it seemed only fair to let you know that you'll be under a certain degree of surveillance the whole time you're here.'

'I see.'

'It won't interfere with the purpose you gave for wanting to come to Malia.'

'That's all right then,' Frere shrugged. 'Ten years as an internationally accredited foreign correspondent would be a very lengthy and elaborate subterfuge to cover some purpose other than reporting on Malia's progress since independence.'

'That's what was decided; but you could hardly expect us to treat you just like any other journalist, Mr Frere.'

'Perhaps not.'

'It goes without saying that you'll make no attempt whatsoever to get a bandit's-eye-view of the situation here. Any move to contact the bandits or any of their couriers will result, at the very least, in your immediate deportation.'

'Oh, I understand that.' Frere held out his hand for his passport.

'We'll keep it for you. It will be returned on your departure.'

Frere hesitated a moment and then said with a wry smile: 'Thank you for looking after it for me. I am a bit careless.'

'We're not, Mr Frere – not at all.'

'That's my impression, too – that you can't afford to be.'

The policeman opened the door for him and Frere left the office. The other passengers had gone and his suitcase stood by itself in the customs area. He picked it up and glanced questioningly at the inspector who waved him through the barrier.

He stepped out into the glare and looked around him at a scene made insubstantial by heat waves, shielding his eyes from the sun with his free hand. A battered car painted bright yellow started up in the shade of a mango tree and coughed and spluttered to a point just opposite him. 'Taxi?' the driver asked.

'If that's what you call it,' Frere grinned, opening the door and swinging his suitcase inside. 'Tanners Hotel.'

'You mean Freedom House?'

'I was told in London that it's still Tanners.'

'It says "Tanners" on the sign in front,' the driver admitted; 'and everybody calls it "Tanners"; but it's supposed to be Freedom House.'

'Well,' good-humouredly, 'Freedom House then.'

'Of course, if sir would prefer Tanners.'

'I'm easy. Take me to whichever you fancy yourself.'

At the hotel there was some delay while he explained that his passport was with the police and that he could not remember its number to put on the hotel register. At last, after a good deal of discussion all around, it was agreed that the clerk would get the number of the passport from the police and tell Frere so that Frere in due course could enter it in the register.

Frere practised his Indomalian on the young man who had picked up the suitcase and was leading him up to his room on the second floor, asking him questions about what part of the country his family belonged to and what conditions were like for hotel staff. From the width of the young man's smile after placing the suitcase on a stand it could be supposed that he had been over-tipped.

Frere deposited his clothes in the high teakwood almirah. He lay down on the bed, fingers laced behind his neck, and watched the revolving blades of the large ceiling fan, surmising that this old colonial hotel with its high, whitewashed rooms suited him better than the smarter, fully air-conditioned International which occupied one of the new high buildings in the centre of town. That was not, however, the reason he was staying at Tanners.

Over the next few days he made much of interviewing various middle-rank government officials, visiting the sites of local industries and booking appointments a week or so away with several very senior ministers, including a short session with President Samad himself.

He also did some fairly conspicuous sightseeing: joining a guided tour of Government Palace, which had been the elaborate home of the royal family of Malia before independence had turned them into highly paid pensioners and it into the offices of state; walking around the gold-spired Great Pagoda taking pictures of the brilliant riot of painted gods and daemons.

He was looking through the viewfinder of his camera when he became aware that the attractive American woman who had flown in on the same plane was quickly moving out of the way.

'Please stay where you are,' he looked up to urge. 'You make a very pleasant foreground to a monument I've already taken too many snaps of.' She stood there smiling and then came over to him.

'You're Colin Frere,' she said.

'Have I denied it?' he asked with a smile.

'Well no, but you've certainly made yourself scarce. I thought you'd be staying at the International but your name isn't on the guest list.'

'I'm at the old hotel where everybody used to stay – Tanners.'

'Didn't Somerset Maugham stay there once?'

'I believe he did.'

'The reason I wanted to see you was I thought you might tell me a bit about this country – just as one reporter to another. I've read up on it, of course, but – '

'I doubt if I can help you much. It's my first visit here too, you know.'

'But you know southeast Asia. I've read pieces of yours on Thailand, on Malaysia, on Vietnam – '

'If you'd like to come back to my hotel I could probably tell you everything I know about Malia over tea.'

'Thank you. Does it have to be tea?'

'Oh, I think they could rise to something else.'

'I'm Clare Wallace.' She held out her hand. 'I'm with the *New York Dispatch*.'

'Ah yes. I've read pieces of yours, too.'

He summoned a cycle rickshaw and they were soon sitting in a cool recess of Tanners with two tall iced drinks before them, her fair hair just faintly stirred by the perpetual fan.

She said straight away: 'Your brother Matthew was killed out here, wasn't he? Fighting on the side of the bandits.'

He looked at her a moment. 'I don't know that I'd have put it like that.'

She bit her lip. 'I'm sorry. I said "bandits" because that's the way they're always described officially here. To make my position clear, let me say that I'm totally opposed to my country's war in Vietnam.'

'Good for you.' He lifted his glass in a brief toast.

'It's why,' she added, 'the *Dispatch* won't send me there. They don't seem to mind so much if I'm critical of the way America supported what your government did here.'

'That's something we liberal-minded journalists working for papers in imperialist countries soon learn,' he said with a laugh. 'Our editors can be quite sympathetic to pieces indicting some other country's colonial crimes.'

'Right. The people in imperialist countries ought to be made to read each other's newspapers.' And after a pause, 'Have you come here now because, well, because something's about to happen?'

'I've come here now because this is the first time the Government of Malia has allowed me to enter.'

'But I thought Britain still had a lot of influence out here.'

'It would have been British influence that kept me out.'

'Because of your brother.'

'Yes. Malia was still a colony when my brother Matthew – or Matt as everyone always called him – when Matt was captured by British security forces and murdered. "While trying to escape" was the usual formula for such deaths.'

'Why did the British Government change its mind about letting you come here? Did you finally convince them that you had no sympathy at all with, with – '

'With the real independence movement, you mean – those under the leadership of Secretary General Lee who want real independence for Malia? I think it's more a case of the British Government's deciding that the Malian Liberation Movement is not so much of a threat any more.'

'Do you think they're right?'

He smiled. 'That's what I'm here to try to find out. With all that's going on in Vietnam – '

'Like the Tet Offensive, for example.'

'Exactly. Well, Malian affairs have taken rather a back seat.'

'Have you come as a reporter or as a brother? – to, well, kind of pay your respects to his memory.'

He laughed. 'There can't be any doubt about what you're here as!'

'Sorry if I sound so inquisitive. Would it make any difference if I said my interest is as much personal as professional?'

Colin Frere looked down at his glass and was so long in answering that she must have felt she really had pressed him too hard. 'We weren't all that close, you know,' he said at last. 'There was ten years' difference in our ages. By the time I was old enough for him to take much notice of, he was away at war. His war kept him in this part of the world for years, first in Burma then here in Malia, right up to the time of the Japanese surrender. He was only back home a year before he was off back here again.'

'Didn't you get to know him during that year? I mean he must have had lots of adventures to tell you about.'

'Oh yes, plenty. He was decorated and all that. But he never liked to talk about himself. And we young men who just missed the War, we didn't want to go on hearing about this great event in which we'd played no part.'

'And now you feel guilty about not getting to know him, then?'

'He wasn't an easy person to get to know – Matt. The woman he married during that year he was back and then walked out on – she never really got to know him either, nor why he left her.'

'You thought you might get to know him better if you came out here?'

'I suppose so. I seem to have been circling about Malia for the last ten years, accepting assignments in countries all around it in order to get to know southeast Asia better. I spent several years north of here where Indomalian is spoken, getting to know the language. I'm not fluent but I probably speak and understand it better than most of our colonial administrators here ever did.'

'And now you're here and, incidentally, in a position to be of great help to a colleague who's got just a couple of weeks to learn all about Malia.'

'Ah,' he muttered noncommittally and got up. 'Come. I'll walk you back to your hotel.'

'Isn't it pretty far?'

'Not the way I'll take you.'

He led her through the main bazaar area, which was just coming stridently alive in the early dusk. The fronts of tiny shops had burst open with an explosion of green light from acetylene lamps and had spilled their beautifully crafted goods out for passersby to finger and haggle over. The raucous din of a loudly amplified Hindi film tune was the sound equivalent of the clash of gaudy colours overflowing the counters and the competition of pungent odours from spice and incense shops.

Clare laughed. 'Thank you for bringing me back this way. It's marvellous.'

'Yes, it's fun. Why is it that I quite like this unselfconscious vulgarity and can't stand our own snide world of television ads?'

'I don't know. I hadn't thought about it. Maybe it's because our world of media kitsch permeates everything and there are fewer and fewer of us left outside to criticise it and keep it in place.' She looked around her. 'This wonderful noisy market is so nicely limited to one part of town.'

He glanced aside at her face, eyes alight, lips parted like a child unwrapping a present. 'How did you escape it – that world of kitsch?'

'Have I?'

'To recognise it is to have escaped it.'

'I wanted to be a foreign correspondent – a good one. I wanted to find out things about our world and tell other people. You wouldn't think that would be so much of a challenge to a woman in our day, would you? But it has been. Each time I overcame some obvious form of male chauvinism, I found myself grappling with a subtler form of it. Anyway, to be forced into rebellion, even on such a narrow front, must make you a little bit suspicious of the value system most people around you just take for granted.'

'That must be it.'

'And you?'

'Me? I don't know. I certainly haven't ever rebelled. There's never been anything I wanted enough. Perhaps that's been my problem – not wanting anything much. Nothing with a price tag on it, anyway. And if there was nothing that didn't have one?'

'You sound like some kind of an ascetic.'

'Just apathetic, I'm afraid. Apart from necessities – and my basic needs are simple enough – anything I could acquire just by putting up a certain amount of cash didn't seem worth bothering with. I kept thinking that I was bound to come across something I wanted that wasn't for sale.'

'Well, it sounds like asceticism to me – like one of those desert fathers perched on top of his column, only in southeast Asia instead of north Africa.'

'Those desert fathers found this world disgusting in the light of the other world they knew was to come. But if there is no other world – !'

'Your brother thought there was.'

'Yes. Matt thought so. He died believing it.'

They had walked out of the bazaar and could see her hotel at the end of the street. 'Was he wrong?' Clare asked. 'Was your brother wrong? After all, in spite of the crimes your government committed against this country as a colony, it was going to grant Malia its independence.'

'Only because the liberation movement was growing so strong. And what kind of independence? By vesting political stooges with power and placing the economy in the hands of compradors my government created the illusion of independence. Nothing has changed.'

'Oh, I don't know. Look at the hotel where I'm staying. It could be a hotel anywhere in Europe or north America.'

He stopped and looked at her directly. 'Do you want to see something? If you don't mind quite a bit more of a walk.'

'Try me.'

He turned off to the right and led her past the spacious bungalows with large gardens belonging to senior government officials and well-to-do merchants to a straight road leading from the centre right out to the far edge of town. They walked along this road for a way, past several blocks of flats housing middle-grade civil servants, and beyond that the road narrowed and almost seemed to stop altogether at some strange obstruction not much higher than a man's head but stretching away to right and left as far as they could see. But as they got closer they saw that the road did not stop there: it drove on through a divided Red

Sea of shanty dwellings which threatened on both sides to drown it in miserable humanity. Huts, made of crumbling mud bricks or flattened petrol tins or sacking hung on wooden frames, crowded in out of the dark with only the odd guttering lamp for light. The well-lit road carved a bright swath through the settlement, laying open many of the closest huts for them to look inside.

In some of them women cradled babies too hungry and exhausted to cry and looked up with hopeless stares as they passed. Pot-bellied little children came to the edge of the road and stood there, fingers in their mouths, at this unusual sight of people from the town walking along this road. There were several groups of men in rags huddled together hardly talking at all. Very occasionally they might be passing from one to the other a bidi which glowed briefly as someone took a drag and handed it to the next.

Somewhere a baby was crying, on and on until it lost any semblance of a human sound and then there was another baby taking up the cry and another. Once or twice Clare spoke to the children but they simply stared at her empty-eyed; and once, when she made a compassionate move toward some of them, they ran back into the night.

They heard a car coming and stepped off the road practically into one of the huts as a car from town drove through at speed.

'Good God!' Clare exclaimed. 'They'll kill somebody driving through here like that.'

'I should think they often do.'

She looked down the road after the retreating lights of the car. 'How long does it go on like this?'

'Oh, for several miles.'

'I don't think I can stand any more.'

'I'll take you back to your hotel.'

And when they had moved out of the bustee, she asked: 'If you've never been to Rani Kalpur before, how did you know that awful place existed?'

'It exists on the outskirts of most towns this size all over the colonial world – which means a good deal of Asia and Africa and practically all of Latin America.'

'Yes, I suppose I knew that. I just hadn't seen it so close before.' She remembered the stench. 'I suppose there's no proper waste disposal or anything like that.'

'None.'

'And water?'

'They'll get it from the river, though it probably isn't fit to drink. For those children we saw there will never be enough to eat, to say nothing of medical treatment or education. Very few of them will ever reach their teens. And all that hasn't changed since the granting of what you call independence. Indeed it's probably got worse.'

'Oh, it's too terrible. I can't bear to think about it.'

'But we have to think about it. Our part of the world in its quest for cheap labour has cheapened humanity itself, all over the rest of the world it controls economically. That's what we've been looking at.'

'And all just so that we in America and you in Europe can live our television-ad lives.'

'You could put it like that. The same thing is happening inside our respective countries, too – the rich getting richer and the poor getting poorer. There are the beginnings of what we've just seen here in many of our largest cities. But of course that internal difference hasn't yet reached anything like the catastrophic proportions of the difference between rich metropolitan countries and these poor semi-colonial countries of the capitalist world empire.'

'An empire headed by us,' Clare said quietly.

'I remember the first time I really saw a huge shanty town – it was actually on the outskirts of Mexico City, which was particularly distressing because the people of Mexico had revolted so courageously against their vicious exploitation from the north. I stood there and I could not but think of the merest chance which had got me born in such favourable conditions instead of in that awful wasteland where human life itself has been deprived of value. For our birth in reasonably comfortable circumstances with every chance of leading useful lives we can't claim the slightest moral nor rational responsibility, can we? When we think of it like that, all our achievements are accidental and we've no right to any pride at all.'

'Unless it would be in trying to narrow that awful gulf,' she said. 'Is that why you're here?'

'Sorry, I shouldn't have bothered you with all that. It was just… But here we are at your hotel. You must be exhausted.'

'Not at all; but I am hungry, even if I've no right to be,' she smiled. 'Will you join me for dinner?'

'Thank you, I will.'

The restaurant was on the second floor. They found a table and ordered.

'Were you ever stationed in Mexico?' she asked.

'Only for a few months. Most of the time I've been out here.'

'You must know a lot about it,' she prompted. 'Over dinner I hope you'll share some of that knowledge with me.'

'I have to sing for my supper then?' He laughed.

'That's about it.'

'I think you're going to be short-changed.'

'I'll just have to risk it.'

He told her about how the whole region, in spite of certain national differences in language, dress and customs, had a kind of identity which must have begun with the Indian civilisation washing over it and leaving behind as it subsided Hindu and Buddhist temples, Sanskrit names for many towns and places and a certain pattern of life with strands of a passive idealistic religious philosophy woven through it like saffron-clad monks weaving in and out of a crowd in a bazaar. Superimposed on this multicoloured map were pools of Muslims where Islamic missionaries had brought in a new religion which had flowed into the most stagnant reaches of the old society to be drunk up eagerly by those whose pitiable conditions made them thirstiest for some fresh draught.

And in the towns, of course, there was the overflow of China's millions, industriously handling much of the small trade and coming often to have in the eyes of the people the character of an immediate exploiter who was ethnically distinguishable – like Indian shopkeepers in Africa or Jewish merchants in small mid-western American towns.

'Then came British or French imperialism,' he told her. 'On the divide-and-rule principle they stirred the embers of old racial rivalries and sectarian divisions. When it suited them they fed the flames of communal violence. Unlike previous empires of the flesh or spirit they have raised no marvellous monuments like Angkor Wat or the Golden Pagoda. Instead they spread over the land the characterless buildings of Western commercialism, like those ugly skyscrapers beginning to sprout here.' He broke off suddenly in some embarrassment. 'I'm sorry. It makes me so angry to think about it that I – '

'No, please go on. It's just what I wanted to get from you. Isn't it what America's trying to do in Vietnam?'

'With Britain's help,' he said bitterly. 'The lessons we learned about fighting a guerrilla war in Malaya are put at America's disposal, as are hospital and leave facilities in Hong Kong.'

'Are they going to win?'

'Your Americans?'

'They're not mine personally, remember,' she said a little sharply.

'I don't think so. I believe the revolutionary muezzin that enabled the Chinese People's Army to defeat the American-sponsored Kuomintang has made the Vietnamese unconquerable. And it can be heard also in the Malian jungle up north.'

'Is that why you're here? Are you expecting something to happen?'

He looked around him for a waiter.

'That's all right,' she said. 'It's been put on my hotel bill.'

'I want another cup of coffee.'

She signalled for the waiter and then: 'Do you think those who hear your muezzin will liberate themselves or merely become imprisoned by a new illusion?'

'I've no right to doubt that they can win through to something better than they've had from us. Whenever I start doubting, I'm appalled at the company in which I find myself.'

'Not mine, I assure you, Colin.'

'I know. Won't you let me pay for this?'

'You can buy me a drink up on the top floor.'

Up there were a bar and a spacious lounge which could be used for dances and receptions encased in walls of glass which gave an all-round view of the capital city – the domed Government Palace, the floodlit spire of the Great Pagoda, partially masked by one of the characterless skyscrapers, the bright area of the bazaar and, just beyond it, a huge dark patch like a great black blanket with a few tiny specks of light on it which had been spread over the northern rim of town and the contiguous countryside.

'That's where we were,' Clare said.

'We crept under the near edge of it.'

'It makes me shudder to think about it.'

'It's the price that has to be paid for being part of the capitalist world.'

She lifted her glass in salute and drank. Then she asked: 'Is your hatred of Western imperialism part of your not wanting anything very much?'

'I suppose it is. I was always conscious when I was growing up – whether I was buying sweets from the tuck shop or having a good innings at cricket or taking some girl to a film for the first time – of my brother, Matt, out here somewhere in the jungle, fighting for something he had to believe in very much. Matt living on a handful of rice, Matt burning off leeches, Matt with a couple of bullets in him. I think it had the effect of turning all pleasures slightly sour.'

'Didn't it stop when he was killed?'

'Not altogether. You see, nothing I found in work nor in personal relationships nor in anything, really, seemed to measure up to whatever it was Matt found out here. It was as though I moved only among the things Matt had rejected for something better.'

'So everything became second-best.'

'I suppose so really.'

'And you've come here to write about it?'

'To understand it so that I can write about it. I only have a month.'

'That's enough for me. I only have two weeks. I hope you'll let me benefit from what you learn during that time.'

He put down his glass and looked at his watch.

'Would you like another?' she asked.

'No, I must go.'

They took the lift down to her floor and he walked with her to her room. 'Well, ' he said with a smile, 'good night.'

'Just that?' holding out her hand which he took. 'Is that good enough in the world we live in now? I had my reasons for not letting you into my room all worked out. I think you owe me some explanation for my not getting to use them.'

He kept smiling and did not say anything. She remembered something he had said in the bazaar. 'It can't be because you think there's some kind of a price-tag on me.'

'Not at all. I'm trying to think of how I can be ungallant without its reflecting in the slightest on your attractions.'

'I don't think you are ungallant. Just careful. You want to stay uninvolved. That suggests to me that something is about to happen. Is it?'

'Not yet. It's very generous of you to pretend there's so much you can get from me. You're very clever, Clare. You have the right feelings, too. There's nothing you need from me.'

'All the same, I intend to keep in touch with you while I'm here.'

He gave her hand a squeeze and released it. He turned and walked a few steps down the hall. Then he stopped and turned back.

'I think I'd like to kiss you good night.'

'Yes, I'd like that, Colin.'

He kissed her and, holding her by the shoulders, looked into her eyes. Then he shook his head, smiled and, releasing her, walked down the corridor.

'Good night,' she called after him.

2

The message Colin Frere was expecting was delivered with his coffee early the next morning by the boy who had brought his suitcase up to the room that first day. A small piece of paper folded under the cup had typed on it: 'Vimla is well worth a visit. A coach leaves at 7am and reaches Vimla late in the evening of the following day. Let the police know that you are going there to do some sightseeing and that you will be returning soon to Rani Kalpur. Anyone visiting Vimla will want to sample the excellent food and scented wine at the Inn of Heavenly Delight.'

He informed the hotel of his intention of being away for a few days but told them he wanted to keep his room. He would be leaving his belongings there except for toilet articles and a change of clothing. Perhaps they would be so kind as to inform the police that he was visiting Vimla and would be back by the end of the week.

During that day he was careful to avoid the area around the International Hotel or any place else where he might run into Clare Wallace. He left word at the desk of Tanner's that he was to be called at half past five the next morning.

The day was still fresh when he left the hotel carrying only a BOAC handbag, but it would be hot before noon. He walked to the coach terminal just beyond the bazaar, which was completely quiet at this time of the morning. A queue for the Vimla coach was beginning to form under some trees on the grass verge outside the building.

Against the clear blue sky was the delicate purple tracery of jacaranda blossom. The people around him, mostly women in bright sarongs, kept up a lively scherzo of talk and laughter to a counterpoint of querulous complaints by the hoopoes hopping about on the lawn.

Frere, while looking the other way in order not to seem to be eavesdropping, listened carefully to the women's talk to see how much of it he could follow. English was still a lingua franca in spite of protestations about replacing it with the majority language; but for his purpose Frere had to become completely fluent in Indomalian.

The driver arrived, grinning a little sheepishly over his tardiness, and clambered up into the seat where he signalled that he was ready to take their tickets. Frere hung back as the others climbed on board and began stowing their various belongings in the racks on both sides. He had chosen the single seat in front, across from the driver, as the one he wished to occupy for whatever breeze might sift in around the door.

Just before the coach started there was a heavy banging on this door which, when it was opened, admitted a rather fat, unshaven man who Frere supposed must be the policeman detailed to accompany him. The man shot a look at him and Frere gave him back a broad wink which was at first disconcerting. Then it made the man laugh aloud as though they were in some kind of collusion and he pushed his way to the back of the coach to find a seat.

On its way out of the capital city the coach went along the road dividing the shanty town in two, and Frere was able to see just how extensive this blighted area of miserable poverty really was. Thousands upon thousands of peasant families driven from the land by the changes in farming brought about by the capitalisation of agriculture had collected here to try to survive on the meagre wages of part-time unskilled labour bolstered up by begging. Little flocks of the skeleton--limbed, pot-bellied children would look up as the coach passed and gaze at it out of large unblinking eyes from which they did not seem to have the energy to brush away the flies.

Frere looked around the coach and saw that none of the other passengers, by no means well-off themselves – the well-off in Malia did not travel by public transport – that none of them was paying any attention to the pitiable plight of those all around. Was it that they had got used to the sight or that they were trying to avoid being aware of such appalling conditions that could so easily engulf any of them who fell ill or lost a job or in any way ceased to be of use to those who rode about in motor cars?

He looked at a last group of hungry children as the coach drove out of the bustee and he closed his eyes tightly as if to impress the sight so firmly on his mind that he would never forget it until some change occurred that began to mitigate all that pointless suffering.

The road curved along beside the Andor until the hills were left behind and then roughly followed the river in its straighter path across the plains. At noon and again at evening the coach stopped at a village where there were long wooden tables under the trees. The passengers sat there eating the food they had brought with them or being served bowls of savoury rice and cups of aromatic green tea. It was very hot and not a breath of air stirred the leaves overhead, nor did a single bird or lizard disturb with a flick of motion the heat-arrested scene.

Colin Frere liked the feel of it. He often said he only opened out in the heat – like one of those highly compressed Japanese paper flowers which blossomed exuberantly when dropped in water. He glanced about good-humouredly at his loquacious fellow passengers whom eating did not deter from a constant run of animated talk. Several of them had got sufficiently over their suspicion at finding someone like him in their midst that they smiled at him rather tentatively and, at last, an old woman, finding that he knew Indomalian, entered into conversation with him about the terrible things that were happening to the country when they had all thought it was going to get better. All night the coach drove on, through a darkness rarely interrupted by any light except the scattered lamps of some of the larger villages, and then at dawn they reached Bandhal at the foot of the mountains. Many of the passengers got out here. Then, with a change of drivers, they made their way upward through valleys and passes until, with the setting sun blocked out of sight by a high peak, they arrived at Vimla.

Frere booked in at the only suitable hotel and went up to his room. He stood a while at the window looking down a steep slope that fell over a thousand feet to the bottom of the Andor gorge. The river at this point was only – far, far down – a white-frothed, rock-shredded mountain stream.

He had a shower, put on a clean shirt and threw over his shoulders the jacket he had brought with him for the cool heights. He went out and walked along the main street of the town. The sky was still light behind the nearby saddle-backed peak which in the clear luminous air of evening looked almost close enough to be a suburban feature. Characteristically, the buildings and dwellings were mostly of wood except for some large stone houses on the edge of town which would soon be occupied by well-to-do and politically important citizens from below seeking refuge from the summer heat. There was a rich blossoming everywhere of the elaborate wood-carving which customarily decorated the shops and houses of hill stations.

At the edge of town the main street changed itself into the country road which wound down toward the southern plains. On the side away from the flank of a mountain was the Inn of Heavenly Delight. The fantastically ornamented structure, like something whittled by a Titan out of a huge hardwood block, propped up by none-too-substantial-looking wooden poles, jutted far out over the lip of the gorge.

Frere had a strong inclination to choose a table, few of which were occupied at this early hour, as near the roadside wall as possible; but a round-faced man with a smile as benign as the name of the inn insisted on seating him at a table in a gaily painted bay window, so that he was perched far out over a thousand feet of nothingness. 'We are honoured by your arrival. Will sir have some delicacies and a cup of tea while reflecting on the dinner of his choice?'

'Thank you. But I think I'm going to leave it entirely up to you to decide what would give me the happiest memory of this charming place.'

The man smiled broadly at the challenge. 'It will be something very special.'

As he withdrew, Frere saw the policeman come in, look around the room and spot him in his carved-wood niche. Frere waved. The policeman took a seat where he could watch Frere and beamed back at him, obviously pleased with the expenses he was going to be able to claim for this trip.

Frere nibbled at delicious concoctions and sipped fragrant tea while night turned the mountain peaks black against a starry sky and from deep down in the gorge the sound of rushing water drifted up faintly. Under the third dish of a six-course feast he found his second message, which he slipped quickly into his pocket without letting the policeman see him do it. There was little enough he could consume of the last two or three courses; but he did not like to get up and leave before the policeman had finished what must for him have been a rare treat.

When the policeman stopped eating and sat back with a look of contentment, Frere got up and said to his smiling host that he did not know how any sum at his disposal could possibly pay for such a marvellous meal but all the same –

And his host waved his offer aside with the assurance that such a perfunctory performance on the part of the chef was quite worthless; but if so distinguished a guest should consider coming again... It ended with Frere slipping a wad of Malian currency under a plate, bowing slightly to the genial proprietor and saying good night to the policeman as he went out.

Back in his room after a nightcap at the hotel bar he unfolded the piece of paper. It read: 'Go to the office of Sami Usman opposite the hotel. He is the manager of several enterprises in the region, including a carpet factory in Kotal Bargh, some fifteen miles up the gorge. Tell him you would like to do a story on the carpet factory. He will drive you to Kotal Bargh. Be sure to be in your room at the government tourist house there from 2pm on.'

When Frere walked into the building across from the hotel the next morning, he was expected. A young man greeted him by name and took him straight into the main office. A big man in a Western-style linen suit got up from the desk and came around to shake Frere's hand.

'Welcome. Welcome. Sami Usman, at your service.'

'Mr Usman, I – '

'Call me Sam. Everybody calls me Sam, including the Prime Minister.'

'Right you are, Sam. The thing is, I want to do an article on how some of the local crafts are faring since independence and – '

'And you'd like to have a look at my co-operative carpet factory. So you shall, er – '

'Colin. Call me Colin.'

'So you shall, Colin. Tomorrow morning I'm driving up to Kotal Bargh. You must come with me.'

'Thank you, Sam. There is the problem of the policeman who's been given the job of keeping watch on me.'

Usman laughed. 'Nobody's going to think that anybody in Sam's company has to be watched. I'll take care of the policeman.'

'Splendid.'

'We'll set forth about 9am. Meanwhile, you must have lunch with me at this restaurant of mine which is known far and wide for its excellent Chinese cuisine. But, of course, you dined there last night.'

The next morning when Frere left the hotel, Usman, large panama hat in hand, was waiting for him beside a shiny black Mercedes parked outside his office. 'Right on time,' Usman said. The driver opened the door so that Usman and Frere could sit together in the back seat.

As the car glided smoothly up the narrow street, Usman laughed heartily. 'You're wondering about this car, eh Colin? It was part of an aid deal with West Germany. Ministers and businessmen in Rani Kalpur don't like to be seen living too extravagantly so I took it off their hands – as a favour.' He laughed again. 'I'm always doing people good turns like that.'

Once they were out of town the powerfully purring Mercedes gave Usman's driver an even stronger dose of the aggressive abandon which seemed to infect every Malian behind the wheel of someone else's car. Frere entered into conversation with Usman in order to be less aware of what was happening immediately in front of them – particularly when they were speeding around hairpin bends up a road used also by peasants and straggling flocks of goats.

'How did the carpet factory get its start?'

'The mountain women around here have woven carpets on old hand-looms for many generations. There's a special strain of sheep in these parts that's just right for the job. When a country begins to attract foreign capital for industrialisation, these are the skills that can be lost.

So I suggested to my friends in the Ministry of Economic Development that they ought to let me collect the women together in a suitable place equipped with powered looms, so that they could produce fine carpets on more of a mass scale. Just the thing for export and for the tourist trade.'

'And the enterprise has flourished?'

'If Sam's involved with it, you can bet it's flourishing. Why every journalist and television team doing a report on "Whither the New Malia" visits my carpet factory.'

'I'm glad I'm not setting a new trend,' Frere said.

'In fact, my carpet factory may be the only thing in Malia that really *is* flourishing. One hundred per cent, I mean. Every so often the Government tries to get me to let someone else run my factory while I take a job in one of their ministries; but I always turn them down. I tell them they'd end up with a carpet factory no more successful than the Ministry of Economic Development.'

Frere laughed. 'Do they know you pass your opinion on how badly they're doing to those visiting journalists?'

'Of course. But what can they do? I and my factory are better known all over the world than they are. Every time anybody puts together a magazine programme on Third World development there'll be a couple of shots of my carpet factory. It's the "co-operative" that does it. Makes it sound like something in between out-and-out collectivisation on the one hand and free enterprise on the other. Sam's factory co-op is the answer to communism. All I have to do is hint that it would be too bad if the answer to communism could no longer be heard in Malia and not only does the Government stop criticising anything I do, a lot of foreign governments queue up to give me a helping hand financially.'

'And what about the women who work in the factory?'

'Oh, they love me. They love Sam. They'll work all the hours God made for their Sam.'

'And do you think you have got the answer to communism?'

'That's not what I say. That's what people say who don't like communism. For all I know the communists may be saying that my co-operative carpet factory is the answer to capitalism. Me, I'm just a born organiser. Let either a minister of economic development or a commissar of state industry show me a job of organisation to do and give me room to get on with it and – hey presto! I could produce a dozen factories like that showplace in Kotal Bargh which you're about to see.'

'And you don't mind if I quote what you've been telling me?'

'Of course not, my dear Colin. If you put together all the quotations that have been attributed to me by all the reporters and foreign delegates I've been interviewed by, the worst you could charge me with is being all things to all men. But isn't that what any religious leader or successful businessman tries to be?' Frere laughed.

'The one lesson for capitalist West or communist East,' Usman added, 'for industrialised North or developing South is simply: "it pays to advertise". Get yourself known. It's not only good for your product; it makes it harder for them – whoever they may be – to act against you.'

'I'll try to remember that, Sam.'

They drove directly to the factory, which was a new white-washed bulbous building clinging to the slope below the little town like a huge human-made wasp nest. 'I designed it,' Usman admitted as the car stopped in a parking space hollowed out of the hillside.

As they approached, some tired-looking women workers were marshalled into two lines on each side of the pavement leading to the main entrance. 'Smile!' a young man who must be a kind of foreman urged them in the local dialect. 'Look happy!' And one or two of them did manage perfunctory little waves of greeting.

Inside, more of the women formed a semicircle around Usman and his guest. The young man hastily withdrew from this welcoming group some workers who were mere children and shooed them away. A young woman stepped forward and put garlands around the necks of Usman and Frere.

When Usman patted the girl's cheek paternally, there was a camera flash indicating that the visit would get its proper mead of publicity. He spoke to them, saying how glad he was to be with them again, how they were not working for him but with him for the good of Malia and how they were all to receive a little bonus to mark the occasion.

They applauded and were then ushered back to the looms on the floor below. The tour of the factory was an extravagant exercise in public relations, with Usman's personal photographer snapping pictures of Frere leaning over the shoulder of a woman at one of the looms, making up a pattern with one of the women designers which was then punched out on a small computer and having tea in the factory canteen surrounded by women who by this time were able to make a better show of appreciating their good fortune in working there.

And just in case Frere might be getting the idea that the factory was more for the purpose of publicising Usman than actually producing carpets, he was presented at the end of the tour with a beautiful, prayer-mat-size example of their automated handiwork.

They drove to the government tourist house where Frere was booked in for a night's stay. Then they had a very good lunch, including lamb cooked in a way the district was famous for. Afterwards Frere looked at his watch and said he would quite like to have a bit of a rest in his room before doing anything else. Usman agreed so readily that Frere almost thought he might be in on the scheme. 'Of course, my dear Colin. I have some work I want to do at the factory and then I'll pick you up later in the afternoon.'

From his room on the first floor Frere could look down on the town square, the fountain in the centre and the police post on the other side. The brightness of the early afternoon sun and the emptiness occasioned by the heat made it look like a film set. And when it all began, it seemed to Frere like a movie being made – the actions of the men in green attacking the police post had that kind of careful deliberation of actors and the few townspeople in the square behaved like bystanders as though a film were being shot on location.

What shook Frere into a sense of the reality of what was happening and a recollection that it had something to do with him was the burst of a grenade in the doorway of the police post. The door and part of the adjacent wall lifted away from the building and then came the sharp crack of the explosion. One of the men in green trotted forward and lobbed another grenade through the gaping entranceway and then moved back into line with the three others as there was a dull boom inside.

Three policemen rushed out and, seeing the four attackers with assault rifles pointing straight at them, threw down their weapons and held up their hands. A shot came from a window and attracted a burst of fire from one of the men in green. A policeman whose chest was bloody stumbled out of the gaping doorway and fell face down.

Two of the men in green then entered the building and there was a muffled burst of fire inside. Several minutes later they came out, assault rifles slung over their shoulders, arms filled with machine guns and ammunition belts which they piled near the fountain. One of them looked at his watch and a few seconds after that there was a huge boom inside the police post and the roof caved in, sending up a cloud of dust and smoke.

Suddenly, behind Frere, the door of his room burst open. He spun around, hands gripping the window ledge behind him, and saw a small wiry man with a large pistol in his hand and a big grin on his face.

'Are you the reporter?' the man asked.

'I'm the reporter,' Frere answered with relief.

'Come.'

Frere followed him along the corridor, down the stairs and out through the empty kitchen. Behind the tourist house were servants' quarters and in back of those a path climbed steeply up, through fir trees, to the ridge which bristled above the town. Frere was soon panting as he kept up with a guide who, by his thickly moulded calves and corded neck muscles, must have been one of the mountain men, used to carrying heavy loads suspended from bands around their foreheads straight up the steepest slopes. The man turned his head every so often to make sure Frere was close behind, smiled companionably and strode on rapidly upwards.

Frere was just beginning to think he would have to ask to be allowed to rest a bit when the man disappeared. He had turned off into the trees and entered a hut which could not be seen from the path. Frere pushed aside the sacking curtaining the doorway and went in too, blinking to accustom his eyes to the interior gloom.

Two others were in that dark room – a large man with a beard, big chested and heavily paunched like a sumo wrestler, the butt of a machine pistol sticking out of his belt, and a lithe young man with a rifle in his hand and bandoleers crossed over his shoulders.

'Here he is,' the mountain man said gaily.

'Well done, Kuk,' the young man complimented him.

There was a flash of white teeth in the matted, grey-streaked beard and the big man said to Frere with a resonant chuckle: 'Consider yourself captured by a detachment of the People's Liberation Army.'

'I think I'd rather consider myself liberated from the Puppet Government,' Frere responded with a laugh and shook hands with each of them.

The big man, who enjoyed an easy authority, said: 'I welcome you, Comrade Frere, on behalf of the Central Committee of the Communist Party of Malia.' Then he added in a more personal way: 'I was a close friend of your brother's. Matt Frere was a great man and a great fighter.'

Moved, Frere grasped this man's hand again and held it firmly a moment. The big man nodded toward the slender young guerrilla. 'Somewhere under all that armament is Comrade Ahmed. He will accompany you back to our base camp. The man who brought you here from the tourist house is Comrade Kuk. He will be your guide till you're out of the mountains. I won't be going with you. I have to attend a briefing session of our Bandhal cell and will return to base by a different route – very likely arriving there in time to be part of the official welcoming committee.' Frere recognised the polite reference to the fact that he would probably slow up the party he was with.

The big man slapped Ahmed on the shoulder. 'Take good care of our honoured guest.' He gave a raised fist salute to Kuk, parted the sacking over the door and was gone.

Frere stood there a moment looking at the place where he had disappeared. 'Was that the great Kuan?' he asked Ahmed.

'You've heard about Comrade Kuan then?'

'Oh yes. His exploits against the Japanese and then against our British imperialist forces after the War were legendary. We haven't heard so much of him since independence.'

'Everything we do is much more secret since our phoney independence. Besides, the Puppet Government would never advertise our successes.'

'No. Of course not.' Frere shook his head in a kind of wonder. After all these years he had finally managed to cross a divide and find himself moving among the people of his brother's world, that world which had always been his too, but only in his imagination.

He looked at Ahmed and at Kuk. He smiled and shook his head again at finding in these two strangers members of what he could only regard as some kind of brotherhood. 'What do we do now?' he asked them.

'Now,' Ahmed explained, 'we turn ourselves into merchants.'

Kuk brushed the dirt away from boards covering a compartment under the floor. He took out several loose nondescript garments such as an itinerant band of traders might wear.

Frere put on the one handed him and did a couple of turns like a model in a dress show. Ahmed donned his as well, arranging the folds to cover the bandoleers and suspended rifle. He reached down in the compartment and brought up a revolver, which he gave to Frere.

'You won't need it, but, well, just in case – '

Frere looked at the arms carried by the other two. 'It keeps me from feeling under-dressed,' he said.

'That's the safety catch there.'

'Oh, I can handle a Webley,' Frere assured him with a laugh. 'This must be one of the weapons my own country has supplied you with.' He flicked the catch on and off with his thumb, checked to see if there were bullets in the gun and dropped it into the pocket of his jacket underneath the robe.

'You can pull the burnous over your head when we're moving in the open,' Ahmed explained – 'to conceal your Western-style haircut.'

'What am I supposed to be selling?'

'You'll see,' Ahmed said with a grin. He motioned to Kuk who led the way out of the hut and up over the crest of the ridge.

In a hollow halfway down the slope on the other side there were four donkeys with loaded panniers and the men Frere recognised as having carried out the attack on the police post.

Ahmed introduced Frere to them and they made him feel welcome at once by showing that they knew who he was and were glad to see him. Then Ahmed lifted the canvas covering of one of the panniers, which was full of weapons and ammunition that had been 'liberated'.

'That's what you're peddling,' Ahmed told him, 'if anyone should get close enough to ask. But they won't. Goh Tun will see to that.' And pointing to the guerrilla who had led the attack. 'That's Goh Tun.'

Frere shook this sturdy young man's hand and Goh Tun said: 'I'm honoured to meet Matt Frere's brother.'

'Goh Tun and his band,' Ahmed explained, 'will be just out of sight and never far away from you. They will discourage anyone from getting close enough to inspect our wares.'

'A pity. I rather fancied my chances of becoming a rich arms dealer.'

'Well,' Ahmed said, 'let's be on our way.'

Goh Tun and the rest of his little group disappeared into the stand of high pines and, with Kuk leading the way with one of the donkeys, Frere and Ahmed, driving the other three donkeys before them, walked along behind.

3

At night, while two members of the guerrilla band were always on guard, the other three would join Frere, Ahmed and Kuk for an evening meal before they all turned in early in order to be on their way again at first light. Two of the group were brothers, still in their teens, who came from the high plateau country in the far northwest. They were Meis and spoke very broken Indomalian. Ahmed gave them lessons whenever the opportunity presented itself and Frere let it be known that he would be glad to benefit from such instruction himself. Sometimes on the march, circumstances permitting, the two brothers would walk with Frere, helping him drive the donkeys and all practising their Indomalian together, while Kuk laughed mightily at their mistakes and corrected them in his own mountain accent. Frere became very friendly with Ahmed, whose extreme courtesy suggested that he belonged to one of the older landowning Muslim families. Ahmed explained to him that quite a number of those who went inside came from wealthy and important families.

'"Going inside",' Frere took it up. 'That means joining the active liberation fighters in the jungle base camp?'

'That's right.'

'When did you go inside, Ahmed?' Obviously referring to his youth.

'Only about a year ago. In another year I'll have done my active service stint and it will be decided whether I go back into the world again or stay on for a further period at base camp.'

Frere looked puzzled.

'You see,' Ahmed explained, 'there's a regular pattern now for young people who join the Party to do a couple of years "inside" and then go back into ordinary life again. Many of us are recruited as trainees while we're still at school. We attend study meetings where we learn about Marxism and we're given jobs to do – running errands and delivering messages, collecting things needed for those at base camp, distributing leaflets and the Party paper.'

'I read *Das Vani* whenever I can get hold of a copy. It's the way I acquired my reading knowledge of Indomalian.'

'Then when we become full Party members we "go inside" for two years to learn how to shoot and how to maintain weapons, we study guerrilla tactics and begin to take part in actual operations.' He looked at Frere and said modestly: 'This is my third.'

'I'm glad I'm in the charge of such a veteran.'

Ahmed laughed. 'Well, Comrade Kuan was really in command until the raid was successfully carried out by Goh Tun's band. But I'm responsible for getting you back to base camp safely.'

'May I wish you the very best of luck then in your present venture! Tell me, how old is Kuan?'

'A lot older than he looks. It's one of his jokes that if the enemy have had all this time to hit a target his size and have failed to do so, how can they possibly hope to win?'

'Isn't he very important to have come on a mission like this?'

'Oh, Kuan's important all right – a founder member of the Party and one of the original band that first went inside with Secretary General Lee in 1947. The reason he came on this Kotal Bargh operation was to welcome you in the name of the Central Committee.'

'I see.' And then: 'I had no idea such weight would be given to my visit – which means that I did not fully appreciate the standing my brother enjoyed.'

'Comrade Matt was one of that original band too. We learn about him when we're studying the history of the Party.'

'It must be very unusual – for a citizen of the imperialist country to be so prominent in the anti-imperialist struggle.'

'It may be unique. It says a lot about your brother.'

'And about Secretary General Lee also.'

'Indeed.'

'But you were saying something about returning to the world outside.'

'After our guerrilla training most of us go back to take jobs and join in the life of our semi-colonial country – as field operators for one of the big foreign companies or as junior officers in the state administration, as factory bench hands or teachers or members of the village service teams. Anything that keeps us in touch with workers and peasants and young people generally.'

'But is that so easy – to disappear for a year or so and then go back and walk into a job?'

'It's getting easier all the time,' Ahmed answered with a laugh. 'It gets easier as more and more of the personnel managers, school inspectors, village service directors and even some army officers and security police are themselves people who have done their spell inside. They're just waiting for the day when we all, inside and outside, can wear quite openly the same green caps with the red star on the bill.'

'But I still don't see –'

'How we come and go? There are organisations – most of them associated with British colonial rule – like the Boy Scouts and Girl Guides or various religious youth movements, Christian, Buddhist or Muslim, which are really exit and entry points for dropping out of ordinary life and then returning to it. In fact,' Ahmed laughed again, 'it's the size and vitality of these youth movements that help to convince foreign businessmen with capital to invest that Malia's a stable society.'

Frere laughed too. 'And there I was thinking that the whole insurrectionary force had been whittled down to a few thousand hard-core guerrilla veterans penned up in the deep jungle straddling the frontier.'

'Things did get bad for us for a time when we were granted nominal independence. It was all staged with such pomp and ceremony that many people were taken in for a while. But Secretary General Lee knew how quickly that corrupt gang installed in the People's Palace would expose themselves. The Party was ready to take advantage of the disaffection that became apparent within months of their taking over. Of course, I was only a schoolboy then. There are those at base camp who can give you a detailed account of how the infiltration scheme was started and how successful it's been.'

Frere looked at him curiously. 'You know, Ahmed, you talk to me very freely.'

'I was told as part of my briefing that you were to be treated as one of our movement's closest friends. Comrade Lee himself issued that instruction.'

'I see. What's he like, Secretary General Lee?' Ahmed hesitated. 'That's rather a large order. Just tell me how he strikes a young man like you.'

'Well, he seems to speak especially to youth. He tells us: "The world is yours as well as ours, but ultimately, of course, it is yours. You young people, so full of vigour and life, are like the early-morning sun. Our hopes for Malia's future rise with you." That's what he says to us. But then I've heard old men say that he speaks especially to them. You could say he speaks especially to all who have joined the movement, to women as well as to men. Women themselves, of course, say more to them than to men. They say he has talked to women as no leader ever has before. He seems sometimes to speak especially to us who have been to a university. He's a great poet, you know. But he seems to speak just as especially to illiterate peasants; and his speeches are often illustrated with the most homely folk wisdom. Factory workers, farm labourers, all when they listen to him have the look of someone in the closest conversation with an intimate friend.'

'All things to all men, you might say.'

'Hah! You who have seen how he's described by the newspapers of this country and of your own know better than that.'

'What makes it possible for him to speak to people like that?'

'I think it's his profound love for this land.'

'So he's a nationalist.'

'He's an internationalist. He says we must unite with the working class of all the capitalist countries to overthrow imperialism, which is their enemy too. But he also says that all patriotic Malians must want above everything else to liberate their own country. Wait a minute. I'll read you just what he says.' Ahmed reached under the folds of his robe and brought out a little book which he thumbed through and quickly found what he wanted. 'He says: "In wars of national liberation, patriotism is applied internationalism."'

'What's that book?'

'It's a collection of Secretary General Lee's observations on various aspects of our struggle. I carry it with me always. Most of us do.'

Ahmed handed him the book and Frere riffled through the pages. 'I'd like to read it,' he said. 'Do you suppose anyone has a spare copy?'

'Take mine.'

'I couldn't do that.'

'I'll get another copy when we get back to base camp. I almost know it by heart anyway. I'd like you to take it.'

'Thank you, Comrade Ahmed. I'll keep it as my own. Will you write something in it for me?'

Frere returned the little book and handed him a biro. Ahmed thought for a moment and wrote on the flyleaf: 'To my English friend who has helped me understand who the enemy is – one we share.'

Frere read the words and smiled. 'That says rather a lot.'

'Too much?' Ahmed asked with a raised eyebrow.

'No-o-o-o,' Frere answered thoughtfully.

Ahmed looked at the biro before returning it.

'And you must keep that from me,' Frere told him.

Throughout the second day and during the morning of the third they were descending gradually through thick pine forest from the high ridge on which Kotal Bargh was perched. In the afternoon they emerged from the trees and saw before them a broad strange valley running north and south as far as the eye could see.

The valley was of karst which had been lifted by some great geologic upthrust and then carved into fantastic shapes by the sculpturing winds and waters. The river Gandhal, which for hundreds of thousands of years had been the main agent of this weird landscape, curved lazily among huge limestone monoliths towering hundreds of feet in the air like a tired old artist relaxing among the great creations of his youth and middle period.

A little way upstream these mighty obelisks rearing abruptly out of the paddy fields on each side of the river clustered thickly in a forest of stone peaks, each honeycombed with hollows and caves, rounded off by the erosion of centuries and softened by a green mantle of plant life sprouting from wind-blown seedlings – so that they looked like a monstrous Manhattan of carious skyscrapers.

Nearer to where they stood on the rim of the valley was a massive chunk of rock so perforated and tunnelled by water eating into the carbonate stone, so oddly shaped by wind and rain scouring its outer surface that Frere was reminded of a temple he had seen in India, carved out of a stone mountain by human hands working away over the years to remove all the material in excess of the shape the holy place was to have. This whole valley was like that, but on an infinitely vaster scale and sculpted to some mysterious design that could only seem wildly chimerical to the human eye.

'Magnificent,' Frere said a little breathlessly to Ahmed. 'But isn't it – in spite of all those marvellous rock towers – a little open for us to move across in daylight?'

'Not the way we go.'

They went down a barely discernible path which headed straight for that extravagantly moulded rock. A deep cleft ran from top to base and at the bottom of this perpendicular wound there was a thick growth of saw grass and bamboo.

The Mei brothers plunged into this tangle and parted it to let the donkeys be driven toward the rock wall where they simply disappeared. Following Ahmed, Frere soon saw that there was a mouth in the rock admitting them to a cave which had been dug out of the stone thousands of years ago when the river had been at a higher level.

They walked stiff-legged down a steep slope to a place where Ahmed felt along a ledge and found the switch to turn on a row of dim lights glimmering away through a wonderland of limestone stalactites and glistening columns and folded sheets of stone like great tinted curtains in some long hall where no breeze stirred.

It was as though the fantastic formations rearing out of the earth above were here turned upside down in a mirror world of dependent shapes. The way through this jungle of gleaming rock spires and dripping icicles of stone, beneath ceilings black with bats, was reasonably level and they made good time driving the donkeys before them until the slippery-looking rock floor slanted up toward a now-visible hole of light. Ahmed switched off the lights and with utter blackness behind them they continued toward that glow ahead, coming out fairly close to low wooded hills on the other side of the awesome valley.

Frere turned to look back, where the tops of the giant monuments caught the horizontal yellow rays of the dying sun. They stood there majestically, rising up out of the paddy fields which were squared off in workable plots. 'It's like a huge chess board,' he murmured to Ahmed. 'With colossal pieces set out to be played with by gods or devils.'

'It's called the Garden of the Asuras, that place. There's a saying about it. No one goes out of the Garden of the Asuras as he went in.'

'I can believe it,' Frere said. 'I have a feeling that having come into your land by that gate I may never go out again.'

The closer they got to base camp the denser the jungle became. There was no longer any need for the guerrilla fighters to provide protection as outposts for the tiny caravan. They joined Frere and Ahmed – Kuk having already left them when they came out of the mountains – and together they pushed along a path that was only recognisable as such to those thoroughly familiar with its tortuous route.

Frere had the opportunity now of getting to know Goh Tun, who had led the guerrilla band in the attack on the police post. This young man was intimidating to look at, having a heavily pock-marked face down one side of which ran a deep scar from hairline to jawline, just sparing the eye; but he grinned a lot and turned out to be very amiable. Ahmed had told Frere that Goh Tun was one of the toughest and most resourceful of the younger liberation fighters and had already been decorated for bravery several times.

'And will you also be going back into the outside world at some stage?' Frere asked him.

It made Goh Tun laugh. 'Me? With this face! It's too well known. I belong to the jungle.' He thought for a moment and added without a touch of self-pity: 'I never leave the jungle. We know each other, the jungle and I.'

Ahmed said: 'Comrade Goh Tun got that wound from the sabre of an imperial officer in the old days. When he was just a boy he was one of a group of protesting peasants ridden down by cavalrymen.'

'I got my own back a few years later,' Goh Tun said with a laugh. 'One of the imperialist soldiers raped a woman in our village and I killed him with a mattock.'

'And that's when you went inside?'

'Well, not at once. They caught me, you see. But they did not kill me straight away. That's where they made a mistake. They put me on trial instead and were going to hang me. Then they made another mistake. They wanted everybody to know about it and my picture was posted up all over the country as an example.'

'And what happened?' Frere asked.

Ahmed took up the story. 'One of Secretary General Lee's first followers, Comrade Tuck, saw the picture and decided that Goh Tun was just like the boy he'd been himself. Nothing would do but that he'd mount an attack to free Goh Tun a few days before the scheduled hanging.'

'I remember my brother mentioning Tuck,' Frere said.

Goh Tun placed his finger on the scar. 'Comrade Tuck said I was marked for the revolution and had to be saved for it.'

Two days later they crossed a sluggish, shallow, reed-choked stream which seeped rather than flowed through the matted jungle and reached the outskirts of the base camp. A member of the guerrilla band led the donkeys away to approach the camp by an easier but more circuitous route which passed by the supply depot. Ahmed and Goh Tun from this point on frequently consulted each other to make sure they were following the current unmined path to the camp's main entrance. Soon they began passing outposts where the exchange of challenge and correct response for the day was followed by light banter about what they had been doing on their tour outside.

The jungle headquarters of the Communist Party of Malia had been referred to often enough in news stories about this part of the world, without ever having been seen by any of those reporting on it, to have acquired a somewhat legendary character. Whatever Colin Frere expected, the actuality struck him as at once grander and at the same time simpler than anything he had speculatively imagined.

At a height of some fifty feet above the ground there was a continuous roof of closely woven reeds and vines, waterproofed with resin, which spread over several acres. Under this roof all secondary growth had been cleared away, leaving only the boles of the larger trees sustaining the whole structure, like the columns of a limitless arboreal cathedral stretching away in all directions.

Set in this expansive roof were naked low-power light bulbs, always lit, which gave the whole area the subdued look of permanent dawn or dusk. There was also, circulating continuously, a very light breeze, cooled by sprinklers in the roof at regular intervals; and under these sprinklers were moist patches of earth where edible tubers and fungi grew.

The power for the giant-bladed fans which kept the air gently moving and for the lights which glowed permanently Frere associated with a perpetual hum to be heard on the camp's northern boundary which proved to be, in fact, the sound of two primitive petrol engines functioning in tandem.

The water for the sprinklers and for general camp use from gravity-operated taps at various places was supplied by several large rain-catching reservoirs above the roof. And above that, Frere was told, thick-leaved, vine-threaded upper branches met and intertwined in a great green live spread that covered the whole camp and shielded it from the sight of even low-flying spotter planes.

It was all rather like, Frere decided, one of those science-fiction cities under a great dome of glass, with artificially controlled lighting and atmosphere – only here that same futuristic effect had been achieved by many hands working together over the years with the most natural materials and processes.

Within the area covered by the vast roof there were numerous huts made of lattices lashed together and plaited with reeds. They were grouped around a dozen or so communal centres where larger buildings served as store rooms and meeting halls. In the centre of camp was an open space called the Red Quadrangle where the whole personnel could assemble, with at one end a high platform from which announcements and speeches could be made and at the other end the camp hospital. It reminded Frere of a university with the various colleges clustered around an administrative core where they could be fused into unity at need without losing their separate identity.

Goh Tun and those who had been with him in the Kotal Bargh attack went off to the operations hut to make their report. Ahmed led Frere to his own commune, where some twenty-five or thirty people, mostly young, were having their evening meal at a table made up of long planks supported by a pair of trestles. They got up and stood there as Ahmed announced: 'Fellow members of the June Tenth Commune. You all know about Comrade Frere, one of the heroes of our struggle. This is his brother.'

Somebody clapped and there was a round of applause. Frere assumed it was for Matt and joined in the clapping. They smiled at him and saluted him with raised fists and made him feel completely welcome.

A young woman asked: 'Won't you join us for supper?'

Ahmed laughed. 'It isn't exactly Tanners, of course.'

'Your hospitality is worth five stars, at least,' Frere said.

A place was made for him across the table from Ahmed and next to the young woman who had spoken to him. She said: 'I'll get some food for you and Comrade Ahmed.'

'Please don't disturb yourself. Can't we get it ourselves?'

'Tonight you are our honoured guest.' She slipped nimbly from the table and came back shortly with two bowls of hot soup which she set down before Frere and Ahmed. Then she brought them two tin plates of rice with tiny portions of some kind of fowl. Frere drank some of the soup and ate heartily of the food.

'Is it all right?' she asked.

'It's just fine.'

'Walking here from Kotal Bargh is pretty good sauce,' Ahmed said.

When they had finished the young woman went away again and returned with a great pot of green tea from which she helped all those at the table who held out their cups. She took her place beside Frere once more, saying, 'Our Commune is proud that you are staying with us. My name is Leela.'

He looked at her and for a moment was speechless. Then he managed: 'I am Colin.'

'Coleen?'

'Well, that's close enough. Is it,' he hesitated nervously, 'is it your job to wait on the comrades of this Commune?'

Ahmed laughed. 'We all take on that duty by turns. Comrade Leela is a graduate of the University of Rani Kalpur.'

'I'm sorry,' Frere apologised quickly. 'I didn't mean – '

To help him over his embarrassment Leela said with a smile: 'If you are with us long enough, you will take your turn also at waiting on the comrades and cleaning up afterwards. But tonight you are our distinguished guest, the brother of Comrade Matt, invited here by Secretary General Lee.'

'Thank you.' He glanced at the huts grouped around them. 'Why is it called the June Tenth Commune?'

'It was on June Tenth, 1946, that a demonstration in Rani Kalpur was fired on by the colonial police, killing fifteen young comrades. All the communes are named after important dates in the history of our liberation movement.'

'I see.' Frere glanced at the small shapely hand resting beside her cup. 'You must have come here straight from the university.'

'Oh? And just how old do you think I am?' she asked with amusement.

'About twenty?'

'I'm twenty-eight.' She laughed. 'A veteran.'

'Comrade Leela is one of the regulars,' Ahmed explained – 'one of those who do not go back to the outside world. She runs one of the Marxist study workshops. She is also an excellent shot and has taken part in armed operations against the enemy.'

Leela turned away with a slight frown at this praise, giving Frere the opportunity of studying her more closely. From under her peaked cap with the red star on it short thick black hair curled against her cheek and the line of her cheek curved gracefully down to the full swell of exquisitely shaped lips. Thick dark lashes were lowered modestly and just the faintest little quiver, as when a child keeps her eyes closed against an impulse to look, agitated the tender lids. But, oh, that melodic sweep of the line from cheek to lips, like the dying fall of a beautiful adagio!

The olive-green jacket and slacks did not give a very accurate account of her figure – except that it was slender and firm. But what Frere mainly took in, with a sharp sense of the kind of wild incongruities a radical political movement could encompass rationally, was the idea of those small tapering fingers of that delicate-looking hand beside her cup squeezing off bursts from a heavy assault rifle.

He had been struck by Leela's beauty the instant he saw her. And then he had wondered if it was not the excitement of arriving at the base camp, of being among those who had lived and fought beside Matt, of having come successfully through the first stage of this dangerous enterprise of his which had singled out one of these Malian women, who tend anyway to be quite lovely, and endowed her with exceptional beauty. That was why he looked away and then looked back again to see if the charm of the situation had not misled him.

'If I'm here long enough to take on the duty of waiting on the comrades and washing dishes, perhaps – well, maybe I could sit in on one of your lectures in Marxism.'

'There are no lectures such as you may be used to in your Western universities,' she told him. 'We are learning to liberate philosophy from the classrooms and the text books so that it may become a useful tool and a sharp weapon in the hands of our people.'

Then, drawing any sting out of what she had said with the most charming smile, she got up and carried on with the tasks it was her current duty to perform.

Frere asked Ahmed: 'Was that a snub?'

Ahmed laughed. 'That was Comrade Leela telling you firmly but kindly that here at base camp there's no, what-do-you-call-it, flirting?'

'Well, I've certainly never thought of myself as a flirt,' Frere said somewhat ruefully. 'But if I'm here any length of time I may have to change my mind about myself in many respects.' He looked at Leela as she collected plates and cups. He shook his head a little sadly for the way beauty of any kind inevitably makes one think of the evanescence of everything.

'You must be tired, comrade,' Ahmed said sympathetically.

'Exhausted,' Frere admitted. 'I'm absolutely exhausted. It's moving through the thick jungle around the camp – I was floundering about like a non-swimmer thrown in at the deep end.'

'It's a knack – like everything. With practice one's body slides through the undergrowth like a snake instead of flailing about like a blind langur – I'll take you to our sleeping quarters.'

They entered one of the thatched huts which had three-tiered bunks along two sides providing accommodation for six people. Frere was to find that, while there were other types of housing, including separate huts for married couples with children, all, whether for Central Committee members or for the newest recruits to the movement, were alike in their extreme simplicity and in having no locks, bars, or bolts of any kind and no lockers, chests or containers for individual belongings. Personal possessions everyone had, but nothing private in the sense of being unknown to others.

And yet at the same time as there was this complete openness throughout the camp, as though to allow the same fresh communal breeze to blow gently on them all, there was adequate provision for the most fastidious privacy in respect to bodily functions. There were shower compartments near the running-water taps and scrupulously clean latrines hollowed out of the jungle all around.

The circumstances of many diverse people thrown together in a fortuitous intimacy under the banyan tree-like roof of the camp – all held there by the same high purpose of founding a just and decent society whose character must be anticipated by the community of those who were to establish it – was bound to entail certain taboos generally acceptable. Before going to sleep Frere thought with embarrassment about his gaffe with Leela in blundering into one of those taboos. He really had been interested in attending one of her classes but he supposed it sounded like some male anywhere in the world trying to date a pretty girl. And on his first night in this place he had been trying to get to for years!

He threw himself fiercely on his other side in an attempt to force this stupid mistake out of his mind and did manage for a few minutes to see that lovely face serenely unruffled by anything he might have said before physical exhaustion plunged him into deep sleep.

4

Frere could judge what the journey to the base camp must have cost him physically from the soundness of his sleep on a not-very-soft mattress of rushes from early the evening before until right up to the stirrings of his hut-mates at dawn. Goh Tun, whom he had not seen since their arrival, was one of these. Ahmed introduced him to two others, both very young men who were doing their military training inside before returning to play some part or other in the semi-colonial, capitalist society which was the 'official' Malia.

While they were waiting for someone, they talked to Frere about what they would probably do in that Malia outside while it lasted. They told him some of the current jokes about the extent to which it was only the crypto-communists in the state administration who were propping up the rickety structure. 'If you meet an official or a policeman who won't take a bribe, he's certainly one of us'; or 'The only soldiers who can shoot straight are, fortunately, those who are secretly on our side'.

They told Frere about whom it was they were waiting for – the veteran comrade who presided over the June Tenth Commune and who shared their living quarters but was away at present attending an early morning session in the operations hut.

'He's taking us out on a training exercise.'

'Tell me about him,' Frere requested.

'Oh he's one of the great veterans of the movement. He must be at least fifty, but he's as tough and resilient as any of our young recruits. There isn't a major campaign since the mid-Forties he hasn't been in on. He knows everything there is to be known about weapons and guerrilla tactics.'

'Peasant stock and absolutely unbeatable,' the other said with an admiring shake of his head. 'Has a terrific sense of humour, too. Things that would scare most of us to death just make him laugh. He – ' The young man broke off quickly at a sign from Ahmed and a sturdily built middle-aged man strode into the hut. He looked around him and then broke into loud laughter. 'Talking about me behind my back, eh?'

He walked over to confront Frere, laughed again and put out his hand, which Frere shook warmly. The man said: 'You must be Comrade Frere. Sorry I missed you when you arrived. I was at a meeting which we had to finish off this morning.'

'And you must be Comrade Tuck,' Frere said.

'You see,' turning to the others, 'my fame has spread to the world outside. He spotted me at once.'

'My brother told me a lot about you.'

'Ah, Comrade Matt. We were very close, you know. I was with him on the last operation he led.' He grinned broadly, disclosing a front tooth of gold.

'Yes, Matt described you to me perfectly.'

'Did he mention my gold tooth?' Tuck opened his mouth and snapped the tooth with a forefinger. 'It may be the most famous tooth in Malia.'

'Tell him how you got it,' one of the young men urged.

'During the War when we were fighting the Japanese, I knew this Tommy who would bet on anything. "Put your money where your mouth is" he was always saying. So after the War when I got a windfall that's exactly what I did.'

Frere laughed. 'I'd like you to tell me about that last operation of my brother's.'

'Oh, we'll talk. These young fellows will tell you, I like to talk about the time when we first came inside. They'll volunteer for anything to get out of listening. But now,' he looked around with a chuckle, 'now there's somebody here who *wants* me to talk about the old days.'

'That'll be nice for you both,' Ahmed said with a smile.

'Oh,' with a wink at Frere, 'I don't think our English comrade will mind if you join him when I'm talking about our victory at Param Belor, for instance.'

'Which we know every detail of,' one of the young men said good humouredly – 'it being one of the seven model guerrilla operations we have to study carefully.'

'For that, my boy, you can show our guest around the camp till lunchtime.'

'Is showing me about the camp such a punishment then?' Frere asked playfully.

'Missing his turn firing at the butts is Salmi's punishment,' Tuck answered. 'That's what all the young men like doing best. I have to keep reminding them that "power may grow out of the barrel of a gun, but the Party rules the gun, the gun doesn't rule the Party". They don't want to admit that there's a lot more to making a revolution than knowing how to shoot.'

'I'm sorry to be doing you out of your turn,' Frere said.

'That's all right,' Salmi assured him. 'He'll probably think of something worse for the others.'

'Just remember when you're showing our English comrade around,' Tuck said light-heartedly, 'it's no use you telling him bad things about me. He's not going to believe you when he knows all about me from his own brother.'

After a breakfast of rice cakes and tea Salmi led Frere about the camp, pointing out proudly various ingenious devices for their general comfort and security. Frere would stop from time to time to study more carefully some mechanical arrangement like the intricate system of buckets on a chain worked by donkeys driven around a circle and used during the dry season to top up the water tanks from wells or the application of some scientific technique like the chemical means used to keep the water potable and the air breathable in spite of the hazards of so many people living in such a confined space.

'People come inside from all over the country,' Salmi explained. 'If they come from villages, they bring with them a knowledge of primitive hydraulics learned from many generations of making water work for them in the paddy fields. If they come from town they know about germs and chemical hygiene. We learn from each other, mixing the old and the new in a common reservoir, like those tanks up there, on which we can all draw.'

That sort of social process was apparent in the large, clean sick bay which had attached to it a small but well-equipped operating theatre. There was a dispensary stocking everything from the latest sulpha drugs to such, for Frere, fantastic remedies as tiny dried frogs.

Salmi told him how they were constantly hearing of plants or practices that were supposed to be therapeutic and how tests were carried out to sort those that were old wives' cures from those that were old wives' tales. 'But the same thing must happen in your country.'

'I'm afraid not,' Frere told him. 'Such remedies would be too cheap for it to be worth anybody's while to make them available.'

'Of course, the best remedy of all,' Salmi said, 'is to catch ailments before they get a start. There's a health card here for everybody in camp and we have check-ups every three months.'

'We've been promised preventive medicine for years but we never get sufficiently ahead of the game for it to be installed. What about those wounded in action? Is that operating theatre – '

'Oh yes. It's fully functional. We always have several skilled surgeons here.'

Frere expressed interest in the facilities for propaganda and was taken to the place where the weekly newspaper was produced. There was a small litho press and a plate-making machine, both of which had been smuggled in part by part and assembled inside the structure raised to house activities in connection with publishing the Party paper, *Das Vani*, and also leaflets and posters as required.

Separated from the printing room by a bamboo curtain was an editorial office containing a large round teakwood table with three people, including an older man who seemed to be in charge, sitting at it. They had been in animated discussion but stopped and got to their feet as Salmi and Frere entered. The older man knocked his cup off the table with his elbow as he rose. 'I'm always doing that,' he explained.

Salmi told them that Colin Frere was a guest of the Party and a foreign correspondent for a London newspaper.

'Oh, we know all about Comrade Frere,' the older man said. 'You're very welcome.'

Frere shook hands with each of them.

'In fact,' the older man went on, 'we are to have the honour of an extended visit from Comrade Frere when we shall be glad to tell him all about our work here.' He made a sweepingly inclusive gesture which swept to the floor a file of photographs from the shelf behind him. 'Don't bother. We'll pick them up later.'

'When I was in Rani Kalpur,' Frere said, 'there were several shops where I could get copies of *Das Vani* from under the counter, as it were. Is it like that all over Malia?'

'Oh yes,' the young woman of the group told him. 'Even though it's a serious crime to sell it, or even to be caught with it in one's possession, the Puppet Government has practically ceased trying to stamp it out.'

'They say,' the young man remarked with a laugh, 'that there's a secret circulation within the administrative offices themselves because *Das Vani* provides the only reliable information there is about conditions in the rural areas or even what actually happened in the latest encounter between our forces and theirs.'

Frere said he would wait for his official visit with them to find out more about what they were doing, and they said how much they looked forward to being able to talk to him and perhaps even to ask for his advice about improving the quality of their work.

After that Salmi showed Frere something of the elaborate defence works surrounding the camp. He was struck again by the complete trust everybody showed in him – going far beyond any mere briefing that would enable him to write well-informed articles about the status of the liberation struggle in Malia.

In one of the command posts he was shown how the defence system was controlled to allow the coming and going of individuals on various missions or the passage of regular patrols setting out for those parts of the country under the influence of the Communist Party. The alarm system set off by any alien intrusion was explained to him. He even had spread before him a map of the thickly sown minefields radiating outwards for more than ten miles in all directions. Safe pathways through them were changed often enough to render any plan which might fall into the wrong hands useless.

'Do you mean to say I walked through all that when I staggered into camp yesterday?' Frere asked in amazement.

Salmi laughed. 'You were in good hands. Goh Tun, in fact, could take you through quite safely blindfolded.'

'Are there ever any accidents to your own people?'

'Very, very rarely. I can't remember one.'

'I suppose the possibility of being blown to pieces does wonderfully concentrate the mind.'

That afternoon Frere was taken by Comrade Tuck to the office of the Central Committee of the Communist Party of Malia, housed in a grass-roofed bamboo structure no different from the propaganda or operational huts except for its location in the very middle of the compound.

Tuck led him inside, where seven men sat in chairs like those of students with oblong writing surfaces fixed to the right arm. The chairs were arranged in a rough circle, thus obviating any question of rank and Frere only recognised Secretary General Lee from the pictures he had seen of that kindly ascetic face.

They stood up and each shook hands as he went around the circle, being greeted with a deep chuckle by the huge, bearded Kuan whom he had met at Kotal Bargh and by a quizzical look from a man with dark, opaque eyes, lank hair still, for all his age, pitch black and drooping wisp of a moustache who must be the one his brother had spoken about called Ang. The others were cordial in their greeting; but no names were given him on presentation – out of a lifelong habit they all shared of not making too free with real names. Indeed, throughout the movement the names by which certain comrades became best known and were to go down in history were appellations assumed along the way for the purpose of concealing their true identity.

Lee smiled gently at Frere and gestured for him to take the one empty chair in the circle. Then he turned his benevolent look on Tuck.

'Do you wish to stay with us, Comrade Tuck, or would you prefer to be doing something useful with your beloved weapons?'

Tuck grinned. 'The Comrade Secretary General knows what I'd prefer so well that no chair has been provided for me.'

'Have you talked to our English friend about that last operation in which his brother took part?'

'Not yet. Not yet. But I will. I will.' Then with a sly glance at Kuan and the man Frere had assumed to be Ang:

'I'll let others tell their version of it. Then I'll tell Comrade Colin what really happened.' With a wave of his hand and a last laugh he turned and left.

Lee said to Frere: 'You are very welcome. I hope our means of getting you here haven't been too risky or too uncomfortable.'

'Not at all. I felt perfectly safe at all times, and everyone connected with my "capture" has been most considerate.'

'You'll be glad to know that we've already declared our responsibility for your disappearance. Our news release said that we found out about your visit to Kotal Bargh and decided to capture you so that you would have first-hand knowledge of the aims and methods of our movement.'

'But are people going to believe that I didn't arrange to be in the right place to be captured?'

'Your visit to the Government Carpet Co-operative was official and was covered in their own newspaper – with pictures.' Lee looked around the circle and a small man wearing glasses held out a copy of a newspaper, folded to show a photo of Frere and a beaming Usman surrounded by women workers.

'Besides,' Lee continued, 'we have given further credibility to the story of your capture being entirely our idea by stating that you will not be released until an article about the Malian Liberation Movement, written by you, is published in the Puppet Government-sponsored newspaper in this country and syndicated by the news agency you work for.'

'But won't they say that you've simply dictated what I was to say?'

'Not if we're going to release you on the fulfilment of their part of the bargain. You would simply say that you had been coerced into writing about us as you had. No, we have made it clear in setting forth our terms that you will be free to see what you like, talk to whom you please and write what you wish.'

Frere thought about it a moment and then looked at Lee with a smile. 'What can I say, except thank you? I got word to you many months ago that I wanted to come here, meet you all, find out as much as possible about the liberation struggle and still be able to leave afterwards and carry on with my journalistic profession in a normal way. You seem to have thought of everything. Except possibly –'

'Yes?' Lee's eyebrows lifted slightly.

'Except,' Frere said with a laugh, 'thinking that delaying my release is going to put pressure on the agency I work for. There have been times recently when they'd have paid a substantial sum to break my contract and get rid of me.'

'Ah, but that was before you became known worldwide for having been captured by the Malian bandits.'

'Of course. You turn me into a nine-days' news wonder to command the widest possible audience both here and abroad for what I write about you.'

'That's it,' Lee said gaily. 'Not only will it get good coverage for your article: it will ensure the acceptance and marketability of the book you will undoubtedly write on your return.'

'True enough,' Frere acknowledged the likelihood of such a venture; 'And yet – well, don't you think that my being Matt's brother somewhat discredits any claim that I was not in collusion with my captors? Won't it also cast doubt on the objectivity of what I write about a movement he gave his life for?'

Big-bearded Kuan answered that. 'We considered that, Comrade Colin. What we mainly concluded was that being the brother of the notorious Matt Frere would give what you said about us even more publicity. Furthermore, the more subtle of them will make us seem thoroughly disreputable in capturing and holding for a price the brother of someone who died for our cause.'

'You know them very well,' Frere said.

'We've been fighting them a long time.'

'The question for us, ' Lee said, 'was whether we could manage things in such a way that you could go back into your world again without suffering any disadvantage.'

'Yes, I think I can,' adding with a smile: 'You've had a lot of practice in placing people back in the world – people who will serve in some way the cause you're committed to.'

Lee laughed. 'Comrade Colin has seen through us. But it's a good bargain: you get the publicity which will sell the book you're going to write: we get the advantage of having a good account of our movement made available to young and progressive people in different countries. One hand washes the other.' He looked good-humouredly around the circle of faces.

'A very good bargain! Perhaps there *is* a bit of the bandit in us.'

'In me too,' Frere laughed, 'if I'm to turn it all into a bestseller.' And after a thoughtful pause: 'And how do you know that what I write will be favourable? Is it confidence born of the fact that I'm Matt's brother?'

'The confidence is in ourselves. We know that any reasonable and fair-minded person – '

'Such as we know you are from reading what you've written about this part of the world,' Ang put in – 'that any such person who has the opportunity of getting to know us well and to understand our determination to liberate our people from imperialist oppression will see that our means are just.'

'We are Malia's only hope,' Kuan said – 'as communism is the only hope of any of the colonial and semi-colonial peoples.'

'Let me ask you a question,' Lee said, as if they were now considering a new aspect of Frere's sojourn among them. 'Did you first propose coming to see us to learn more about your brother, enough to write a book about *him*, perhaps? Or was it not also to learn more about us, to learn what it was that drew your brother to our side?'

'Both,' Frere answered at once. 'The two things are inseparable.'

'That's what we thought. So we say to you now: feel free to ask anyone in this base camp anything you want to know. If you think that, on questions of policy, the comrades of the Central Committee might be the most helpful, approach any of us. But do not hesitate to ask anyone you like what they think of what we've told you.' He looked around the group and they all nodded in affirmation.

'Comrade Kuan you've already met,' Lee said. 'Comrade Ang you must also talk with. He, too, was with your brother just before he was wounded and captured.'

The man with lank black hair Frere had already identified nodded just perceptibly. 'Yes, I would appreciate that,' he said rather gravely and then surprised Frere by adding: 'You may help me to understand Comrade Matt even better.'

Lee then said: 'In finding out what you want to know, you may also find out things you want to criticise or comment on. It would be helpful to us if you would tell us about them.'

'From someone with so little experience of the actual waging of an insurrectionary war, wouldn't that be impertinent?'

'No, a fresh look. You might spot something we've missed. Have you, for example, seen our propaganda centre? Have you met Comrade Chin, the editor?'

'I looked in this morning, briefly.'

'We want you to study this branch of our activity and let us have your opinion of it. We intend very soon to publish a monthly magazine, in English, which will be our account to working-class organisations all over the world of what we're doing here in Malia. We have got so much from the West, Marxism itself, that we ought to render in return our account of the results of applying a Marxist line to our conditions here.'

'I'd be very interested in hearing about such a publication.'

'We'd particularly like your criticism of the standard of English we're using.'

'Of course.'

'That will be very satisfactory for me,' the round-shouldered, bespectacled man who had shown Frere the newspaper photo said dryly. 'My name is Hadar. I'm the Commissar for Propaganda. I want you to get to know the comrades who produce our weekly newspaper. We would be very glad to benefit from your criticism of our clumsy efforts.'

Frere nodded without being convinced that in this case his views were being all that urgently sought nor quite knowing whether it was toward his own staff or toward this foreigner that Hadar was being a bit patronising.

Those who had not been specifically designated nonetheless entered into friendly exchanges with Frere; and then Lee, by way of ending the meeting of welcome, said: 'In the next day or so I'd like you to come to my own private – ' he paused an instant to stress the word humorously – 'hut where I can take up several other matters with you.'

'Certainly.'

'Perhaps I ought to warn you in advance,' Lee said with a smile, 'that we Asian communists make rather a thing of frugality and those of us who have any authority wished on us are expected to outdo all others in this respect. So don't – '

'That's hardly a true account of the matter,' one of them interrupted. 'We have to plot against the Comrade Secretary General constantly to keep him from adopting on his own an asceticism actually dangerous to his health.'

'Still,' Lee continued imperturbably to Frere, 'if you can put up with the Spartan character of my quarters and the fare I can offer you, we can have a useful informal chat. There are several things I can tell you and one important thing I'm going to ask of you.'

'Do ask it of me now.'

'In good time. In good time.'

'Well, there's certainly a lot I want to ask you – and foreign correspondents are used to roughing it, you know. Indeed our copy rises in value to the extent that we can boast of discomforts in obtaining it.'

Kuan heaved his great bulk erect and announced that he would like to take their English friend to operational headquarters. 'I can show him on the map exactly where Comrade Matt was captured.'

As Frere accompanied Kuan to a structure not far from the Central

Committee pavilion he asked: 'Were you close to my brother?'

'As close as anyone,' Kuan answered after a pause. 'I don't think anyone was all that close to Matt, except Lee perhaps – and Anna of course.'

'That would be Anna Lau, who was hanged?'

'Yes.' Kuan's voice went hard. 'Your government did that. They took that lovely young patriot out of a cell at dawn and they strung her up! But,' he added with a triumphant laugh, 'they never did anything like that again. The reaction throughout the country, indeed, throughout the world, rattled their teeth for them, I can tell you. It made them all the more eager to get out of Malia and leave their native stooges to run it for them.'

'Matt was difficult to get to know, then.'

'He never seemed able to let himself go. He always seemed to be holding something back. Not out of meanness. He was the most generous of men, giving everything he had freely – even his life. But there seemed to be something inside him he held back because he had never made it his to give.'

'He was not at ease with himself.'

'That's it. He was not at ease with himself; therefore he was never altogether at ease with others, with us who loved him and respected him and would have done anything to put him at his ease.'

Almost as if he wanted to relieve Kuan and the other comrades of any feeling of not having done enough to give his brother a sense of inner peace before he was killed, Frere said: 'Matt was like that with me, too – his own brother. Something in him, for which he did not seem to be entirely responsible, got between him and others.'

'Sometimes we thought it was just the way Englishmen are.'

'No. There was more to it than that.'

'I guess there has to be. No other Englishman has ever thrown his lot in with us the way Comrade Matt did.' And with a look at Frere, 'Not up to now anyway.'

A single liberation fighter in his red-starred cap, machine gun cradled in one arm, stood at the entrance of the operations hut. He raised his fist in salute as Kuan stopped in front of him.

'This is a friend of the Party's from England,' Kuan explained. 'He can go where he likes, Comrade, and should be given any help he asks for.' The soldier grinned and extended his hand in the western form of courtesy. Frere shook it warmly and grinned back.

The main feature of the room they entered was a large metal cabinet with deep shelves on which large maps could be kept flat, protected by close-fitting doors from insects and damp. Kuan pulled out one of the large ordnance maps.

'This is something we're grateful to your government for. They were made to enable the imperialist troops to keep us in order while our land was ransacked: we use them to take our land back. They cover the whole country and with them we can plan an attack anywhere down to the last detail.'

'And that's the key to guerrilla victory – careful planning.'

'The key to victory is morale. That may be one of Comrade Lee's greatest contributions to revolutionary theory – the overwhelming importance of morale. But of course the knowledge that all our operations are carefully planned by those with plenty of practice in guerrilla struggle enhances morale.'

'Yes, of course.'

'Men are more important than weapons. To start with, we had no weapons but those we took from the enemy – '

And now?'

'Now, it's true, we get weapons from both the Soviet Union and China; but only because we have proved that we can win, that those fighting a just war like ours must win, that a people's war, involving workers and peasants, men, women and children, is always a just war and that a just war is invincible. The American troops pouring into Vietnam have the most powerful weapons in the world – and the lowest morale. Nothing can save them from humiliating defeat.'

'How often are major guerrilla operations carried out these days?'

'It's not so much the frequency as the absolute decisiveness of each engagement that counts. As we move toward a qualitative change in the character of our liberation war we have to raise our own morale to the highest pitch while completely demoralising the enemy.'

'I see.'

'In an earlier phase of the struggle, when Comrade Matt was in action with us, we used guerrilla tactics just to survive. We had, at all costs, to avoid confrontation with a large enemy force; but we had, at the same time, to launch attacks, like the last one your brother was engaged in, to capture the arms we so desperately needed and sometimes the cost was too high. It's different now. We use guerrilla tactics to tilt the balance more firmly in our favour before going over to the strategy of all-out positional warfare. These days we never go into action except when we can concentrate such forces at a particular point that we have something like a five-to-one advantage. The initiative is entirely with us. We fight when we choose and the result is always the same – very light to no casualties at all for us, annihilation for the enemy. Now that enemy only has to glimpse a red-starred cap moving through the undergrowth or hear the strains of the Internationale on one of our jungle amplifiers to be thrown into panic.'

'What I don't understand is why a major assault, including massive aerial bombardment, strongly backed by Britain and the United States, hasn't been launched against your base here.'

Kuan grinned. 'I've mentioned one reason. Vietnam. The US is getting bogged down there and doesn't dare get involved in military adventures anywhere else. And as for Britain, the government knows the British people wouldn't stand for a large scale re-involvement of British troops here after the granting of nominal independence. It would be Suez all over again.'

'But surely the Puppet Government has been supplied with the arms for such an attack.'

'Oh, it has been. And they've been provided with the funds for acquiring arms elsewhere as well. But such is the corruption in the relationship between any imperialist power and its semi-colonial territories that much of the so-called defence fund finds its way into the private pockets of businessmen there and compradors here. Those arms which are actually bought and delivered are often unsuitable for the kind of war that's being fought and those that are useful aren't properly maintained. Aircraft and tanks rust away in hangars and depots. Bombs and shells and small arms ammunition are stored so insecurely that we usually manage to blow up at least one huge dump as part of the general merrymaking in connection with the Great Spring Festival or Christmas or Eid.'

'That's jolly! But haven't I read from time to time that Malia and her northern neighbour were planning to launch a joint attack on this camp which straddles the border between them?'

'They do mount such attacks occasionally but mainly to try to convince the West that they're doing something about the menace of communism. Remember, it's very difficult for two semi-colonial countries to be on good terms. They're in competition for aid and it suits the imperialists to keep them divided and suspicious of each other. In joint operations each thinks the other is skimping and quietly cuts back its own effort. On one occasion,' Kuan said with a deep rumble of laughter, 'we arranged for their two armed forces to wage a week-long battle with each other, thinking on each side that they were hotly engaged with us while we were right here in camp, listening to the distant gunfire and cheering when our scouts brought in news of some particularly bloody exchange.'

Kuan beckoned Frere to his side and pointed at the map he had spread out on the table. 'Do you see that clearing in the jungle, not far from the village of Param Belor? On that last operation your brother took part in we surrounded a whole company of imperialist troops there, just after arms and supplies had been dropped to them from the air. Comrade Matt had staged an ambush near Khangtu itself and led the hot pursuit force across the swamps, over the Black Escarpment and right into our jaws, there!' Stabbing at the place on the map with a blunt finger. 'It was one of the worst defeats ever suffered by Loring, who's a general on the Imperial Defence Staff now, I believe. But it cost us the life of our comrade, your brother. He was wounded and captured, as you know. The story is that Loring himself shot Comrade Matt in a rage at having been made such a fool of.'

5

Kuan took Frere to the entrance of the operations hut. 'I have some work to do here. You're staying in Comrade Tuck's Commune, I believe.'

'Yes. The June Tenth.'

'Can you find your way back there all right?'

'I can. And thank you for telling me about my brother.'

It was the first time since his arrival that he had been left quite on his own, free to wander where he would and see what he pleased. And it was a Central Committee member himself, the great guerrilla leader, Kuan, a legend in that part of the world, who with a cordial farewell had bestowed on him this freedom.

It was partly their tribute to Matt, he supposed, that they would not be seen by so much as the slightest precaution to have any doubts about him. But it was also that supreme confidence in themselves derived from the conviction that theirs was indeed a just war and, therefore, invincible. Was such a conviction not a little like the faith of warriors on jihad for whom the very possibility of defeat had been ruled out by heaven's will, merely substituting for 'Allah is with us' the equally talismanic 'History is on our side'?

That, in fact, was just what it was not like. It was not an article of faith but a formulation of reason that people's war, which by its very nature could not be waged aggressively in someone else's land, was just. It was a demonstrable truth that the consciousness of fighting a just war was a powerful weapon to be found in the arsenals of ordinary people everywhere, no matter how poor or oppressed. The people who took up that weapon were not the pawns of history: they had begun to make history themselves – even if their development through class struggle to the point where they revolted was entirely historic.

But there was something else at the back of Frere's mind about the latitude allowed him. Was it not becoming something to do with him, with Colin Frere in his own right, and not simply with him as the brother of an heroic comrade? Did it not represent in anticipation the way they would treat him if he should become something more than a foreign correspondent professionally exploiting a chance relationship with them? There was that one thing Secretary General Lee had spoken of wanting to ask him.

Almost as if that reflection had called it into being, the propaganda hut appeared before him as he rounded a corner. Attracted by the sound of copy being hammered out on typewriters, he drew near the door, was seen and invited to enter.

The young woman and the young man Frere had seen that morning were typing articles in the romanised script which had been established about the turn of the century. Two other young people were laying out the four-page weekly paper on slanted glazed-glass screens, lit by lights underneath to make the guide lines show through the large sheets of paper.

The young woman who had asked him in told him he was welcome to look around. 'We're getting the pages ready for making the plates,' she explained. The plate-making equipment was on the other side of the room from the press. 'We'll be printing tomorrow morning.'

This was a world Frere knew something about and he stood there with a faint smile for the satisfaction of knowing that in some forms of liberation struggle he could participate usefully.

The older man wearing glasses pushed through the bamboo curtain from the editorial room, knocking his glasses askew on his nose in the process. He straightened them with a finger of the hand that was not clutching corrected copy. When he saw Frere, he held out his other hand, dropping the pages of copy and banging his head on the edge of a table when he stooped to pick them up.

'Are you hurt?' Frere asked.

'Not at all. I do that several times every day.'

'It's Comrade Chin, isn't it?'

'Yes. Yes. It's good to have you back with us so soon. I hope my young friends have received you courteously.'

'Indeed they have. They've explained that they were just putting the next issue of *Das Vani* to bed.'

Chin peered over the young man's shoulder at the front page and read a bit of the lead story. 'That's rather good,' he said – 'that piece telling us into whose pockets the aid from Britain actually goes.'

'You wrote it yourself, Comrade Chin.'

'Oh did I?' in some confusion. 'There are probably some mistakes in it then. I hope you checked it carefully.'

'Everything you said was confirmed by the latest information we've had from Rani Kalpur.'

To Frere Chin said: 'We've been bringing out *Das Vani* for six years now. It almost produces itself. There's plenty of material. We have people high up in army and government circles who leak all the scandals to us.'

'I've often wished an English version of it could circulate in Britain.'

'Great care is taken to see that it doesn't! It's probably too localised, anyway, to appeal to anyone who doesn't have your special interest in Malia. That's why there's this project of bringing out a periodical called *Workers' World* – something which would be of interest to workers everywhere. Militant workers, of course.'

'Yes, Hadar mentioned it when I was seen by the Central Committee.'

'We're supposed to have the first issue ready soon,' Chin said gloomily.

'There are problems?'

'I may be the problem,' with a despairing shake of his head. 'I taught English for many years, at the King Edward School and at the University. But teaching young people to speak English and appreciate the great English writers isn't quite the same as addressing a worldwide audience of workers.'

'Don't worry about it,' Frere told him. 'I wrote articles for a trade union journal for a time. The only people who ever criticised the language were employers who complained that the style was too high-flown for industrial workers to understand. People can usually understand anything they're convinced it's in their interest to understand. Still, if you think it would help if I – '

'Oh I wish you would, dear friend. I've been told you might be willing to look at some of the articles we've collected for that first issue.'

'Comrade Hadar did mention such a possibility and I'd be glad to – '

'To read them and tell us what you think? Excellent! Excellent! Comrade Hadar has been somewhat contemptuous of my own efforts so far.'

'As the employers were of mine,' Frere observed with a laugh.

Chin was not sure that he ought to join in the laugh but he looked enormously relieved at the offer of help. 'That copy I spread over the floor just now is intended for that first issue. I've just been proofreading it. If you *would* just have a look at it.'

'Of course.' Frere accepted the galleys of four or five articles and rolled them up. The young woman gave him a rubber band to put around them.

'Would you like a cup of tea?' Chin asked gratefully.

'If you're all having some,' Frere answered. He walked over and looked at the completed front page, with the big black *Das Vani* heading and, in the top right hand corner, the Party insignia of crossed rifle and mattock within a five-pointed star.

'Are most of the articles written by the comrades in camp?'

'They come from all over the country. Some of them have to be rewritten, of course. The editorial is usually supplied by Comrade Hadar who has discussed it with the Central Committee. But if we have an idea for an editorial we can submit it to him for approval. There's a regular column devoted to the words of Secretary General Lee which we compile among ourselves – drawing on extracts from his speeches or from papers he has circulated among us. Chips from his revolutionary workshop, we might call them.'

'Several of the comrades have shown me a little book of quotations under various headings which they carry with them at all times.'

'Yes, we made that up by going through a number of issues and picking out the best and most relevant of the Secretary General's remarks. Then with his amendments and additions we printed many thousands of copies. Sympathisers in other countries have heard about them and are asking for copies for themselves.'

'There will be lots more orders,' Frere said, 'when you begin distributing *Workers' World*.'

'All the comrades in base camp are encouraged to write articles, even though only a few of them will actually be used. They write about the world situation or aspects of our own struggle in Malia or even about things that happen here in camp. Secretary General Lee always says we can understand better what we're doing and how it fits into the whole scheme of liberation if we have wrestled with concepts and made words convey to comrades the essence of some task we're responsible for.'

'It's a good discipline,' Frere agreed. 'We often think we know something till we have to write an account of it others can understand.'

'You must write something for *Das Vani* about what you've seen here,' Chin urged.

'When I think I understand it,' Frere temporised.

He said goodbye to the young people, shaking each of them by the hand, and he told Chin he would be back soon with his comments on the articles in English he was taking away with him. 'Only as to their language, of course.'

'Why wouldn't you comment on their content as well, if you thought some point was politically questionable or not well substantiated? After all, *Workers' World* is intended for readers like you.'

'Well,' Frere reflected, 'perhaps I might wish to discuss certain issues – but only to learn more myself about the views held here.'

Chin smiled. 'You speak as though all of us here hold exactly the same views.' He turned to the young people. 'If only it were as simple as that, eh comrades? But that's dialectics and out of dialectics comes truth.'

Frere returned to Tuck's commune, where no one was about. He entered their sleeping quarters and found Tuck sitting on the floor before a bench he had rigged up with vice, drill and appropriate tools at the back of the hut. Spread around him were the parts of an automatic rifle he had taken to pieces.

Frere laughed. 'It's almost as though you'd staged this scene to substantiate the Secretary General's remarks about you.'

Tuck grinned as he tested the ejector mechanism. 'It's no act, friend Colin. Even yet, when something goes wrong with a gun, when rounds are getting jammed or something, they bring it to Tuck.' He cocked his head to one side and frowned. 'You don't suppose they damage the guns themselves and bring them here just to humour me, do you?

'It makes them seem very nice if they do.'

'But it makes me seem like an old fool.'

Frere sat down on the bottom cot which had been assigned to him. 'You said you'd tell me about that last operation my brother was on – once I'd heard from the others who were there. I've met Ang and Kuan now.'

'Kuan wasn't with our party. He commanded the force deployed around the dropping-zone in the final action. There were four of us with Comrade Matt – Ang and me, and Kirin.'

'I remember my brother's mentioning Kirin.'

'He died several years ago. He was quite old, was Comrade Kirin. And very, well – almost holy you might say. Sometimes he was called Comrade Monk and all he needed was a saffron robe. A saying of his is often quoted: "We must persevere and work unceasingly and we too will touch God's heart. Our God is none other than the masses of Malia." He did not take part in any further guerrilla actions after that but he continued to teach here in camp.'

'That's three,' Frere said.

'Well, the next time you're in Rani Kalpur you must go to the Khandev Academy and see one of the masters there called Tinoo.'

'Tinoo? I don't think my brother ever mentioned him.'

'No, he wouldn't have. Tinoo was just a boy then, on his very first jungle mission. When we attacked the troop transport, he was hit in the shoulder. Your brother Matt half-carried him for many miles with the enemy snapping at our heels. Then we had to leave him on a little island in the midst of the swamps. Before the battle in which Comrade Matt was wounded and captured, the last thing he said to us was to go back as soon as the battle was over and get Tinoo.'

'And he was still alive?'

'Yes, he was. Only just, though. They had to cut off his arm and part of his shoulder; but he's alive and active today. When he was completely recovered we managed to slot him back into the world outside.'

'Is he still with you? – In spirit, I mean.'

'Of course! Loyal as they come is Tinoo. And not just in spirit either. He writes articles for *Das Vani*. Very theoretical and thoughtful. Sometimes I think I can catch the sound of his voice in something of his I'm reading. He briefs us too on likely lads to come inside. You must see him if you ever get the chance. He'd like to tell you what he feels about your brother.'

'Yes, I must see him – some time.'

Tuck, as though he had grown a bit bored with it, hastily re-assembled the rifle and somewhat doubtfully tested the firing mechanism. 'I don't think much power will grow out of the barrel of this gun.'

'It's one of those weapons men are a great deal more important than,' Frere suggested.

Tuck laughed. 'Comrade Lee has made fun of those who are always quoting him. He has threatened to go through his works pointing out all the statements that just seem to cancel out.'

'Ah,' Frere said, 'that's dialectics.'

The others came back to the hut from whatever tasks they had been engaged in during the afternoon, Ahmed, Goh Tun and Salmi. They asked Frere about his meeting with the members of the Central Committee.

'It went very well. They weren't at all – you know, stiff and stand-offish.'

'That's the way it is when you've all, at some time or other, cowered together from enemy bullets,' Tuck said.

Frere asked them about what they had been doing and then they went out to the long table in the square space enclosed by the June Tenth huts. Frere was pleased when Leela took the place beside him which she had occupied before.

He had wondered if her manner to him, when he saw her again, might not be somewhat reproving; but there was nothing but friendliness in her glance and smile.

'How have you spent your day, Comrade?'

'Oh, just meeting Secretary General Lee and the members of the Central Committee is all,' he made light of it.

She laughed and it was for him the sound of a breeze gently tinkling strips of glass.

'And then,' he added, 'I spent some time with the comrades in the propaganda section.'

'You've met Professor Chin then.'

'He was a professor?'

'Oh yes. He occupied the chair of literature in the University of Malia when I was there. But he refused to name students of his who were involved in an illegal demonstration five or six years ago and he had to come inside.'

Frere shook his head in wonderment. 'It's very strange to someone from my world. Everybody here dresses and acts and lives the same; everyone is addressed the same way and is treated exactly the same; and yet the person sitting beside you may be a tribal from the northwest plateau just learning to read or a – or a,' with a smile, 'distinguished philosopher.'

'And it may be the philosopher who has most to learn,' she said with a smile also.

'Last night after we'd eaten, I was so exhausted I went straight to my bunk. What usually happens after supper? I suppose people work so hard during the day that they turn in very early.'

'Not at all. Often there's entertainment in the evenings, folk music and folk dancing. Or plays may be put on. We have something like cabaret sketches in which the imperialists and their puppets are made fun of. And we have a projector, you know. Films are shown.'

'But are films the right thing for – '

'Serious-minded communists? You're thinking of Hollywood films. We have Soviet films, the great films of the late twenties and thirties. We have Chinese films and films from Vietnam. Films are a particularly good medium for showing collective historical action on a grand scale. As Comrade Lee has said: "We let breezes from all quarters blow through our house; but we put up our shutters against the corrupt gale from the West.'

Frere started to protest at quite so sweeping a cultural dismissal of his part of the world and then remembered how his part of the world had to look from here. 'Is anything happening tonight?'

'You'll see, after we've eaten – if you think you can stay awake.'

'I might just manage it, if you were explaining it to me as we watched.' The moment he had spoken he regretted it. Would it not sound to her like another clumsy approach where such things were frowned upon?

She hesitated a while. Then she said a little distantly: 'We've been told to do what we can to make your visit a success.'

'For me or for you?'

'It couldn't be a success for the one without being a success for the other.'

'No, of course not.' He thought for a bit and then with a wry smile: 'I don't think I've ever been the object of someone's communist duty before.'

She replied with a smile of her own: 'I hope I'll always do my communist duty whatever personal sacrifice it implies.' And having ticked him off to that extent she was able to add in a friendlier way: 'We are told that communism comes through ever more comrades acting like communists while still living in class-divided society.'

'Would it be by Secretary General Lee that we're told that?'

'But of course,' she said. 'We'll go now to the camp centre.' She got up and walked away, leaving behind a little wake of champak scent.

He got up to follow, recalling some lines of Sanskrit poetry he had read in an Indomalian translation: 'I remember the day we met on the banks of the Andor. Today the sweet breeze blows. The mulati blooms and the champak flower, drenched with dew, sends out its fragrance, and you, my beloved, are present before me here, and so am I before you, the same that I ever was. But yet does my heart long for union with you in the shades of the cane-bowers on the banks of the Andor.'

6

Over the next week Frere spent most of one day with Tuck in the camp armoury being introduced to the arsenal of revolution, from First World War weapons right up to the latest Soviet Kalashnikov automatic rifle and also the Chinese version of it. There were long-barrelled guns with telescopic sights for distant sniping and there were short-barrelled sub-machine guns with large magazines for liberally spraying near targets in jungle fighting.

Another day Frere was shown around the forced-growth truck farm and the pool of water beyond the camp confines where fish were harvested like crops.

He spent a day with the comrades in the propaganda section talking about the copy for the first issue of *Workers' World*. And one day, at his insistence, he did his stint of waiting table and cleaning up when the comrades had finished eating. 'What, no tip?' he had asked at the end to general laughter.

He was waiting for a summons from Secretary General Lee when time was found for a private meeting. He was just getting up from a noon meal of rice and fish when he was saluted by a young woman in Liberation Army uniform who asked him to follow her to a bamboo hut near the Red Quadrangle.

Inside this structure, which was no different from any of the other living quarters, stood Lee, beaming benevolently and waving Frere toward a cane chair facing the one he had just got up from. When Frere was seated, Lee sat down and, taking up a pot on the little table between them, poured green tea into two porcelain cups, his hand, for all his sixty-five years, perfectly steady.

While the lowered, eastern-lidded eyes gave him the chance, Frere studied that kindly face. What he was looking for in that bland, rather mystical countenance was some sign of the toughness which had enabled him to endure five years of close imprisonment and torture, which had kept strong his confidence in the liberation movement when its forces faced annihilation, which had armed him against critics in his own party who argued for a policy of liquidation and reformism and which had preserved him against all flattery and enticement once his leadership was unassailable.

Had some resolution of conflicts within his own nature brought him such inner integrity that it could not but shine through the smooth, transparent skin of his face like a general benediction? Or had he learned to cultivate such an appearance because it would comfort and reassure those in the struggle when the prospect of final success seemed almost hopeless? But then, could one convincingly pretend to be certain of the ultimate victory of justice and truth against all odds without being, in a large measure, just and without having got hold of, to a considerable extent, truth – so that the pretence, assumed for the sake of others, had validated itself and become his own inner peace?

It was almost as if Lee had been protracting somewhat his ceremonious filling of the two cups to let Frere have his searching look. He smiled now and invited Frere to drink.

'Thank you. I'm beginning to love this aromatic tea.'

'I know what you're thinking,' Lee said with a smile.

'What's that?'

'You're thinking that for all my talk about frugality I serve tea in rather exquisite ware. You see, the comrades felt that I shamed them when I entertained visitors from fraternal countries with tea in tin mugs so they gave me this set for special occasions.'

'Thank you for considering me a special occasion.'

'Very special, Colin.'

Frere held up his cup to look at the light-bulb through the transparent rim. 'It does seem rather a long way from what I've been hearing about earlier operations – jungle fighters carrying only water to drink which, as a special luxury, they'd have hot when it was possible to make a fire.'

'And only a handful of rice to eat,' Lee chuckled. 'Our guerrillas have somewhat better rations now. It's like the change in our weapons which, I'm sure, Comrade Tuck has told you about. At first we set killer-wasp booby-traps for the enemy and bent back branches edged with sharp fragments of broken glass. We perfected concealed pits with pointed stakes fixed to the bottom and we filled holes with poisonous snakes and covered them with leaves. Now we are supplied with the most modern weapons, by our friends who give them to us freely and by the enemy from whom we take them willy-nilly.'

'Yes, I was shown the well-equipped armoury.'

'And we eat better now; but not too much better,' Lee said with a laugh. 'We must never forget that lean hungry people make good fighters. It's what disturbs the sleep of rich fat people.'

'You should sleep well,' Frere said. 'There can't be an ounce of fat on you.'

'I'm not rich either, if that doesn't sound too complacent. At least not in money.'

'In wisdom?'

'In my comradeship with the people of this country. It's from them any wisdom I may pretend to comes from.'

'But they're mostly peasants, aren't they? Didn't Marx draw his wisdom from the working class of an industrialised country?'

'That's true,' Lee nodded; 'but remember, I know that part of the world, too. I've been a dishwasher in a London restaurant and a page in a Paris hotel. I first read Marx in English when I was picking hops in Kent.'

'I didn't know that. Oh, I knew you'd been abroad but I didn't know you'd worked at jobs like that.'

'I joined the Party in London. I wrote several articles on imperialism in southeast Asia for the *Marxist Quarterly*.'

'I do know that. They're part of my collection of works about Malia.' He paused for a moment and then, somewhat tentatively: 'One of the problems often discussed back home, discussed, that is, by left-wing intellectuals, is how a proletarian revolution can be made by backward countries – well, backward in the sense of not having a large organised urban proletariat.'

'I know,' Lee smiled. 'Some of those intellectuals would even have us postpone a revolution we are capable of making until we have the kind of organised working class to be found in Britain. I point out to them that such a working class hasn't made a revolution there yet. Such a postponement might be for a very long time indeed.'

'Why hasn't there been a proletarian revolution in any of the older, highly industrialised countries? Is it because the proletariat in an imperialist country loses its revolutionary zeal through being associated in the exploitation of colonial peoples?'

'That's another thing your left-wing intellectuals often say. Capitalists try to share the ideology of imperialist exploitation with the working class but they don't share with them the fruits of exploitation. In a period of imperialist expansion it is possible for the organised working class to win concessions through struggle. That turns them into social democrats. But that period has come to an end in Britain.'

'Why has it ended?'

'Because Britain will soon have no empire. Even new colonies like Malia are in revolt. Bereft of an empire, the class struggle between metropolitan capitalists and the abysmally low-waged workers of their foreign possessions becomes internalised in an intensified struggle between capitalists and native workers at home.'

'I like "native" workers!' Frere laughed.

'It's important to understand the relationship between a liberation struggle like ours against capitalist imperialism and a class struggle like that of British workers against their own finance capitalists. Your left-wing intellectuals do not understand that relationship. According to them we are too poor and backward to make a revolution: British workers are too corrupted by the easy living of an imperialist country to make a revolution. So no revolution.'

'Maybe they don't really want one.'

'Maybe not. Your Western analytical thinkers can take things apart and study them but they can't put them back together and act on them. They can use abstraction to see things separately but separate things don't interact and develop. Only seeing things as internally related in some larger unity enables us to compare and contrast them in their conflict with something else. That's dialectical thinking. Fortunately Marx was not a Western analytical thinker. When it comes to a question of which of two groups of workers is revolutionary, an either-or logic tells us neither instead of each by turn.'

'That's good,' Frere mused. 'Either-or always equals neither instead of both.'

'In a country like Malia the people are exploited by both an imperialist power which still dominates the economy and by compradors and corrupt officials who rule locally. The working masses can only liberate themselves from this double exploitation by revolutionary means. But that revolution has its effect on the metropolitan country. There the possession of an empire to provide great quantities of cheap labour and a huge free market for mass-produced goods abroad has already led to the decline of industry at home. An increasingly large section of the working class is permanently unemployed, and the main drive of the capitalist ruling class is directed more to the making of money than of things. In other words, the change from industrial to finance capitalism – which is capitalism's final phase.'

'And stripped of its colonies,' Frere took it up, 'the uncompetitiveness of the metropolitan country's industry with that of newer capitalist countries plus all the economic deformations at home of the imperialist domination of overseas trade have to be paid for – by the working class, of course. And that's in addition to the normal expropriation of surplus value they always suffer. So they, then, can only liberate themselves from their double exploitation by revolutionary means.'

'Ah, you are a Marxist, Colin.'

'I try to be.'

'That's just what happens. The extra exploitation the imperialist country exported to its colonies flows back to the metropolitan country with the collapse of empire. But there's another problem. Exporting exploitation overseas has attracted a considerable number of the worst victims of that exploitation back to the imperialist country where they are welcomed by employers looking for cheap labour at home. These "foreign invaders" can then be blamed for the deterioration of working-class conditions in the metropolitan country.'

'So that there is an alternative to working-class revolution. Fascism.'

'If the ruling capitalist class gets its way. So we begin to see how everything fits together and how changes here in Malia are related to changes all over the world.'

'Thank you, Comrade Lee. You've helped me understand better, not just the relationship between Britain and Malia, but between Europe and the rest of the world.'

'I think I've only helped you sort out your own ideas. That's all we can ever do.'

'But there's one thing that still puzzles me. Even if British imperialism has created a revolutionary situation here, won't there be a shortage of working-class cadres in the early stages of establishing socialism? Isn't the proportion of organised workers too small to set up a working-class dictatorship?'

'There are several things to be said about that. A prolonged revolutionary struggle in which peasants fight under a working-class banner has a proletarianising effect on them.

'And then, after the physical revolution has been won and we've begun to institute a socialist society in which the means of production belong to the people and the products are fairly distributed amongst them, it may be possible to promote a kind of ideological revolution which will bring the customs, habits, motivation and ways of thought of the masses into closer accord with those new socialist relations of production. But there's something else that may be quite special for us Malian revolutionaries. Such is our security in our jungle stronghold, thanks to the support of the rural people round about, and such is the chaos and corruption in the Puppet Government and its army that we've been able to carry out infiltration on a considerable scale.'

'Yes, I've heard something of that.'

'Quite a few of our people will have had some years of playing by no means unimportant roles in actually operating the neo-colonial system in all its aspects before we take control and replace it with a socialist system. It could mean that those involved in this process are acquiring a political sophistication which will be invaluable in organising that ideological revolution I mentioned.'

'But might it not mean that those who have assumed high posts in the administration, army and police, with all the temptations they'll be exposed to, will be seduced away from their loyalty to the revolution?'

'That will have happened in some cases. But not as many as you might suppose. And anyway, friend Colin, it's better that such betrayals should occur at this stage than when we have taken power.'

'That's true, of course.'

'You might also bear in mind what Chairman Mao has to say about revolutionary change in countries with a predominantly peasant population. There can be a two-stage revolution.'

'Yes, I've read about that. To begin with, the revolution establishes a people's democratic dictatorship which only later is transformed into a full-scale proletarian dictatorship.'

'That's it. But I think we have to be careful about the use of that word dictatorship. It's only applicable while the class enemy is still able to resist forcefully. As soon as possible we have to think in terms of working-class democracy – working-class rule exercised not by the Party on behalf of the working class but by the working class itself. Dictatorial methods must only be used against a class enemy capable of damaging our working-class democracy. Chairman Mao helps us with that problem, too, with his distinction between antagonistic and non-antagonistic contradictions.'

'I'm sorry I haven't been taking all this down,' Frere said. 'My journalistic instincts seem to have deserted me.'

Lee laughed. 'Oh you'll hear what I've just been saying often enough around here. The important thing is not to become too engrossed in what's going to happen *after* the revolution when we've still got a revolution to *make*. That would be most un-Marxist.'

'And when do you think it's likely to happen?'

'Later than our own people hope, sooner than the enemy expects. It's not entirely in our hands. It ought to come after some particularly vicious attack on us – demonstrators shot down in the streets, massacres in the rural areas, something like that.'

'And if nothing like that occurs, will you provoke it?'

'Never, friend Colin! Never! The people wouldn't forgive us if we collaborated in their suffering to make them rebel. It wouldn't be necessary anyway. The present administration can only rule on the basis of terror.'

'But with so many of your own people infiltrated into the Government and army, don't they get involved in terrorist attacks?'

'They warn the people who are to be attacked when they can; they sabotage the efforts of soldiers and police; they act so as to make the Government look as ineffectual as it is brutal.'

'All the same I can imagine some terrible crises of communist conscience in that world out there.'

'To be sure. But we aren't talking about a permanent state of society, are we? Only a highly volatile and relatively short period of transition to full-scale armed revolt throughout the whole country. It won't be long now – and that brings me to the question I want to ask you.'

'I can guess what it is.'

'You've thought about it then?'

'I have to admit – it's a unique opportunity for a journalist, to be able to cover the revolution in Malia at first hand. It's like – well, it's not unlike John Reed's being on hand for the October Revolution.'

'Yes, it is like that. Does the idea appeal to you?'

'Very much.'

'And is that all there is to it?'

'No. It's being involved with something for which my brother gave his life. And it isn't only that either. It's also something I myself have come to believe in – passionately.'

'I've realised that, from reading your articles on various parts of southeast Asia.'

'Was that what was in your mind when we first began exchanging messages on the possibility of my visiting the base camp here – that I might stay on and report the Malian revolution through the news agency I work for?'

'A bit more than that, my friend. I discussed it with the Central Committee and we all agreed that if you came here, we would ask you to take over the editorship of *Workers' World*.'

'What!'

'It may not seem a very important post for such a well-known correspondent but – '

'You know it isn't that, Comrade Lee. I know so little of your movement, so little of Marxism, for that matter. What qualifications have I for a job like that? Why it's – well, it's almost ridiculous. Or is it just that you want to use my name for a periodical others would write?'

'Oh come now, Colin, we wouldn't ask you to put your name on something you had not helped to create. We think it's very important to launch an English language monthly for worldwide circulation at this very time. We must begin preparing our friends in many countries for what we are about to do here.'

'Yes, but – '

'Think how important such a publication could be to us. Remember how British dock workers blacked ships which were carrying arms for the interventionist troops invading the Soviet Union. Might not the labour movement there come out in opposition to the dispatch of British troops to Malia? The labour movement helped to force the British Government to suspend the attack on Egypt.'

'But – '

'That's not the only reason for wanting to bring out *Workers' World*. We want our struggle here to give encouragement to workers everywhere. We want them to know of our awareness that in fighting for our own liberation, we are playing a part in ending the exploitation of the working class generally. We want them to hear from our own mouths, not from their capitalist press, why we're fighting and how we're organised for it.'

'Oh I know how important it is,' Frere managed to break in and say. 'People *must* know what actually happens when imperialist rule is finally challenged. I've already gone over some articles Comrade Chin wanted me to see and made some suggestions about style and vocabulary which I hope are helpful. But being editor – !'

'Isn't the risk ours? Don't you realise we've thought about it very seriously? Haven't we gone over it again after meeting and talking with you?'

'I don't know. I just don't know. I wouldn't like to replace Comrade Chin.'

'You won't be. He edits *Das Vani*. You edit *Workers' World*. You work very closely. Comrade Chin knows about the proposal and agrees with it completely. He will help you in any way he can. But while his name does not appear on the front page of *Das Vani*, your name will appear on the cover of *Workers' World*. That's what you have to think about. You don't have to worry about whether you're politically qualified or not. That's our problem. All you have to think about is how the rest of your life may be affected by your open association with the Malian revolution.'

'I think I'd already begun to think about that when I first decided to come here. And Comrade Hadar – does he agree entirely with my appointment?'

'No,' Lee said carefully – 'not entirely. He does not think we should trust an outsider with such a post. But he does agree that if we are going to make such an appointment, you're the only person we could possibly choose.'

'I see.'

'Do you want more time to think about it?'

Frere suddenly grinned. 'No, of course not. I don't know why I'm pretending this has all come to me as such a great surprise. When you took my proposal of coming here seriously, I knew it had to be more than just giving me an interview or letting me write about the sanitary arrangements of the base camp. I knew, really, that something like this was in the offing and I must already have decided deep down what I'd do about it.'

'So you'll take over the editorship?'

'Yes.'

'Tell me, Colin. Do you have any immediate family to consider? Anyone dependent on you?'

'No one. I might almost have been getting ready for this assignment years ago. Perhaps from the time I heard about my brother's death.'

Lee ran his fingers through his fine grey hair, leaving it rumpled, so that it caught the light of the suspended bulb behind him like a halo. 'I know. When a very close relative is completely involved in something, it's like a legacy when he dies. Not a few of our young people here are the sons and daughters or nieces and nephews of those who have been killed in the fighting.'

'I wonder if it's more that with me or more that I'm simply grabbing at the journalistic scoop of a lifetime?'

'Sometimes we can only know what our motives really are,' Lee said reflectively, 'by seeing how what they prompt us to do turns out. But there are easier and safer ways to make a name for yourself as a journalist than by identifying yourself completely with someone else's revolutionary struggle. Nor do I think you've made your choice *because* of Matt. It's *through* Matt that you yourself have learned that it's with us that you belong.'

'I hope so,' shaking his head a little doubtfully.

'I'm sure of it. We're sure of it.' Lee reached inside the loose tunic he wore and drew out a folded sheet of paper which, when opened out, showed the official heading of the Government of Malia. 'Now that you've taken your decision to stay, this becomes academic.'

Frere read the response to the demands made by the Communist Party of Malia for his release. The Government refused categorically to print anything he wrote about the 'illegal insurrection' in the Government-sponsored press and on no account was he to be allowed to speak over the radio or to appear on television before his enforced deportation from Malia. However, the Government did understand that World Press, the news agency he worked for, in order to facilitate his release was willing to syndicate an article on his experiences since capture, provided that it was made clear that the article had been written at 'bandit headquarters'.

Frere laughed. 'Even if I'm not released, my employers will exploit the article I'm going to send them. And when it's learned that I'm editing *Workers' World*, they'll publicise the fact that I've been on the writing staff of World Press. In fact, what it means is that they'll get their special coverage of the liberation war in Malia – and without having to pay me a salary!'

Lee and Frere, as by mutual agreement, stood up; and Lee took one of Frere's hands in both of his and shook it warmly. 'Thank you, Comrade Colin, for acceding to a request that's very near my heart.'

'Thank you, Comrade Secretary General, for feeling that there's a part an outsider like me can play in your glorious struggle.'

They embraced and then Lee said: 'Now that you're going to remain with us, would you like to move into the wooden building near the communications centre where we put up guests from fraternal countries?'

'I'd rather stay in Comrade Tuck's commune, if that's all right.'

'Of course.'

'I already know some of the young comrades and,' grinning, 'it would be foolish to move out now when I've just done my stint of menial chores.'

7

Urged on by impatience to begin as soon as possible this important task which had just been assigned him, Frere went directly to the propaganda centre. Chin was not there but two of the young people he had seen before were busy, the young man typing and the young woman checking copy on the backlit glass screen.

'Don't stop work because of me,' Frere said when the young woman turned around to face him.

'Oh we're well ahead with the next issue,' she told him and then presented herself. 'I'm Siti.'

He did not know quite what gesture to make and she laughed and reached out and shook his hand.

The young man got up and shook hands, too. 'I'm Swee Meng. You are very welcome, Comrade Frere.'

'This morning we went over with Comrade Chin the articles you returned with corrections,' Siti told him. And then with a little frown: 'You didn't suggest all that many changes. Comrade Chin wondered if you were simply being kind.'

Frere laughed. 'I've had too many stories of mine ripped to shreds by sub-editors to pass up a chance of doing the same if I thought it was justified. No, apart from some corrections of idiomatic usage I didn't think there was much need for change. The style seemed to me about right – very clear, not too stiff and formal but not too colloquial either. In something that's to be read in different countries it wouldn't be possible to strike a common vernacular note. And, best of all, they were wonderfully free of jargon.'

'Yes, that's something Comrade Chin is very insistent about.'

'You know what struck me when I was reading those pieces? It suddenly seemed so strange that people stuck away here in a southeast Asian jungle should have something to say to workers in a Manchester factory – and the language in which to say it.'

'English is compulsory in all our schools,' Siti reminded him.

'Which only a few of us have the privilege of attending,' Swee Meng added.

Siti continued: 'Just as we took weapons away from occupying British forces which we could then use against them, so with *Workers' World* we'll be using against the imperialists the language they imposed on us.'

'But the language that enables us to talk to workers everywhere,' Swee Meng argued, 'is Marxism.'

'Wouldn't that mean,' Frere asked, 'that before Marx it was impossible for people suffering different kinds of exploitation in different parts of the world to communicate with each other at all?'

And while Swee Meng thought about that, Siti answered: 'We mean that the different languages of exploited people at various times and in various places, once capitalism had united the world, became one language Marx had a sensitive enough ear to appreciate. By analysing the nature of exploitation he was able to set forth the philosophical grammar of that common language.'

'Yes,' Swee Meng nodded. 'That's probably what I meant.'

'But let's not forget our good fortune,' Siti said, 'in having to hand in English a language that's almost as universal as the language of Kalashnikov rifles.'

'It's interesting to think what Macaulay would have made of that,' Frere laughed. 'You people here seem to have thought such a lot about Marxism.'

'No, Comrade,' Swee Meng said, 'we're living it. That's a very different thing.'

'Yes,' Frere reflected, 'yes I suppose it is. Just thinking about Marxism, lecturing about it and writing books about it, can be very exclusive and divisive. It has the effect of turning Marxism into an academic fad. We've had a lot of that back home just lately.'

'And no two purely intellectual Marxists ever agree with each other,' Siti observed. 'Just thinking about Marxism brings out differences and separates us. Living it is something we can do together. Practising it can unite a whole community.'

'That's why the Central Committee decided that *Das Vani* wouldn't be a theoretical journal but a newspaper,' Swee Meng pointed out. 'It's made up of factual accounts of what's happening in various parts of the country, written in such a way that the political lesson is implicit. Each news story has a kind of built-in editorial.'

'That doesn't mean that the Central Committee doesn't provide us with explicit editorials – often written by our Secretary General.'

Standing beside Siti, Frere considered the column of print she had been proofreading. His knowledge of Indomalian was insufficient yet for him to read comfortably an abstruse philosophical argument but he could cope satisfactorily with a straight news story.

'This happened recently?' he asked.

'The day before yesterday,' Swee Meng answered. 'Kholay isn't all that far from here and couriers bring in important news items very quickly. There's a code that can be used for getting stories to nearby villages by telephone from all over the country. Then they can be collected and brought to us.'

'And written up here?'

'Only if need be. We try to teach our correspondents to give their material the right shape themselves and not tack onto the end of an article like that one some such observation as: "And so we see how important it is to support the Revolution with all our might so that the time will come when puppet troops won't be able to carry out massacres of those protesting against shortages of food and medicine."'

'For a while,' Siti said, 'we made it a practice to cut the last paragraph of every article submitted – to get comrades out of the habit of tagging a political moral on the end.'

'And does that often happen?' Frere wondered. 'Men, women and children mowed down by machine-gun fire for demonstrating against intolerable conditions?'

'Not as often as it used to. The troops began to run into fierce ambushes on their way back to their encampment. Indeed those who carried out the shooting at Kholay have some way to go yet. We'll see what happens to them.'

'This piece,' Frere tapped the story with his finger, 'seems to me to be very well written. I can't think of any way it could be improved.'

'Perhaps the conviction that the worst evils of this land can be cured lends our people a natural eloquence,' Siti said. 'And, of course, our Secretary General, whom so many of our people have read, is a great poet as well as a great Marxist.'

'I've heard that.'

'While he was in prison and had no reading matter and no writing materials of any kind, he used to make up patriotic poems in the traditional sloka style.'

'Have any of them been translated into English?'

'There's a collection of fifteen of the best known, translated by an Australian comrade who was in Malia during the war. I can get a copy for you if you'd like to see it.'

'Yes, I would.'

'So you see,' Siti explained, 'we've had a very good example to follow when it comes to writing concisely and elegantly. Secretary General Lee says somewhere: "Treat language with the consideration you would show to a very dear friend and it will always bear true witness for you".'

Just then Chin came through the curtains and, seeing Frere, rushed over to shake his hand, bumping into the lay-out screen and dislodging the copy.

'Oh I'm sorry, Comrade Siti,' he apologised.

'That's all right,' she said with a laugh.

'That's always happening to me,' Chin said philosophically. 'I'm off there concentrating so hard on keeping my thoughts in order that my limbs take advantage of my absence to do what they like. I think it's because my parents wanted me to become a sort of mandarin, set free from all practical tasks so that I could work out what was practical for everyone else. I'm not the type to be a mandarin, of course, but I am quite hopeless at anything practical. I always feel uneasy when I'm reading Chairman Mao's "On Practice".'

'Me too,' Frere agreed, 'if for somewhat different reasons.'

'At the University, you know, Friend Colin, my students started a breakage fund for me – to pay for all the things I knocked over or stepped on.'

'And just before Comrade Professor came inside,' Swee Meng told Frere, 'the fund was closed out to buy compact editions of a few books the students knew he would want to take with him – on the grounds that in breaking the rule about informing the authorities immediately of any left-wing activities among students he had achieved his greatest breakage of all.'

'Here in camp,' Chin admitted with a gesture that hit the carriage release of the typewriter and rang the bell, 'I'm not allowed to have anything to do with the actual printing of the paper. I'm not allowed within a hundred yards of the armoury. I've heard talk of a plan for infiltrating me back into the world outside, just before our final uprising begins, as a manual operator in the central power station.'

Frere laughed. 'I'm so glad to see you, Comrade Chin. I've just been talking with the Secretary General.'

'And you've agreed to edit *Workers' World*! I'm delighted. Absolutely delighted.'

'How do you know I agreed?'

'Oh I can tell from the way you look, the way you speak about your meeting with Comrade Lee.' He turned to Siti and Swee Meng. 'Do tell friend Colin how pleased we are that he's joining our staff as editor of the new publication.' And to Frere again: 'It's such a relief to me! It solves the problem of how the national newspaper and the international periodical can be complementary without my being responsible for both.'

'Was that your problem?'

'Yes, I kept trying to be two different people producing publications for two different readerships.'

"You can imagine what that did to any breakables in the Comrade Professor's vicinity,' Siti observed.

'Well it was very worrying, I can tell you. And very confusing. Now that my responsibility has been halved, I can sort out my worrying better, you know, establish a better order of priority in the things I worry about. It's the lack of that, I think, which has been worrying me the most.'

'And there I was,' Frere said gaily, 'worrying about whether you might resent my taking on the editorship of *Workers' World*!'

'I couldn't be happier.'

'As I was saying to these two comrades, the articles you gave me seem very good. How soon do you think it might be possible to bring out the first issue?'

'Soon. Quite soon. I like the introductory paragraph you put at the beginning of the main article. Where is it?' He put on the glasses suspended around his neck and looked through the papers piled on one of the desks. 'Yes, here it is: "The spectre that has been haunting Europe can now be seen rousing up the people of southeast Asia; and all the imperialist powers have entered into a grim alliance to exorcise it." That's nice.'

'Secretary General Lee should be asked to write something special which can be put in a box on the first page – some kind of greeting to workers the world over from revolutionaries at the base camp of the Communist Party of Malia.'

'Yes, of course. I'll mention it to Comrade Hadar.' Chin, frowning, thought about this for a moment. 'No, I'll tell you what would be best.' He beamed at the idea of it. '*You* mention it to Comrade Hadar.'

'And exactly when,' Frere repeated the question, 'do you think we can bring out the first issue? The articles I've checked and the material already agreed by the Central Committee, together with some photos of our guerrillas in action and with some graphics to brighten up the appearance, could fill an eight-page edition now.'

'That's true. Well,' rubbing his hands together gleefully, 'when you tell Comrade Hadar about the message you want from the Secretary General, why shouldn't you tell him also that we've got the first issue of *Workers' World* ready for publication?'

'That's the easiest commission I ever undertook. You comrades have done all the work; I look it over in a supercilious way, put my name on it as editor and we're launched!'

'We try not to think in terms of individual effort,' Siti said. 'You've helped us a lot already.'

'You'll earn your keep when *Workers' World* achieves regularity of publication,' Chin chortled. 'And I'll be able to think of all the work and all the worry you're involved in as what I'm not!'

'One thing I've wondered about,' Frere said. 'I understand now how *Das Vani* appears each week all over Malia, even though you're presumably bottled up here in the jungle; but how will *Workers' World* be distributed to various foreign countries?'

'Ah,' Chin explained, 'that's a positive feature for us of the unfortunate split in the world communist movement. Anything we want worldwide circulation for we only have to get both to Moscow and Beijing to be sure that they will vie with each other in distributing it for us – each hoping to win us over for that side.'

'Is the Communist Party of Malia absolutely impartial?' Frere wondered.

'Well,' Chin answered shrewdly, 'there are similarities in the ideas of Mao Tsetung and our own Secretary General. How could there not be when for both it's a question of applying Marxism to industrially backward countries with large peasant populations which for many years have been economically dominated by highly industrialised imperialist powers? They have arrived at similar solutions to the same kind of problem quite independently – rather like two of my students coming up with the same answer to an examination question I've set them and without passing notes to each other which they don't think I see. But then, on the other hand, the Soviet Union is still the country of the October Revolution, the classic example of the first workers' state; and Lenin, after Marx, is the father of us all.'

'But isn't there considerable pressure on you to plump for one side or the other?'

'Well the Chinese don't put much pressure on us so it's hard for the Russians to. It suits us very well to have them competing for our favour. As to who is the more sincere – well, a gun handed to us by way of paying lip service to the revolutionary ideal kills just as deadly as one given to us out of genuine comradeship.'

'Still, I'd have thought people here at base camp would have strong views about whether Moscow or Beijing has the right of it.'

'Our Secretary General urges us not to make the mistake of so many communists in the West who quarrel and split over which side is right instead of getting on in concert with the task of revolutionising the working class in their own countries. He says we can't enjoy the luxury of strong views about anything but making our own revolution in Malia.

So we get on with it.'

'Very wise,' Frere approved. 'And what I must get on with is seeing Comrade Hadar.'

'Right,' Chin agreed.

'Do I just go and ask for him?'

'Why not?'

'I mean his being a member of the Central Committee and all that.'

'There's no protocol here. This place started as a refuge for a few hundred comrades and, as it grew, the easy style of that original retreat was maintained. It's simply taken for granted that no one would seek out a member of the Central Committee without sufficient reason and that no member of the Central Committee would ignore any comrade who thought he had a matter of sufficient import to raise. That will all change, I suppose, when we achieve state power – which,' Chin added, 'is something else for me to worry about.'

Frere said goodbye to his young friends at the propaganda centre and made his way to Hadar's hut. Hadar was there and bade him enter without quite accepting it as such an ordinary incident of base camp life as Chin had suggested. 'If I'd known some time in advance that you were coming,' he said with his rather crooked smile, 'I could have risen more suitably to the occasion.'

'That would have been to give my visit a greater significance than it has.'

'Please sit down. At least I can offer you some tea.'

'No thank you. I had some at the propaganda centre which I've just left.'

And when they were sitting facing each other, Hadar said: 'The propaganda centre, you say. So you've lost no time in taking up the offer of editorship?'

'Naturally I feel that my becoming editor of *Workers' World* has to be conditional on your approval as head of the propaganda department. That's part of the reason I'm here.'

Hadar had a tiny self-contained smile for that. 'Are you suggesting that I might go against the Secretary General's wishes in this or, indeed, in any matter?'

'Well, I wouldn't like to work for you just because Comrade Lee thought it was a good idea.'

'Here we don't work *for* others. We work *with* them. I assure you there's no difference between the Secretary General and myself on this question. I've already told the staff at the guest house that they're to expect you to move in.'

'Ah, that's another matter I had a word with Comrade Lee about. I'd really like to stay in the commune I've been in since my arrival. The June Tenth presided over by Comrade Tuck.'

'Is that because he's a special friend of yours?'

'He was a special friend of my brother's. But more than that it's because I want to live exactly as if I myself were a Malian who had come inside out of conviction in the justice of the liberation movement.'

'I see.'

'It seems to me that if I move into a building normally reserved for foreign visitors, it could keep me from feeling sufficiently a part of the life of the base camp to write other than superficially about it.'

'But that's what you are – a foreign visitor who's to stay a little longer and work a little closer with us than is usual.'

'I think I must try to be more than that. I think I have to live in such a way as to identify myself completely with the struggle of the Malian people – if I'm to write about it from the inside.'

Hadar paused a moment before answering. 'If you live just as we do, won't it, rather, emphasise the fact that you're not a Malian who's taken up our cause in the most natural way? Surely it's better for you and for us to accept your separateness – and then do everything we can to help you and ourselves to begin to ignore it.'

'If I intended to live in Comrade Tuck's commune while doing very different things from what they're doing, then that would, indeed, make my separateness more obvious. But that was not my idea, Comrade Hadar. It was my idea that I should attend the same study sessions as Ahmed or Salmi or Goh Tun; that I should take my turn firing at the butts and learning about guerrilla tactics and that I should do my stint in the routine work of the camp.'

'Is it your idea, perhaps, that you should go on an inspection tour with one of our patrols or take part in a food or weapon-collecting mission? And why should it stop there? Perhaps you would even wish to accompany one of our fighting units in the field.'

'Why not? If I'm to report to the world on the liberation war here as it moves into its final phase, won't I need to have learned how to accompany fighting units for observation purposes without getting in their way?'

'That's not why we've gone to considerable trouble to get you here. It's not what the Secretary General meant in terms of your writing for others about our liberation struggle.'

'Oh? I'd have thought it's very much what he meant. He insists always on our testing our theories by social practice. I have to be involved in both the theory and the practice of your revolution to write about it at all profoundly.'

'Aren't you tending to make practice an end in itself? Practice validates our theory for achieving some goal – for us the liberation of

Malia. Your goal is to edit a periodical explaining that revolution to the outside world. Each of those goals determines its own form of practice.'

'You mean that the liberation of Malia can't be a goal for me because I'm not Malian? Neither was my brother, Comrade Hadar.'

'That's rather different. Your brother came to know Comrade Lee during a war in which they shared the same limited goal – driving the Japanese out of our country. It was on that basis that he was able to rejoin Comrade Lee for a greater goal when Britain subsequently broke its wartime promises to us.'

'I think my case is similar to my brother's. I start by sharing with you the limited goal of producing a periodical which will inform workers in other countries of the revolutionary struggle of the Malian people. But reporting a revolution isn't like covering a bank robbery. It's only to the extent that I share in that revolutionary goal that I can carry out adequately the specific task Comrade Lee has asked me to assume. It's only by identifying myself with all aspects of the preparations for radically changing Malia's history that I can begin to share in the goal to which the periodical I'm to edit is dedicated.'

'Well, I shall put your views to the Central Committee.'

'And meanwhile as to my quarters – ?'

'Meanwhile you're free to stay where you are.'

'Thank you, Comrade. And now I'd like to put to you a proposal Comrade Chin and I have agreed upon. We think we have enough articles, all of which, I believe, you and the Central Committee have seen, to go ahead with the first issue of *Workers' World*.'

'You have an odd sense of priorities. I'd have thought that the question of actually bringing out the introductory edition of the new periodical took precedence over the question of your personal circumstances here.'

'But that grew out of the question of whether you approved of my appointment as editor or not. I could hardly raise the matter of bringing out the first issue till I knew the answer to that, could I?'

'But you should have realised that I'd go along with what Secretary General Lee wanted.'

'Which reminds me of something else. Shouldn't the first issue have a message from Secretary General Lee? A message to the world, as it were? Probably in a box on the front page.'

'Would I have forgotten something like that! You can be sure that an appropriate text from the Secretary General will be provided.'

'Then can I tell Comrade Chin and the other comrades that we're to go ahead with the first issue?' Frere started to get up.

'The Central Committee will be pleased to know that my instructions for launching *Workers' World* have been carried out so promptly that we can go ahead. But, Comrade – ' Hadar held Frere there a while longer. 'There is something I'm sure that, with a little thought, you can appreciate. For many generations the people of Malia have had it dinned into them that the foreigner from England was better at everything than they were. Learning to rely on themselves, gaining confidence in their own abilities is as important as arming themselves with the enemy's weapons. If we sometimes seem to you somewhat ungrateful for what you feel you have to contribute – '

'It would be entirely understandable, Comrade Hadar; but I assure you that everyone I've met has expressed gratitude for my modest offers of assistance and has treated me with a courtesy far exceeding anything the skills I happen to possess would merit.' He had answered stiffly out of a feeling of resentment and he got up abruptly to be on his way. Then he sat down again, frowning deeply and clenching his fists. At last he splayed his fingers as though he had solved some inner problem and said: 'I'm sorry. There is something I've been forgetting. I know what I think my feelings for this country and for you comrades who serve its best interests are. But why should those who have suffered so much humiliation and violence from my countrymen accept me as completely different from them? How can the comrades be sure that I'm on their side when people have so often tricked and deceived them? I must never forget that I'm, in a sense, on trial here. If I do seem to forget it, I hope the comrades will always remind me.'

8

When Frere returned to the hut in the June Tenth Commune which he had been arguing was the right place for him to stay, he found Ahmed and Goh Tun waiting for him there.

'So it's arranged then?' Ahmed asked.

'What?' Frere asked.

'That you'll be staying here with us.'

'How could you know that? I've only just this minute got permission.'

'We knew you'd ask to stay here.'

'But how did you know they'd let me? Perhaps Comrade Tuck put in a word on my behalf.'

'No, I didn't,' Tuck said. He had been lying on his bunk and Frere had not seen him. 'If I had said you ought not to be whipped off to the guest lodge, they would have accused me of being bolshie again and moved you over there straight away. You could say I put in a word for you by keeping my mouth shut.'

'Well thank you.'

'What I'm going to do now,' Goh Tun told Frere, 'is to take you off to the firing range, so that you can begin to familiarise yourself with some of the weapons we use.'

Frere was surprised. 'That, too, is something I've been arguing for as hard as I could – the right to participate in everything the comrades here are up to. Now I'm told that we're off to the firing range just as though there had never been any question about my joining in. I seem to have been struggling frantically for the last hour or so to achieve what was going to happen anyway.'

'It's like,' Ahmed said with a laugh, 'it's like making a big effort to express some particular feeling you have, only to be told that it's what someone with your class background was bound to say anyway.'

'If your father's a big land-owner,' Goh Tun said jokingly, 'you quite like it when something of your past – your manners maybe or the way you speak – slips out like that.'

'We can't all be blessed with the background of an illiterate serf,' Ahmed pointed out with a comic hauteur.

'We'll try to be patient with you,' Goh Tun assured him good naturedly. And to Frere: 'Come. We're off to the butts.'

'Wait a minute,' Tuck told them. 'I'm coming with you.' He went over to the gun stand where there were always rifles or machine guns he was either working on, studying the mechanism of or merely fondling in an absentminded sort of way. He picked out a light twenty-two calibre rifle and handed it to Frere. 'This is just the gun for a bit of target practice.' He slung over his shoulder the sling of his own personal Kalashnikov automatic rifle.

Goh Tun saw Frere looking at Tuck's weapon and patted his own. 'This is the Chinese version of it. A better gun, I think.'

'Is that the remark of a politician or an armourer?' Tuck wondered. As they left the hut he said to Frere: 'On that last operation with your brother we captured a Bren gun. All the time Comrade Matt was helping the wounded boy keep ahead of the troops right behind us I was nursing this heavy Bren gun through the jungle. It sawed at my shoulder and snagged in the vines but I wouldn't leave it behind. A good gun, like a comrade, is worth saving, I told them. Good guns were not so easy to come by in those days.'

'A Bren gun isn't a weapon I like to wrestle through thick jungle,' Goh Tun said.

'That's why I had to stop carrying it,' Tuck agreed. 'But when you open up with a Bren gun it certainly clears away everything in front of you.'

'Oh we all like that feeling of firepower claiming all the ground in front of you,' Goh Tun admitted, 'but in our kind of war it doesn't usually have to include more than an arc with a fifty-yard radius. A short cartridge, such as this fires,' he held up his own automatic rifle for Frere to see, 'does the job – just as long as there are enough of them pouring out per minute.'

'Being taught how to suck eggs by one's own grandchildren,' Tuck observed, 'is one of the things one learns to put up with in my job.'

Frere asked to look at Goh Tun's Kalashnikov, which had an identifying mark burned in the hardwood butt. He took the gun, hefted it to judge its weight and handed it back.

'Me,' Ahmed said, showing Frere his own weapon, 'I prefer this Czech Skorpion. It's a machine gun you can handle just like a pistol.'

'It's a nice toy,' Goh Tun said a bit scathingly.

'Depends on the kind of children you play with,' Ahmed retorted.

As they approached the area outside the camp where fields of fire had been cleared of undergrowth they could hear the regular, tree-muffled crack of individual shots loudly interrupted from time to time by the sustained crash of the automatic rifles.

'And everyone in camp,' Frere asked, 'has his or her own personal weapon?'

'Yes,' Goh Tun said. 'That's partly what we're doing today. Fitting you up for the right fire-arm.'

'Which,' Tuck added, 'can be modified in certain ways to suit individual preferences.'

'I'll get you to do that for me,' Frere said. 'I knew I was picking the right bunch to bunk in with.'

'Comrades learning to look after their own weapons is an important part of basic training,' Tuck said. 'It's with us and guns the way it is with you in London or New York and motor cars. Although they're put together on an assembly line and look identical, each car has certain special characteristics a good driver gets to know. That's the way it is with guns, too. They may look exactly alike but each one of them has peculiarities we have to know about. Our lives and the lives of comrades may depend on it.'

'Take this AK47 of mine,' Goh Tun said by way of illustration. 'In a burst of a dozen shots or more I know just how far, however tightly held, the barrel will climb upward and to the right. So I point the gun at the appropriate lower left hand part of whatever I'm shooting at and the muzzle rides diagonally across the middle of it.'

'And blows it away,' Ahmed said. 'I've seen him in action.'

In a trench closest to the line of targets a dozen young people, some only in their teens, were taking pot shots with twenty-twos. Tuck handed Frere the gun he had brought and said: 'You try.'

The young people made room for him to get down in the trench with them but he preferred to shoot standing up. He adjusted the loop in the sling around his upper left arm to help steady the gun.

'It's easier if you shoot down here,' a boy who did not seem more than eleven or twelve said. 'You can rest your elbows on the edge of the trench.'

Frere smiled but remained where he was and lifted the gun to fire when he got the signal. He had good vision, particularly at a distance, and he knew from experience with a rifle club he had once belonged to that if he waited until the sights were lined up exactly on the black circle at the centre of the target, held the gun still and squeezed off his shot carefully there was no reason why he should not score a bullseye.

He lowered the rifle, squinted at the target and then looked up at the leaf cover overhead. 'It's not very bright here.'

'These are the conditions we usually fight in,' Tuck reminded him.

'Of course.' He lifted the gun again and got the signal to fire. He shot twenty times in fairly rapid succession. The target attendant signalled back that every shot had been in the black.

'Expert! Expert!' The boy in the trench called out, looking back admiringly at Frere.

'You should have told us you're good at this,' Goh Tun said with a laugh.

'Only at target practice,' Frere disclaimed.

After a while he was given a Thompson submachine gun to try his luck at hitting man-shaped targets that suddenly poked up into sight somewhere at the other end of the firing range. There was no time to aim: it was simply a question of feeling when the cradled gun was in the right attitude for at least some of the spray of bullets to strike home. He looked at Tuck and shook his head.

'Not so good,' he said.

'Not bad, eh comrades?' And to Frere: 'You just need more practice.'

But what Frere liked best was the sense of controlled firepower he got when they moved back farther from the target line and he tried his hand with Goh Tun's assault rifle. Letting rip with a sustained burst using up most of the thirty-round magazine and watching a wooden target fly apart in splintered disintegration gave him the hint of a feeling of what it might be like to be in a real battle.

When they had finished Frere's first lesson on the firing range, some of the young people accompanied them back to camp, the bolder asking Frere about the place he had come from and what the people there thought of the Malian liberation struggle. And he asked them in turn how they came to be in an armed camp in the middle of the jungle when they were so young. Several were orphans from round about, whose parents had been killed in the earlier fighting. Several were there with a mother or father who had come inside. Three or four had actually been born there of couples that had met and married in base camp. All of them expected to see active service. Indeed some of them already had. One of the youngest put his hand in Frere's as they walked along and Frere was deeply touched.

The next day Frere spent with the comrades at the propaganda centre, discussing articles for the second issue of *Workers' World*. He wondered if it would be possible to run a correspondence column so that working people in any country the periodical reached could write in with their questions and ideas. He was told that there would be no problem about supplying addresses in both the Soviet Union and China to which their correspondents could write and have their letters forwarded to base camp.

After one of his sessions with Siti and Swee Meng he took a somewhat circuitous route back to his hut and encountered a group of young people weeding and caring for the large garden of mainly tubers and fungi which supplied much of the camp's food. It was when he saw Leela among them that he stopped and watched. All the time they worked they carried on a spirited colloquy, with Leela taking the lead in keeping it going while working alongside them. She would ask them what seemed a perfectly simple question about some problem they had encountered in their work and they would talk about it. Then she would get them to analyse it into its principal contradictory feature until they understood the nature of the main obstruction to achieving the goal of that particular piece of work. When they had done so, the solution of the problem would be clear to all.

'But remember,' she told them, 'when we know what we have to do to solve some contradiction we've run into, we don't proceed straight away with the solution. Because that might interfere with the solution of some more important contradiction to which the first contradiction was secondary. We wouldn't increase the amount of vegetables we could grow to feed the comrades here in camp by chopping down the trees and letting in more light, would we?'

They laughed at that.

'Every time we act on a decision it's part of a whole hierarchy of more or less secondary contradictions leading from the most trivial right up to what is for us the major contradiction of all, which is...?'

'That between the people of Malia and the imperialists who exploit us,' they answered in unison.

A young man brought from a shed fertiliser which had been made in camp and this was sprinkled over the ground. Then another youth sprayed the whole garden with insecticide.

'And what is the "green revolution"?' Leela asked.

A young woman answered quickly: 'It's the use of modern technology to increase agricultural production.'

'Did the imperialists introduce the "green revolution" into Malia so that all the people of Malia would have enough to eat?'

'No,' the same young woman answered promptly. 'They introduced the "green revolution" to try to prevent our "red revolution".'

Keeping his distance so that he would not interrupt the work and the discussion Frere studied their faces. There were tribals and peasants and those from the towns as well, mostly youths of both sexes – though one or two quite old people were there, also, working away and obviously enjoying being together with the youngsters.

He appreciated the fact that considerations of a very simple kind would often reach the level of philosophical disquisitions you would only get in institutes of higher learning in Britain – as if to demonstrate the point Secretary General Lee often made: that the ideas and experiences of working people down the ages in their struggle to survive had been concentrated and codified in dialectical materialist philosophy which, given back to them, they could recognise as having their own mark on it.

But that was not the only nor, indeed, the main reflection in Frere's mind as he watched the rapt faces of those young people who enjoyed that easy relationship with Leela. What struck him forcefully was that no one but himself seemed to make anything at all of her being a remarkably beautiful woman. Not so much as a glance exchanged between any two of the young men nor the slightest sign of envious resentment in the looks of any of the women nor any fleeting recognition marked by lips parted in wonder that among those fresh young countenances one happened to be outstandingly lovely marred the gay seriousness of their work-study session.

He shook his head for the way it emphasised that loveliness for him more than ever. It also made him realise that he could never even want to achieve the degree of dedication to what held them all there that made largely irrelevant the shapeliness of the lips forming the words of commitment or the sweet clear tone of the voice sounding them.

In the midst of his musing Leela suddenly saw him and said to the others: 'We have a visitor – a comrade from that imperialist country we've been talking about. Perhaps he will join in our discussion.'

Frere stepped forward and held up his fist in salute. They turned and looked at him in a friendly way that invited some contribution.

'I'll tell you something about that "green revolution",' he told them. 'Aid and technological advice was provided for the farmers of Malia so that agricultural output could be increased. And it worked. But only for the richer farmers. It was too costly for the poor farmers. As a result of the lower prices for farm produce, these poor farmers could no longer make a living. They lost their land and it was bought up by the rich farmers. Former land owners became landless labourers. Moreover, with the introduction of farm machinery on the larger holdings the number of landless labourers without even part-time employment increased. Thousands of people in the rural areas, homeless and hungry with no prospect of work, began to crowd into the towns and cities where they formed huge slums on the outskirts, asking for work, begging for food and sometimes driven to crime.'

He stopped, looking about him apologetically. 'I only tell you what you've already heard from Comrade Leela and others. But what I've seen with my own eyes is the misery of that huge bustee attached to the north side of Rani Kalpur like a hideous cancer. Hopeless mothers with almost lifeless babies in their arms. Empty-eyed children with skeleton limbs and pot bellies who are starving to death. I've seen, I've seen – ' He broke off, too moved for the moment to go on. Then he waved his hands dismissively. 'But that's what we have to put an end to, isn't it?'

They were silent for a bit and then someone there clapped. They all clapped and stood up looking at Frere.

'Thank you, Comrade,' Leela said. And to them, 'It's what our Secretary General has told us: science in the hands of the imperialists is a weapon to destroy us. We must take science away from them and use it as a tool to serve the people.'

They had stopped working. They put the hoes and pitch forks and tins of insecticide in the shed and moved away in twos and threes. Frere waited until they had gone, wondering if Leela would consent to walk back to the June Tenth Commune with him.

She was aware of his standing there expectantly. 'Was there something you wanted to ask me, Comrade Frere?'

'Well, nothing specific. It's just – '

'Yes?'

'I was wondering if I might get help from you sometimes. When I'm working on articles for *Workers' World*.'

She frowned slightly. 'Why me?'

'Well, you seem to have such a grasp of the Secretary General's ideas.'

She began walking back through the camp and did not seem to object to his accompanying her. 'I think that could be said of most of us here.'

'I'm sure that's the case but, but I have met you, that is, we are acquainted as members of the same – well, I've heard you speak now and it seems to me – '

She laughed. 'It seems so strange that you should be looking for someone to interpret the ideas of Comrade Lee in the very place where Comrade Lee himself actually is.'

'But he must be too busy to – '

'You won't find Comrade Lee ever turning people aside because he's too busy. And anyway the base camp is full of his writings. You have a copy of the Quotations, I know. There are several books as well and any number of hand-bound volumes of his articles. If you would like me to tell you someone who could – '

'Oh there's a complete set of his works in the propaganda centre which I've been dipping into regularly. It's just that – ' He felt helplessly exposed, his request, which he had thought at the time was perfectly genuine, shown up as a ruse to claim her company.

She looked at him, smiled and relented to the extent of saying: 'I'm glad you came by when you did. Your description of the Rani Kalpur slums was just what was needed.'

'It's something I feel deeply about,' he quickly assured her – almost as though he had to defend everything he had done to find himself here from being put down as no more than a ruse to get to know her.

'Oh that came across – your sincerity.'

'I really do think,' still defensively, 'that the capitalism planted here by my country has to be got rid of – the way those young people in your workshop were getting rid of noxious weeds.'

'It will be. What we're seeing here now isn't the first stage of capitalism in Malia: it's the last stage of capitalism in Britain. When we get rid of imperialism's stooges and puppets, we'll have got rid of capitalism.'

It seemed to Frere that there was just the slightest element of hostility in her rejoinders to anything he said. Perhaps there was nothing personal in it. Perhaps a woman like Leela in a situation like that of the base camp would have had to adopt a somewhat aggressive manner to make her position of wishing to preserve a sacrosanct inner integrity perfectly clear, so that a hands-off attitude of keeping everyone at bay was quite habitual. It presented him with the problem of convincing her that she had nothing at all to fear from him without its seeming like indifference.

'What was it that made you come inside?' he asked her. 'I don't mean what made you enlist in the fight for freedom: I mean what made you cut yourself off from that world out there to fight for it from in here?'

'I wonder if you aren't a little obsessed with individual motives. Surely the point is whether we are serving the right cause, regardless of how or why we're serving it.'

Again he sensed that hint of hostility. 'Do you mean that scientific socialism has no room for ethics and motives and all that?'

'No. That's positivism. Scientific socialism is an analysis of how society in general changes according to the interplay of opposites, so that we can understand our own society well enough to be called upon to change it, and to change ourselves in the process. That's a moral appeal.'

Every attempt at anything personal seemed to end in a philosophical exchange in which he was bested. He gave it up with the observation: 'I suppose that a purely mechanical interpretation of social change is what's called revisionism.'

'That's right. The idea that the demise of capitalism will be brought about automatically as a result of its own internal contradictions, so there's no need to go to the trouble of making a revolution.'

'To which Mao retorts, doesn't he? "If you don't push it, it won't fall!"'

She glanced at him with more respect. 'Exactly!' And then looked away again.

But he felt he had merely exposed himself once more as having pretended to know less Marxism than he did in order to get her to help him.

He started to say something to absolve himself but she was still thinking about what she had called the moral appeal of communism.

'Class conflict,' she said, stopping and looking at him directly, 'has to be fought through and resolved to find our real humanity. In every age and in every place that class struggle has a particular form. History is nothing but the forms, here or there, now as in the past, which that struggle takes. Living a meaningful life is simply a question of understanding the particular form of class struggle which characterises one's own time and place and committing oneself to it with all one's heart and all one's mind.'

Frere stood there taking her in, her lifted face, her eyes fixed on a point above and behind him, her hands clinched into fists at her side. He had thought she was playing intellectual games with him to bring about his discomfiture; but that was because he was simply not accustomed, in the world he normally inhabited, to this use of the intellect to lay bare the very springs of one's most intimate being. He had thought she was avoiding an answer to his question by retreating into a philosophical digression but she was, in fact, answering his question, and at a deeper level than he had asked it.

He shook his head respectfully. Was it the profession he had followed so long, writing about movements and the people caught up in them from the outside, that always made him seem somewhat detached from the passion and devotion and commitment of others? Or was it something in himself, something in himself that would always separate him from – well, from Matt?

She lowered her eyes and seemed instantly aware that she might appear to be striking a pose. She said a trifle casually: 'Those of us who have learned our Marxism from Comrade Lee don't think of it merely as an academic discipline, you know. It's, it's a kind of social poetry.'

'Yes. I've been reading some of Lee's own poetry. It's magnificent. But – '

'But?'

'You obviously feel it, Leela, that compassion for people, just ordinary people, that can have the intensity and the concern and all the sweetness of – well, of the romantic love between woman and man. I wonder if it's in me to any degree.'

'Would you be here if it weren't?'

He did not answer.

'When I was at school,' she recalled, 'I used to pretend to like things I had no taste for yet – like the copy I used to carry around with me of our great epic, *Arien Nemastabadh*. It was composed by a woman, you know.'

'Yes. Narmala. I've read a translation of it.'

'Anyway, through pretending to like it because I wanted to be thought to, by always carrying it with me so that I could be seen reading it I came to love it. I know great chunks of it by heart.'

Frere laughed. 'So it's just a question of carrying people about with me until I come to have the right feelings about them.' And there was one with whom he would have been delighted to institute such a practice.

'But you do carry them about with you. You showed us the people of the Rani Kalpur bustee you carry about with you.'

He did not tell her that there was a difference between loving people and feeling guilty about them.

They had come to their commune and she was about to move on to her own quarters. He held her there with asking: 'Does it ever seem to you a little sad that winning over that world out there by a successful revolution means destroying this idyllic world inside? I can't tell you what it's like to come here, to this camp of like-minded people in the midst of the jungle, from the selfish, uncaring world London is becoming. It's – I don't know.'

'We're not utopians, Comrade Frere. Not – what do you call them in England? Hippies – opting out of society instead of transforming it! We didn't come inside to escape from that world out there but to gather the strength to change it.'

'Of course, but I was thinking of something Comrade Chin said the other day about how easy all relationships are here, how there's no protocol about seeing anyone from Comrade Lee himself down – '

'"Up", he would put it,' she corrected with a smile.

'Or, at least, sideways.'

He looked around them. 'So much of this will have to change, won't it?'

'Yes. In order to change that world out there. This is an idealised version of what we want that world to be. And those of us who have dreamed of what that world can become will have to adjust to the fact that our new reality will in many respects fall short of what we've imagined. We'll have to remember to take as one measure of our achievement the way that new reality will look to those who pay heaviest for the world out there as it is now, those people you were reminding us of who barely exist on the edge of starvation, whose whole lives are only a short stagger from birth to early death.'

'I know,' he said soberly. And then brightening: 'But don't you see, Leela. In this little talk we've had you've given me just the kind of help I was asking for.'

'There are others who could help you as well – or much better. You ought to talk with Comrade Pir Dato. Have you met him yet?'

'No, I haven't.'

'He's an alternate member of the Central Committee and about the same age as you. He was very much involved in making the selection of quotations for the little book I see you have a copy of.'

'Pir Dato?' There was reluctance on his part to seek any other tutor, not only because of his satisfaction with what he had got from her but also, he realised with some surprise, because of an instant stab of utterly irrational jealousy.

'Yes. Comrade Chin was right, you know. You can search out any of us whatever our position and expect us to help – particularly when it's to assist you in bringing out *Workers' World*.'

'I was wondering if you might not write something for it yourself. Something about teaching Marxism through practice to those who can make the best political use of it.'

'Comrade Dato is the person you should see about that.'

'Oh.'

She looked at him just a moment, seriously, and then smiled and turned away.

9

The time Frere could spare from working with the comrades in the propaganda section getting another issue of *Workers' World* ready for the press he spent attending courses on arms maintenance and guerrilla tactics. He took part in jungle movement and deployment exercises, being sent into the swampy region to the west of camp to rendezvous with a comrade waiting in concealment there or, having reconnoitred a thickly grown sector, he would be expected to make a rough map of the area showing the main trails.

Tuck took an avuncular interest in Frere's progress as a jungle warrior under training. Once when they were returning to camp after taking part in a game rather like 'tag', played in an almost impenetrable maze of vine-threaded secondary growth, Tuck complimented him on his reactions. 'You move like a very young man, Comrade Colin. You would have made a good jungle fighter.'

'That's just it. "Would have!" I'm only playing at soldiering. Those young comrades I was playing with, they're getting ready for war. It's not the same.'

'It's what you asked me to get permission for you to do – to go through the same kind of training as our guerrilla fighters do. So that you could write about our struggle with a greater knowledge of its details.'

'But to go through that training with those young comrades and then to stand aside when they go into action will divide me from them more than ever.'

Tuck grinned. 'You're very clever, Comrade. You realised that if you could make them agree to let you take the first step then it wouldn't make sense for you not to be allowed to take the second. I know what you want now. You want a chance to take a shot at one of our enemies – to make you really one of us.'

'Well,' Frere qualified, 'I'd like to be shot at by your enemies to make them my enemies, too. There's a special kind of bonding that comes from having been under fire together.'

'I don't think they'll agree to that. They'll say you can write very well about our struggle without having been in action yourself.'

'But it won't put my relations with those I have to write about on the right footing – my relations with Goh Tun and Ahmed and with you, Comrade Tuck. Admit yourself that if I were never in action you'd never feel the same about me as you felt about – well, my brother.'

'Yes, I can see that, but – '

'I wouldn't be easy in my mind associating with men who'd been in a real fight – '

'Women, too,' Tuck interrupted.

'That makes it worse. Associating with those who'd been in danger, who'd been wounded even, when I myself had never fired a shot in anger nor ever been fired at, talking to them about their experiences – well, it would all seem a bit ghoulish.'

'But as a journalist you must often have written about things happening to people that had never happened to you.'

'I often felt like a ghoul too. And this is different. I'm not supposed to be writing about the comrades here. I'm supposed to be writing from inside – from inside the people here to all those toiling people out there with ears cocked for something happening somewhere that could encourage them in their own struggles.'

Tuck shook his head. 'They won't like it, the Central Committee. They'll say it isn't necessary for everyone to do everything.'

'But Secretary General Lee would never ask comrades to do anything he hadn't done and wouldn't do himself.'

'That's so; but you're not in the position of asking anyone to do anything.'

'Only myself. To know what I really feel about Malian liberation, I have to know if there's anything I might ask myself to do in its name that I couldn't do.'

'But nobody doubts that you could take part in guerrilla action. We're all having a hard time restraining you. After all, you're Comrade Matt's brother.'

'There you've put your finger on it,' Frere said ruefully. 'That's always stood between my brother and me – being in action, putting one's life on the line in a military engagement. When I was growing up, my brother was out here, fighting with the Chindits, winning an MC. And then, afterwards, he was back here again in the even more romantic guise of fighting with the Malian "bandits" – as you were always called in our press. All the while I was in school or at the university or beginning to work in Fleet Street. I believe that if I'm in action, if I've fired at an enemy and been fired at myself, it will help to remove a barrier that's always existed between Matt and me. Do you see what I mean? About getting closer to someone who isn't here any more?'

'I think I do. I remember when I was scraping a living in that shanty town on the outskirts of Rani Kalpur – if I'd done something rather clever or rather wicked, I'd tell myself: "say hello to your father". That's what he must have been like.'

Frere glanced aside at Tuck. 'Did he ever speak of me?' he asked. 'Matt? Did he ever mention having a younger brother?'

'No, he didn't. He never talked about any of the people he'd left behind. When he came to us it was as if he'd blotted out everything before in order to start all over again.' Tuck walked on a few paces in silence and then he said: 'Maybe I can persuade them to let you come on a raid with us now.'

'Thank you, Comrade.'

And so it was that a few days later Frere went to the operations hut just after the evening meal. There he was joined by Goh Tun and Salmi and shortly after that by Tuck himself. Tuck was grinning broadly enough to display his gold tooth advantageously. 'Comrade Kuan himself has supported the plan I've worked out. Overcoming the resistance of the Operations Committee is often the main obstacle. After that, overcoming the enemy is just fishing with dynamite.'

'If we're going to blow up something – ' Goh Tun began.

'Only a manner of speaking,' Tuck cut him off. 'What we're setting out on tomorrow is a shopping tour.' He explained to Frere, 'A shopping tour is when we go out and do three or four different things in a particular region, things taken from the operations list of tasks which need to be taken care of some time within the next month or so.'

Tuck pulled out a large map of the region to the south and west of base camp and pinned it to the map stand. 'Only this shopping tour makes a bit more sense than they sometimes do because I planned it myself. Some of the tours look like the dashing about of a Mei woman on her first trip to town.'

Salmi, Goh Tun and Frere came up close behind so that they could see the map over his shoulder and follow the route he traced with his forefinger.

'We start out before dawn tomorrow going west – '

'Along the Mau Lin highway,' Salmi told Frere. 'We call it that because we travel it so often on raids in that direction.'

'We go into Mau Lin, leave some propaganda for distribution and pick up a young fellow who's waiting for an escort to come inside. We'll take him with us on the rest of our tour, just to watch, of course. It will be good for him. Then we go south to Teipur where a local militia officer is causing a lot of trouble to the villagers by pretending to be one of us.'

'Do we try him for his crimes?' Salmi asked.

'The villagers will try him. We'll carry out the sentence if he's convicted.'

'Good,' Frere said. 'I'd like to see one of the people's courts in action.'

'Then we go southwest from there to Kalibad – not to go into town. There's a police station a couple of miles north of town that we haven't hit for some time. I think you were with the raiding party that last visited it, Goh Tun.'

'That's right. They're probably feeling neglected. It's the headquarters for the area police. They have an armoury which we cleaned out.'

'We're going to clean it out again. In fact, there's a drive on just now to build up our stocks of weapons and ammunition as much as we can.'

'Oh,' Frere wondered with interest, 'is there any particular reason for that?'

Tuck shrugged. 'I don't know. Still, we can always use any weapons we can get our hands on. There's talk of a new American fifty-calibre machine gun which is being supplied to the puppet troops and police. We'll just see if any of them have filtered down to out-stations like Kalibad.'

'And then – ?' Salmi asked.

'What more do you want?' Tuck demanded in mock indignation. 'We haven't been told to finish off the war – just to tidy up a few loose ends.'

'If we're cleaning out the armoury...' Goh Tun began doubtfully.

'That's been taken care of. In the nearby jungle there will be comrades with half a dozen donkeys. All the arms we take will be loaded into panniers and brought back here. It's not like the old days, you know. Like the time I had to carry that Bren gun from one end of the country to the other. I can never bear leaving anything behind that can shoot. I'm haunted by the idea that it might one day kill one of my friends – or worse,' with a laugh, 'me!'

Salmi said to Frere: 'You'll have to be careful about using stories told you by members of the old gang like Tuck in *Workers' World*. They sometimes enlarge on them just the tiniest bit.'

'Only to teach a stronger political moral,' Tuck insisted good humouredly. 'Only that.'

Frere's carefully suppressed excitement about the guerrilla raid he had managed to become a part of went off like an alarm clock just before four the next morning. He got up and dressed, anticipating by ten minutes or so the boy sent around by the night-watch to make sure they were up. The other three were awakened and in the pre-dawn stillness Frere could hear the rustle of green cotton combat jackets being donned, the chunk of canteen against hip or the careful metallic clang of weapons being withdrawn from lockers.

The four of them sat at the table outside the hut, glancing at each other and fleetingly grinning, while Melee, the young woman on kitchen duty that day, served them rice cakes and hot tea. She smiled at them as they got up from the table and they waved to her as they marched off to the western perimeter. Tuck reported to the night guard at the beginning of the trail to Mau Lin.

When first light trickled down through the leaves and vines to dilute the darkness through which they had been somewhat tentatively striding, they were already several miles on their way. With the greater ease of walking along the now dimly-lit trail, which had originally been an animal track then a path which numerous human travellers had hollowed out with their matchete-wielding hands and paved with their rope-soled feet, their tongues were loosened and an exchange of observations and reflections took place up and down their single-file line.

'You must be thinking of the times your brother set forth like this in the grey light,' Tuck said to Frere.

'That's just what I was thinking, Comrade. And you must know the thought that came to me immediately afterwards.'

'Oh you don't have to worry about matching up, Comrade Colin. I've been at this game a long time now. I can look at a man and tell how he'll be under fire. I can't say how much fear he'll know. We all keep that to ourselves. But I can judge in advance what he'll do – whether he'll stand his ground if that's what's required or, if quick violent action is wanted, whether he'll find the instant muscular response and, most of all, whether he'll stick by his comrades to the end.' He turned and slapped Frere, who was right behind him, on the shoulder. 'You'll do fine.'

That night they moved off the trail into a little clearing of the undergrowth where a lean-to in good repair kept the ground underneath it dry. The small camp was often used and there was a store of food on which they could draw, keeping the rations they carried for the later stages of their raid. Hot tea was welcome and they turned in early in good spirits.

Several hours before dusk on the following day they came to the edge of the jungle and lay up within the sheltering fringe to wait for dark.

Goh Tun complained about the wait. 'It's not like Comrade Tuck to misjudge our time like this.'

'He thought I'd hold you up more than I have,' Frere guessed.

Tuck laughed. 'Yes. I thought you'd give my poor old bones an excuse for going slower; and you let me down.'

'What will you do,' Salmi asked Tuck, 'when we've seized power and there are no longer enemies to mount raids against?'

'Old Tuck will be needed more than ever, my boy. The imperialists using the bad elements we've overthrown and the bad elements in neighbouring countries will be mounting raids on us! All the cunning I've acquired in moving secretly against them will provide a battle plan of what they'll try to do to us. Don't worry about Tuck being out of work.'

'Have you ever thought about how much the imperialists would pay you to go over to their side and do the job for them?' Salmi asked with a wink at the others.

'They've robbed us blind for years and lots of other countries too; but I don't think they've got anything like enough cash in their coffers to buy my defection!'

'We'll just have to go on putting up with him,' Goh Tun said affectionately.

Frere took advantage of the break in their talk to ask: 'Do you find it restricting on your military operations, the way Secretary General Lee often talks about winning socialism as cheaply as possible in terms of the violence used?'

Tuck laughed and said to the other two: 'See, I'm being interviewed for *Workers' World*. I'll become famous in countries you don't even know how to spell, Goh Tun.' And to Frere: 'Comrade Lee knows the basic price of socialism. If it came any cheaper, there'd be a lot more of it about.' He paused and grinned; and then he told Frere: 'You can quote me on that.'

'I may at that. So the cost of the revolution is justified by the benefits won for the people?'

'I wouldn't put it like that,' Tuck objected. 'It isn't the end justifying the means sort of thing. Revolution isn't a bad thing we have to go through to get to the good – like those fierce stone daemons guarding the Garden of the Asuras which we have to walk between in order to enter that marvellous place. It isn't like that. It's like a forge in which we who are making the revolution are tempered. It's the means by which we're purged of the impurities in our minds and hearts inherited from the past and become like toughened steel in the fight against exploitation.'

'And can I quote that?' Frere asked a little doubtfully.

'You can,' Salmi answered, 'but you'd better credit it to the Secretary General. Because that's where Comrade Tuck got it.'

'It just shows I study the little book.' Tuck took his copy out of his pocket and waved it. 'I was testing to see if any of you did.'

'You don't think it sounds a bit – well, moralistic,' Frere prompted to see what they would say. 'A bit like the line taken by the missionaries who brought Christianity to Malia.'

'It doesn't sound like that to me,' Goh Tun assured them, 'and I was a long time in a mission hospital when my face was split open. They were all getting ready to go to heaven and they wanted everybody else to get ready too. But nobody's come back from heaven to tell us what it's like and whether it's worth going to. People have come to us from the October Revolution and from the Chinese Revolution, though, and it sounds pretty good. That's something worth getting ready for.'

Frere smiled, somewhat wistfully. 'I wish the young people of my own country could hear you and Salmi. The October Revolution and the Chinese Revolution are events that seem such a long way off to them. I suppose it's why the radical enthusiasm of those who are marching up and down in protest takes such anarchic forms. And the others, those who have been convinced that there's nothing they can do about the world they're inheriting – if they could just share the faith in revolution that unites you young people here, whatever your background. A faith in the future they're helping to make. It's so fresh and, and – ingenuous. It's what any movement needs and what the young people in my land need – so desperately! I only hope,' he looked at Salmi and Goh Tun and held up his own little book, 'you'll all go on believing in this.'

'You make it sound as though Comrade Lee had just made it all up because it was a good tonic for our youth to take,' Tuck said, 'like the herbal medicines old women make up for children whether it really cures them or not.'

'Or like the old stories we tell the children,' Salmi added – 'not because they're true but because they've got such a good moral at the end.'

'Mind you,' Tuck held up one finger, 'we don't mind if those people out there do think it's all just some kind of a myth. One fine day they'll wake up and find that this myth can bite.'

Frere smiled. It was not quite what he had meant. 'I think I know what Comrade Colin is thinking about,' Salmi said. 'In his country for young people to believe in revolution and to fight for it is the hard thing. Here it's the easy thing. A lot of us have no alternative. But what if things changed? What if it became the hard thing for us? – To maintain our revolutionary discipline when the revolution had won us the possibility of an easier life? Is that what you're thinking?'

'I suppose I was. If the revolution succeeds and things get better, won't that mean that the impulse which gave rise to the revolution will no longer be there to make people defend it? What do you think, Goh Tun?'

'How can anybody say?' He shrugged. 'It's like knowing how you'll act under fire when you've never been shot at. You just have to take up your gun and go ahead. What happens when the battle's over – well, I don't guess I've ever thought about it myself.'

'Our Secretary General has thought about it,' Salmi reminded them. 'He writes somewhere about the danger of falling to the sugar-coated bullets of peacetime temptations when we've won the revolutionary war.'

'He thinks ahead, does Comrade Lee.' Tuck nodded in approval. 'There he is worrying about how we're going to preserve a revolution we haven't even made yet.' He looked out and saw that it was dark enough for them to move. 'All right, we can get on now with our little piece of it.'

It was unlikely that there would be any enemy elements anywhere in the neighbourhood but movement across open ground was habitually cautious. They pushed their way past fronds of jungle fern and the last few vine-trailing trees and crossed broad fields that had been cleared in ages past, bent low and moving along the hollows so as never to be silhouetted against the still luminous skyline.

This careful approach hardly prepared Frere for what they encountered when they passed through an opening in the thorn hedge at the bottom of a gently sloping meadow and came to the village of Mau Lin, lit up as for a festival. There were coloured lanterns hanging in the trees and a large fire blazing in the square around which the houses were clustered. In this square, their faces glowing flickeringly in the orange light of the flames, the whole population was gathered expectantly.

'It's usually like this when someone comes inside,' Tuck explained to Frere. 'The villagers like to organise a bit of a send-off.'

'What about the authorities?'

'Oh, they're not invited.'

'I mean, isn't there a danger of their finding out about what's going on and – ?'

'No. No. Mau Lin's security is guaranteed by regular patrols of this area. We like to show how openly we can operate in whole regions of Malia – particularly at night. Most of Malia already belongs to us at night.'

The young man who was to join the liberation force inside sat on a dais, his beaming face almost obscured by the garlands of flowers the girls of the village had hung round his neck. In front of the dais some children, clutching tiny wooden replicas of assault rifles, were marching up and down and singing a patriotic song. When the song was finished they formed a semicircle around the young man and, raising their toy guns in the air, shouted three rousing hurrahs.

A local official stepped up on the dais and, standing by the new recruit with a hand on his shoulder, spoke of who his parents and grandparents were, told some anecdotes about the family which everybody there would know and then recounted something of the youth's achievements in studies and sport at the village school. He stopped and peered past the fire to the place where the four armed men from the base camp silently stood.

Tuck stepped forward and raised his arm. 'Greetings from our Secretary General to the people of Mau Lin.'

The official motioned for the young man to rise and then conducted him around the fire and presented him to Tuck. 'This is Kawan who wishes to join your ranks in the fight to liberate Malia.'

Tuck embraced the young man and said to the other three: 'This is Kawan who has become one of us.' Each of them embraced in turn their new comrade in arms.

The crowd of people around them applauded and then, parting in the middle and withdrawing to either side, disclosed a long table which was heaped with food. However difficult times might be, Salmi explained to Frere, for wedding ceremonies and such the villagers would always contrive a spread like this.

Frere found himself engulfed in a hospitality which made nothing at all of any difference in his appearance and took not the least notice of his somewhat stilted speech.

He had wondered in the past if he really did have any feeling about people, ordinary working people, which nourished the left-wing views he had always professed. Where did those views come from if they did not spring from such feelings? Or had he simply inherited the views from Matt? His life up until then had not presented him with so many occasions which would have proved one way or another whether he had strong feelings about fellow human beings or merely felt the pull of a strong sense of duty.

He regarded himself as working class in so far as he, like any worker, lived by the sale of his labour power. But if the fact that what he marketed was a mental rather than a manual skill did not alter his relationship to the means of production, it did alter the form of his association with fellow-workers. Never for him the socialisation of labour in factory, mine or mill; and meetings of the Union of Journalists, in which he played an active part whenever he was in England for any length of time, were probably not much like the meetings of the unions of engineers or miners – which he supposed would be much freer of individual competitiveness.

As for his family and friends, such personal relationships as he had were intensely individualised and quite detached from any social context like church or club. He was not sure why he had never married and rather supposed it had something to do with his having been constantly on the move. No, nothing of the nature of this village ceremony, like a tribal initiation of a youth assuming adult status, seemed ever to have figured in his past.

Now, as pretty girls garlanded him and smiling matrons pressed food on him and laughing men pumped his hand up and down like a long-lost brother, he felt the stirring of a response directed not toward ideas about people but toward a group of people themselves and it was not entirely unlike the first stirrings of a romantic passion for an individual attractive woman of whom he had just become aware. He thought fleetingly of Leela and wondered if what he believed he might be starting to feel for her was a reflection of whatever it was he was feeling about these exotic people in this remote part of the world who had suddenly become like next-door neighbours or whether some poignant puncture she had made in his outer rind was letting in these present feelings about ordinary people.

When, with Kawan accompanying them, they reached Teipur, a three-day march away through thick jungle, the people of this region showed him a different face. Tuck had sent Salmi and Goh Tun ahead to make sure it was perfectly safe for them to enter and, when it was dark, they went into the village and Tuck was soon in close conference with the serious-faced members of the *panchayat*.

It was arranged that the trial of the police officer should take place early the next morning in a clearing outside the village. By avoiding the publicity of a show trial in the centre of Teipur it was thought there would be less likelihood of bringing down reprisals on the heads of village elders and citizens. Soon after dawn a crowd gathered, made up of as many women as men but no children. They waited, grim-faced and patient, not chatting or moving about and, while noticing the five armed guerrillas standing there with the headman, they made no attempt to greet them or ask why they were there.

The headman explained to Frere and the others that outrage at the assaults on the women of Teipur district had made them take action. They had appointed a group of tough village men to kidnap the police officer from the barracks at Kalibad so that he could be dealt with. When the man claimed to be a secret member of the Communist Party, it was decided to hold a people's trial at which representatives of the Communist Party of Malia were present.

The police officer in rumpled uniform was dragged forward by two villagers and stood there, hands bound behind him, eyes fixed on the ground. The headman pointed at the officer and called for anyone who had anything to say against him to come forward. There was a long pause during which no one spoke and no one stepped out of that rigid half-circle of villagers all staring intently at the man held there between the headman and themselves.

Tuck became impatient. 'See here, comrades. We have marched many miles through the jungle because we understood that you had serious charges to make against this fellow. But when you're invited to speak, the only sound I hear is the chattering of monkeys in the trees overhead. Are his only crimes against them?'

A man from the Kalibad district said: 'It's like this. His worst crimes have been against women. We men feel it's not right for us to speak first when women have a far greater right.'

Then a middle-aged woman spoke up. 'The young women abused by this bad man do not like to speak of the shame he's brought on them. But I will speak. My sister's daughter, Shenti, when she was bringing water from the well at sundown, was taken by two soldiers of this pig. They smashed her chatty and dragged her away to his quarters where he beat her and did bad things to her.'

After this several older women from the region between Kalibad and Teipur told of similar attacks on friends or relatives and then some of the young women themselves who had been sexually abused came forward and, pointing their fingers at the police officer, accused him of violating them. The man did not look at them but kept his eyes lowered. He made no effort to rebut the accusations but, surprisingly, Frere fancied that a smile played around the man's lips.

Tuck asked the headman what the police officer had said when he had been taken prisoner.

'At first he said it was all lies. Then he said that, although he wore the uniform of a police officer, he was really a member of the Communist Party. And in fact, when we searched him, we found a Party card in the lining of his jacket. He said he had been sent to this district to recruit young people for special assignments. He said young girls were needed to entice policemen and army personnel and worm secrets out of them.'

'And what did you say to that?'

'We said we thought he was using his Party membership to satisfy his lust. Things had got so bad no women, particularly no young women, dared venture out alone and men had to be taken off work in the fields to act as escorts.'

'And when you found what he claimed was his Party card – ?'

'We sent word to base camp.'

'Very right and proper. Well, comrades,' Tuck lifted his voice, 'I can assure you that this pig is not and never has been a member of the

Communist Party of Malia. I have looked at the card he carried and it's a forgery. Knowing the respect you villagers have for our Party, maybe he thought that if he got into trouble, just producing the card would get him off.'

Some of the people nodded at this and they began talking to each other about whether it was what the police officer had thought. The headman held up his hand for quiet and Tuck continued:

'Or maybe he was sent here with a card so that he could do bad things to discredit the Party.'

Other people seemed to think this was more likely and there was more excited talk.

'But it doesn't make any difference,' Tuck said loudly to reclaim their attention. 'Whether he was using the card to get him off doing bad things to our womenfolk or whether he was doing bad things to our womenfolk to discredit the Party doesn't matter. He has done bad things to our womenfolk and that's all there is to it.'

Suddenly the police officer looked up. He glared around the half-circle of angry faces and he said: 'It does make a difference. If I was disobeying orders to do what I wanted to with these women, that's one thing. But if I was sent here officially to do a job and you punish me for it, you'll bring down on your heads the full weight of the Government!'

'It's thoughtful of you to tell us,' Tuck said; 'but we've been bringing the full weight of the Government down on our heads for many years now and they seem quite unbowed.'

'When it's known where I'm being held,' the officer shouted, 'a force will be sent to come and get me.'

'It won't be necessary,' Tuck assured him. 'When these people have finished with you, you'll be sent back to your own lot – as a warning.'

Tuck turned and nodded to the headman who spoke to the people crowding about. 'You have heard of this man's crimes from those he's laid his hands on. What should be done with him?'

The crowd shouted in a single voice: 'Kill him! Kill!'

'So be it, ' Tuck said. He beckoned to Salmi and Goh Tun. 'Against that mud wall beyond the well I think.'

'Wait! Wait!' the police officer called out in terror. 'You can't shoot me like that.'

'Why not?' Goh Tun asked him. 'We've got the guns and the bullets and we've got you. Where's the difficulty?'

'But I have the right to a trial.'

'You've just had it. This people's court has tried and sentenced you.'

Goh Tun and Salmi helped the two men holding the police officer drag him toward the wall.

Frere said quietly to Tuck: 'Do you intend me to be part of the execution squad?'

'It's entirely up to you, Comrade Colin. You told me you wanted to go on an operational patrol and I arranged it for you. This carrying out of a sentence passed by our friends here is the sort of thing we do on such patrols.'

'Of course.'

'I'm not telling you to take part in the actual shooting. You told me you could only write about such things by doing them yourself. You said you didn't want to be just a foreign correspondent writing about a war you were assigned to.'

'That's so.' He could write theoretically about the way there was more indignation in his part of the world over the execution of one rotten landlord or corrupt official than over millions of people suffering poverty and injustice for many generations; he could write about this trial he had just seen; but that would never be the same as actually involving himself.

'And yet you want me to order you to take part, don't you?' Tuck asked him.

'Yes. I wanted to participate while at the same time absolving myself of any responsibility. I request that you allow me to be part of the firing squad.'

'Request granted.'

Meanwhile they were having difficulty in propping the whimpering police officer against the wall. His legs were trembling so that he kept slumping down and Goh Tun had to hoist him erect again and again.

'Am I supposed to hold him up like this when you shoot him?' Goh Tun enquired with grim humour.

'Let him die in whatever position he prefers,' Tuck said. 'If he wants it to happen while he's grovelling in the dirt, so be it.'

He turned to the new recruit, Kawan. 'You can use an AKM?'

'I've never really fired one,' the young man said, adding eagerly, 'but I know how it works.'

'Good. We've brought one for you. This way you'll begin to get used to it – killing two birds with one stone as they say. We never waste stones, you know. All our stones are paid for by the people.'

Goh Tun and Salmi left the man on his knees, his face in his hands, his shoulders heaving. Kawan took the assault rifle that had been brought for him and switched from 'safe' to 'fire' and then back to 'safe' again. Tuck formed them up in a rough line some fifteen yards away from the cringing police officer. 'When you get the signal, a three or four second burst. We don't want any doubt about this.' Then he stepped into line himself and said to the headman: 'You give the order and we'll fire.'

Suddenly there was an enormous silence which seemed to borrow its absolute quality from the expected noise of the guns about to shatter it. In that stillness the sound of five rifles being switched to automatic fire was loud and then – Frere was wondering what it was going to feel like, shooting at an unarmed man in cold blood; and then – the headman raised his arm, held it aloft a moment and then – Frere was still waiting to see what it was going to feel like when there was a throbbing roar of sound and it was all over. He was standing there wondering what it was going to be like when the man, after being slammed back against the wall, fell forward in a bloody mess and lay still. There would be some feeling; but then it was as if he could not feel anything about a body emptied of life because he had not been quick enough to feel anything about it while the man still cowered and sobbed.

Perhaps much later, Frere thought, some image of the bullets driving the man back against the wall and pinning him there for a few seconds spouting blood before slumping forward would return to him, charged at last with an appropriate emotion. But even as they left Teipur early the following morning there was nothing. Was it possible, he wondered, to think something through so thoroughly, ordering his ideas about popular justice, marshalling his arguments for it and eloquently vindicating the practice, that when an example of it occurred which involved him, there was no further comment his feelings were called upon to make?

He was to find that experience repeated in the days ahead. He was aware that anyone from his old life would say that his sensibilities were becoming numbed and soon the bloodiest acts his political commitment might call for would be executed without a qualm. He was learning instead that, given time, the mind can settle moral issues so finally that one is unaffected by the kind of scruples imagined by those who will never find themselves in such a situation.

And, of course, there had been the casual communalism of their all firing together like that – his own reflections on shooting a human being for the first time merely part of his awareness of Kawan's youthful excitement, of Tuck's easy authority and of the practised professionalism of the other two. That might be the real reason the episode never came back to haunt him. Since they all acted together under the same conception of shared goal and the only way to it, he could surrender his conscience to the common will. Nothing about that democratic and efficient elimination of an enemy of the people gave him the slightest urge to withdraw his personal conscience from the Party's deposit account in order to pay individually for his part in their common act.

When the five of them took the trail to Kalibad not all that far away, the nature of their progress changed. For guerrillas to be moving in the direction of a government outpost was an act of war and they advanced accordingly. They made a show of leaving Teipur along a track running south and then cut through thick jungle to make a wide laborious curve to the north where they spent the night in a tiny clearing hollowed out of the brush.

Just after noon of the following day they came to higher ground where the undergrowth thinned to show them a shallow river valley with cultivated fields spread like a patchwork cover over the gentle folds from which the jungle had been gradually pushed back. Kalibad straddled the river with three small bridges pinning the two halves of the town together.

Tuck led them along a low ridge, keeping well below the sky-line, to a place of concealment some five hundred yards above the police station – a square, squat structure of cement – and they spent some time studying the building and the ground around it, occasionally exchanging quiet remarks. Then Tuck turned and summoned the other three to join them, all now peering down through a last thin curtain of grass and leaves at the solid shape of their objective.

'You see,' Tuck pointed out holes in the ground to the right and left of the building, 'those are cossack posts for defending the station in case any naughty "bandits" should take it into their heads to attack. You can see the muzzles of the fifty-calibre machine guns on swivel mountings poking out of the holes. Those must be the new American guns we've heard about. The word is that those flanking machine gun posts are only manned during the hours of darkness.'

'Because,' Goh Tun said with a laugh, 'as everybody knows, "bandits" only attack at night. They haven't the guts for daylight raids.'

'We'll see if we can't dispel that myth this very afternoon,' Tuck said with a grin. He explained the plan he had worked out with Goh Tun. 'At this time, in the heat of the day, all of the men stationed down there, some seven or eight of them, are inside – most of them probably asleep. So Salmi and Goh Tun will slip down and take over those two machine gun posts. Then, under the cover they provide, you, Comrade Colin, will crawl along a way Goh Tun will show you to the west wall of the station, just under that ventilation grill you can see quite clearly. You throw a grenade through the grill and then lie down close to the wall to be out of the way.'

Frere had been shocked by the realisation that the attack on the police station was not something to be talked about and thought about until everybody was thoroughly ready for it but was going to happen now, in just a few minutes. And then, compounding the shock, had come the further realisation that he himself was to play an active part in that action which was only those few minutes off.

'It'll be all right,' Goh Tun assured Frere. 'I've attacked this station before and you can crawl right up to that wall without being seen by anyone inside.'

'When the grenade goes off,' Tuck continued, 'those who are not knocked out by the blast will either run out of the front to be picked off by Salmi and Goh Tun or rush out of the back to seek concealment in the brush – to be met, of course, by Kawan and me who will be waiting for them right here.' He looked at Frere. 'All right?'

'All right,' Frere answered in a way that sounded to him a bit tentative. 'Do I, do I take my assault rifle as well as a couple of grenades?'

'We keep our weapons with us always. Unless, as in the case of Goh Tun and Salmi, we're arming ourselves at the enemy's expense.'

'And when will our attack begin?' Kawan wanted to know.

Tuck looked at his wristwatch. 'Oh not for another five minutes.' Frere was hit again by the blow of immediacy. He could only hope that if there was not time for him to steel himself for what was about to happen there was not time for fear to clutch and thoroughly discompose him either. He held his hand out to see if it was steady and then quickly put it down again. After living around armed violence so much of his professional life as a journalist, after years of flirting with it, as it were, he was about to embrace it himself. And it was strange how different it was. Taking up a gun for the purpose of shooting someone with it was an entirely different thing to simply being where guns were going off around one. No more dangerous, perhaps, but a definitive crossing of the barrier that separates the combatant from the non-combatant, a joining of the ranks of the warriors, an entering into the fellowship of those who down the ages in just and unjust wars have taken on themselves the supreme arbitrament of the lives of other men.

And then, of course, he thought of Matt. For him Matt had always been the brother on the other side of a kind of metal screen where life was different because it was the stake everyone in battle constantly played with in the ultimate game. No other life had quite that quality and, therefore, the professional soldier was just that, over and beyond everything else, and could only figure somewhat dimly in any relationship but that of comrade-in-arms.

He felt that in emerging from these shrubs and ferns and moving down toward that squat ugly cement fort he was going toward an encounter with Matt and it was that which was determining his present mood more than any personal hazard. If he conducted himself as a good soldier, then it was going to be like the meeting with his brother which he had often, as a boy, perhaps turning over in his fingers the medals won in Burma, imagined and always been cheated of, the meeting which being a war correspondent or anything else but an armed fighter ready for action could never vouchsafe him.

He hefted the Russian assault rifle which had been his from the time it was decided that he should be allowed to participate in an operational patrol; he removed the magazine, tested the tension on the cartridges and replaced it; he swung it up toward the branches overhead with one hand to see how easily he could manage it while keeping the other hand free – to lob a grenade through a two-foot square perhaps. He looked around, saw the others watching him and smiled sheepishly.

Tuck patted him on the back affectionately. 'Not this time, Comrade. You won't be doing any shooting this time; but make that first grenade count.' Tuck nodded to Goh Tun and Salmi and they moved away to right and left, going very quietly through the strip of brush and then on elbows, belly and knees wriggling toward the two machine gun emplacements, taking advantage of every hollow, rock or bush.

Frere watched Goh Tun's progress carefully to be able to take exactly the same route himself. Tuck handed him the two grenades and he fastened them to his belt, at the back to be out of his way as he crawled along hugging the ground closely. Goh Tun first and then Salmi reached their respective holes, slid in headfirst and then moved the guns on their swivels to show both posts were manned. Frere looked at Tuck. Tuck winked and nodded. He was smiling broadly as though he and Frere shared a highly comical secret between them.

Once Frere had left the protection of undergrowth and was moving down the slope toward the gun Goh Tun had taken charge of, he found that the effort to remember the precise path, to keep low and move quickly without the slightest sound took too much of his attention for him to be able to decide whether he was afraid or not. He soon reached the lip of the hole, was greeted with a touch on the shoulder before Goh Tun's finger pointed out the way he was to move to the wall of the police station.

He set out again, wriggling forward on elbow and opposite knee until he reached the wall just under the ventilation grill. He pulled himself as close into the wall as he could and paused to get his breath, forcing himself to fill and empty his lungs slowly so as not to be heard.

It was very still. He had not realised how still it was until he was in a position where the slightest sound he made could be disastrous. Suddenly he heard voices inside the building. A question asked and a sleepy answer. Then a louder call and the sound of movement.

Had they heard him? he wondered in a kind of panic. Were they about to start rushing out of the building? Was he going to be caught cowering there? With a trembling hand he detached one of the grenades and almost dropped it. He raised it to his mouth and primed it with his teeth. He stood up, aware that his legs were shaking violently, and flung the grenade through the vent.

He threw himself down again in time to hear the muffled roar inside the building. He thought he could feel something of the force of the explosion through the wall next to his body. Then there was a piercing scream and shouts and the pounding of feet making for the door.

Frere stayed very still, watching intently that sharp edge of the wall around which one or other of the men might take it into his head to run when Salmi and Goh Tun opened up on them. But where was the fire from the two machine gun posts? Survivors of the explosion must be running out of the station now and not a shot was to be heard! Should he see what was happening – even if it exposed him to attack? But what if he got in the way just when Salmi and Goh Tun were about to open fire! Something must have gone wrong. Was he to go on lying there while the scheme went to pieces? He had never known such an agony of indecision. It was shaking his whole body.

And then with what was at once shout and groan he leapt up, stood there tense a moment and ran around the edge of the building.

Something very strange happened. It was not exactly a change in tempo with all movement slowed as in an action replay: it was more like a tableau presented in such exquisite detail that time seemed to have stopped while he took it all in. Three men had come out of the station and were arrested in flight by his precise apprehension of them, the last looking back over his shoulder, face fixed in fear, the one in front of him carrying a rifle but as yet unaware of Frere, and the farthest one, arms outstretched, feet kicking out to the side in an ungainly run, simply putting as much distance as possible behind him.

There were shouts from Goh Tun and when Frere shot a glance in that direction Goh Tun was waving his arms in frantic frustration. For a fraction of an instant Frere thought Goh Tun wanted him to move out of the way so he could shoot. But he was not in the way. Was the gun not working? And why was Salmi not firing?

The three running men hardly seemed to have moved when Frere looked back at them, lifted the rifle and found that he was firing. He had wondered for an instant, as his finger closed on the trigger, if he had switched to automatic and then there was the controlled leap of the rifle in his hands and his bullets were hitting the man with the gun. He fired a second burst of four or five shots at the man who was farthest away and it was as if someone had given this man a powerful shove in the back with both hands and knocked him flat. The nearest man, still with the expression of fear on his face, had turned around completely and was raising a pistol to shoot. Frere squeezed the trigger once more and three little explosions of flesh and blood angled up the man's chest and he took several stumbling steps backwards as though jerked from behind by a rope, his flailing arms describing circles in the air to regain his balance and the pistol flying off to one side. Frere looked away to see the man he had shot first scramble to his feet and in a limping run disappear behind the station, still carrying his gun.

There was movement behind him and Frere spun around, covering the entrance of the station just as a dimly seen man was about to emerge. A burst of fire drove him back inside and Frere, reaching behind him with his left hand, unhooked the other grenade, pulled out the pin with his teeth and lobbed it through the door. He was running toward the opposite side of the station from that behind which the wounded man with the gun had vanished when the second explosion boomed inside.

Frere ran right out behind the building and, not knowing how many bullets he had left, switched his rifle to single fire. He was levelling it at the back edge of the station house when the wounded man staggered into view. Frere shouted at him to drop the gun but the man swung it up as if to fire. Frere shot and hit the man in the side, spinning him around. But he was still on his feet and tried once more to raise the gun. Frere's next shot finished him off and he lay there crumpled and still.

Frere switched his rifle to 'safe' then back to 'fire' as he walked around toward the front of the building. He lifted his right hand, which had been trembling badly when he threw the first grenade. It was perfectly steady. He shook his head.

He was standing outside the entrance listening carefully for any sound inside when Goh Tun ran up and urged him to back away. Salmi joined them then and also told Frere not to go inside. By that time Tuck and Kawan were there too.

Goh Tun started to explain to Tuck what had happened. 'You don't have to tell me. That point fifty had been left out there without maintenance, for months maybe, and wouldn't fire.'

'Neither would mine,' Salmi said.

Tuck laughed. 'What a joke on us if one of our own people sabotaged them!'

'It was almost a fatal joke,' Goh Tun said, looking at Frere.

'That's right,' Tuck said – 'if it hadn't been for our one-man guerrilla army.' He slapped Frere on the back.

'Shouldn't we, shouldn't we look inside?' was all Frere could say.

'I'll have a look first,' Goh Tun said, taking his rifle from Kawan who had brought it down along with his own. In a minute or so Goh Tun shouted that it was safe for them to go inside.

The acrid smoke and thick dust made it difficult to see and the heavy sulphurous fumes hard to breathe. Just within the door lay sprawled the man Frere had shot just before throwing the second grenade; and slammed against a wall by the force of the blast was a man in a sitting posture, head lolling. In the sleeping quarters there was one body half out of a bunk and another staring open eyed at the ceiling as though undisturbed by all the noisy action.

Tuck went over to a wall rack and said: 'These weapons seem to be all right but we'll have to give them a good going over.'

'Maybe none of them will shoot,' Frere said. 'I don't remember anybody getting off a shot at me.'

'You were just too fast for them.'

Frere started to say something and then did not. When they had gone outside again Goh Tun inspected the two men Frere had killed in front of the station. Each time he looked up from one of the bodies he gave Frere a thumbs up sign.

Tuck said to Kawan: 'There are some lessons to be learned from this, my boy. Not just by you. By all of us. In the first place, think not only of what's likely to happen in any attack but also of the most unlikely thing that might happen and plan on what you'd do about that as well. I made a major mistake in not considering the possibility that neither of those machine guns would be in working order – and I know how badly puppet troops treat their weapons, too. I know how troops whose heart isn't in the fighting can commit acts of intentional or accidental sabotage. So one of the unlikely things that could always happen is that some veteran leading an operation may have failed to take into account the unlikely things that might happen.'

'But how could anyone have guessed that both of those guns would be out of action?' Kawan wondered.

'They were, though,' Tuck reminded him. And with a shake of his head: 'They certainly were. What you have no right to plan on,' he continued, 'is that one of your comrades will rise to an unlikely situation the way Comrade Colin did. Action like that is a bonus we have no right to take into account. I hope you noticed the way he did that, my boy. First he takes out of the battle the man with the rifle; then he shoots the one farthest away before he can get to the cover of those big rocks; and then, finally, he takes care of the man closest to him.'

'You could see the whole thing?' Frere asked.

'We could see it. And then when the man who was only wounded runs around the side of the police station, Comrade Colin doesn't simply chase after him. Oh no. He bottles up any that are left inside the station and runs around the other side to surprise the run-away head on and finish him off.'

'That's right,' Goh Tun said in hearty agreement. 'It was done beautifully. It was a beautiful thing to watch; and that's all Salmi and I did – just watched. It was like being in the front row for seeing a shadow play back at base camp.'

Frere still did not say anything. Their approval made him very uneasy. Not because he was modest but because the way they described it was not the way it had been for him at all. He had not thought about the order in which he would shoot the three men before him nor had he realised he must seal up the station with his other grenade. From the moment he had let loose with his first burst something or somebody seemed to have taken him over and dictated everything he had done. It was that thing or that person, whatever or whoever it was, that they were praising. He did not think he liked the experience, the experience of being possessed like that. He looked at the two dead bodies. No, he did not think he liked the way that thing or that person had taken charge and made use of him.

'You know,' Tuck said, 'your brother would have been very proud of you today.'

That was what it must have been, Frere thought – Matt the professional soldier must have possessed him and directed everything he had done, not speaking to him, any more than he ever had spoken to him, but simply seeing what had to be done and, out of the experience of having done it countless times before, simply doing it.

He felt differently about having been taken over that way once he thought of himself as having been in Matt's care. In some sense, on the field of battle, he had met his brother. He walked over to Tuck and warmly embraced him and in holding to him Matt's old comrade-in-arms he felt closer to Matt than in his entire life.

10

When the caravan of donkeys laden with captured arms arrived at base camp several days after the return of Tuck's patrol, something of an occasion was made of it. Even Secretary General Lee was involved to the extent of saying a few words about the special importance at this time of keeping high both their morale and their state of armed readiness and about the way the raid under Comrade Tuck's command had contributed to both.

Tuck climbed up on the platform and addressed those gathered in the Red Quadrangle, giving a humorously self-deprecatory account of the battle of the Kalibad station.

'So,' he told them, 'the new fifty-calibre machine guns from America didn't work. But the new comrade from Britain worked very well indeed!'

There was some laughter and applause at this and those in Frere's vicinity winked and beamed at him. He looked down at the ground, still feeling that he really had no right to any commendation for the way the fight had gone.

When he got back to the June Tenth Commune that evening, there was a message for him from Hadar asking him to report to the propaganda centre first thing in the morning, which, apart from the time he had been away from camp with Tuck's patrol, was what he did every day.

Although he went straight to the centre as soon as he had finished his breakfast of rice cakes and tea, Hadar was already there, and sitting on stools ranged around him were Chin, looking uneasy, and Siti and Swee Meng looking as though they would like to be getting on with their work. Standing by the bamboo curtain was Masuri, who was the camp's wireless operator and expert on communications equipment.

Frere felt that it had been made to look as if he had kept them all waiting. Hadar motioned him to an unoccupied stool as a teacher might direct a late pupil to a seat. 'I was telling the comrades that the Central Committee has been considering the first few issues of *Workers' World*.

It had been hoped that Comrade Frere would be there for the discussion; but apparently that had not proved possible.'

'I'm very sorry, Comrade Hadar. I certainly wish I could have been present. When was the discussion?'

'Four days ago. I expressed regret that you preferred taking part in an ad hoc operational exercise to being present when the periodical for which you have assumed responsibility was up for consideration.'

'I had no way of knowing the Central Committee was going to discuss *Workers' World* when I asked to go on a patrol.'

'The Central Committee doesn't post its agenda in advance,' Hadar said.

'But if I could have been told that the subject of *Workers' World* was coming up in the next few days – '

'The Central Committee has other things to think about than harmonising its business with your revolutionary predilections, Comrade Frere.'

'Of course. But I don't think my going on the raid with Comrade Tuck was unconnected with my editorial responsibilities.'

'Perhaps you think members of the Central Committee should be out on patrol instead of remaining in camp planning for the liberation of this country.'

'Certainly not.' Frere did not add that, all the same, he would have much less faith in that planning if most of the members of the Central Committee had not, at one time or another, been engaged in guerrilla action or, in Comrade Lee's case, actual wartime service.

'I'm afraid I was never convinced by your reasoning that, in order to understand that enemies of the revolution must be dealt with firmly, you had to go out and kill a few of them yourself. Although,' he conceded niggardly, 'I believe that having arrived at that illogical conclusion, you did conduct yourself most acceptably.'

Frere started to say something and then changed his mind and merely murmured, 'Thank you.'

'So without the benefit of Comrade Frere's presence,' Hadar addressed them all, 'the Central Committee did consider the issues of *Workers' World* that have so far been published.'

They waited for Hadar to say more and when, for the moment, he did not, Chin asked: 'Would you say that, on the whole, the Central Committee took a favourable view of the line of the new periodical?'

'Isn't that line agreed with me as the Central Committee member responsible for propaganda? How then could the Central Committee not take a favourable view of it? However – ' He took from a cardboard folder a carbon copy of a page of typewriting. 'However, the Central

Committee does have certain alterations and improvements to suggest. They are written here.' He handed the paper to Chin. 'Study them carefully and then think how best you can incorporate the suggestions in future issues.'

'Comrade Colin and I will go over them, with the rest of the staff.' Chin made a point of associating himself with Frere in this editorial response.

Hadar got up to go and almost as an afterthought before departure: 'Congratulation on your good work, Comrades. The Central Committee is well pleased with your efforts.'

When he had gone, Frere shook his head doubtfully. 'That's not quite the point,' he said of Hadar's commendation. 'Of course you, Comrade Chin, and you too,' taking in Siti and Swee Meng with a glance, 'have put in good work on the new publication. When have your efforts *not* deserved praise. The question is whether the Central Committee thinks *Workers' World* is performing the interpretive function for the international working class I'm supposed to help it achieve.'

'I think you can take it,' Chin said, 'that the Central Committee *does* think it's striking the right note, that it is translating the aims and ideals of our liberation movement into terms which workers in struggle anywhere can appreciate. Don't forget that our Secretary General has worked abroad himself. He can draw on his personal experience for knowledge of the kind of approach that might appeal to European workers.'

Frere reached for the paper Siti had taken from Chin. 'Perhaps,' he said, 'the suggestions they've made will give us a clearer notion of what they think of it up to now.'

'I've looked at the points they've made,' Siti told him. 'Most of them are things we'd already thought of ourselves.'

Frere glanced at the sheet and nodded. 'We'd better keep it on file, though.' And then to Chin, trying not to make too much of it: 'Either Comrade Hadar doesn't like me much or doesn't trust me. I'm not sure which.'

Chin thought for a moment, brow wrinkled, before answering. 'There's something you may not have taken into sufficient account, Comrade Colin. Some of those here like Comrade Tuck or Comrade Kuan or Secretary General Lee himself have simply accepted you as the brother of our brother, Comrade Matt. But to others Matthew Frere is just a name. To them it might seem a little questionable that someone from the imperialist country which for so long held this land in chains and our people in contempt should be taken at once to our bosoms. We who have worked closest with you, these two young comrades and myself, and Masuri, too, we know and trust you, completely.

And, besides, we like you.' They all nodded in enthusiastic agreement. 'Which can sometimes be just as important; but you see – '

Frere held up his hand to stop him. 'Please don't say any more, Comrade. I've been guilty of that same stupidity before – of not realising the kinds of doubts that are bound to exist about me. Isn't it an example of that very imperialist attitude that I'd think I had only to declare myself to be of your camp, for everybody to treat me at once as a long-lost brother?'

'That's the way we *do* think of you,' Siti assured him.

'It's that warm and comradely reception I've had from some and, particularly, from you whom I've worked with so closely that's my excuse. That's what has made me forget that I ought to be regarded with the greatest reserve until I've had time to prove I'm not, at best, just a hired journalist who will go to any lengths for a good story and, at worst, well, a spy!'

Siti laughed. 'You must allow us to flatter ourselves that in the kind of discussions we've had about the contents and presentation of *Workers' World* we'd have spotted any mere pretence at revolutionary conviction.'

'I don't know,' Frere demurred. 'My own country and the United States must have acquired some expertise in espionage. They've been at it long enough.'

'But, Comrade,' Chin objected, with good humour. 'Our side has always had the best spies. You have to believe in something besides your pay cheque to be a good spy.'

'That's true,' Frere had to agree. 'Ideological conviction is necessary. It isn't possible to believe in capitalism – only what it can get you.' And then with a wink: 'But isn't that just what a spy from the West would have been briefed to say?'

'And isn't our assurance to you of our trust,' Siti answered, 'just how we'd treat a suspected spy?'

Frere laughed and was serious again. 'Joking apart, there is a sense in which I'm pretending to be one of you, trying to convince you and even myself that this is where I belong. There's something individualistically willed and, therefore, arbitrary about my being here – so that I feel the need to justify myself and prove my right to be treated like any of you.'

'Which could mean,' Swee Meng said, 'that you could be the most reliable of us all since you would be constantly striving to be what we, more naturally simple, are.'

'This is an amusing conversation,' Chin said, 'but it doesn't get articles written or front pages laid out.'

'Or printing presses inspected,' Masuri said and pushed his way through the curtain into the back of the hut.

Siti and Swee Meng returned to the tasks that had been interrupted by Hadar's arrival.

Chin said to Frere: 'Any feeling Hadar may have about you as an Englishman who has to prove himself is only part of it. Several times I've managed to go over Hadar's head to get the Central Committee to agree to set aside some ruling of his I thought was questionable. On each occasion he treated me just as he treated you this morning.'

'Thank you, Comrade Chin. That helps.'

But Frere wanted to have some more direct knowledge of what the Central Committee thought of the first few issues of *Workers' World* than Hadar's report had provided. He remembered that when he had been received by the Central Committee, Ang had said that he thought Frere might help him to understand Matt better. It had surprised Frere at the time and he had thought that he ought to follow it up. In doing so he might also get more information about the Central Committee's appreciation of his journalistic efforts.

And a few days later Frere, having passed a request for a meeting through the Secretariat, was invited to Ang's hut for tea. Ang rose as Frere stepped onto the wooden platform which raised most camp structures some six or seven inches above the ground. The woven reed sides and roof were like all the other residential quarters and enclosed the same small space.

'We Central Committee members rather pride ourselves on the simplicity of our existence,' Ang said with just the ghost of a smile; 'but, as you see, I've lost out to the extent of these two magnificent cane chairs. I always insist that I only make use of them when I have a distinguished guest; but that makes it a claim I can't substantiate.'

'Nor they refute,' Frere said. 'Am I then a "distinguished guest"?' as Ang motioned for him to be seated.

'Certainly,' Ang said and sat down himself.

'I shall say,' making himself comfortable, 'that in the name of hospitality you bore the luxury of these chairs with all the fortitude of a faqir on his bed of nails.'

Ang laughed but it did not change that black opaque surface of his eyes from which one's glance seemed to bounce off. He set about the preparation of two cups of tea. 'I congratulate you on your exploits during one of Comrade Tuck's forays.'

'It was largely accidental. I just happened to be in the right place at the right time.'

'These things never just happen, Comrade Colin. Back in the days when I was an active guerrilla fighter I remember thinking – and this was at a time when our casualties were murderously high – that even death doesn't just happen. It seemed to me that men died when they acquiesced in their death, when exhaustion or illness or despondency, perhaps, weakened muscles, slowed brains or destroyed morale to open the way for death.'

Frere accepted a cup of tea and sipped it.

'Have you got to liking it yet – our aromatic tea?'

'Yes, I do.' He put the cup down. 'Is that what happened to my brother? Did he acquiesce in his capture?'

'Not in the sense of *letting* himself be captured. Comrade Matt would never give up. But – '

'Yes?'

'I don't know. His mind and will seemed somehow divided on that last action we carried out together. Instead of feeling that we would have to fight on and win, whatever the odds against us, because we were right, I think he'd begun to wonder if the fact that we were *not* winning, not then anyway, meant that we were in some way wrong.'

'He could doubt the cause of national liberation!'

'Not the cause but the means by which we were trying to achieve it. Your brother was a – I think you'd have to call him a humanitarian.'

'Not a Marxist?'

'Not in the sense of working things out theoretically. He felt when things were right. And his feelings did him credit. Oh he understood that the violence we used to free ourselves was simply the violence used to keep us in subjection turned inside out. But he was always much more concerned with what had been done to us than with what we were doing about it. He came to us to begin with more as a protest against all the barbarous acts committed by your country against the people of Malia than out of a conviction that whatever we had to do to liberate ourselves was justified.'

'I can understand that. He hated the imperialist occupiers of this country, the way they bribed the very people they'd treated with such contempt to fight against the Japanese invaders and then, after the war, broke all their promises. He hated them enough to kill and in killing them he possibly felt that he was killing that in himself which he felt was like them.'

'Perhaps that was what made him seem somehow divided that last time we were together. I'd never got to know him very well before that. He was not at all a violent man, you know.'

'But he was a soldier all his adult life.'

'Yes, and always with that inner contradiction between what he thought he ought to do and his natural peaceful inclinations.'

'Poor Matt.'

'Don't pity him. It was because he was acting against his nature that he was such a good soldier and guerrilla fighter. In action he was like a machine – quite fearlessly doing exactly the right thing without even having to think about it.'

'You know,' Frere said excitedly, 'that's just how it seemed outside that police post at Kalibad – as if Matt had taken control of me and was doing exactly the right thing, quite automatically. I didn't feel anything at all while it was happening.'

'There must be the same thing in you that was in your brother before.'

'Maybe. I've never experienced anything like that.'

'Your brother always seemed to be acting against the grain to do what he thought was right. He might have his doubts about whether our struggle would ever be successful but he would never have stopped fighting on our side. That's why I regarded him as a hero – even though I never told him. We were so different it was hard for us to communicate. I think I was a very *dogmatic* Marxist in those days. While Matt – well, there's something about him I think I understand better since we've been talking. Matt Frere came to us after the war of his own free will, as a volunteer. That made him feel he was personally responsible for everything he was involved in – because he'd chosen that precise involvement.'

'Like me.'

'Yes, like you. That's something I hadn't thought about before. For me, indeed for most of us here, it hasn't been like that.'

'How do you mean? Surely everybody has to make a choice whether to fight or not.'

'The choice can be forced on us. Take me. I was the spoiled son of a rich merchant who threw me out of the house for being disrespectful. I became a drug addict and a petty criminal, completely demoralised. Do you know how I came here from China? I stole an old man's steerage ticket. That saved my life; but I've never thought of that life as being mine. It belonged to that old man and all like him. All the poor and wretched of this world. There have never been any alternatives for me. From the moment I got to know about Comrade Lee and the Marxist theory of how the poor and the wretched could liberate themselves, they claimed me – body and soul. Whatever they asked of me needed no other justification.'

'No, it wouldn't be like that for Matt.'

'He could never see that a class war – and liberation struggles are only a special form of class war – in a class war the gulf between the two sides, between the exploiters and the exploited, is too great for nice humanitarian generalities to stretch across. They strain and break or become quite meaningless. Matt could never accept that.'

Frere shook his head. 'I'm like him in certain ways. But I don't have that problem. If I tried to apply the most humane principles to the situation here, I'd have to say that they can't begin to have any meaning till they've been translated into the liberation of the poor exploited people of Malia from imperialist oppression.'

'Thus giving those general humane principles a specific class content,' Ang nodded in agreement – 'without which they're to a large extent irrelevant to any particular situation.'

'That's not my problem. My problem's different. Matt hated killing. But he hated the people's oppressors more. He could kill *them*. I don't seem to have in me the hatred that could justify killing – which must mean that I don't have the love for the oppressed that he had.'

Ang looked at him and smiled very faintly. 'You seem to have done very well the other day.'

'But I've told you. It's as though Matt took me over and did those things through me. I did not seem to have then and I do not find in myself now the hatred or the love my brother must have had.'

'It's there. It's there, Comrade Colin. You may not have fully recognised it yet; but it's there. You wouldn't be here if it weren't.'

'How can you be so sure? I think about things a lot; but I don't seem to feel much of anything.'

'Just think about *why* you're here, Comrade. You found that in a world that doesn't need love, where everything that's done gets done by the interplay of individual desires in a dog eat-dog world, your spirit was wasting away. You got out. You saved yourself. Just as I did. But you can't expect in a few months to be emotionally whole again.'

'No, I guess not.' Frere shook his head and looked at Ang and smiled. 'How wrong we can be about people! I was thinking that you must be a bit of a fanatic, the sort of person people in my part of the world imagine as a hard-line communist. And yet – you know, I think we may be rather alike – if that doesn't sound presumptuous.'

Ang laughed. 'Not at all. I think so myself.'

'I can see how Matt might have found it difficult to understand us and how we'd find the same difficulty in understanding him. But even though I don't know whether I'll ever thoroughly understand him I know I love him. Indeed, there's a sense in which it's my feeling for Matt that made me get out of that world you describe as loveless, that world inhibiting any love I might have felt for anyone in that world.'

Ang was thoughtful for a little while, almost to make Frere wonder if he had been presumptuous. Then Ang set his tea cup aside, got up and came over and took Frere's hand, which he held tightly for a few moments. Then he sat down again. 'Yes, Colin, I think you're right.' He corrected it. 'I *feel* you're right. We may be very much alike.'

'I'm glad *you* feel like that, Comrade.'

'You know,' Ang said reflectively, 'there's one thing I always wished that I could have told your brother before they killed him. He made me promise that as soon as the battle at Param Belor was over a party would be sent back to find the boy, Tinoo, we'd had to leave behind. None of us thought he'd still be alive; but we went back and we found him and he was alive. Thanks entirely to your brother he survived. He's a loyal member of our Party and Movement to this day.'

'Yes. Comrade Tuck told me about it. I look forward to meeting him one day.'

'I wanted Matt to know about that; but your meeting Tinoo when Malia has been liberated will be the next best thing. Let me give you some more tea.'

And when Frere had drunk from the fresh cup, 'Something I'd like to know from you, Comrade, is what the Central Committee really thought about *Workers' World*.'

'I can tell you quite honestly that we like what you're doing with it. We appreciate the fact that we have a worldwide audience now of those involved in struggle, too. All struggle against exploitation is related. Ultimately we all have the same enemy. That leads me to make just one suggestion.'

'Yes, please.'

'I think it could be a bit more overtly Marxist. I don't mean writing the kind of jargon you get from academic Marxists. I'm not talking about Marxism as just another interpretation of the world; but Marxism as a method of analysing and understanding the world so that we can change it. It's that Marxism which is the international language of the working class. It communicates the ideas of the struggle against exploitation which, when they've *seized* the working class, become a material force.'

'I'll remember that, Comrade.'

But ever since he had got back to camp it was with Leela that Frere had hoped to be able to talk. Somehow no occasion seemed to arise when they could exchange more than a few words and he did not dare fabricate some excuse for a proper meeting. She would see through it at once and deal with him quite disdainfully.

If he could only explain to her that it was not purely personal, his wanting to establish some sort of a relationship with her. That if some feeling he had about her was not unconnected with the feeling he was beginning to have about the people of this land, then such a relationship was justified in terms of the more caring, loving person it could make of him. And the personal feeling for her that had started the process would become absorbed in a generalised feeling for all those united in struggle and thus assume a form that she would find perfectly acceptable. He would be on the verge of thinking that perhaps he had the grounds for seeking her out when it would occur to him that it was probably just another fabricated excuse which, though it might be capable of fooling him, would not fool her for a moment.

And then a day or so later at their evening meal she turned to him quite naturally and explained that in their methodology session that day a question had come up about the role of *Workers' World* in the Malian struggle. Perhaps he would be free to join in the discussion on that question the following morning.

The next day he went to the propaganda centre early and left some articles he had been working on for Siti to type. When he got to the operations hut which was being used by Leela to introduce some young comrades to the politics of waging peasant war under working-class leadership, a young man was reading from the *Selected Quotations.*

'We use the tactics of guerrilla struggle to build up our strength in the villages and countryside and this enables us eventually to go over to the strategy of surrounding and taking the cities – mainly, Rani Kalpur itself.'

'And what was it you were asking yesterday?' Leela prompted him.

The young man looked at Frere and then said: 'I don't see what putting out a periodical in English has to do with all that. It's sent to Britain and America and to various European countries; but the British have been our enemies ever since they invaded us. The Americans are bombing our comrades in Vietnam now.'

'Perhaps the editor of *Workers' World* can help us provide an answer to that,' Leela said.

Frere reminded them that the force in Rani Kalpur they would have to defeat was armed and supported by the capitalist ruling class in Britain. The working class in Britain was exploited by that same class. 'Therefore, the liberation movement we belong to here in Malia has the same enemy as the working class in Britain. Should there not be some form of communication between us then? Are there not ways in which we might be able to help each other fight that same enemy?' He was aware that it was a somewhat mechanical answer and probably not all that helpful.

Another of the young people wanted to know if there had not been members of the British working class in the ranks of the soldiers that had occupied Malia after the war.

'Aren't there workers and peasants here who don't support our liberation struggle?' Leela asked. 'There will be fewer of them as we move into the next and final phase of our armed struggle.'

And then, taking them with her all the way on the basis of their own answers to the leading questions she put, she got them to elaborate themselves a more dynamic relationship between the anti-imperialist struggle here and the class struggle in the homelands of capitalist imperialism. It was agreed that capitalism could not be defeated by all-out war between the capitalist and the socialist powers; it could only be defeated by the working class in the capitalist countries once those capitalist countries had been weakened by liberation struggles in their economic empires.

'So,' Leela concluded their discussion, 'our struggle here in Malia is the first stage of working-class revolution in Britain and America and all those other places to which copies of *Workers' World* are sent.'

When the young people dispersed, Frere, with no particular effort on his part, found himself walking back toward June Tenth at Leela's side. He almost asked if she would like him to carry the papers and charts and the copy of the Quotations tied together and slung over her shoulder and then, realising that it was turning a guerrilla stronghold into a school yard with a shy boy making up to a pretty girl by offering to carry her books, he laughed.

'What is it?' she asked.

'Oh nothing.' And then: 'I'm afraid I wasn't much help.'

'Surely you recognised the editorial I was basing the latter part of the discussion on. I think you probably write better on political subjects than you speak.'

'Well, it's my trade, isn't it? – Writing *about* things. Indeed, I've sometimes felt that writing about things instead of experiencing them directly has turned me into something of a political voyeur.'

'I'd have thought your exploits with Comrade Tuck which I've heard so much about were direct enough.'

'I've been wondering what you'd think about that. When I tried to decide what I thought about it myself it always took the form of my trying to explain it to you.'

'But why?'

'Why did I think it necessary to explain it to you?'

'Why did you think any explanation was required at all? Isn't it what we're here for – to defeat the enemy?'

'Yes, but suppose it was an act of bravado on my part? Or even suppose it was what I said it was – being involved with comrades in military action so that I could write about liberation war from inside?

Killing seven men just so I'd know what it felt like the next time I was writing up the account of a successful raid!'

'If we're the kind of people who look back critically on everything we've done, we can always find discreditable motives.'

'But what makes some of us look back critically on what we've done? Isn't it some arbitrary quality about our actions? When I realised that I wanted to talk to you about what I'd done, I also realised that one of the reasons I'd done it might be so that you'd stop regarding me as a – well, an outsider. Then suddenly it came to me that there was more to it than that. It was as if – ' that earlier figure of himself recurred to him – 'It was as if I were a schoolboy in my part of the world riding a bicycle with no hands when he thinks a pretty girl he likes is watching.'

She started to laugh and then checked herself, as a Christian might at some remark which was slightly blasphemous.

'You see,' he said, 'that's what happens when we're not sure about our motives. We implicate others – without meaning to.'

'Why do you think your motives are so different from anyone else's on that patrol?'

'Because I've no reason in terms of my own life experience to hate the minions of the Puppet Government the way you do. They've never done anything to *me*. Indeed, they seem to me to be victims also of what I really do hate – British imperialism.'

'Does one have to hate to kill?'

'To kill without questioning your motives – yes, I think you need to feel a righteous hatred for that. To kill without it is like – ' he hesitated a moment and then continued, somewhat doubtfully: 'Well, it's like having intercourse with a woman you don't love.'

Her silence made him think he had certainly gone too far and then she surprised him by asking: 'Has that happened to you often?' She stopped and lowered her eyes to the ground and was probably wishing she had not asked that.

'Hardly ever,' he said quietly. 'It was not a pleasurable experience.' Then he realised the need for amending what he had just said. 'I don't mean that killing should ever be *pleasurable*, whatever one felt – only, perhaps, justifiable.'

Suddenly she showed impatience, as much with herself for that expression of personal curiosity as with him for this perverse muddying of the springs of action. 'We can't go on endlessly analysing what we do. We have to learn to assess our acts in terms of their objective consequences. If you hadn't killed those men what would have happened to your comrades? What would have happened to the weapons we need to take from the enemy?' She began walking again.

'Oh I know that,' resuming his walk beside her. 'But still, if one of the results intended was to influence someone's feelings about us – ?'

'Isn't that a kind of emotional blackmail, Comrade? I'd never be prepared to accept responsibility for an action I hadn't even known about till it happened.'

'Not even if it was an act of which you approved? An act you had, to some degree, inspired?'

'Not even that. I don't think we ought to be inspired by anything but the justice of our struggle.'

'But suppose you'd helped me to understand the justice of that struggle in a way I never had before?'

'Well, I hope that's something all those who take part in our Marxist method exercises get out of them. But they don't have to thank me for that, do they?'

And then, blocked in every attempt to find a natural way through the interests they shared to the question he wanted to put, he simply asked outright: 'Tell me, Leela, could you possibly, do you think – Oh not yet, of course, but some time – could you see yourself getting to the point where you regarded me the same as any man here in terms of, well, some personal relationship?'

She did not answer at once and then: 'I hope I'm not prejudiced in any way. I –'

'I'm not talking just about comradeship. And I'm not asking you to commit yourself in any way, to anything. It's just – think of it almost as a philosophical question – could you imagine yourself, well, liking me?'

'Yes and no.'

Frere's laughter had the slightest tinge of bitterness in it. 'Ask a Marxist philosopher to treat a question as philosophical and what can you expect but a dialectical answer.'

'It's a dialectical question. Since you have been so frank in asking it, I must be as frank in my reply. In terms of the kind of relationship you seem to have in mind I have to say that what's strange and different about you both attracts and repels me. I'm glad to think that our movement should have drawn someone to our side from the ranks of our enemies but – '

'But you could never trust such a person completely.'

'Oh but I do, Comrade – completely, as do all the comrades who have shared with you the work and now also the fighting. But you say you're talking about something other than comradeship.' She looked at him and he did not dissent. 'As far as that is concerned those cultural differences you've mentioned might intrigue me but would not seem to provide the basis for an enduring personal relationship. And if you ever became so familiar to me that no differences seemed to separate us any more – '

'There would be nothing at all to attract you to me either.'

She looked at him and then looked away again, obviously wondering whether she ought to qualify his conclusion in any way. 'There's something I must say to you. Since you've raised the subject, I must tell you what I'd tell anyone here – what I *have* told anyone here for whom it was appropriate. I've decided categorically not even to think about any personal relationship until Malia has been liberated.'

'That seems to me completely in character,' Frere said. 'If I promise you sincerely never so much as to hint at what you've been kind enough to talk to me about today, if I never so much as idly speculate about any personal disposition you may come to at some time in the future, will you continue to count me among your comrades?'

'Even among comrades I have friends, you know. I respect all comrades equally but I have my likes and dislikes. I shall regard you as one of my friends, Comrade Colin.'

'Thank you.'

'In fact, since you came I have been finding out more about your brother. We all know of Matt Frere as one of the heroes of our movement; but I wanted to know more about him as a man. You know that he was in love with a young woman who was hanged by the imperialists soon after his death.'

'Yes, Anna Lau. Are any of her family still around?'

'Her mother's still alive. She lives in a home for the aged in Rani Kalpur.'

'I must see her if I can. You know, for a moment I was thinking of it as giving her some message from Matt. It's hard for me to think of him as dead.'

'He could not have died better – nor could Anna. Their two deaths were heard about all over the world. Mao says somewhere: "Countless revolutionary martyrs have laid down their lives in the interests of the people, and our hearts are filled with pain as we the living think of them – can there be any personal interest, then, that we would not sacrifice nor any error that we would not discard?"'

'I didn't mean that it was hard to think of Matt's death because the thought is painful – just that because, at the most impressionable period of my life, my mind was full of a brother I never saw, now when my thoughts are so often turned in his direction by constant reminders the fact that I don't see him does not suggest to me that he's dead.'

'Some who knew your brother best say that just before setting out on that last guerrilla operation he seemed troubled. It was a difficult time, of course. Our movement was at its lowest ebb in those days. But whatever it was that was disturbing him must have been settled in the fighting around Param Belor. He never gave way to the pressure on him to recant after his capture. That's why they had to kill him.'

'One of the reasons I wanted to take active part in a military operation was that I thought it would bring me closer to my brother, the warrior.'

'Did it?'

'Yes and no,' with a smile for giving the same answer she had given. 'Certainly that kind of active military involvement made me feel very close to him indeed. As I've told others, it was almost as though Matt took control of me and handled the Kalibad affray with his own expertise. But I'd thought that if I got close enough to him, I'd find out how he felt about the killing.'

'Did you?'

'Not really. Was he so intimately involved with Lee and the others – they'd fought together against the Japanese during World War Two, you know – that their enemies were simply his enemies? Did he feel the kind of hatred for those enemies that meant he didn't have to question his motives – any more than Comrade Tuck does or Goh Tun?'

'And do you think he did feel that?'

'I don't know. There's a distinction in our positions, you see, Matt's and mine. When he came back and joined Lee in the Malian liberation struggle, he was fighting the troops of his own country, the forces occupying Malia after the betrayal of the wartime promises of independence. For them he probably did feel that kind of hatred. I think I share it with him. But at Kalibad I was killing Malians, and even if they were the enemies of my Malian comrades here, killing Malians is too much an imperialist action for me not to have doubts about it.'

'And that's what's been troubling you?'

'You and I know, Leela, that those who profess a love for the people and don't hate their enemies must feel a very tepid love indeed. If I don't feel the right kind of hatred, the kind that you don't have to wonder about for a second, then do I really love anybody? Have I simply been won over by a logic I accept? Or is it something else which has brought me here but will never make a passionate revolutionary of me? I don't know. But I don't think I want to do any more shooting at people until I find out.'

'I understand now. I can't help you with that, Comrade.'

'I hoped Matt could. But I've heard about him from Ang and from Kuan, from Tuck and from Lee himself. And just now you were telling me something about him too. But these different accounts don't add up to a single recognisable person. They seem – well, contradictory.'

'But isn't that because there were contradictions in his own nature? Different people giving varying accounts of the same person would be true of all of us. We're all "yes and no" people. Indeed, the most active, resourceful and adventurous people are precisely those in whom the internal contradictions are strongest. That inner opposition keeps generating the controlled explosions which drive such a person forward. I believe you're such a person.'

'Well, thank you; but – ' He shook his head. 'But I don't think so. I seem to be a very cold running engine. It may determine rather strictly the nature of my usefulness.' Then taking up the subject of his brother again: 'There were five in that attack on the army lorry near Khangtu. Tuck and Ang I know. Tinoo I understand is a teacher at an academy in Rani Kalpur. I hope to meet him some day, like Anna's mother. But there was another – '

'Yes, Kirin – a gentle, lovable man who had been a teacher himself before the war. That he could bear arms in struggle just shows how little we can judge what people will do solely on the basis of their personality. He was too old for active service when I came inside but very much involved in training and worked closely with Comrade Chin in bringing out *Das Vani*. He died several years ago.' She paused and then asked: 'Are you thinking of writing a book about your brother and about the early stages of the liberation struggle?'

'I don't know. I might. Some day I might. But at present I'm only concerned with getting on with what we're presently engaged in doing.'

11

There was so little change in the temperature from season to season in the largely human-made climate of the base camp that Frere was scarcely aware of the passage from autumn to winter and then from winter to spring. There was a steady flow back to them now from different lands of letters, comments and contributions to keep them from feeling, as they had at first, that publishing *Workers' World* from inside this thick jungle was about as effective a way of spreading the word as blowing hard on a dandelion boll. Indeed, articles in *Workers' World* were sometimes quoted in the polemics between Moscow and Beijing.

Sometimes when he was hard at work correcting articles or writing an editorial he would think about the way people committed to some great end like revolution or national liberation can become so future-orientated that all present day-to-day tasks are robbed of their validity and seem to lose their connection with the very end they were organised to bring about. It was like gazing at a mountain which looks so close in the clear upper air that the smallest details can be observed and yet when the eyes are lowered to the mist-concealed river, the great tumbled rocks and the thick, sharp-thorned brush which separate the observer from the mountain base, it is hard to believe the peak will ever be reached. One simply concentrates on immediate problems with a kind of blind faith that their solution is taking one in the right direction. And then something will occur that reminds one forcefully of the precise relevance of what one is presently doing to that after all not-so-distant goal.

It was in March, nearly a year after Frere had come inside, that a sound was first heard which for many in the camp was an entirely new experience. It started as a distant and ominous hum which increased in volume as it approached until just above their protective roof of plaited branches it was a deafening roar which seemed to shake the whole camp. Then it gradually subsided as it moved away to the west.

People all over the camp stopped whatever they were doing and simply stared at each other in awful astonishment.

Soon one of the look-outs came down from his high tree perch to report that six huge bombers had flown over the camp in line abreast at about two thousand feet. The markings on the wings were stars in circles, which must mean that they were American bombers – probably the giant B-52s which had been in action in Vietnam. But what were they doing here? Another of the look-outs substantiated this report.

Neither of them had been aware of any bombs being dropped but both had seen trails of vapour streaming out behind each aeroplane. One of the camp doctors took this up immediately.

'Vapour, you say?'

'Like long clouds of steam which seemed to be settling slowly toward the earth.'

And then someone pointed to the mouth of one of the drains for disposing of rainwater. From it was dripping a steaming moisture which made a faintly hissing pool on the ground beneath.

'Don't touch it!' the doctor called out to those who were nearest the smoking trickle. 'Don't let it fall on you. It's some kind of toxic chemical.'

By this time Kuan was on the scene. 'Shouldn't the water reservoirs on the roof be covered?'

'It's very likely too late. The water up there will already be infected.'

'Get word around camp,' Kuan ordered, 'that no water is to be taken from the taps. Water for drinking purposes will have to be drawn fresh from the wells.'

Masuri, who operated the camp wireless, was summoned and told to inform as many of the villages as possible along the flight path of the bombers about the precautions they must take.

The following day about the same time there was another attack by the six bombers, this time some five miles to the south. And on the third day the formation appeared again, on the horizon some ten or fifteen miles south. It was obvious that there was a plan to fly successive east to west sweeps until the whole northern jungle area had been covered.

The base camp roof of interwoven reeds and branches water-proofed with tar provided some protection from whatever the bombers were spraying over the land; but those who had been out on patrol and some of the nearby villagers complained of the effects on their lungs of breathing the chemically polluted air. The camp doctors were unable to suggest any remedy; but word was spread among the villages farther south that breathing through damp cloth during and for some while after one of the bomber flights overhead would enable people to avoid the worst consequences.

And then Masuri began to pick up on short wave an explanation of what was happening. Bulletins appeared on the camp billboard around which comrades gathered to read and discuss. Copies of these bulletins were provided for the Secretariat and the Propaganda Section.

A Statement from the Samad Government said that it had been agreed that Malia would offer training and leisure facilities to the American troops supporting the South Vietnamese democratic government in its war against communism. This would be a boon to the Malian economy; and the citizens of Rani Kalpur, where the major leave centre for American troops was to be established, would benefit in particular. 'But, of course,' the statement continued, 'for this scheme, so important for the people of Malia, to be carried out it would be necessary to eliminate the threat of the guerrilla bandits hiding in the northern jungle. Therefore, with the full approval of the democratic Government of Malia, the United States Air Force would spread defoliants over the jungle area to deprive this communist remnant of shelter. These defoliants are harmless to people but have the effect of stripping jungle trees of their leaves, thus exposing the enemies of Malia who are cowering there.'

It was a very busy time for all the comrades concerned with bringing out *Das Vani* – not only covering the news of the attacks by the American bombers but also printing editorials on the vicious betrayal of the people of Malia and of Vietnam by the Puppet Government of President Samad. Each issue contained the Central Committee's declarations to the world pledging that 'Malia will never be allowed to serve the interests of American and British imperialism against the people of Vietnam. Our allies and friends in Vietnam who have waged such a magnificent war against the major enemy of the world's people can count on us not to permit the brutal invaders of their land to find a moment's peace and rest in Malia.'

Frere, too, was very busy preparing a special issue of *Workers' World*. He had not so far used many photos in the monthly journal since care had to be taken not to give the Malian authorities any hint of the exact location of the base camp; but one of the look-outs had managed to get some good pictures of the six giant B-52s with circled star markings and he was going to use one of them on the front page of the March issue.

He was glad to know that there were a number of Contact cameras which had been collected for the purpose of the fullest possible photographic coverage of the final all-out phase of the liberation war. He attached one of them for immediate use and arranged for a young man who knew how to work it to act as photographer for *Workers' World*.

As he said to Chin and the others: 'There won't just be these flights spreading defoliants. That's only the first stage and wouldn't make sense without more to come. We have to get ready to deal appropriately with that "more to come".'

Chin told him: 'The Central Committee is of your opinion. Through Comrade Hadar I understand that other forms of attack must be expected. We shall soon be hearing what our Party's response to this has to be.'

A week after the first defoliant-spraying B-52s appeared came attacks by fighter-bombers dropping napalm and anti-personnel explosives on any villages that had been spotted by reconnaissance aircraft. There were simply not the facilities for dealing with burns and shrapnel wounds on the spot and many of those who could be moved and were not too far away were brought into the base camp. The hospital was soon full and comrades doubled up in the residential huts to make room for the wounded men, women and children who kept flooding in.

Teams were made up in camp to take what medicines and bandages could be spared to deal with those too badly injured to be moved or too far away to be brought into base camp.

Chin and Siti and Swee Meng were working day and night to bring out daily issues of *Das Vani*. Frere had finished the March issue of *Workers' World* and only wanted some more pictures of the hideous atrocities perpetrated by the American Airforce with the complete agreement, no doubt, of the British Government. He summoned the young man, Dipo, who was going to take pictures for him and, equipped with camera and medical supplies, they joined one of the parties taking aid to the region to the south, around Teipur.

On the way they passed through Mau Lin and what Frere saw there, where not many months before he had participated in the happy send-off of young Kawan, filled him with such an ache of sadness that he had to keep clearing his throat as he told Dipo where to point the camera. A trench had been dug and into it were being laid bodies burnt beyond recognition, mutilated bodies with limbs missing and some bodies of women and children so little damaged that their death seemed all that greater a tragedy. They were not being dumped into the deep furrow but laid out tenderly and a record of who was buried there was being kept to fix to a post at one end.

Cries were coming from a pavilion in the centre of the village and lying on the floor were some thirty men, women and children – lying there exhausted staring up at the roof, twisting about in pain or whimpering quietly. A few people from base camp moved among them, dispensing what medical help they could and trying to comfort the children. A woman gave sharp little cries as bits of shrapnel were removed from her back without any anaesthetic.

Frere nodded to Dipo to take pictures of the distressing scene, wondering if it was like other times in his journalistic career when he had witnessed terrible sights of human suffering. But it was not like that. Those other times he had been aware of a feeling of guilt because he almost seemed to be preying on their misfortune for the material he would be paid for. It was not like that now. These people were his people. Their burns and wounds hurt him in the same way the afflictions of a close relative would – so much so that suffering the pain himself would hurt less. There was no question of any feeling of guilt now as a mere observer. There was a growing sense of anger that he had to share with someone or it would choke him. He said to Dipo:

'Now we're seeing before us the essence of the relationship between the capitalist world of Europe and North America and the undeveloped world of Asia, Africa and Latin America. In their endless search for cheap labour the imperialists have cheapened human life itself – the lives of all the people of the hinterland who count for nothing but the money that can be made out of them. If they're passive, they're worked to death. If they resist, death is rained down on them from the skies.'

'We have to resist,' Dipo said. 'We have to put a stop to their crimes against us.'

'You don't know how I envy you, Comrade. You have not to the slightest degree ever benefited from that awful abuse of fellow human beings. No matter what I do, I'll never be able to say that. And those in my country are fooling themselves who think that just by marching up and down waving a few banners they can dissociate themselves from –' he shook his head miserably – 'from all this.'

'I know,' Dipo said and took one more picture before they turned away.

Almost to himself Frere said: 'When you think of the millions who have perished through slavery, the millions who have died of hunger when their lands were carved up and their economy twisted to yield profits to their conquerors, when you think of the use of the most sophisticated arms to murder in their hundreds of thousands any who tried to set up in opposition a decent society for the native people or the delegation of slaughter on a mass scale to those who could be bribed to use their sophisticated arms to do their killing for them – .' He laughed bitterly. 'When you add all that up, it makes even the wildest exaggerations they make up about the crimes the revolutionary socialist leaders are supposed to have committed look too trifling to bother about for an instant!'

Near Teipur they actually witnessed an attack by fighter-bombers dropping napalm on a collection of straw huts. Dipo took many photographs of the planes skimming along low with a trail of flames exploding behind and then zooming away leaving the huts in flames. Two children came running toward them screaming, their clothes burning and smoking. Frere and Dipo held out their jackets and each catching a child to him wrapped his jacket around the tightly held child to put out the fire. Some older people who had also been burned in patches but made nothing of their injuries hobbled up and thanked them. They laid the children on the ground and tried to comfort them. They seemed to be the only people left alive. Frere explained that they would get medical help from the next village.

On their way back to base camp Frere put his hand companionably on Dipo's back. 'You've got some good pictures there. They'll help us show the people of the West what they're really like!'

'I got some pictures of those poor children too.'

'Good! Good! That's just what I wanted for *Workers' World*.'

The day after they got back to base camp there was an announcement by Secretary General Lee of a meeting that very afternoon in the Red Quadrangle. Everybody in camp felt the excitement of the occasion. Their look was somewhat distant and reflective as they thought about what was probably going to be said and each wore a careful smile in expectation of what they had waited so long to hear. Frere remembered how he sometimes thought of the liberation of the country as a distant mountain peak toward which they were constantly striving without ever seeming to get any closer. As the entire personnel of the camp gathered in the square, the benign countenance of their beloved leader looking down on them from the platform was suddenly like a firm shape hewn out of the solid rock of the mountain, giving a human face to that goal and making it appear much nearer.

Lee stood there waiting for the last to arrive and join the others, his contemplative smile linking together all that charged expectancy and putting them all in tingling touch with each other – as though altogether they shared some huge secret joke and were only just able to stifle an outburst of laughter.

He did not keep them waiting long. He raised his palm for quiet and as soon as it was perfectly still he simply announced: 'Our great spring offensive for the final liberation of Malia will begin on March Twentieth, the day after tomorrow.'

There was a moment's hush while Lee continued to beam down on them without immediately saying anything more. Then there was a massed shout of joy and a forest of fists filled the Quadrangle.

When it was quiet again Lee continued: 'March Twentieth, of course, because on that date back in 1947 the first shots were fired at the imperialist occupation forces. On that day began our liberation war against Britain.'

Another pause and then: 'In the past few weeks, at the instigation of British imperialism, the United States, which our Chinese comrades rightly call the main enemy of the world's people, have rained down toxic chemical defoliants on the part of Malia we have already liberated. This attack is designed to strip our liberation headquarters of its jungle defences and expose us to massive aerial bombardment – a bombardment which has already begun on many of the villages loyal to the Liberation Movement. With customary savagery where the people of the developing world are concerned, enormous numbers of napalm and anti-personnel bombs have been dropped to hideous effect. Many, many hundreds of Malian men, women and children have been killed or maimed.'

There was a rumble of anger running through the crowd and Lee put up his hand to still it. 'We would have to act against this barbarous attack whatever our circumstances.' He looked up at the green roof of the camp and made a gesture to take in all that was under it. 'This shelter which has served us so well will soon be no protection. We could not fail to begin our final campaign against those responsible for this latest affliction of death and suffering imposed on our people. It would almost seem that the British have been able to set the time for the last phase of our liberation war – with all that this might mean in terms of our basic unpreparedness. Such, Comrades, is not the case.'

There was something like a whispered sigh of relief. 'We on the Central Committee,' Lee assured them, 'together with the heads of all the executive committees concerned with preparations for all-out war, have long been planning to make this March Twentieth, 1969, the date of the beginning of the last phase. Our enemies must have come to suspect that we were getting ready for something and decided that time was running out for them. The British have not set the time of the final struggle: we have set the time of their last desperate act and it will only serve to strengthen our determination to sweep them out of Malia completely.' There was another cheer at this.

'And remember, Comrades, we shall also be sweeping out all the compradors and collaborators who have enabled Britain to go on exploiting our land in spite of the charade of independence. We are not freeing the people of Malia from British imperialism to be the victims of native exploiters but to take in their hands their own destiny. Our war of liberation is also a revolution. That is why March Twentieth, 1969, will be celebrated not only by us and by our children but also by working people the world over.

'While you are listening to me now, word of the beginning of our last big battle is going out all over Malia to our own people wherever they may be, whatever job they may be doing.' With a sudden grin he added, 'And many of you will be very surprised to learn who some of our own people are! It is you Comrades, and those like you in many parts of Malia, who by your selfless dedication and conscientious work have set the date of our revolution.

'And don't forget what Marx has said about revolution. It is necessary because the ruling class cannot be overthrown in any other way. But it is also necessary because the class overthrowing it, our class, can only in revolutionary struggle succeed in ridding itself of all the muck of ages and become fitted to found life anew.

'Let us also remember at this time all those dear comrades who have nobly laid down their lives so that March Twentieth could dawn for us. They will be in our hearts as we charge forward to victory.'

There was no communal shout as he ended but several minutes of quiet, each person in the Quadrangle, Colin Frere of course included, being affected in some particularly intimate way by that reminder.

Lee stepped back and his place at the front of the platform was taken by the more than life size Kuan, who held up his clenched fist and let out an appropriately huge bellow of triumphant laughter. 'This is it, Comrades; this is it! Let the great advance begin! Thanks to our leader, Secretary General Lee, thanks to all of you here, thanks to the thousands of comrades throughout Malia waiting for this call, we are ready to embark on the best planned, best prepared seizure of power by force of arms in history. As you have been told, the timing of the final phase of our struggle is not theirs but ours. For years we've been assembling the forces and the arms for all-out positional war. For years we've been organising the underground movement to sap the enemy's strength at the right moment. All this will allow us to sweep to victory in the shortest possible time with the least cost in comrades' lives. We cannot spare one of you. We need all of you for the task of laying the foundations of socialism in our liberated country.'

He continued: 'The dispatch of field commanders to the three main assembly areas in the country, the supply of special weapons to those in various parts of the country with specific tasks to perform, the preparations for surrounding Rani Kalpur from the outside and undermining it within – all of this has been set in train. Do not be anxious about the communications brain in Rani Kalpur with its tentacles stretching all over the land. Its destruction will be one of the first actions on the Twentieth. Radio and television transmissions, telephone and telegraph services, postal deliveries will all go dead. The base camp here, relieved of the pressure of the last few weeks by our spreading the liberation war all over the country, will be the only communications system left, the military and political nerve centre of the revolution. That will continue to be the case until we are in control of the country and can take over in the people's name, without fear of counter-attack, all the media installations of the capital. No later than tonight you will be contacted by the heads of the different sections in which you have been working and told precisely what you have to do in the execution of the overall plan for liberating Malia.'

Kuan paused and looked around at the upturned faces. Then he held up his clenched fist again. 'Comrades, to our certain victory!' And again there was a tremendous roar and an upsurge of clenched fists.

Then Ang came forward and spoke to them in the same flat, controlled voice they had heard when he was explaining some aspect of Party discipline. He told them that they would soon have completed the liberation of their country from the last vestiges of colonial rule – rather as he might have announced that a new order of camp routine was about to be brought into operation.

Frere thought that it probably had a calming effect on them to have armed conflict treated as a rather tiresome chore that must be got through so that they could get down to the real work of establishing a socialist Malia.

Ang told them that as it became obvious that their liberation movement would be victorious 'there will be attempts within and without to set up non or anti-communist groupings pretending to have been for liberation themselves all along. We must be vigilant, Comrades. Everyone has a right to play a part in our revolutionary struggle but no one will be allowed to take over its direction. That remains the responsibility of the Party and the Party alone – until such time as the liberated people of Malia, under the Party's guidance, have developed their own political organisation. And what gives us this right?'

Ang answered his rhetorical question like a teacher reciting a lesson the class could not possibly have forgotten. 'What gives us this right is simply the fact that the Party line is nothing but the ideas of the Malian masses concentrated into revolutionary theory. Now, at this moment in our history, we take those ideas in their new form back to the masses for action. When ideas grip the masses they become a material force – the material force which will sweep imperialism and its corrupt agents out of Malia forever and make of our land a beautiful place in which human beings do not exploit one another.'

They no more cheered this than they would a practical demonstration of some physical law in a school laboratory.

Secretary General Lee returned to the podium and, holding up his hands rather in the manner of a benediction and smiling broadly at them for a moment or so, he then dismissed them in the characteristic way he always ended meetings: 'To work. To work.' And then they cheered, loudly and long, before breaking up to hurry off to whatever part of the camp their duties took them.

Frere realised that at some point he had stopped thinking about what these announcements and speeches and the excited reaction to them meant simply in relation to Malia's liberation and was almost more concerned with what it all meant in terms of his own editorial responsibilities. Lee's electrifying declaration of all-out revolutionary war was becoming the April issue of *Workers' World* with its splendid cover, bold main article and actual words of the leaders of the Communist Party of Malia on the eve of battle, illustrated with appropriate photographs.

More copies than usual had been printed of the March issue and it must be seen to it that they were dispatched at once before all means of transport and communication had to be devoted entirely to the needs of the imminent military campaign.

Frere went straight to the propaganda centre where he found Siti and Swee Meng talking together animatedly. They, too, were thinking about what it all meant in terms of the work of their department. Soon they were joined by Chin, who was looking very worried.

'Aren't you pleased with the news?' Siti asked him.

'Oh yes. We already knew it was coming; but yes, I'm pleased. Only – '

'Only what, Comrade?'

'Only it's such a great responsibility. Somehow we, we four individuals in this room – Oh, there's lots of help from others, of course, from our leaders on the Central Committee, from our comrades in camp and our reporters in the field, from everybody in the Movement really – but all the same we four are nominally in charge of chronicling one of the great events of our era.'

'It's so exciting!' Siti exclaimed, eyes shining and hands coming together in a clasp like the attitude of prayer. 'Well, yes,' Chin admitted, 'it's exciting. But when the spotlight of world history is suddenly focused on you what will you be doing? I know what I'll be doing in all probability. Accidentally knocking printer's ink over a lay-out or letting a little light onto – not some difficult aspect of our struggle but photographs being developed in the darkroom.'

Frere laughed. 'What the spotlight's more likely to discover is you in the act of polishing an article on the tremendous significance of what the Malian people have stepped on the world stage to do which I'll turn into a dreary tract to be tossed aside as irrelevant by a lathe-operator in the British midlands or a West Virginian coal miner.'

'I suppose it's only among communist journalists,' Swee Meng observed, 'that you get this heated competition in modesty.' He slapped his thigh as though he had just suddenly realised something for the first time. 'Just think! When the next issue of *Workers' World* comes out and is being read by workers in different countries, here in Malia our revolutionary war will be raging. Some of the major battles will already have been fought!'

'Yes!' Siti lifted her clasped hands to her chin.

'I take it that we'll go on putting out *Das Vani* and *Workers' World* from here in camp,' Frere said.

'Yes,' Chin nodded. 'Once the struggle has begun in earnest all over the country and becomes concentrated around Rani Kalpur, it will take the pressure off the base camp. There won't be any more air attacks on the northern jungle. I have some instructions here from Comrade Hadar.'

He took a folded paper from an inside pocket and opened it out. 'It says that we will continue to carry out all our functions here in camp as usual. We will continue with the policy of putting out as frequent issues of *Das Vani* as considered necessary. *Workers' World* will come out at the same intervals but till further notice the print run will be doubled. It says that we will continue to use the same equipment and enjoy the same facilities until such time as there can be an orderly transition to the capital where we will begin to use the liberated machinery of the national papers.'

Chin looked up with a wry smile. 'You see. They put off as long as they can letting me anywhere near the national communications centre and those great presses.'

'It will be like old times,' Frere said, 'to have a desk I can put my feet on.'

Siti smiled. 'To think of words of mine revolving with a roar on those huge rolls to come streaming out in thousands and thousands of copies.'

Something occurred to Frere. 'Since this camp is to continue to be the main base of the armed struggle, it must mean that as quickly as possible communications will be established between any liberated area and headquarters here. That being so, why can't some of us act as correspondents in the field – attaching ourselves to this unit or that and sending stories back here for use in either of our publications?'

'It's interesting you should have raised that question,' Chin told him, taking up the paper again. 'It says right here. "Very likely our guest editor will want to exploit his lately acquired military prowess by acting as a frontline reporter. I see no reason why he should not do so – as long as it does not interfere with his more serious responsibility of getting our monthly English language publication out on time".'

'And my friend here as well?' Frere asked when he saw a look of disappointment on Swee Meng's face.

'Not just him,' Siti said of Swee Meng. 'Me also. Comrade Colin hasn't been with us long enough to know that in our revolution there are no jobs reserved for men. We women have proved that we can do anything men can do.'

'Usually better,' Chin said. 'They don't take anything for granted. Well, you'll both be glad to know that, subject to the greater demands made on us by *Das Vani*, you also can act as reporters.' He was thoughtful a moment. 'It looks as though I may often be here on my own. What a prescription for minor catastrophes that will be! Still, I can't do as much damage here as I could in the middle of a battlefield. Oh, and another thing I believe I mentioned before. You're all to have the new Contact cameras and you're to practise with them until you know exactly how they work. We want to have as fine a pictorial record of this great historical event as possible.'

When Frere got back to his own hut before supper, he found Ahmed, Goh Tun and Salmi talking and laughing in a spirit of jolly camaraderie – just a bit forced perhaps as far as Salmi and even, to some extent, Ahmed were concerned but a genuine expression of Goh Tun's delight at the prospect of action on such a grand scale.

They greeted Frere and he said: 'You look like athletes whose training has brought them to the peak of condition just as the starter's gun is about to go off.'

'We're ready,' Ahmed agreed.

'As ready as we'll ever be,' Salmi said.

'Me,' Goh Tun declared, 'I've been ready for years. I've had to wait for the rest of you to catch up.'

'Where's Comrade Tuck?'

'He's been at a briefing session all afternoon. No doubt they've got something very important in mind for Comrade Tuck.'

'We've decided,' Ahmed explained to Frere, 'that the best way we can help him in this important task is to make sure he gets the right people to go along with him.'

'And we've chosen them,' Goh Tun assured him – 'ourselves.'

'I've something to contribute, too,' Frere told them. 'I can make sure that Comrade Tuck's task force has as chronicler of its successes in the field none other than your old bunk-mate – me.'

'At least he knows how to spell our names,' Ahmed said to the others; and to Frere: 'Wouldn't you rather be coming along as a fighter?'

'As a writer will have to do me. Haven't you heard it said that the pen is mightier than the sword?'

'I don't believe our Secretary General ever suggested that power flows out of the nib of a pen.'

'He might, if Comrade Colin wielded one the way he wielded an AK47 the day we attacked the police post at Kalibad.'

'The day he attacked the police post at Kalibad.'

'That's what I mean.'

'Well,' Frere told them, 'I'll also be carrying a camera. Just be sure you smile triumphantly if I point it in your direction.'

He looked around as Tuck came in beaming, his gold tooth like a bright nugget in the stream of words that suddenly gushed forth on the subject of his briefing.

'It's agreed. It's agreed,' he burst out. 'I'm to have the main responsibility for the final battle of Rani Kalpur.'

'Who else could do it as well?' Ahmed wondered – 'particularly since you'll have us to help you.'

'And who decided that?'

'We did,' Ahmed told him. 'We thought about it very seriously and we agreed that nobody knows as well as we do both your strengths and your weaknesses and can, therefore, render you the assistance you need for such an important assignment.'

'Well,' Tuck laughed and said, 'I did think of you three. You're certainly keen. But then I remembered,' with a wink at Frere, 'how your impetuosity could sometimes make you take on the enemy with guns that don't shoot.'

Salmi took him up. 'Which reminds us of something you ought to know, Comrade Tuck. If your plan of attack goes wrong at Rani Kalpur, you won't have Comrade Colin to get us out of trouble. He'll be coming with us – but armed with a camera.'

'Of course,' Ahmed said, 'he could take pictures of any confusion there might be for a manual we could get out later on how not to fight a liberation war.'

Tuck gazed at them good humouredly. 'On behalf of Comrade Kuan and the operations section may I thank you for planning our final campaign against the enemy? May I also express my personal gratitude for your consideration of my failures in leadership which you're prepared to put up with for my own good? Of course, an impartial observer would say that you put your request for accompanying me in the form you have because you think it's too dangerous and you hope I won't choose you.'

'You know better than that as far as I'm concerned,' Goh Tun said.

'Well,' Tuck said blandly, 'the matter doesn't arise. Each of you is to be attached to one of the columns converging on the capital. I suggested that it would be a good idea to have you all separated so you wouldn't be able to plot together how your brigade ought to carry out its mission.'

'And you, Comrade Tuck?'

'I'm to go to Rani Kalpur secretly – well, first to Gongor, the little fishing village nearby, in order to make the right contacts. And then to the capital itself to begin organising the subversion which is to break out in all its fury just when the forces you're with have surrounded the city.'

'You're going by yourself?' Goh Tun asked.

'There are plenty of comrades on the spot I can work with.'

'All the same, you ought to have somebody to act as your bodyguard while you're doing all that.'

Tuck thought for a moment. 'You may be right. I might need someone like you, Comrade. Maybe it's what I got you out of jail for, eh? I'll mention it to Comrade Kuan.'

Tuck turned to Frere. 'Is that true? Are you going to be carrying a camera?'

'We all are, all of us reporters. We want to get a lot of good pictures of Malia's liberation war. When we've taken over the publishing facilities in the capital, we'll be putting out newspapers and periodicals which can include excellent half-tone photographs and even colour. We'll want to get out a well-illustrated book as soon after we've won as possible.'

'Ah,' Tuck said in appreciation of the wisdom of the operations section, 'that's why they've put me in charge of liberating the capital. They want me to do the job in such a way that all that equipment doesn't get knocked about too much.'

During all these months Frere had respected Leela's wishes and refrained from anything but friendly greetings and amiable exchanges of good wishes. But he felt that the special circumstances of this day perhaps allowed him a little more leeway. They got up from the communal table after supper and he found the opportunity of speaking to her.

'I wonder if I have the right to ask you – in the most general terms, of course – what you'll be doing on March Twentieth.' He realised in some confusion that it almost sounded as if he were asking if she were free that night – to take in a film perhaps! 'What I mean is have I the right to know – well, how dangerous whatever you'll be doing is likely to be?'

She paused a considerable time before answering. 'I don't think you do have the right, Comrade Colin, to single me out for your concern.'

'Being concerned about you isn't something which is under my control. Neither of us can decide what I'm to feel about you, Leela. We can only decide together what form the concern I feel can be allowed to take.'

She was silent again, as though to test the validity of his observation as she might have judged the practicality of an answer of a young comrade to some problem they were discussing. She smiled then and said: 'A number of teams are being formed to go into areas liberated by our fighters and help reorganise communal life there – to see that food and shelter is available and that medical care and schools are established as soon as possible.'

'Are the re-organisation teams under the administration of an Alternate Member of the Central Committee?'

'Of Comrade Pir Dato? Yes they are,' she answered without comment.

Frere was sufficiently encouraged to ask: 'Do you, do you wonder at all what I'll be doing on March Twentieth and immediately thereafter?'

And yet again there was a very long pause and then the thick-fringed lids dropped over her eyes and she said quietly: 'Yes, I've thought of what you might be doing and I've been pleased that your editorial duties here would keep you away from any reckless display of courage, Colin.'

It was the first time she had ever used his first name by itself like that. In the necessarily puritanical atmosphere of base camp and from someone of such seriousness of purpose this simple use of his name sounded almost like an affectionate endearment.

He reached out and took her hand. Her eyes opened with a flutter and he was engulfed in their warm dark depths.

He started to say something, thought better of it and merely smiled. He squeezed her hand gently, released it and turned to go back to his own quarters.

12

The grand strategy of Malia's revolutionary war, which Frere came to understand better through having to write about this or that tactical aspect of it, was really very simple. From a situation in which the neo-colonial forces held the major towns, besieged by a guerrilla army occupying the countryside and existing among the people like 'fish in water', a new situation was to be brought about in which the guerrilla forces, acting in unison with those who had infiltrated the military and public services at all levels, defeated the puppet forces in their town strongholds and expelled them to find themselves in the midst of the people who had come to hate them. In this way the people would be actively involved in the last stages of the war and revolution would not be something imposed on them from the towns but something they had helped to bring about themselves in the rural areas.

The attack on Rani Kalpur from within was to be the set piece of this strategy. If Tuck, working with all those inside the city who were alerted to disrupt communications, to issue conflicting orders to the forces still fighting in the countryside, and to organise crowds of civilians to occupy certain buildings or barricade certain streets, could succeed in capturing command of the army encampment in the northern part of town at the same time that the various reinforced shock brigades surrounded the capital, then not only would the strongest force loyal to the regime have been rendered *hors de combat* but also the remaining resistance in the rest of the country would have been beheaded and left to thrash about on its own in a dying paroxysm.

Frere was engaged from early morning until late at night in roughing out a plan for the major issue of *Workers' World*. It was to come out in a month's time and present the Malian Revolution of 1969 to the world. It meant getting from the Secretariat copies of the speeches of Lee and the others on the day the March Twentieth launching of the final phase was announced. It meant going through masses of Central Committee minutes to pick out what was most useful in explaining the revolutionary aims of the Party. It meant clearing with Hadar his own interpretation for the international working class of the general line of the social transformation of Malia.

He was in a hurry to get all this done as soon as possible because he wanted to be free to go with Salmi when he joined one of the shock brigades which was forming in the Baidan area. And, of course, everybody he came in contact with was acting under the same sort of compulsion. The whole atmosphere was electric with the tension and excitement of an event they had all, individually and collectively, been shaping their lives toward for many years. There was the kind of hush that comes over a theatre as a stupendous resolution is about to burst on the audience like a thunderstorm.

That was it. The narrative prose of a movement evolving over three decades was being dramatised and building toward a great revolutionary climax which would change the entire face of Malia and would not leave unchanged the changers themselves. Everyone seemed to be living between the flash and the thunder clap.

And then came the evening of the 22nd of March when Salmi and Minto, the Deputy Commander of the Second Shock Brigade, having received the latest orders from the Operational Section, took the trail for Mau Lin. In a well concealed depot beyond Mau Lin there was a jeep which was to take them to Baidan. It had been agreed that Frere was to go with them and remain for a time attached to the Brigade as it fought its way south.

It was the trail Frere had followed with Tuck and the others that time he had got involved in the action at the Kalibad station. He suddenly realised that he had not thought about that experience of actual fighting for a long time, must, indeed, have thrust it right out of his mind. But now he was not sure why. Now he was glad that it had happened. He smiled as they walked rapidly through the dark, clutching to him the memory of that occasion, when for a while he had been in the thick of the action and conducted himself well, like a ticket which would gain him comradely acceptance by the guerrilla force at Baidan as their reporter and photographer.

They did not talk much on the way to Mau Lin. They had to make good time and it was all Frere could do to keep up and avoid as much as possible tripping over roots and rocks and being caught by the backlash of some branch Minto had pushed aside. Salmi led them along a side trail that avoided the little town and just before noon they reached the small depot where there was only the one jeep.

Food was prepared for them and they rested through the afternoon. When it was dark enough, Salmi climbed behind the wheel of the jeep and motioned for Frere to get in beside him. Minto with the map case, several canteens and a hamper of provisions got in the back.

The road to begin with was no more than a dirt track twisting among trees. Salmi, in spite of the fact that the hooded front lights of the jeep threw only the dimmest of beams ahead, was driving at a fast clip, hurling the car about expertly to follow the bends of the road and avoid the encroachments of forest.

'I hadn't realised,' Frere said at one point, 'that the greatest danger to life and limb of joining the Second Brigade was just in getting to it!'

Salmi laughed loudly. 'The Comrade doesn't know that I drove a taxi for years in Khangtu. Trees are easy: they stay in the same place. You should try driving when every other cabby is trying to force you off the road.'

'I didn't even know this road, if you could call it that, existed.'

'Usually it's heavily mined,' Minto informed him from the back. 'The mines were removed when mobilisation in this area began.'

'I hope they got all of them,' Frere remarked a little doubtfully.

'I hope so, too,' Minto said with a chuckle.

They drove for a time in silence and then there was a better road and less throwing of the jeep from side to side punctuated by jabs on the brakes. Frere said: 'I hope Comrade Tuck is getting on all right with organising things in the capital.'

'I hope so, too,' Minto agreed.

'And what will happen if for some reason or other the expected rebellion in Rani Kalpur doesn't break out on time?'

'I can only answer that with something Comrade Tuck himself has often said: "We'll cross that bridge when we've burnt it behind us."'

'That sounds like Tuck all right,' Frere laughed. Shortly after sunrise they reached Baidan. Salmi drove around the little town to an encampment on the other side and parked the jeep under the cover of some high bushes. There was an almost smokeless fire between two trees and over it were suspended from an iron rod two large metal containers of boiling water from which tea pots were continuously replenished. Milling about, drinking tea and chatting together, were several hundred members of the Second Shock Brigade.

Minto went off to report to the Brigade Commander. Frere and Salmi got themselves cups of tea and queued up for some hot rice. Talking with those standing about they learned that all resistance in that area had been suppressed. The two police posts, which only existed on sufferance anyway, had been wiped out and the Brigade was ready to begin its southward march on the following morning.

While Salmi was absorbed in the preparations for this advance across open ground, Frere went into Baidan – or what was left of it. All the shops in the centre of the town and most of the wooden houses round about had been burnt out, some of them still smouldering. There was no one at all about, the survivors of the napalm raids who could walk having obviously sought shelter in relatively undamaged villages in the neighbourhood.

In a warehouse one end of which was left standing he found the badly burned and wounded lying on the hard earth floor in two rows and being tended by one of the medical orderlies from base camp.

Frere talked with him and learned that there had been no more raids since the general uprising all over the country. There was enough food and medicine but, of course, no one knew what the long-term effects of the toxic chemicals which had rained down at the start of the attack might be.

He walked with Frere between the rows, pointing out what various of those lying there, for the most part in patient agony, were suffering from. He assured Frere that there was no reason why he should not take some pictures.

Frere tried to think that the terrible suffering he was freezing in time at its most painful by photographing it would be given its true significance by a victory in the liberation war. These pictures he was taking on their own would merely add to the endless representations of the misery inflicted all over the world by imperialistic greed, serving only to prompt from some few people a charitable response which would change nothing. But a victory over the forces of that empire which freed a whole country from its vicious grasp – Ah, that would give meaning to that sad sight of tortured bodies and fixed faces. These pictures would at last make sense when printed alongside those of triumphal celebrations in a liberated Rani Kalpur.

And yet when he looked up and down those two rows again, he shook his head. Had there not already been more than enough suffering to justify any action that was necessary to relieve people from that awful exploitation from abroad? In their going as in their coming the imperialists were to be guilty of the same extravagant waste of human life – like, in the time between, the extravagant waste of the natural resources on which human life depended.

He slung his camera over his shoulder and took one last look. With clenched fists he muttered to himself. 'Just let it end! For humanity's sake let it end here now!' He waved to the medical orderly who was comforting a child and walked back to the encampment.

The next day they moved out, sometimes advancing quickly in columns of threes and then, when approaching some place where there might be resistance, spreading out widely in a skirmish line.

But there was not much resistance. Obviously as soon as the March Twentieth offensive began it had been realised that the whole northern region would rise in support of the Liberation Army. Police posts and even an army barracks had been abandoned in panic, leaving weapons and equipment behind.

On the second day the British finally put in an appearance. Although they had been behind the attacks by American aircraft to force the bandits out in the open, although they were behind the moves by 'the Government of Free Malia' to ring Rani Kalpur with 'a wall of steel to keep the bandits at bay', there had as yet been no direct intervention by them.

The column of liberation fighters was marching along a country road that climbed a low hill, with forest a hundred yards to their left, when the sound was first heard – the throbbing beat of helicopter blades beyond the hill. And then they came in sight, a dozen Royal Air Force gun-ships in line astern.

For a moment the column halted in surprise and then, at shouted commands up and down the line, a large proportion of the force ran off the road and made for the shelter of the forest. Others were organised into units to concentrate rifle and machine-gun fire on the helicopters. But before those running toward the trees could get there the heavy machine guns firing from side bays in the helicopters were raking the ground between road and trees.

Frere saw a shallow hole and jumped into it, turning over on his back so that he could get some pictures of the helicopters flying by. When the last of them had flown past him, he stood up and looked back where the helicopters were still pouring fire at those who were only just beginning to disappear into the forest. There was answering fire from groups who were shooting their rifles in unison but they seemed to be having little effect; and Frere saw one of the groups scythed down by one of the gun-ships.

He had not had time to be afraid and now all he felt was a terrible despondency over the killing, which seemed to go on and on whatever people tried to do to stop it.

And then, far down the road near where the tail end of the column would have been, he saw one of the helicopters explode in a huge puff of black smoke. Then another.

He shaded his eyes with his hand, trying to see more of what was happening now a considerable way off. He could still hear the whish of the helicopters and the intermittent sound of firing, punctuated by several more explosions. And then far off on the other side of the road from the forest he saw three helicopters flying back the way they had come.

In the space between road and trees there were many dead and dying whom comrades from farther back were moving amongst and doing what they could to help. Frere walked toward a tangled collection of bodies where one of the earliest groups had formed up to focus their fire on the helicopters. Something familiar made him go to one of them who was lying face down, grip his shoulder and turn him over. It was, indeed, Salmi, who had taken a point-fifty shell full in the chest.

Frere squatted there, his feeling of despondency growing with the sense that the death of his friend had given a name and a personal history to all of those who had been killed in this attack.

Minto joined him in mourning Salmi's loss.

With others they set quickly about moving the wounded under cover of the trees where they would be looked after by those with medical skills accompanying the Brigade. Then they began the lugubrious task of carrying the bodies into the forest, too. There a clerk took down their details before they were buried in a trench hastily dug for the purpose.

'They'll get a proper burial when it's all over,' Minto told Frere.

Frere just shook his head.

'It's too bad.' Minto put his hand on Frere's shoulder. 'But we won quite a victory, you know.'

'Victory!' Frere exclaimed.

'Oh yes. We didn't know about their helicopter gun ships and that took us too long to sort out. But then they didn't know that we'd been supplied with ground-to-air missile firing weapons by our Soviet friends. We had a detachment armed with them at the rear of the column.'

Frere looked up eagerly at this. 'How many of them were shot down?'

'We got nine of them. Two crash landed and we took some prisoners. The others were destroyed completely.'

'Good!' Frere said. 'What will be done with the prisoners?'

'There's a holding camp near Khangtu for puppet troops who are captured or surrender. But British pilots and soldiers are different. They'll be useful in any negotiations with Britain after the war. We'll take good care of them.'

When the advance was resumed on the following day, the detachment of ground-to-air missile launchers was split up and scattered along the column; but there were no further attacks by British helicopters. The Brigade's wireless operator had made sure that news of the destruction of the nine helicopters got back to Britain where, no doubt, it would be the subject of lively debate.

Frere, walking along reflectively at the rear of the column, sometimes had a slight twinge of guilt about not continuing to feel the loss of his friend as deeply as he thought he should. He would be trying to get rid of a vague sense of depression by thinking of how they would all celebrate the final victory in Rani Kalpur, he and Tuck and Goh Tun and Ahmed and Salmi, when he would suddenly realise that Salmi would not be there. And he would have to accuse himself of having taken Salmi's death so lightly that he had momentarily forgotten about it.

And then he wondered if part of the bonding of those who were under threat of death together might not be a kind of anaesthesia in respect to the loss of any one of them, a kind of rapid closing of ranks as though nothing all that terrible had happened to them. It seemed to him that he had acquired this soldierly attitude to life and death as naturally as he had picked up a soldier's instant responses in a violent engagement that day at Kalibad – almost as if in this case, too, Matt the professional man of action had simply taken his brother over.

When on the third day they reached Makhan, which was only about forty miles north of Rani Kalpur, they found that the local puppet commander was determined to make a stand. Scouts reported that the local government building was strongly occupied and that four light tanks were stationed at the four corners.

The Shock Brigade commander threw a ring of liberation fighters around the town who then advanced to occupy the dwellings on the outskirts. There was no resistance. The townspeople welcomed them. Once in position surrounding the civic hall the liberation fighters shot off their guns and gave every sign of being about to attack. Then under cover of darkness heavy charges of explosives were planted around the centre of town and under the civic hall itself. Amplifiers were set up and demands of surrender were broadcast followed by a burst of the liberation song 'Malia Forever'.

There was no response from the puppet commander and all the explosive charges were set off. The broadcast surrender demand was repeated and the puppet troops came streaming out of the building with their hands up. It was learned later that they had shot their commander.

There was a circle of tanks and self-propelled guns at a ten-mile radius from Rani Kalpur. This defensive ring was intended to hold off the liberation forces closing in on three sides; but the gaps between the sources of fire power were wide enough to offer ample opportunities for infiltration to an army of trained guerrilla fighters. The Brigade bivouacked just out of range of the guns and those who had tasks to carry out in Rani Kalpur itself simply slipped through the defences at night and entered the city.

Some of the buildings, including the Communications Centre, had already been liberated by undercover supporters of the revolution who had grabbed up their hidden arms on March Twentieth and come out on the streets. It was agreed that the Communications Centre, which was on the main square not far from the Government Palace, would be the ideal place from which Frere could observe the progress of the battle for the capital city.

A young man who had already penetrated the defences several times was appointed to be Frere's guide. It turned out that this young man, Fazar, had been a student at the Khandev Academy and one of his masters had been Tinoo.

'That's how I got to know about your brother,' he told Frere.

'One of the first things I'm going to do when Rani Kalpur is ours is to find Tinoo and get to be friends with him. But it's a bit early to be thinking about that when we've yet to get inside a city still occupied by the enemy.'

Fazar assured him there was nothing to worry about on that score. 'Except for a pretty long wriggle on elbows and knees till we're past the tanks and guns.'

'I think I can manage that all right.'

Just after dawn they reached a guard post which had been set up by the inner-city forces on the outskirts of the largest liberated area. Frere was expected and he and Fazar were waved on. They walked through deserted streets hearing the sound of firing to one side and then to another, mostly sporadic rifle fire. But farther off there was the sustained hammering of heavy machine guns punctuated by the crump of mortar shells.

As they got closer to the centre of town there were increasing signs of damage, buildings from which the sides had been peeled away, revealing the intimate interiors of offices or bedrooms, shop fronts with the plate-glass show windows blown in, rubble piled high on the pavement to clear the streets for personnel carriers and ammunition vans which occasionally rumbled past them.

Coming toward them were bands of city fighters, men and women, with only red bands around their arms and forage caps with a red star on the bill to mark them as part of the Liberation Army. Some of them had bandaged wounds which were too slight to keep them out of further action. From them Frere and Fazar would gain the latest information on the situation in the streets just ahead, whether mines had been cleared and whether there were any snipers still about.

'There are no mines from this point on,' they were told by one lot. 'The puppet troops were in too much of a rout. They simply fled into the Government Palace.'

'And the Communications Centre,' Fazar asked, 'is it still in our hands?'

'Yes, but it's being raked with fire from the tanks in front of the Palace.'

And soon they could hear the muffled boom of tank cannon on the other side of a big building just ahead from which came an answering rattle of rifle and light machine-gun fire.

Fazar tapped Frere's arm and pointed upward. From a shattered transmitter mast on the top of the building fluttered the red flag with its crossed mattock and rifle. 'That's the back of the Communications Centre.'

There were guards stationed at the rear entrance who had to seek permission by internal telephone for Frere and Fazar to be admitted.

'Be careful,' one of the guards told them. 'Stay away from the front of the building on all floors. It's under fire from the tanks. And don't go near the left side of the building which is in ruins.'

'Where do I find whoever's in charge?' Frere wondered.

'On the top floor, at the back. You can use those stairs there.'

The man in command of the Centre, Rahman, had been a senior administrator in the State Broadcasting Service. On March Twentieth he had taken over, arresting all those loyal to the Samad regime and immediately sabotaging all communications so that no message of any kind could get out.

He shook hands with Frere and welcomed him.

'You knew I was coming, then?'

'Yes. We're in constant touch with base camp. You must know Masuri.'

'Oh yes. He's our Chief Wireless Officer.'

'Well, he's here and he's in charge of the technicians who are bringing various services back into operation as we need them.'

'What's the situation here?'

'Not too good,' Rahman answered. 'General Ozman has made Government Palace, just across the way, the headquarters of their resistance. There are at least two dozen tanks guarding the main entrance. They've destroyed the whole left side of this building with tank fire and there are glancing shots along the front every so often.'

As if to underscore this remark there were two sharp explosions of tank cannon accompanied by the thud of the shells along the front of the building and the sound of falling masonry.

'He's got a lot of his best troops inside the Palace,' Rahman continued, 'but they can't get at us because we've got the space between covered by our mortars on the roof. But we can't let the stalemate continue because they're gradually eating away this building with their cannon fire and we'll soon have to retreat.'

'Which would be too bad,' Masuri said as he joined them. 'We don't want to lose all the equipment here.'

Frere shook hands with him warmly. 'No, of course not. It's the only way to get news all over the country.'

'To say nothing of re-establishing contact with the outside world.'

'When did you get here, Comrade Masuri?' Frere asked.

'Comrade Masuri was on hand at the very start,' Ali Rahman told him. 'He'd slipped inside the city and come to us before the Twentieth.'

'What's happened at the army depot and barracks north of town?'

'That's just it. We haven't heard anything. We aren't in touch and nobody's been able to get past the camp guards.'

'I hope Comrade Tuck's all right.'

Rahman shook his head. 'If Comrade Tuck had gained control he'd have let us know before this. It doesn't look good.'

Frere addressed Masuri. 'Can I get material back to base camp for *Das Vani*?'

'There's no problem about that. A lot of information about what has happened here since the Twentieth has already gone back. By this afternoon we'll be able to broadcast all over Malia a message from the Secretary General urging Ozman's forces to lay down their arms and give themselves up at the nearest Liberation command post.'

'If we're still here,' Rahman said gloomily.

'Can I go up on the roof and have a look?' Frere asked.

'It's not safe. They're lobbing mortar shells up there ever so often – to get at our mortars behind the protection of the parapet. However, there's an observation post from which you can get a good view of the Palace and the Square.' And to Masuri: 'You can take Comrade Frere to have a look.'

Masuri took him to a room on the same top floor whose windows had looked out on the Square. Now the whole front wall had been blown away, leaving the room completely open on that side. A large mirror had been set up in the middle of the right wall. In the corner of the room to the left of the doorway through which Frere and Masuri entered, three observers were sitting in small straight-backed chairs, a young woman with a note pad on which she was scribbling and two young men with binoculars swinging from cords around their necks. One of them lifted his binoculars and looked steadily at the mirror.

One of the young men got up and Masuri explained to him who Frere was. Frere was looking at the mirror, which was tilted at the right angle to reflect the front of the Palace and the tanks drawn up in front of it.

'We've lost some comrades to snipers,' the young man told him. And with a gesture at the mirror, 'We rigged that up this morning. It won't last long but for the time being we can watch the Palace without danger.'

'Ingenious,' Frere said. 'If I could get just a bit closer, I could get a picture of the tanks through the mirror. There must be nearly thirty of them.'

'Twenty-eight.' The young man took Frere's arm and guided him as close to the mirror as it was possible to get without being exposed to sniper fire. Frere took several pictures and then, putting the camera aside, he moved about just enough to bring reflections of various sections of the Square and the buildings around it onto the mirror.

There were trees and flowering shrubs in the park at the centre of the square and a lot of holes and smashed paving stones where mortar bombs had exploded. The great domed Government Palace took up all the left side of the Square. On the opposite side from the Communications Centre were office buildings with great scorch marks on them which must house various government departments.

'Do they still hold those buildings over there?' Frere asked.

'There's nobody inside. They're completely burned out. We did that the first day.'

On the right side there were more buildings, divided in the middle to allow a wide avenue bordered by jacaranda trees to flow into the square.

'That's Independence Avenue, isn't it?'

'Yes,' the young man answered. 'If you go three miles along there you come to the main army barracks.'

'And no word has come from there in all this time?'

'We've had reports that there was a lot of firing earlier on and two nights ago there was an enormous explosion when one of the ammunition dumps blew up. But we've no idea what the situation there is.'

Suddenly there were three heavy crumps of cannon fire from the tanks and three jarring crashes of shells hitting the front of the Communications Centre, one just below the open observation room where the five of them were.

'That was close,' Frere said.

'Very,' one of the young men said. 'If they really open up on us, we'll have to move out of this building.'

'Why don't they?'

'Like us, they're waiting to see what kind of a force comes down the Avenue from the armoury.'

Later, when Rahman had time, Frere interviewed him about the way the uprising in Rani Kalpur on March Twentieth had worked. At first everything had gone according to plan. General Ozman's forces had been taken completely by surprise. Small detachments of them, cut off from each other and surrounded, had shown no will to fight. Hundreds of them had been disarmed and herded into the athletic stadium where they were now under guard.

It had even been hoped to capture Government Palace and take President Samad and his cabinet prisoner. But Ozman had called up an armoured battalion in the neighbourhood and had the tanks in position when the liberation fighters broke into the square.

'That's when we had our worst casualties,' Rahman told him. 'Three of our liberation fighters managed to get right across the square. They clambered up on top of one of the tanks, pried open the hatch and dropped a grenade inside. But they were wiped out by machine-gun fire from some of the other tanks. So we pulled back into this building to wait for support from Comrade Tuck.'

'And you're still waiting.'

'We thought we had a big enough "fifth column" in the army barracks to take over the tank depot without any trouble.'

'That's something I've wondered about,' Frere said. 'When I was describing in *Workers' World* the way our people have been infiltrated for many years into the towns and into the Samad Government service itself, should I refer to them as a "fifth column"? For a lot of our readers that term's associated with the fascists in Spain, you know.'

'It's like a gun,' Rahman said with a laugh. 'It depends on who's shooting it at whom whether it's a good thing or not.'

'And now everything depends on whether Comrade Tuck has been able to take over the army barracks.'

'Well,' Rahman said very seriously, 'ending the war quickly with the minimum loss of life to our people depends on it.'

'I can hardly imagine Tuck not accomplishing something he has set out to do.'

'Nor can I, but – '

Neither Frere nor anyone else got much sleep that night. Firing could occasionally be heard from other parts of town; but the guns in front of the Palace were silent. It was as if all the people in the two buildings were waiting for something with heart-throbbing intensity, as if they were all looking down on that green square between them like a gambling board on which a single roll of dice, depending on the numbers that came up, would determine their respective fates.

The next morning Frere was beginning to feel that the coup to take over the army depot must have failed. Surely if Tuck had succeeded, they would have heard something by now. But he was careful not to betray this growing despair to anyone and being unable to share it made it all the worse.

No shots were fired from the tanks in front of the Palace. Not even any small-arms fire from other parts of town could be heard. The whole city of Rani Kalpur breathlessly waited.

It was not by anything heard or seen that something was at last felt to be about to happen but only by a sense that such hushed expectancy could not go on any longer. And then from the observation room came word that they had picked up with their binoculars the approach of some kind of army vehicles far up Independence Avenue.

'I'm going up on the roof,' Frere said.

'It's too dangerous up there,' Rahman warned.

'Not now. They won't be paying any attention to us now.'

When he climbed the stairs and came out on top, there were already several lookouts, including one of the observers with binoculars, crouching behind the parapet.

The young man with the binoculars let Frere have a look. He could identify the movement now as a column of tanks.

'But who's in them?' the young man asked with a helpless gesture of his hands. 'Their troops or ours?'

Preparations across the way showed that they were equally aware of some force coming down the Avenue. Several tanks which had been around the sides of the Palace were moved in front and so placed as to increase the overall firepower while leaving room for the tanks behind to fire through the intervals.

Frere looked back up the Avenue again; and, as he had noted before when looking back at something eagerly expected and finding no sign of movement, the tanks seemed to be no closer at all. Others, taking advantage of the concentration of everybody's attention on that column rolling toward them, had come up on the roof. Some of them even stood up without attracting any notice from the Palace.

The rumble of tanks could be heard now. 'But who are they? But who are they?' was in everybody's mind and on everybody's lips.

There they came, the tanks, moving quite leisurely, two by two, down the broad Avenue between the rows of jacaranda trees, as formally dressed as if they were part of some ceremonial display. And still there was no sign of whether these tanks were joining the force in front of the Palace or about to attack it. One of the defending tanks which was directly across the Square from the entrance of the Avenue shifted about, rather like a nervous man taking a last puff of a cigarette. 'They'll have to declare themselves soon,' someone pointed up the Avenue and said, 'or they'll be fired on anyway.' And then, just when the front of the column was in good firing range, one of the leading two tanks ran up on an improvised mast, at the same time that both tanks fired their guns, the crossed mattock and rifle standard of the Liberation Army.

Frere joined in the cheer that went up from those on the roof as he noted that two of the government tanks had been hit by the shells fired by the two lead tanks of Tuck's force. And then he watched a very skilful military tactic beautifully executed. The two leading tanks, having fired one shell each, turned ninety degrees in opposite directions to move away from each other along the last street crossing the Avenue before the open area of the Square was reached. And the moment the two tanks immediately behind were unmasked they both fired and then also turned in opposite ways to follow in single file the lead tanks moving east and west along the side street. Then the third pair fired, using the broad mouth of the Avenue to swivel their guns left and right in a sweep of the centre of the defensive line of tanks.

This manoeuvre obviously confused the tank commander of the Palace force. Four of his tanks had been knocked out and his other tanks were too far off to each side to bring their guns to bear on the Liberation force tanks still coming down the Avenue. As these tanks at the ends of the line were hastily moved in front of those which had already been destroyed, they came under instant fire from successive pairs of Tuck's tanks which also fired once and turned away to each side.

Now there were seven or eight wrecked tanks in a useless jumble, several of them belching smoke, right in the middle of the defensive line and getting in the way of other tanks being brought up to fill the gaps. As the hatch of one tank was thrown open and the crew tried to get out, they were cut down by accurate rifle fire from inside the Communications Building. Those on the roof ducked behind the parapet in case there was answering fire.

By the time all the still-serviceable government tanks were regrouped in front of the entrance to the Avenue, the Liberation tanks had completed their manoeuvre of firing by twos and turning opposite ways along the side street. There was nothing for the government tanks facing up the Avenue to fire at while the two files of Liberation tanks, having turned back toward the Palace from the ends of the side street, came into the Square from two directions in a double flanking manoeuvre that completed the confusion of the defensive force. Shell after shell was fired into the muddled mass of tanks in front of the Palace until not one of them was firing back.

Frere had a fleeting recollection of something about Tuck which had been called up by this brilliantly planned and executed attack. Was it something about Tuck and tanks? And then it came to him. In the early days of the armed insurrection Tuck had captured a Bren gun and had remarked that the British were providing them with better quality weapons than before. Someone had said: 'Next you'll be wanting a tank' and Tuck had replied in the most natural way in the world: 'Why not? They'll just have to realise that nothing's too good for us!'

Frere could not remember the source of the story. Had Matt told him? That seemed unlikely. He must have heard it since going inside himself. Well, now Tuck had got his tanks and what marvellous use he had made of them!

The battle was over. The hatches of the few undamaged tanks in front of Government Palace were thrown open and the crewmen climbed out clumsily while trying at the same time to hold their hands above their heads in the sign of surrender. They grouped themselves in front of the Liberation tank which flew the revolutionary standard. On each side of it the other tanks under Tuck's command all had their guns trained on the columned facade of the Palace.

Frere looked up at the great dome and saw a door at the base of it open. Three men came out and began climbing up the stairs that curved up to a tiny platform at the very top.

A single shot cracked from inside the Communications Building, making the three men duck. Rahman, realising what the men were about, shouted for the liberation fighters to hold their fire.

When the men were on the top of the dome they pulled down the national flag and raised in its place a large white square of cloth at whose bellying out in the breeze an enormous cheer went up from those inside the Communications Building.

The hatch of the tank with the standard opened then and Frere saw Tuck climb out and stand on top. It was too far away for Frere to see it but he clearly imagined the gold tooth shining in the midst of Tuck's grin of triumph.

Tuck turned from side to side, bowing his acknowledgement of the cheers and applause from fellow fighters inside the building and from those who had been engaged in various parts of the city but were beginning to stream into the Square now.

Tuck raised his joined hands above his head in the traditional gesture of a successful prize fighter and then – somehow Frere had known an instant before that it was going to happen, so clearly that he always felt afterwards that he might have shouted a warning – and then, on the stroke of Frere's premonition, a shot cracked out of a high window of the Palace. Tuck was knocked back on the tank and then rolled off to fall on the pavement. He lay there motionless.

The cheering and laughter stopped – there was one moment's absolute silence – then it turned into an angry moan above which Rahman's voice could be heard ordering an assault on Government Palace. From the Communications Building and from all sides of the Square came a concerted rush. Liberation fighters who had climbed out of the tanks were led by Goh Tun in an attack on the grand front entrance of

President Samad's citadel. The moaning sound of grief in the throats of all those men and women crossing the open space became a mighty roar engulfing the Palace and swamping any last flicker of resistance.

Frere had wondered whether he ought to join them in this final attack; but he was too far away. He put his hands on the parapet and looked down and he was suddenly aware of the camera swinging from a cord around his neck. It struck him almost like a bullet. He had taken no pictures! Not of Tuck standing there triumphantly. Not of Tuck reeling back from the shot. There, right before him was the cover of the celebratory issue of *Workers' World*. More important, there waiting for him to take it was the photograph he would have cherished always of Matt's friend at the moment of victory in the liberation war which had taken Matt's life too. This irrevocable failure on his part to record an event which was so significant at once in Malia's history and in his own personal life made Tuck's death almost unbearable.

He had never wondered for an instant whether Tuck had been killed or not. He knew that Tuck was dead in the same way that he had known an instant before it hit that the bullet was on its way. It was as if all Tuck's life had become more and more narrowed into that single path which, through many battles and adventures, through many changes in himself from social discard to seasoned agent of social revolution, led to this place, to meet this bullet in front of the high-domed building that had been the symbol of imperial power, then of semi-colonial dependence, now of revolutionary liberation!

When he reflected on it Frere thought he understood why he had been so sure it was going to happen. As meaningful an event as Malia's liberation had to be paid for and in the moment before the shot he must have realised that, as far as he was concerned, the most plausible payment to meet the high price of victory was Tuck's life. What was it Mao had said? Heavier than Mount Tai was the death of a comrade who died for the people. It was particularly heavy for Frere because he felt that one of his last few ties with Matt had snapped. It was as ironic as it was inevitable that the liberation of Rani Kalpur, which he had always thought of as something that in some spiritual way he would be celebrating with Matt, had cost the life of the person through whose mediumship Matt had seemed closest to him.

The random firing from the Palace was quickly silenced as the liberation forces rushed inside. After a few minutes two women and two men came out of the door on the Palace roof and climbed the stairs to the top of the dome. There they hauled down the white flag of surrender and raise the crossed mattock and rifle banner of the Malian Revolution.

Frere did get several pictures of that; but it only made him regret the more the pictures he ought to have taken. He stood there looking at the red flag streaming out in the breeze, his eyes prickling with an unwonted tendency to brim, and he pledged: 'To you, Matt; to you, Tuck and Ang and Kirin, and to you, Tinoo, whom I may soon see now; to all of you who by fighting on when the cause seemed hopeless have gloriously realised the Secretary General's ideal of a land in which the people of Malia are free to determine their own destiny!'

13

On the evening of the day General Ozman surrendered there were victory celebrations in many parts of town. Frere managed to find Goh Tun and they talked together while all around them singing and speeches and general merrymaking marked Rani Kalpur's release from the grip of the Puppet Government.

Frere told Goh Tun how Salmi had been killed in that one vicious attack by the British helicopter gun-ships.

'Poor Salmi,' Goh Tun said with a slow shake of his head, then, brightening: 'But you gave it back to them with a vengeance!'

'They never attacked again. Was there anybody close to Salmi we ought to tell about what happened?'

'Salmi was like me, orphaned by poverty, I don't think he had anybody except us comrades.'

But it was of Tuck that both of them were thinking most.

'It's just as if I'd lost my father,' Goh Tun said. 'I wouldn't be alive today if it wasn't for him. He was the only close family Salmi and I ever had.'

'And for it to happen when the battle for the capital had been won,' Frere complained bitterly. 'If he could only have been here now! If he could have witnessed something of this tremendous gratitude we all feel! He'd have loved it – hearing the plaudits of comrades and making jokes about how he had brought it off. To come now when the war's practically over – I don't know; it makes his death seem – unnecessary.'

'Not unnecessary!' Goh Tun denied. 'At the moment of victory our dear comrade, by his death, reminds us of what the enemy is like. We think we've won. We think we've finished with the imperialists. But Comrade Tuck is telling us to think again.'

'How right you are,' Frere had to agree. 'I should have thought of that. Britain will certainly find ways to strike back. Comrade Tuck reminds us that the war against imperialism never really ends – not till there's no more imperialism.'

'Still,' Goh Tun said with a sudden lightening of mood. 'We've won a great battle in that war. And no one will ever think of it without remembering Comrade Tuck. That's a fine memorial for a great fighting man.'

The next day Secretary General Lee, who had been waiting for the outcome of the battle in the village of Gongor only a few miles away, entered the city in a jeep and was driven to Government Palace. From the front steps, where microphone and amplifiers had been installed by Masuri, the Secretary General addressed a large crowd in the Square.

He spoke of his old comrade-in-arms, Commander Tuck, who had been with him from the very beginning: 'That bullet fired under cover of a white flag will remain a symbol of the perfidy of those who sold our country to the imperialists for their private gain. Through the sacrifice of brave comrades like Tuck and all those others who have died in the struggle, our final victory is now assured. There are regions where the fighting goes on – in the foothills around Bandhal, in the highlands of the Mei people and in some of the towns of the south where the bulk of the imperialist forces used to be quartered. But yesterday the back of enemy resistance was broken.

'Soon the Rani Kalpur which has been won back for us, the people of Malia, will be *our* capital city, *our* cultural centre, the base of *our* public services covering the whole land, the headquarters of *our* Communist Party. Soon all of us millions of Malians who have endured so much for so long will act on the realisation that our tremendous creative energy has been released for the good of all instead of having to serve the profit of the few.'

There was no great outburst of cheering as there had been on the previous day. It was as though the Secretary General's words, as well as congratulating them on their victory, were calling on them to apply the same discipline and co-ordinated effort which had liberated their country to the enormous tasks of socialist rehabilitation now confronting it.

With a smile and a raised fist salute Lee turned and entered the building as though to get started on those enormous tasks at once.

Frere had to get back to base camp to finish editorial work on the victory issue of *Workers' World*. Before he left Rani Kalpur, Masuri talked to him about how soon the mechanical facilities of the national press could be got back in running order and gave him a report on the situation for Hadar.

Establishing political headquarters in Government Palace while the base camp remained the command centre for the control of liberation forces necessitated frequent trips between the two by van or coach, escorted by armoured cars. Frere had no difficulty getting a lift back to base camp, which he found largely deserted.

Kuan was somewhere in the northern highlands where there was still intermittent fighting. Ang was in charge of the base camp and Frere sought him out at once.

Ang seemed to be glad to have Frere's eye-witness account of the battle of Rani Kalpur. When Frere finished his description of how Tuck had been killed, Ang said: 'He was a truly great guerrilla fighter. He was also a good friend. I haven't had many friends. I don't make friends easily. Comrades yes; but not friends. Tuck was my friend.'

'Yes, I know,' Frere said.

'You're thinking that of those who were with your brother in the attack at Khangtu only Tinoo and I are left.'

'Yes, I was thinking that.'

It was the most Ang could manage in the way of observable personal reaction. He was perfectly willing to talk quite freely with Frere about political decisions that had to be taken now that the war was over.

'So what's likely to be done with ex-President Samad and ex-General Ozman?' Frere wondered. 'Will they be brought to trial?'

'Probably not. If they were tried before a Western-type tribunal, they would not be found to have broken any law. If they were properly tried by a court of the people who have suffered under their rule, the Western world, including some we may wish to have relations with, would simply call it a barbarous act of Communist vengeance. They've cost us a lot. There's no way they can pay for what they've done to our country. Perhaps we can exact some price for them. Perhaps we can make Britain pay to have their imperial agents returned to them. If they don't, then they'll appear as the meanest of employers as well as the cruellest of imperialists.'

'Which could have an effect on other puppet rulers of the semi-colonial world.'

'Exactly. As for dealing all over the country with crimes against the people we'll apply our Secretary General's formula: "Let the people themselves judge instead of initiating endless legalistic procedures on the people's behalf." Summary justice will be meted out quickly in each district through the people's courts set up by the revolutionary committees – as much to demonstrate that we're living under an entirely different type of regime as to wreak justice on evildoers. Then, when that's over, there's an end of the matter. Crimes and injustices of the past will become history, to be studied by our children so that they never allow Malia to fall under alien rule again.'

'And all the prisoners of war we've taken?'

'For six months they will work at rehabilitation, housed and fed but unpaid. During that time they will learn about Communism and the kind of society we intend that a free Malia will become. After six months they will be given the choice of staying here and being given a sum of money for the work they have done or of leaving this country and going to live somewhere else – like Britain.'

'If Britain will have them.'

'Ah, that's Britain's problem.'

Frere also learned that Pir Dato was supervising from base camp the teams of political cadres who were setting up administrative councils, medical centres and schools in the newly liberated areas. But he could not bring himself to ask what part of the country Leela was working in. Then he happened to run into one of his messmates in the old June Tenth Commune who told him that she believed Leela was with a team up on the plateau where the Meis dwelt.

Frere went to the propaganda centre where he found Chin and Siti. Swee Meng had not returned yet from an assignment covering the action of one of the assault brigades in the Mati. Siti told him excitedly about her adventures with the guerrilla group which had attacked a number of police posts in the area around the base camp, including the one at Kalibad.

Frere told Chin about the report he had given to Comrade Hadar on how soon the printing of *Das Vani* and *Workers' World* could be moved to Rani Kalpur.

'As soon as that?' Chin's forehead crumpled into worried furrows.

'But that's wonderful!' Siti exclaimed. 'Think of those electric typewriters and plate-making machines and huge presses.'

'I am,' Chin said gloomily. 'I like it here. I like the rhythmic hum of our little litho press. It's so soothing. I've managed very well for years on a system of sticking background material on nails and keeping copies of old issues of *Das Vani* in piles in the corner. There will be great metal filing cabinets there in which I'll never be able to find anything. I don't want to go to Rani Kalpur. And the trouble is, Comrade Colin: when deep down I don't want to do something, my body gets up to all sorts of tricks of absolutely devastating clumsiness.'

'No, you'll like it once you get used to it,' Siti assured him. 'Think of the wonderful reproductions of photographs there will be.'

'With such a big daily paper I'm sure to get them on the wrong pages.'

'At least you'll never do anything as stupid as I did,' Frere told him. 'I was in the perfect position to watch Comrade Tuck's brilliantly executed attack on the City Palace and I forgot to take a single picture with the camera you supplied me with.'

'Don't worry,' Siti said. 'We've got some marvellous photographs of that attack. Look at this.' She held up the latest copy of the paper.

But it did not keep Frere from feeling an intense regret that he had not taken a picture of Tuck standing, legs outstretched, on top of the leading tank at the moment of victory. It gave him a fresh shock of the utter irrevocability of death. Tuck had always seemed so indestructible he had to force himself to think of Tuck dead. And then it was difficult to revive in his memory that lively face crinkling in its perpetual gold-toothed grin.

'That reminds me,' Chin said of Siti's holding up a copy of the last issue. 'This was passed on to me by Comrade Hadar. It's from the Central Committee. I was going to wait till we were all here; but Comrade Swee Meng will see it when he gets back.'

Chin cleared his throat and read: '"To the Publications Committee of the Propaganda Department." That's us, of course. "Congratulations on your work leading up to and during the final phase of the revolutionary war. In addition to regular editions of *Das Vani* there have often been as many as five or six special bulletins a day covering all fronts and distributed all over the country. These have played a vital part in maintaining the high morale of our forces in the field. The issues of *Workers' World* describing the tactics and strategy of the Liberation Movement at this crucial time will inform the world of our successful struggle. In the articles, reports and hundreds upon hundreds of photographs, many of them taken in action, we have a complete record of one of the most important events in the history of working-class struggle against capitalist tyranny. The Central Committee has approved of the idea of a well-illustrated book on the Liberation of Malia to be printed in a number of languages as soon as the publishing facilities in Rani Kalpur can be brought to bear on this task."'

'I'll make copies of that for each of us,' Siti said.

Chin looked around him. 'Yes, I'll miss this place. But at least, off there in Rani Kalpur with so much more to do and so much more machinery for me to drop spanners into, I'll be surrounded by the same faces – which must be used to me by now. With their help I suppose I'll be able to blunder on.'

'Are you calling the Central Committee liars?' Siti joked. 'They don't say anything about a poor old man blundering on.'

'Now don't criticise the Central Committee, Comrade. They can't know everything.'

'The victory issue of *Workers' World* is on its way,' Frere said. 'Now we have to start thinking about the next issue.'

'Ah, that brings me to something else. We want to start collecting material on the subject of building socialism in free Malia. It might be a good idea for us to see something of the efforts being made to set up the machinery of popular government in various parts of the country. I can't spare you,' he told Siti, 'until Comrade Swee Meng gets back.'

'I'm free,' Frere said.

'Good. Is there any particular area you'd like to visit and write about?'

'Well, yes. The northwest plateau.'

'The land of the Meis. Yes, that could be very interesting. Buddhism is still very strong up there.'

Frere got a ride on a lorry travelling in convoy to Bin Thi on the edge of the northwest highlands. There he joined a party which would make its way by foot to an ancient lamasery which was being used as the headquarters for the rehabilitation groups working with the Mei people.

Frere was delighted to find that in charge of this party which would carry ammunition and supplies up the steep slope of the B'nal Pass was Comrade Kuk, the tough mountain man who had acted as guide to the guerrilla group with whom he had first made contact. Their fortuitous encounter in such victorious circumstances required celebrating in the inn above Bin Thi where they stopped for the night. Considerable numbers of sugar cakes were washed down with tea flavoured with goat butter and a number of toasts were drunk in the potent spirits of the region.

The next morning, trudging up the dry rocky valley at the head of a column of laden donkeys and a dozen fellow comrades all headed for the lamasery, Frere and Kuk talked about that original meeting.

After watching Frere's progress Kuk said: 'You're in good condition these days, Comrade. You looked quite green.'

'Ah,' Frere laughed. 'Protective colouring for the new life in the jungle I was about to take up.'

'You're a good shade of brown now – just right for the barren plateau above Kotal Bargh.'

'Are there puppet troops still fighting around here?'

'Not in any force. There may be the odd band of soldiers hiding out until they're absolutely sure how the war's going to end.'

'Was there heavy fighting in this area?'

'There was one pitched battle near the big lake where the monks from the lamasery rallied government troops to make a stand.'

'That was odd behaviour for those believing in nonviolence, wasn't it?'

'Oh the monks didn't do any fighting themselves. Apart from that one engagement it was mostly complete panic among the puppet troops, whose main effort was directed to turning themselves into shabbily dressed peasants as quickly as possible.'

'They could still make trouble.'

'For many years to come,' Kuk agreed. 'What's it like in Rani Kalpur?'

'The same thing is happening there. Officials and administrators and army officers all turning themselves into ordinary citizens who were on our side all along. It turns out now that President Samad with only a couple of supporters was holding Malia in the sway of imperialism practically on his own!'

'And what about the British troops in the south? Wasn't there a support regiment?'

'Yes, and a Royal Air Force detachment. But when our people got there they'd cleared out.'

'They're smarter than the Americans in Vietnam.'

Frere wanted to know why they had to cross the ridge afoot when there was a road which zigzagged up to the lamasery. Kuk explained that while there was no organised resistance left, armed bands sometimes preyed on traffic along the road.

Frere dropped back to talk with a veteran guerrilla leader who was returning with fresh instructions to his command on the plateau. From him Frere learned that the problem in the Mei region had not been so much the resistance of puppet troops. There had only been that one major conflict. The trouble was that there had been a lack of response to the call for the people to rise against their oppressors. Most of those living on the plateau had for centuries been under the repressive rule of local landlords backed by the priesthood and whatever might be happening in the rest of the country, the serf-like conditions in this far, high land had gone on and on without change generation after generation.

The next afternoon they reached the top of the ridge from which it was possible to look across a deep gorge to the lamasery clinging to the far cliff side. It struck Frere that, in an area where there was so little social progress, there should be scenes of such breathtaking grandeur – almost as if the fabulous gods who had come here from India had demanded nothing less than the grandest of amphitheatres for staging the feudal subjection of this people.

They camped that night in the gorge, which was like a moat protecting the massive fortress of the high tableland. And the lamasery they climbed up toward in the morning was like the castle of the lord of that land; and the lakes and the fields of grain they saw when they got to the top were like the supplies of water and food a beleaguered host might have stocked to withstand a siege of centuries. Inside the lamasery Frere found those who could give him information about the process of involving the people up there in establishing self-governing communities. He got the impression that it was not going too well.

It was early for supper but he was hungry. He understood that arrangements had been made for members of the liberation force to eat in the refectory. When he got there he found that apart from some monks huddled together at the lower end of a long table the place was empty. From several large pots on a stand near the kitchen he helped himself to a very simple meal which he took to the other end of the table from where the monks were sitting.

He had not been there long when someone entered the room behind him, came straight to where he was and sat down, without saying a word. And suddenly a surge of feeling sang through him. He did not know what it was that told him, the particular rhythm of the footsteps or a faint whiff of fragrance, but he knew she was there. He did not look around at once, saving the sweet shock of recognition for a while but he smiled and the smile grew wider and then he looked. She was not facing him and what he saw was that graceful line of cheek curving down to the slightly parted lips and then the lips smiled and the head turned a little way toward him and she was watching him out of the corner of one eye. He did not say anything but shook his head slowly in rapt appreciation. Then her face came right around and the gaze of those lovely dark eyes simply engulfed him.

She laughed gaily. 'Is this a coincidence?'

'Well, not altogether,' he admitted. 'But to look for and actually find someone in this time of turbulent movement and rapid change requires a lot of luck.'

'I'm glad to see you, Comrade Colin,' she said quite simply. 'So the luck is mine, too.'

'You look so – ' He could not put it into words.

'Tell me what you've been doing since you left our Commune,' she asked quickly.

He told her about the advance of the Second Shock Brigade and about the perfectly executed tank attack on Government Palace in Rani Kalpur. 'Members of the June Tenth Commune have distinguished themselves; but we've had serious losses.' He told her about Salmi's death in the vicious raid by British helicopters. 'And of course there was Comrade Tuck, killed at the moment of victory.'

'Yes, I heard about Comrade Tuck. I didn't know about poor Salmi.'

'Have you heard anything of Comrade Ahmed? He was with the First Brigade I think.'

'Only that he's all right. They're doing in the southeastern part of the country what we're doing up here. It's hard to believe that Tuck's gone. We didn't just respect him as a formidable guerrilla leader. We loved

Tuck, you know.'

'Yes, it's one of my great privileges to have known him.'

'He was your brother's good friend, too, wasn't he?'

Frere turned his face to her but whatever he was going to say was lost, as he himself for the moment was lost in the vertiginous depths of her compassionate look. He asked hesitantly: 'And you, what have you – I mean, how has it been with you, Leela?'

She shrugged. 'I've seen no actual fighting. My little group has come in afterwards and organised makeshift lodgings for ourselves, rather like,' she laughed, 'camp followers. Once we get the people themselves involved in setting up courts to try the worst oppressors, in starting up schools and medical centres we move on – to be followed by those with the skills to link up with the electricity generators and get any workshops or factories running again.'

'And that's what you're doing up here?'

'We haven't really begun yet. It's difficult up here. There's nothing to build on. We're going to have to start from scratch. None of the peasants can read and write. Occasionally young men have left here and found out something about the world down below; but they haven't been encouraged to come back.'

'That's what makes the work you'll be doing up here so interesting for articles on rehabilitation for *Workers' World*. Do you mind if I, well, sort of attach myself to you?'

'Of course not. I've worked out plans for tomorrow and you're welcome to join us. Two brothers from this district who were inside with us are acting as interpreters. They – '

'Oh, I know them!' Frere assured her. 'They first came to base camp when I did.'

'They're twins, you know, and quite inseparable.'

'Indistinguishable too. None of us could tell them apart. They were simply the Mei brothers. On that journey to base camp we practised our conversational Indomalian together.'

She was suddenly thoughtful.

'What is it, Leela?'

'I was just thinking how close we all were together under our Secretary General's personal guidance. Now we'll be spread out all over the country and – '

'Diluted with all the new elements we'll be absorbing.'

'Yes. I hope our revolutionary *ideas* and *ideals* don't get diluted.'

'You always said that as far as working people are concerned what we give them ideologically is what we got from them to begin with and now give them back in a more systematic form.'

'I wasn't thinking of *them* – more of the intellectuals and professional people in the towns who will join us for selfish reasons without shedding the bad ways of thinking about themselves they've acquired.

Frere pushed aside the plate he had hardly touched. 'When we were approaching the lamasery from below, I could see a kind of balcony running the whole width of the building. There must be a magnificent view from there but I haven't been able to find my way to it.'

'Come,' she said. 'I'll show you.'

They walked down stone stairs worn away by the feet of many centuries and along dim corridors which reminded Frere of the tortuous arguments of religious idealism and came at last to a low arch which admitted them to an open passageway. An embrasured parapet ran along the outer edge of the passage and at regular intervals it was possible to look down a sheer drop of hundreds of feet to the bottom of the gorge where tendrils of milk-white mist were forming. The sun was just setting behind the ridge opposite and all that part of the sky was a glorious yellow.

'It's so strange,' she said, 'to think of the exploitation and misery which has existed for these people for so long in such a majestic arena.'

'I know. It's like something I used to think about in England – people who had been forced by poverty to leave their sun-drenched, palm-fringed beaches in the Caribbean, the dream of rich tourists, to come and live in drab, sodden Brixton.'

There was so short a twilight the stars seemed to be treading on the heels of the last bright sunbeams.

Frere reached over and took Leela's hand. It just perceptibly tensed and was quiet. He cleared his throat and said: 'Leela.'

'Yes,' she answered, her voice sounding slightly wary.

'Nothing... I –' He released her hand and they went back inside.

'I must go,' she said. 'We have a briefing session tonight and we want to get off to an early start tomorrow.'

She smiled and turned away, leaving him wondering, as always, whether he had shown too much or too little of his feelings about her.

The next morning they set out for a village some three miles from the lamasery. There were five of them: the guerrilla leader who had assumed command of the forces on the plateau and wanted to see something of this community work; Kuk who was driving two donkeys loaded with food and medical supplies; a young man who knew the local language and was setting up literacy courses; Leela, who was in charge of the party; and Frere himself.

He did not try to speak to Leela on the way. She was discussing with the others plans for extending an administrative network over the whole region. And in any case Frere felt that idle chatter about this or that when both of them knew so well what was really in his heart was too ridiculous.

When they reached the village the Mei brothers had already assembled the people around a huge fire in the central open space. They sat there impassively, some children running about chasing each other until looks or gestures from their elders quietened them. All around were the mean huts in which generation after generation of them had lived. At one end of the little square there was a larger building which must have served as the office for the headman or a commissary for storing farm implements or perhaps what had to pass for a village shop.

It was cold enough at that altitude to make the fire welcome and, though there was a shortage of wood on the tableland, a kind of peat which burned well was plentiful in the valley below.

Frere and the Mei brothers greeted each other warmly and filled in with quick snatches of talk what they had been doing since their last meeting. Then Frere moved back out of the way to observe whatever happened and take notes.

He had brought his camera and he took some pictures – not many. The villagers seemed so indifferent to the proceedings, merely staring into the flames or muttering a few words quietly to whoever was to the right or the left of them, that Frere decided to save his film for later. He did take several rather distant shots of Leela.

Soon the Mei brothers, after exchanging some words with Leela and the young man, walked into the centre of the ring of peasants and, standing on opposite sides of the fire, took turns telling them in their own language what had been happening in Malia since the Twentieth of March.

Frere had the impression that this was by no means the first attempt at an explanation of the revolution and what it ought to mean to them. They listened, but without the slightest indication that what was being described had anything to do with them. It was as if, Frere thought, this was just one more warlord and his cohorts, one more saffron-robed priest and his acolytes telling them that everything was going to be different now when their lives down the centuries proved that for serfs nothing ever changed.

The young man talked to them but they did not seem able to understand what he was saying. He started again in Indomalian with one of the Mei brothers translating, telling them something of the medical treatment that would be available to them and of the literacy courses which would be available to young and old alike. They listened blank faced, showing not a flicker of interest.

The guerrilla leader tried next. He told them that the two biggest landlords in the region were locked up, that the monks had been ordered to stay in the lamasery until some agreement about the future role of religion on the plateau could be worked out. He told them about the men of Mei who had gone down from the heights and joined the revolutionary struggle and how their courageous action reflected credit on this land.

Again, there was nothing to be seen on their faces but puzzled frowns as to why they should be given so much information that had so little to do with them.

The guerrilla leader gave it up and, making his way through a gap in the circle, came over to where Frere was standing.

'I don't know what else to say to them.'

'It's difficult,' Frere agreed, glad that it was not his problem. 'I suppose they've been told so many times down the years that things are going to be better for them only to be bitterly disappointed that they don't dare let themselves believe in the possibility of beneficial change.'

'The ironic thing is,' the guerrilla leader said angrily, 'that the British who overthrew feudalism to put the bourgeoisie in power and constantly proclaim their liberal principles at home were delighted, as imperialists abroad, to accept the gift of this feudal fief. They let the landlords go on ruling it as despotically as ever, as long as they paid a tax to their alien rulers – which, of course, was also wrung out of the hides of their serfs!'

So it was Frere's problem after all. 'I suppose it's a question of convincing them that getting rid of the last vestiges of British rule has rendered their age-old oppressors completely impotent. That there really has been a change this time.'

'But how do we get that through to them?'

Frere shrugged helplessly and looked again at those who were sitting around the fire, their faces as clear of any expression as that vast wind-swept tableland was of any trees. They lived in another world from the one he, for some time now, had been becoming part of and his distance from them was like his distance from that other life before he had gone inside. What were the bridges from one world to another? People, just people. For making his transition to a revolutionary world there had been first of all Matt, of course, and there had been Lee and Ang and Tuck and there had been Leela. Who was there for these people?

He saw Leela take her place in the centre of the ring with a feeling of nervous excitement. He listened with strained attention as she began to speak. It was almost as if she were about to utter the words which would answer any doubts he might still have, any doubts Matt had ever had and might even have died with. It was as if, in finding the right thing to say to these dour, hopeless people, Leela was about to perform in the realm of ideas something like that splendid last action of Tuck's when the column of tanks, two by two, had driven down the Avenue, fired simultaneously and moved off to right and left only to come together again in victory. Leela's words might be deployed dialectically, moving off from thesis to antithesis only to come together again in a synthetic conviction that would unite all of them there no matter how different their backgrounds.

But all Leela said through one of the Mei brothers was: 'Greetings to you all from our leader, Secretary General Lee. You do not know him yet; but he knows you and he intends that you should get to know him. You have been in our thoughts as we purged our land of oppressors. Now we are at your service, you people of the high plateau.'

She turned to the brother who had been translating for her and they spoke together quietly. Then they both walked toward the large building making up one side of the village square. There was a large padlock on the door which the brother smashed with the butt of his gun.

All the heads of the people had turned to watch them as they approached the building and, having forced the door, went inside. Their faces remained turned in that direction like heliotropic flowers fixed on the point where the sun had disappeared. After a few minutes Leela and the Mei brother, his face glowing with pleasure, came out of the building carrying between them a huge roll of sheepskin parchment.

There was an escape of breath from the mouths of the people like a long sigh when they saw what the two of them bore. It was the debt-roll of the entire village going back hundreds of years. For hundreds of years all the borrowings of bad years which the good years never made up for were inscribed on that lengthening roll of indebtedness, as were all the failures to meet the interest charges which kept mounting so that whenever there was a little something left over after the landlord's tallage and the lamasery's tithe had been met, it was promptly seized as a tiny payment on account. That ever-growing roll bore down on their shoulders like the visible form of their feudal yoke.

They watched fascinated as this strange woman and the young man, who was one of their own, made their way through the circle and up to the fire. There was a sharp intake of breath as the two of them lifted the roll above their heads. When they hurled it onto the flames, there was the general exhalation of a relieved sigh like the sound that might come after a lifetime of fruitless toil from those who have crossed a foul stream out of a dark place to enter the sunlit fields of the blest.

Some of them got to their feet and walked toward Leela, holding out their hands and smiling broadly. Then the others got up, too, and they crowded around Leela and the Mei brothers and they were grinning and tears were glistening in the eyes of many and then they were all laughing. And the children caught up the laughter, not knowing what it was about but joining in boisterously. And some of the younger women formed a ring around Leela and began dancing, taking two steps forward and swinging a foot and then two steps back while moving gracefully in a clockwise direction until they had come full circle around her as she stood there laughing with them.

Frere did not know why he was so moved. Somehow this entering of history by people who had hitherto been excluded from it touched him profoundly. It was not simply that it was the radiant Leela who had found the key to unlocking their past and letting them out into a liberated land, although that was part of it. It was more that these people, released from centuries of bondage and only now for the first time beginning to experience what life could hold for those whom no one had a right to exploit were helping him to understand why he had come here and made the communist cause his own. It was the answer to his question about whether he loved people or only hated their enemies. It was possibly the answer Matt had been looking for too. And at the thought that Matt, who had the greatest right in the world to have seen such a sight as this and never would, his own eyes brimmed. He had an overwhelming feeling that it was up to him to see it all for them both and to appreciate it enough for them both to go on being a good communist himself.

His vision of Leela swaying in time with the dancers' rhythm, lips parted, eyes shining, was blurred: it had released some inner spring of repression so that tears flowed down his cheeks. For the first time since as far back as he could remember he was openly and unashamedly crying.

Leela looked over the heads of the girls and saw him. She smiled and waved at him. And he nodded and smiled back and the tears were unchecked. All this time he had been looking for his life's meaning and suddenly here on this high plateau he had found it, among people he could never have imagined encountering and with whom he could only exchange facial expressions of joy and friendliness. Found it for himself and found it for Matt, too. They had both been driven by the sense that they were the unintentional heirs of wealth robbed from people all over the earth and once that realisation had dawned it would let them settle nowhere and nowhere be at peace. So much had been taken out: something had to be put back. Something had to be repaid: some lesson had to be learned.

The awareness of a debt unpaid, increasing down the years, was as much of a burden as the roll of indebtedness Leela had destroyed. It had been a barrier between Matt and others and it had become a barrier between himself and others, too, separating both of them from their own people who could not or would not recognise any such debt. It had made it impossible for them to accept as in some way earned the comfortable consumerism paid for in blood by the colonial world.

It was why Matt and he himself had felt such an intense need to be accepted by these comrades he had for many months been living with and fighting beside. It was as a sign of the blessed forgiveness so desperately sought that Anna's love had meant so much to Matt and the love he had hoped to receive from Leela would have meant so much to him.

But even so he felt that there, on the other side of the world from where he had started in a state of original sin, he knew at least what a state of grace shared with Leela would be like. He was so moved by this passionate revelation that he did not find it possible to join with the others, not yet awhile, and he withdrew into a tiny alleyway between two huts where he could be alone.

He was standing there, head lowered, when there was a touch on his shoulder. He turned and looked down into Leela's face. She was smiling up at him but there were tears in her eyes also.

'I wondered if I would ever see you moved like this,' she said. 'I never really believed in your motives. Not altogether. But now I do. I believe now, Colin.'

'It was you, Leela, and what you were able to do for them. But also for me. I can't tell you all that's been happening to me just now, in this place.'

She touched his lips with her fingertips. 'I know. I know.'

'If I could only explain –'

She touched his lips again. 'I know, dear Colin. I know. The idea of burning the debt rolls came to me when I was thinking about you. How I could make you understand what it all meant and how you'd respond to it. What I did was right for them because it was right for you.'

He held her, his two hands grasping her upper arms, and as he held her like that his eyes drank up the feeling for him he could see in hers, as if the water his eyes had lost when he was watching her win over the village was being restored as the sun draws up moisture from some lovely pond. He held her and gazed down at her tenderly, and then, after a slow shake of his head for the wonder of it, enfolded her in his arms and held her close to him.

PART 2

14

There was a place Colin Frere liked to visit, about ten miles from Rani Kalpur. It was on the river beyond Gongor and could be reached by a bus which left the Square every hour.

He would get down at the bus's last stop and walk up a path which led to the top of a grassy mound above the riverside village. There he would sit cross-legged on the ground, perhaps nibbling on a wild mint sprig, and simply become a part of a scene which represented for him a kind of compendium of this land of his adoption.

The low hills rising up from the opposite bank were terraced in that peculiar Malian way of rimming each step with white stones so that hilly areas were marked by highly visible concentric lines surrounding every rise like a full-sized contour map of the region. It was a touching example of that ancient relationship between human beings and nature, each shaping the other down the ages – like the striated ridges of China or the hedgerow-divided fields of England – which always struck Frere as extremely poignant, a tender record of ecological intercourse that must never be so scrawled over by industrialisation as to become indecipherable.

That had not happened here so far. The lines of barges going up and down the river and the three or four small factories which had sprouted up as part of the Taking-Industry-to-the-Villages Movement fitted into this old setting as naturally as he, on his high mound looking around him contemplatively, liked to think that he did.

One of these little factories, where buttons were made, emitted a quiet grunt from inside and a smoke-ring from its chimney stack with each successive stamp of the press within. Frere had only to think of this tiny factory conscientiously puffing its rings up toward the blue sky, no matter where he was or what strain he might be under, to smile and even, sometimes, to the surprise of those around, to laugh aloud.

For him it was like industry saying: see, a new force has come onto this scene where people and nature have been indicting their mutual history all these years; but don't worry, I don't intend to disrupt anything and you don't have to take me too seriously. I'm not driven by some greedy individual's need to make profits at all costs. I'm simply a new voice to enter into that age-old colloquy and enrich it.

He could not but think again of that absolute dichotomy between those who lived out their lives somewhere in the land of their birth among the utterly familiar which, like comfortable, perfectly fitting old clothes, became as unremarkable as one's own skin and those who planted themselves exotically among strangers with different customs and never, no matter how long they stayed or how fluent they became in another tongue, never ceased altogether to be alien. If the penalty the first lot faced was to be so blinded by the thoroughly known as to be unable to see any more what was all around, that of the second was always to be sensitive to the impact of the new and unable ever to take anything or anyone completely for granted. It was to rest a bit from this constant awareness that he would slip away, very occasionally, and come to this spot which was the closest he could get in this land to the relaxation of the unworryingly and unchallengingly habitual.

It was October, 1977 – some eight years since the revolutionary victory which had put the Communist Party of Malia in power to inaugurate a socialist republic. Colin Frere had reason to think of it because that very afternoon he was meeting at the airport an old friend, the American journalist Clare Wallace, for whom he had obtained a visitor's visa.

She had visited Malia briefly back in 1969, one of the few foreign journalists to be allowed to do so, for the ceremonial installation in the People's Palace of Secretary General Lee as the first head of state; but there had been little time for Frere to see her then. However, they had kept in touch over the years by letter when she wanted some information about Malia's relations with other countries or when he wanted information from her which he needed for some article he was writing for *Workers' World*. Now she was coming to Malia for a longer stay to do some studies in depth on one of the latest additions to the socialist world.

He thought of himself a little as a proud father about to show off his young son to an old friend; and then he smiled at the thought of comparable developments in his personal life he would also be telling his journalist friend about.

He got up, brushed his trousers and walked down to the village to take the bus back to Rani Kalpur. After a quick lunch he spent an hour or so in the *Workers' World* editorial office and then went down to the front entrance of the Communications Building where the large black Russian car assigned to him for meeting Clare Wallace's Aeroflot flight was waiting.

He climbed into the front seat with the driver, whom he knew from other occasional uses of cars from the State pool, and after a few friendly exchanges relapsed into the same slightly smiling somewhat quizzical mood he had been in on the top of his grassy mound, running through his mind all that had happened since he had last met Clare Wallace in anticipation of giving her a brief account of it.

At the airport he went into the lounge where dignitaries from other countries were met. He sat down to wait, picking up the last issue of *Workers' World* and thumbing through it, trying to decide, as he often did in such instances, if, as a foreign visitor who knew little about communism or the problems of underdevelopment, he would get anything much out of the magazine. The pictures were good and it was well laid out. He put it aside and got up as Clare Wallace was led in, her high heels rapping out an unfamiliar tattoo.

Frere walked toward her smiling and holding out his hand for the forthright grasp customary between all Malian comrades of whatever sex and then paused in slight confusion.

'I think you kiss me on the cheek,' she said with a laugh, turning her face for him to do so.

He took a step or so back and looked at her. 'The years can't do a thing about you, can they, Clare? You don't look the least bit different.'

'Nor do you, Colin. Is it because, always following up and writing about what's happening to other people, we're ourselves too uninvolved personally for time to put its mark on us?'

'Well, I'm not as personally uninvolved as I used to be.'

'Oh?'

'I'll tell you about it in due course. And you, Clare? Any additions to your private life?'

'Nope. There's nothing I can't throw in a bag with a few cosmetics and clean dungarees and be on my way anywhere.'

Remembering when it had been like that for him, Frere said: 'It was a good life'.

'Don't sound patronising.'

'I hope I don't. Only satisfied with what I've got now; but I'll let that speak for itself.' He took her arm. 'Come. The car's waiting for us.'

'Just like that? No customs or anything?'

'We aren't too worried about people bringing in a few cosmetics and a pair of dungarees. Your bag will have been put in the car.'

'That car!' as she saw the limousine. 'You must be somebody pretty important, Colin.'

'Not me. You. I'm only assigned a car like this when I'm doing something important for the Ministry of Information.' The driver got out and Frere introduced him to Clare and told her that Makhan might be taking her to some of the places she would want to see.

She shook hands with the driver who then helped her into the car before resuming his place at the wheel. She said to Frere when he got in beside her: 'I hope my visit isn't going to be too official.'

'No. No. I've told them that you weren't to be trundled around to the places it had been decided in advance you ought to be shown. The fact that your visit is on a high level just means that you'll enjoy *carte blanche* in seeing anything or anyone you want to.'

'How did you persuade them to give me such a free hand?'

'It was the quality of the articles you've been writing about this part of the world that persuaded them – that and the fact that the Information Ministry thought it would be a good idea to have the right sort of Western correspondent doing a broad survey of the country at the end of the first Five-Year Plan. All I did was to point out that the person they were looking for is you.'

'Thanks, Colin. It must mean that you think you've got a pretty good story to tell.'

'We do. We do. Of course a lot of journalists think they should only go to places where they're not wanted. That's where the real stories are. But you, Clare – '

'Oh, I like to be wanted. And I'm not afraid of good news. My world could be doing with it.'

'Besides which I wanted to see you again.'

'You've been so cut off here. I can imagine that you'll be pumping me for news about the world out there as hard as I'll be pumping you about what's going on here in Malia.'

'That's true; but I meant that I wanted to see you again as a good friend.'

'Thank you.'

'What I've arranged this evening is that you'll have supper with me – something quiet and homely, after which you'll probably be glad of an early night.'

'So I can catch up on my jet lag.'

'We'll drop you off at your hotel first. Actually it's the hotel you stayed at when we first met here. For some time after the Revolution it was used by the Ministry of Industry; but last year, when we began opening up the country a bit more, it was decided to turn it back into a hotel.'

'And I'm one of the early guinea pigs?'

'Something like that,' he laughed. 'Your greatest criticism is likely to be about the number of times you're asked for any criticism. Anyway, I'll leave you there now.'

'To freshen up I think it's called.'

'And I'll be back in a little over an hour to pick you up and whisk you off to my bungalow.'

When the publication of *Das Vani* and *Workers' World*, together with state book publishing, had all been housed in the Communications Building, just across the main Square from the high-domed City Palace, now the People's Assembly, Frere had been assigned one of the small bungalows in the nearby residential area not far from the Great Pagoda. It had belonged previously to a junior official in the Puppet Government; but Frere had insisted that it was more than large enough for him, even in the event of his personal circumstances not remaining the same as during the pre-revolutionary period.

In the occupation of the capital there had been at that time a good deal of competition among high-ranking Party members for the most modest accommodation; and the assignment of commodious quarters tended to be in inverse ratio to the importance of those taking up occupation, so that Secretary General Lee, who had become Prime Minister though he continued to be addressed by his Party title, could say with relief that the private dwelling of the first chief of state was not too different from the base camp hut which would always be home to him.

The base camp had been preserved pretty much as it was in 1967 when the comrades had emerged from it to take over the country; and Frere hoped to be one of those showing Clare Wallace around it at some stage of her visit.

Having picked her up from the hotel, the big black car dropped them off outside Frere's bungalow and he waved goodbye to the driver.

'I hope we've finished with that,' Clare said. 'It makes me feel uncomfortably CD.'

Frere laughed. 'Crétin Distingué is how we always translated it, remember? I'll see to it that you're provided with something more modest – if, indeed, you don't do a lot of your travelling about by public transport. It's perfectly safe.'

'That would suit me best. It would give me a chance to meet and talk with ordinary people.'

'We're all ordinary people now, Clare.'

'Of course!' with good-humoured reservation.

He led her through a garden, across a tiny verandah and into a small but high sitting room with a ceiling fan just ticking over.

As soon as they entered Leela appeared from the back of the house holding the hand of a five-year-old boy who walked beside her in a dignified way.

'This is my wife, Leela, and my son, Matt.'

'You are very welcome to Malia, Clare Wallace,' Leela said in her perfect English.

'Oh, my dear,' Clare said, clasping her hands on her breast in completely spontaneous enthusiasm, 'how beautiful you are.' And bending down she took the hand that little Matt held up toward her. 'Hello there, Matt. You're named after your uncle, aren't you?'

'Yes, I am.'

Clare said to Leela: 'Do you know how Colin describes having a beautiful wife and such a darling son? As no longer being so personally uninvolved as before!' And to Frere: 'But you never wrote a word about this.'

'I knew that some day you'd get a chance to see for yourself – just as you'd be able to see the changes in Malia for yourself.' And to Leela: 'Clare doesn't believe a word of what she reads in *Workers' World*. Why should she credit my account of domestic bliss?'

Clare and Leela sat down, Matt standing beside his mother's chair, and Frere went over to a table where there was a jug and some bottles and a few glasses.

'Leela and Matt only have fruit juice,' he said, 'but I'm using you for an excuse to have a whisky. I hope you'll join me.'

'All right, I will then,' Clare said and to Leela: 'I want to hear about you. Colin is just a journalist, like me; and that doesn't interest me much. But you, Leela, what do you do?'

'What doesn't she do?' Frere answered for her. 'She's a senior instructor at the Marxist-Leninist Institute, which is part of Malia University. She's prominent in the Women's Union and she's an alternate member of the Central Committee. That's just for starters.'

'How on earth do you manage, with a child, too?'

'We've very good nursery schools.'

'You see,' Frere explained as he handed them their drinks, 'the great problem when we began to build socialism was the shortage of skilled workers, in every field. We had to bring as many women into industry, into medicine, teaching and administration as possible. The only way we could do it was to see that every factory, hospital, school or office had its creche; and nursery schools were established everywhere as the first stage of our system of education. Matt started last year.'

'And do you like it?' Clare asked him.

The boy nodded vigorously.

'And has it worked?' Clare wondered – 'as far as freeing women to take on all kinds of jobs is concerned.'

'You'll see as you travel around the country,' Leela told her. 'You'll see almost as many women factory managers as men; you'll see women engineers, electricians and crane operators; and you'll see rather *more* women than men as doctors, teachers and nurses.'

'*Every* kind of work then?'

'Just about. There are some heavy tasks like coal mining or loading and unloading ships which women don't do but we hope that in time, with technological advances, men won't have to do them either.'

'Equal pay?' Clare asked.

'Absolutely, *and* generous pre- and post-natal leave.'

'Fantastic! You're way ahead of us in the States.' And then: 'But if women do all the jobs, at every level, that men do – ?'

'Exactly,' Leela triumphantly took up the question that suggested itself, 'then why should there be jobs women do that men don't – like looking after children, mending and cleaning clothes, tidying the house and preparing meals? Why indeed! At the last People's Congress, Secretary General Lee addressed the whole male population of Malia on this issue and asked that every man in the country should write to him in the next three months mentioning one kind of "women's work" which he now shares or has taken over altogether.'

'And was there much of a response?'

'Pretty good. It was a test of our improving literacy rate as well.'

'And how does Colin measure up?' Clare asked with a laugh.

'Oh, he's literate enough,' Leela answered, laughing also.

'Now just hold on,' Frere spoke up. 'In about – ' he broke off to look at his watch – 'in about an hour Matt and I will show you how we have something to eat and then get ready for bed, entirely on our own, won't we?'

Matt nodded vigorously again. 'I tell him stories.'

Frere leaned back in his chair and let the conversation about the new Malia run on between the two women. After a bit he motioned to Matt to come to him and the boy left his mother and walked over to post himself between Frere's spread knees, the two of them listening to a feminine dialectic of question and answer as if it only indirectly had anything to do with them.

It was quite obvious that Frere had intended the late afternoon and evening of Clare Wallace's first day to take this form, partly because he thought Clare really would feel that she was getting more out of what a native Malian like Leela told her than anything the naturalised editor of a very committed journal was saying and partly because in watching a fellow journalist interviewing this beautiful revolutionary who was, so surprisingly, his wife, he was able to give that amazing fact more credence – as one might open a morning newspaper to confirm some strange event one had actually witnessed the day before.

Several times Clare asked Leela's permission to take down verbatim, in the notebook she always carried, some account of the way this or that institution was supposed to function in the Malia of today.

'Jot down anything you like,' Leela said; 'but you'll find most of what I'm saying in the pamphlets and documents issued by various collectives and ministries.'

'Journalists are always a little suspicious of anything written down and published for their benefit.'

'You have to be suspicious of what I say, too.' Leela smiled.

'Oh I am! But the *way* you say it, the look that comes into your eyes when you're explaining something, tells me a lot.'

And then as the day beyond the aromatic, water-sprinkled matting in the windows faded, he got up and said: 'This is where Matt and I vindicate the claim made in my letter to the Secretary General.'

Later on, when the three of them were having a light supper consisting mainly of a salad and a particular kind of freshwater fish caught in the Andor which Clare had never tasted before, Frere said: 'And this for me is the best thing of all. We can eat this meal in the confident knowledge that not a single child, indeed that no one at all, anywhere in Malia is going to sleep hungry. You remember the pathetically thin little pot-bellied children, Clare, who used to gather and stare at you in almost any place you stopped. Their eyes haunted me – up to a few years ago.'

'That means a lot. When I'm in Latin America or Africa or India or, indeed, any land ever ruled by your country or mine, those big staring eyes of the hungry children are a terrible reproach. If what has happened here means that for you, Colin, that ghost is laid – '

'We're laying it. In the Soviet Union and then in China and now in Malia it's being demonstrated that no one has to starve, that those who say poverty and undernourishment are the inevitable consequences of industrial backwardness or overpopulation or the collapse of world commodity prices lie in their teeth. That's what we say in *Workers' World* to poor working people everywhere: you see, it can be done; you don't have to go on watching your children die in their infancy; you can organise yourselves against the terrible sacrifice of your dear ones to line the pockets of people somewhere else.' Clare applauded.

'Colin gets carried away,' Leela said without suggesting for a moment that he should not.

All the same, he somewhat sheepishly set about serving their plates and during the meal he again detached himself to some extent from whatever discussion there was in order to observe these two women, representing the two halves of his life, talking together – as if he might in that way discover if his past and his present, each under the rule of such different considerations, could nonetheless be friends.

When they had finished eating, they moved into more comfortable chairs and Leela made coffee for them.

'You say when you'd like me to drive you to the hotel,' Frere told Clare. 'You must be tired after such a long flight.'

'Yes, I will turn in early. I'll tell you what I was thinking about in the plane coming here. As one of the first journalists to be given a free hand in dealing with post-revolutionary Malia – '

'*The* first actually.'

'Well, I'm probably going to be overwhelmed with information about how well it's all going. You say it isn't going to be simply an official tour, that I can see what I like. But every place I go, whether at my suggestion or not, they'll be ready to show me that this "is the future and it works". The only way I can come out of it all with any idea of what's really going on is by thinking of just a few lines of investigation to follow up in order to find answers to a couple of major questions.'

'Like?' Frere asked.

'Like whether socialist incentives can keep workers and peasants doing a good day's work when they no longer have to fear unemployment and dire poverty.'

'It's a good question,' Frere said with a glance at Leela.

'A very good question indeed,' Leela agreed.

'Particularly when revolutionary zeal for emancipation has to give way to down-to-earth communal life over the long haul.'

'Any other questions?' Frere wondered.

'One other. Can factory managers, central planners, state administrators and high-ranking party officials avoid or be stopped from coming to be a different class of people in some sense from the toilers in field and factory?'

'That's a very good question, too,' Leela said.

'You realise,' Clare explained with a smile, 'that I have to be a devil's advocate in all this and express doubts I may not even personally feel.'

'Of course,' Leela smiled, too. 'And you realise also that, however honest Colin and I try to be, we're bound to believe passionately in the possibility of a land from which exploitation is being eliminated.'

'I'm just glad I don't have to cope with your questions on my own,' Frere said to Clare with a laugh. 'The Ministry of Information may not thank me at all for suggesting you as the right journalist to expose ourselves to.'

Clare put down her cup. 'I think I will go back to the hotel now.'

'I'll have a car pick you up.'

'Can't I walk? It seemed such a short distance; and it's a beautiful night.'

'Of course.'

Leela said: 'You'd be perfectly safe. But Colin had better go with you, to make sure you don't take a wrong turning.'

'I wish "being perfectly safe" was something that could be said of many parts of New York at night – or even Washington! Thank you so much for your hospitality, Leela dear. When I've seen something of the new Malia, I'll want to talk to you about it. To sort out my ideas. And may I say,' she paused a moment, 'how absolutely delighted I am that something so beautiful should have happened to Colin.'

'I'll help all I can,' Leela took up one part of what Clare had said. 'And I'm so glad Colin made them realise you were the right person to write about us. You are the right person, Clare.'

On such mild nights, after the heat of the day, many people were out strolling along the palm-lined avenues or having refreshments in one of the pavilions where there might be a performance of a musical drama or a puppet show.

'And how are things in the States?' Frere asked. 'Have they adjusted to their defeat at the hands of the Vietnamese?'

'That will take a long time. There are those who say nuclear weapons should have been used.'

'They probably would have been if the Soviet Union and China didn't both have them.'

'They hit back at Vietnam in any way they can,' Clare dissociated herself from her country's actions. 'They've made every nation in any way connected with them join in a complete boycott.'

'Britain has collaborated up to the hilt on that and got Malia included in the boycott as well.'

'Do you realise,' Clare asked indignantly, 'that Vietnam is the only country in the world that receives nothing from the United Nations – not even information bulletins?'

'The only country except Malia. Britain is better at hiding her tracks.'

'Part of the peace settlement was an agreement that the Unites States would pay reparations. They haven't paid a cent. They claim no payment will be made until every single missing soldier or airman has been accounted for. That in a country where they killed or seriously injured over a million people, a country on which they dropped more bombs than were dropped on Germany in World War Two, including toxic chemicals which have not only rendered millions of acres infertile for decades to come but are causing stillbirths and deformed babies by the thousands.'

He put his hand on her arm to calm her. 'We had a taste of that chemical warfare of America's. Not for long fortunately.' And as if to reassure her on the score of America's uniqueness in revanchism: 'Britain is behaving as badly as it can. The total reserves of Malia, quite a few hundred millions of pounds, were deposited in the Bank of England. They have been sequestrated and there can be no discussion about the release of these funds until all private claims by British citizens in connection with property they owned in Malia have been dealt with!'

'It's appalling!' Clare exclaimed.

'Yes, but the very extent of the vicious meanness of both countries is a measure of the huge success that's been won against imperialism. We like to think we contributed in some small part to Vietnam's success: they contributed tremendously to ours. Thanks to the heroic sacrifices of our Vietnamese comrades Malia has been given the opportunity at relatively little cost to build socialism here.'

He looked around at the city sights they were passing as though seeing everything afresh in terms of the obligation it represented. 'Only by making a good job of it can we express our appreciation.'

'You'll be expressing mine, too, Colin.'

As he walked with her, Frere felt that he was nodding to acquaintances or speaking to friends they passed along the way as though from a slight distance – the result, no doubt, of seeing things through her eyes. 'You know,' he told her with a little laugh, 'I suddenly feel like a foreign correspondent again myself, about to dash around a country new to me and write up my impressions before hopping off somewhere else.'

"Do you miss it? With what you've got here, I don't see how you possibly could.'

'No, I don't miss the life. But sometimes I miss that feeling of detachment, the sense that whatever's wrong with any place one's writing about, it's always somebody else's problem. And you, Clare. Do you think you'd ever like to stop? – If you found some corner that seemed right for you?'

'No. I believe I've passed any such chances by. It's different for a woman, I guess. If she doesn't find the right place before a certain age, she'll probably just keep going.'

'You beyond "a certain age", Clare! You seem to me – maybe because of constantly seeing new places and getting fresh impressions – perpetually young.'

'Childish even,' she laughed. 'That's the way your Leela, with that mature wisdom of hers, makes me feel. I suppose it's knowing exactly who you are, where you come from and what there is for you to do. I still have to make myself up as I go along. Just as you probably used to.

Congratulations, Colin, on becoming a part of reality instead of merely writing about it.'

'I wonder.'

'What?'

'I wonder if anyone as detached from life as you and I have been, professionally, ever gets completely caught up in it again.'

'Well, I certainly got no sense of detachment seeing you with your lovely wife and smart little son this evening. But then they struck me as irresistible. There's just one thing you're going to have to watch, Colin.'

They had arrived at the hotel. 'What's that?' he asked her.

'You're going to have to be very careful that in talking to me in my vagabondage from that domestic security of yours you never sound patronising.'

He held the door open for her with a smile. 'I promise.'

'Thank you for a delightful evening.'

'Come to the Communications Building in the main city square about ten tomorrow morning. I'll be waiting for you and will introduce you to the young woman who will be acting as your interpreter and guide for the whole tour.'

'Right. Good night, Colin.'

He kissed her on the cheek. 'Sleep well.'

'Like a log.'

When he got back to the bungalow, Leela had finished clearing up and was studying some papers. She put them aside and he sat down beside her, taking her hand in his.

'Thank you for the hospitable way you received my friend,' he said.

'She's also a guest of the People's Democratic Republic of Malia,' Leela reminded him with a smile.

'Do you like her?'

'Very much. It's just – '

'Yes?'

'It's something I've noticed about you before when people from your part of the world were here. You – I don't know, Colin – you somehow cease to be entirely with us here.'

'With you and Matt?' For just a moment he wondered if there might be a hint of jealousy in what she was saying and then for another moment he felt a slight regret that it was most unlikely.

'Not Matt and me. With all of us here who are trying to build a new world. You become one of them to some extent, who just happens to know more about Malia than they do. Sometimes this evening it seemed to me that both of you were visiting me in my native surroundings.'

Frere did not answer at once. He weighed her words very carefully because he could be quite crushed by her slightest criticism. 'Clare didn't feel that I was anything but completely immersed with you in everything that's happening in Malia. She did suggest that your being so beautiful might throw a bit of doubt on my motives for getting caught up in Malia's revolution but – '

'I wish people wouldn't say things like that.' She frowned.

'What she mainly expressed was her regret that she was unlikely now to find herself a part of anything the way you and I are.'

'Poor Clare.'

He put his arm around her and kissed her and he wondered if there was just the slightest disinclination on her part or whether it was simply that complete containment of her feelings which sometimes made him feel, him of all people, gauchely over-emotional. 'You don't think that when such visitors are here I, well, distance myself even from you a little.'

'No, it's not that. It's just that your commitment to the revolution and to building socialism seems to become a little provisional – as if you needed them to understand your reasons for being involved here for those reasons to seem valid to you.'

He paused again before speaking. 'I don't think it's any lack of conviction on my part, Leela. I do try, quite deliberately, to put myself in a non-partisan frame of mind when I'm writing something for *Workers' World*. When explaining some new policy that's been adopted, I try to convince that uncommitted self that it's right.' He worried sometimes if he was not getting to a point where he simply assumed that every policy adopted by the Political Bureau was correct. And then he worried about what he would do if, on some occasion, an agreed policy seemed wrong to him. 'You don't see me going through that process at my office – only when outsiders present themselves here. I think it's that ability to see what's going on in Malia through the eyes of a stranger in order to know the kinds of explanations and arguments to use which makes me a good editor for an international periodical.'

'Yes, if by the time you're working on the final copy you're writing with complete assurance.'

Again a pause. 'Has anyone suggested that I sometimes don't?'

'No. Certainly not.'

He kissed her again. 'Shall we go to bed?'

She looked at the papers she had put aside and then left them there. 'Yes,' she said, kissing him. 'Let's.'

15

After seeing Clare Wallace off on her tour of Malia, Colin Frere went up to the *Workers' World* editorial department on the top floor of the Communications building. He had asked for an office looking out over the Square and the great, domed People's Assembly Hall. It was the view he had been privileged to have on the day Rani Kalpur was liberated and People's Hero Tuck was shot and killed after the historic tank battle.

As he entered his office he paused before a framed copy of one of the early issues of *Workers' World*, dated January 1969 – just a few months before the revolutionary uprising which was to lay the foundation for building socialism.

It was not as well laid out as it might have been; and, with no photos or much variation in typeface, it did not present a particularly attractive appearance; but there was a fervour glowing through the articles and the boxed editorial comment which lit up the whole front page in a remarkable way.

That was not so often the case these days. With all the attention to design, the handsome photographs, the regular features and the general professionalism, what often seemed to him to be coming through was special pleading rather than eagerness to break the good news of what socialism was achieving in one corner of the world.

Workers' World now enjoyed a wide distribution, both the Soviet Union and China vying with each other in accommodating it on reading racks in this or that part of the world where their influence was strong. It was popular with the radical youth of the Western democracies eager to see a publication from a country that had recently liberated itself and become part of the socialist world. Frere was perfectly aware of how left-wing political groups in various countries would study new editions of *Workers' World* to see how it could be used to support them in their frenetic debates with other radical groups. It seemed ironic that a country like Malia, which had been so completely subject to the intellectual, moral and cultural sway of British imperialism, should have become an arbiter for politicised youth everywhere, including Britain itself!

He smiled over the advice Secretary General Lee always gave to representatives of such groups when they arrived on delegations. 'Do not expect to get from us answers to the Great Polemic between the Soviet Union and China or to any of the political problems in your own country. All we can offer you is the Marxist method we have used and continue to use in arriving at our own answers for building socialism in Malia – which at every turn will have to be tested by us in practice.' He mused briefly on printing that advice as part of the masthead of the journal, and then realised that it should guide editorial policy and not pre-select the *Workers' World* readership.

Frere sat down at his desk and typed for a while at a leading article it had been agreed was to appear in the next issue. About halfway through he began to feel that he was just stringing words together and after a bit he stopped typing. He sat for a while just staring at the words he had written until they did not have any meaning for him at all any more and then he got up to stare out of the window at the busy Square below to see if some meanings would not come back to him.

After a while he left his office and walked down the corridor. Siti gave him a little wave and smile as he paused briefly in her doorway; but she was working on a special feature for *Das Vani* and he did not want to disturb her. He went on to the large office at the end of the corridor, which was Professor Chin's, and knocked.

At a summons to enter Frere opened the door and asked: 'Are you busy?'

'How kind of you to suggest that I ever am these days,' Chin answered with a broad smile. 'Come in and sit down. Have a cup of tea with me.'

'That would be nice.' Frere was thinking that Chin had begun looking older from the time he had become less actively engaged in the work of the Department.

Chin got up and plugged in the electric kettle on a table by the wall on which there were cups and saucers and a big jar of Mati tea. 'It's the thing I was most glad to make friends with again,' he said – 'the electric kettle. Civilisation means such different things to different people. To me it means an electric kettle and an ample supply of the green tea of the Mati hills without which I don't think real companionship is possible.' And when Frere did not say anything: 'Usually such a disclosure about oneself invites a similar revelation in return.'

'I think civilisation means to me having friends who are always willing to pretend to be at leisure when one feels the need to visit and chat, and to express that willingness in terms of cups of Mati tea.'

'Ah, my dear Comrade Colin, it's no pretence. They made me Editor-in-Chief of all publications to keep me from damaging the orderly production of any one of them. It was really, I think, the first step toward retiring me altogether; but the Central Committee hasn't made up its mind yet on the question of retirement. Should it be on the basis of chronological age or the state of one's health or should good communists simply die in harness, long after they could still pull anything?'

'You add to their difficulty, of course, by keeping so well.'

'The real difficulty, as you know perfectly well, is the venerable age of our revered Secretary General. Nobody can speak on the subject of retirement without everyone's being aware that it's a reflection on the continuance in office of our great leader – including Comrade Lee himself who's repeatedly urged that he really *wants* to stand down and let the existing Political Bureau govern collectively.'

'If it would still be a collective without the Secretary General. No member of the Political Bureau can express an opinion on the matter without appearing to be staking out a claim for himself in whatever pattern of power comes next. And everyone else is bound to feel that no one but a member of the Political Bureau has sufficient knowledge of the Secretary General's real wishes for himself and the country to speak with any authority on the matter.'

'So here I am,' Chin said with a laugh, 'still waiting for a ruling on the question of retirement. I don't worry. There's always that grim person with the reaper who can step in and put an end to that particular debate.'

Frere dismissed that idea with a laugh. 'Did you have your talk with the Information Minister?'

'Yes, I did. I told him that I thought it was the duty of someone as old as I am to step aside and make way for a younger man. The trouble is that Comrade Hadar and I are the same age.'

'So the question of your successor didn't come up?'

'No, even though there are any number of people Comrade Hadar would rather see in the office of Editor-in Chief. But then he knows that to mention the name of one's favourite candidate too early in the game is the surest way of dishing his chances. That's what happened when I was too fulsome early on in recommending Swee Meng as editor of *Das Vani*. It got Swee Meng posted as Secretary to the Gouri District.'

'But what got Kalan appointed editor of *Das Vani* was the fact that he's Hadar's nephew.'

'That may have had something to do with it. Of course, if I were at all devious I might find out who was favoured by Comrade Hadar for my job and then come out openly right now with the most enthusiastic testimonial to his fitness to replace me.'

'Or *her* fitness,' Frere corrected.

'Do you know something then?' Chin asked with raised eyebrows.

'I'm the last person to know anything like that. I'm just putting in a plea for equality of opportunity as between men and women, that's all.'

'Quite right, too. For a time we honoured women who had been actively involved in the struggle, like Comrade Leela, with important posts; but I'm afraid we've slipped back into only thinking of men for advancement. We should be putting forward names like that of Comrade Siti. Only that would introduce a whole new range of suspect motives.'

'All of which reminds me of another question. Is there any chance of getting Tinoo transferred from the Education Department to Publications?'

'I've asked for him a number of times you know. I pointed out that his English is so good that, among other things, he could keep an eye on the translation standards of anything we put out in that language. I was told that the same qualification was vitally important for the Education Department. "Even when English is to be phased out as far as official use is concerned?" I asked them.'

'And what did they say to that?'

'They didn't say anything. They didn't have to. Because they know that I know that English won't be phased out as its continued use represents a claim on the more important posts by an intellectual elite educated in British-type schools.'

'Even though the academic and administrative ranks were supposed to be purged of all those sympathetic to British influence?'

'Well, you know, a lot of those who opted in secret for revolutionary change were simply insuring their future in case it ever happened.'

Frere leant back in his chair and regarded Chin speculatively. 'What do you really think, Chin? Are our revolutionary achievements being frittered away by self-seeking bureaucrats?'

'No, I don't think so. Of course we're bound to have those who are motivated more by a desire to get ahead themselves than to be of service to the people. But you take some poor peasant in the countryside whose children for the first time are not only getting enough to eat but are being educated and cared for medically – he's not going to be worrying about whether the motives of everybody responsible for that are as purely socialist as they ought to be. What counts, I think, is whether a socialist climate is established such that self-seeking has to take the form of giving every appearance of serving the people more selflessly than others.'

'Doesn't pretending to have motives people don't actually have eventually discredit those motives?'

'I think that if pretending to have the right motives works for a particular society, in time people will begin really to *have* those motives. I remember lecturing to a girls' school once. Oh, many years ago. I was telling them about our great epic which happens,' he reminded Frere pointedly, 'to have been written by a woman. I said to them: "Just humour me by *pretending* to like Narmala's epic poetry better than the rubbishy popular novels we get from Britain. Carry a copy of the *Arjen Nemastabadh* around with you and fool me by appearing to read a bit every so often." Because, you see, I knew that if I could make them feel that there was any reason for making out that they liked it some of them really *would* get to liking it very much.'

'I suppose so,' Frere said, rather doubtfully.

'Just remember what there was before – the naked self-interest of the imperialists arguing that if there was poverty and starvation in the land, it was because the poor weren't selfish and greedy enough to improve their lot by their own efforts. You don't have to replace a system like that with perfect socialism, just ordinary old make-believe socialism will do.'

'Perhaps. But might it not be that you have to aim for *perfect* socialism to get *any* socialism strong enough to withstand the re-emergence of the profit motive?'

'That's not a question of individual motivation, Comrade Colin. Having got rid of the capitalists, the compradors and the big landowners we just have to be sure they don't come back in any form.'

'I suppose so,' Frere merely said again.

'Is something troubling you?'

'It's just that when my brother came back to Malia after the War it was to take up arms against imperialism – his own country in fact. To a lesser extent that was true for me, too. That same imperialism still ruled through its puppets and hangers-on. But now when the external enemy has been banished and all the problems are purely domestic ones – well, I'm not so sure I'm the person to write about them.'

'What makes you say that? From all over the world we get reports on how useful and informative the journal you edit is.'

'When the Communist Party of Malia was operating out of a stronghold hidden away in the depths of the jungle, there was some reason for having a fairly well-known foreign correspondent describing the revolutionary emancipation of the country; but now, when Malia is firmly established as one of the socialist powers, why would anyone be interested in what a forgotten journalist of the West has to say about it?'

'Forgotten as a foreign correspondent appearing in various British papers, perhaps; but ever more widely known as the editor of one of the most lively and perceptive of international radical periodicals.'

'Can you honestly say, Comrade Chin, that it's never been put to you that it might be better to have a native-born Malian as editor of *Workers' World*?'

'Every crazy proposition imaginable has been put to me at one time or another. The point is that there's never been the slightest move to act on such a proposal.'

'All the same I wonder if I ought not to make that suggestion to Hadar myself.'

'I wouldn't,' Chin said with a little shake of his head. 'It would just make them wonder what your *real* motive was in bringing it up.'

'Perhaps they'd tell me!'

It was Chin's time to lean back, fingertips together, and regard his interlocutor thoughtfully. 'We become obsessed with motives, I think, when the drive to action has weakened. Back in base camp we knew just what had to be done and that knowledge organised our lives for us. Now we feel that we need a new ideological definition of the tasks ahead to give us a new impetus. But maybe the task of building a socialist society can't be defined in the way that throwing out foreign exploiters can. We can't rush forward in a great upsurge of long-suppressed energy to pick our way carefully across practically unknown territory. You're not the only one who's puzzled sometimes by the kind of problems we're having to face now.'

Frere nodded. 'You're very wise, Comrade Chin.'

'No, just old. We old men have a lot of sound reasons why people oughtn't to throw themselves at their objectives quite so vigorously.'

During the rest of the day as Frere was getting on with various odds and ends of routine work, he kept thinking of discussing these doubts about his position with Leela.

Sometimes he avoided raising with her certain specific issues, like having Tinoo moved over to Publications, because he was afraid that, even if he told her otherwise, she might think that it was a plea for her to use her considerable influence to get something done about it. But this was different. This was trying to understand the peculiar requirements of Malia's development strategy in order to re-assess his responsibilities in relation to editing *Workers' World*.

It had been possible for him to launch and edit a periodical for the foreign market because there was such unity, under Secretary General Lee's leadership, about the need for revolutionary change and about the steps for bringing it about. But what if that unity were broken? What if there were important differences about the way forward now. Would his position not become untenable as this faction or that sought to use *Workers' World* to make its case before an international tribunal of progressive peoples?

And yet it could also be argued that he was in a better position than others to keep the periodical above the fray, as it were, and provide well-wishers of the Malian Revolution abroad with some insight into the vital issues that were being fought over. These were certainly questions to be gone into with Leela. Indeed, it was precisely in engaging her on matters she would recognise as being well worth her most penetrating philosophical thought that he fancied their relationship was deepened and enriched, giving it a dimension few wives and husbands could enjoy to anything like the same extent.

When he got back to their bungalow, Leela had not returned. The sixteen-year-old girl from Teipur who looked after young children in the neighbourhood had picked up Matt from the nursery, given him something to eat and was watching him play on the floor with bangles that had little bells on them, and wooden blocks for beating time.

'Thank you, Lara,' Frere said to her. 'I'll take over now. How are you getting on at the college?'

She smiled and gave him a brief account of her studies. 'I'll go back and do some homework.'

The practice of bringing girls and boys from villages like Teipur to live in the better of the old servants' quarters attached to each bungalow and help out with looking after children or doing other chores in exchange for board and lodging while continuing their education was just one of the ways that had been found of transforming the pattern of life which had originally dictated the architecture and landscaping of this part of the city. The maintenance of flowering trees and green lawns distinctive of this area was attended to by boys who were also taking courses in the college which were not yet available in some of the rural regions. As Frere had said: it was a constant struggle to see whether this part of the city would be properly socialised or would finally succeed in re-imposing the bad old colonial ways on the new inhabitants.

He took Matt by the hand and led him to the shower room where, as was often the case when he was home at this time and assumed responsibility for washing his son, he stripped off his blue cotton boiler suit as Matt climbed out of his shirt and shorts and together they stood under the spray of water soaping themselves and inevitably getting involved in the exciting game of hunting the slippery, elusive bar.

Then while the boy had a bowl of cereal and milk and Frere made a cup of tea for himself, they would exchange reflections on what the day had held for each of them. It seemed that the children at the nursery school were rehearsing a song and dance to be performed on the next

Liberation Day; but some of the children could not remember the words. Matt demonstrated that this had not been a problem for him by standing very straight and going through the song from beginning to end without a single mistake.

Frere in turn told Matt about sending the nice foreign woman he had met last night off on a sightseeing tour.

'Will she see your button factory?'

'I'm not sure that's on the list of things for her to have a look at. And then this afternoon I had a nice visit with Uncle Chin.'

'Did he drop anything?' Matt asked.

'He *usually* drops things, doesn't he? Well, today he didn't; but you know I rather suspect it was only because he wasn't *holding* anything.'

Sometimes in such conversations Frere would switch to English and Matt, without really being all that aware of the change, would answer in that language. They had decided that Matt should grow up bilingual. Even if English was to a considerable extent associated with Malia's colonial past and had to be downgraded from the official position it had arrogated to itself, knowledge of English and familiarity with English literature was part of Malia's own history now and well worth preserving for its usefulness in keeping Malia in touch with world scientific developments and for giving the works of Malian writers, carefully translated into good English, a worldwide currency. The thing was, Frere always said, to see that this linguistic channel never became the means of flooding Malia with the consumerist trash of western Europe and the United States.

As he sat there chatting with his son, he thought of that conversation on the equality of women he had staged between his wife and Clare Wallace as the best way of showing Clare what had happened here in terms of relations between men and women. It occurred to him, not for the first time, that to the extent that women had been liberated from masculine domination, the feminine in men had been liberated too.

Indeed, he was not sure but that he was in some ways a little bit more of a 'mother' to Matt than Leela was. Leela as a lovely girl child whose parents had been killed in the Japanese invasion, as a beautiful young woman in the, for all women, precarious colonial world and then the macho if Marxist world of a guerrilla stronghold, had become accustomed to regarding her own tenderness, to say nothing of her sexuality, as the enemy within which could betray her to the inevitably threatening masculine forces without. An ingrained wariness marked her comradeship with the very like-minded men who were allies in what, for the women in the movement, was a double liberation. And even when the fighting which had united men and women so intimately was over, the defence in depth against male dominance was too habitual, the scars of the struggle for sexual liberation too deep for her to relax completely in the freedom she had helped to win.

He was more aware of these lesions inside her than she was; but he did not think it would help to let her know that she was actually withholding herself even when she thought she was yielding in the most natural way and that he sometimes felt slightly cheated that she never wanted him as desperately as he sometimes wanted her. He simply hoped that love and gentleness would eventually make it possible for her to abandon herself with him in a completely unthinking trustfulness. Meanwhile what he had of her was such a wonderfully fragrant and feminine presence that he could not think of his life with her as other than joyous, nor of that final surrender as other than something he and his entire sex might have forfeited any immediate right to through brutal exactions down the centuries. As one of the walking wounded in a war the women of Malia might at last be on the point of winning, Leela aroused in him such pride and tenderness that he could hardly wish her to be other than she was.

He had put Matt to bed and begun a story whose end slumber did not wait for when he heard Leela come in. He went into the sitting room and kissed her. He explained that Matt was cleaned, fed and storied and that he had picked up a nearly-ready-meal in the Communications commissariat which only had to be heated up.

She laughed and held up a paper bag. 'So did I – from the food centre at the Secretariat.'

'That's a problem about shared domesticity – everything tends to get done twice. Still, houses twice as clean and children twice as well trained in their social responsibilities can't be bad.'

'Can you eat twice as much food tonight or shall we give some of it to the students in the back? Lara's gone, I suppose.'

'Yes, I got back early and released her to do some studying.' He noticed just the slightest crease of a frown between her brows and wondered if she felt that he was overdoing his housewife act by way of a mild reproach. 'Nothing to do with Matt is ever a chore for me,' he lightly waved aside any credit for looking after their son, 'and, besides, at this time when you have so much to do I seem to have rather less.'

While they were eating he hesitated a moment before asking her what she had been doing that day. He had become a little self-conscious about possibly sounding as though he were trying to make up for all the times men over a large part of the globe had returned to recount boastfully or angrily the ups and downs of their bread-winning engagements of the day while assuming that nothing of any importance or interest could have happened in the house. What he hoped he conveyed instead was that he never tired of imagining this intelligent, beautiful woman, who was so unaccountably joined to him, in the situations which she described. It was also true, such was the honour and trust in which she was held by the most important comrades, that her days were much fuller of significant incident than his were. When he did manage to put his question, she answered:

'Oh, they've been at me again to become a full member of the Central Committee.'

'Do you feel that you should?'

'No, I don't. I've told them that I'm not prepared at this time to take on anything that cuts more deeply into my time with a very young child, nor my work at the Institute for that matter. And when they say that what's expected of me as a CC member can be scaled down to what I feel I can manage, I tell them that there can't then be any very pressing need to fill the post now.'

'Are you, are you sorry that you can't take it on, Leela?'

'Not a bit, darling Colin. I have little enough time for you two dear people as it is.'

'Have they ever suggested that you might give up or reduce your work at the Institute?'

'They've hinted at it; but I've always pretended not to hear. You know I'm particularly interested in the work we're doing now on formalising Marxist method. We're putting together for study purposes the results of the problem-solving workshops we've established in factories, on collective farms, in community centres – '

'More of your "liberating philosophy from the confines of lecture rooms and textbooks and turning it into a sharp weapon in the hands of the masses" sort of thing,' he said, referring to the appropriate quotation.

'Exactly. Our young people at the Institute will be able to study how dialectical method yields practical answers which can be tested and also how this method can be applied to the problems of government administration and central planning as well as those of farm and factory.'

'Isn't that turning philosophy back into textbooks again?'

'No, it's taking the solution of problems concerning the whole country away from administrators and bureaucrats and putting it in the hands of the masses. It involves me in working with people who come to the Institute from all over Malia. It means keeping in touch with the people we're supposed to be serving.'

'Do you feel that the comrades in administration or the central planning bureau are getting out of touch?'

'There's always that danger.' She also hesitated a moment before asking him about his day, so obviously not wanting it to sound in any way perfunctory.

'The opposite of yours in a way.'

'How do you mean?'

'There seems to be less and less demand for my journalistic capabilities.'

'But *Workers' World* is as much appreciated as ever, Colin.'

'Perhaps. I rather have the feeling that in the heady days of the revolution and after, we wanted everybody in the world to know about the exciting things that were happening in Malia. Now I think we're too caught up in our own problems here to care very much about what others think of us.'

'That itself could become a problem, if we let it.'

'To be solved by your students at the Institute?' He smiled.

'All I know is I never hear anything but praise for the job you do in publicising us abroad.'

'But will it continue to be the case that what's acceptable here tells readers in other countries what they ought to know? Aren't people out there going to start asking: "Who is this Englishman in the editorial chair of *Workers' World*? Isn't he some foreign journalist patronisingly extolling Malia's socialist progress from outside the struggle?" You see what I mean.'

'I see what you mean; but no one anywhere could possibly think of *you* as outside our struggle. There must be many people out there who completely identify our struggle with the person from whom they've learnt most about it.' She paused for a moment and then asked: 'Has anybody said anything to you that makes you feel like that?'

'No. No. It's just something that's occurred to me sometimes.' And then, suddenly: 'Has anybody said anything to you?'

'Certainly not!' she answered quickly. 'I think you're just imagining the whole thing.'

'Maybe.' He got up and began to clear the table.

'Let me do that,' she said.

'Of course,' he said with a laugh. 'If we don't watch it, I'll be accusing you of mussing up my nice tidy house next.'

He stood in the doorway watching her deal with plates and things and then begin to make tea and, just watching those deft slender fingers moving among various objects like a musician stroking inanimate strings to lively music, just seeing her look once or twice over her shoulder and smiling at him, filled him with such love for her that he could hardly restrain himself from going to her and taking her in his arms.

But he shook his head over what she had said about the continuing importance of his editorship of *Workers' World*. Was there a suggestion in her assurance that it would be difficult for her to be completely involved with anyone who was not in some sense essential to the political movement which meant so much to her? He felt an instant foreboding of what might happen to her love for him if he were ever discarded as of no further use to the cause she lived for.

She handed him a tray with plates of the heated food they had brought back and cups and teapot and he carried it into the other room and set it down between their two chairs.

She had been thinking about something that *he* had said. 'Colin. You must never feel guilty about anything that's happened to us women in the past, you know. You're the kindest, gentlest man in the world!' She frowned. 'When you seem to be trying to make up for something you've never been guilty of yourself, I don't know – it makes *me* feel guilty.'

He thought about it a bit and then said with a despairing little laugh: 'Guilt is something I came out here to get away from. But for someone as marked by life in a greedy, uncaring world as I am, not to feel guilty, of itself, gives me a sense of guilt. All I can do is to try harder not to infect you.'

'We can both see to it that Matt isn't infected. I think about our lovely son that way sometimes – as a child born in socialism who never need know the deforming effects of growing up in an exploitative society.'

'Yes!' he exclaimed enthusiastically. He took her hand and kissed it. 'That's the way I feel about Matt, too. I feel that, without being aware of it, I was being driven halfway around the world to meet the one woman who could share with me the creation of a child symbolising the peace and freedom of a world no longer at odds with itself.'

She laughed. 'That sounds like something you might have written back in your by-line days on a popular newspaper.'

'It does at that,' he admitted. 'Maybe there ought to be a socialist equivalent of a tabloid.'

She poured more tea for them. 'And Colin.'

'Yes.'

'Don't worry too much about that sense of losing way a bit. We all feel it. You can't experience something like a revolution without feeling a sense of letdown afterwards. It's probably why an Extraordinary People's Congress is being called.'

'Oh, it's the first I've heard of it.'

'It's only been discussed in the Political Bureau. Even the Central Committee hasn't had a chance to consider it yet.'

'Is it the Secretary General's idea?'

'It is now. Apparently he wasn't too keen to begin with. He felt it might be just another exercise in popular adulation which he's becoming more and more critical of.'

'I know. He's warned us in Publications to go easy on crediting him with all Malia's successes. If it were anybody but Secretary General Lee, I'd say it was a cunning way of adding to the cult of approbation by seeming to abjure it.'

She frowned slightly. 'Are *you* a bit critical of the way we use his popularity to mobilise people? Printing thousands of copies of *The Fifty Essential Sayings,* for example, which people can keep about them at all times?'

'You know very well, Leela, that I myself worship the man just this side of idolatry. And feeling the way I do about him if he says that the affectionate reliance on him is becoming excessive, well – '

'But what if he's allowing his natural modesty to interfere with his playing the part he and he alone is capable of at this stage of our development? Malia's not like your part of the world, Colin. People aren't used to thinking. Revering someone whose understanding of Marxism Leninism enables him to make judgments about what's best for this country is the first step toward judging things dialectically oneself. To love and respect a supremely logical man is the beginning of a respect for logic. That little book of the *Sayings* – I've seen people with some serious problem, perhaps even a personal problem, poring over it sure that an answer for them must be there.'

He smiled but did not say anything. When differences, usually of emphasis or of forms of expression, occurred between them, Leela would often, in the nicest possible way, treat him as one of her better students and he, conscious of the fact that his not being a native Malian always placed him in a somewhat junior position in all matters of that kind, would gracefully accept that role. He rather enjoyed the pleasure it gave her to feel that she had explained something to him so clearly that he could earn from her the pat on the head which took the form of a tender kiss she was delighted to bestow.

He accepted her kiss now and turned it into something a little more personal than the reward for an attentive pupil. It was a scholarly charade played out many times with the grateful assurance they both had that no difference between them could ever be fundamental. At least that was the hope he felt safe in entertaining. And the basis of these little academic exercises of hers, the never-to-be-entirely-eliminated fact of his strangeness as hailing from another land, reminded him most agreeably each time of his long courtship which, in spite of her not being able to decide whether his being something of an alien was an attraction or not, had nonetheless eventually come out happily in the end. That was what the kiss was all about.

'Anyway,' he said, 'an Extraordinary Congress is something to look forward to.'

'As a communist or a journalist?'

'Both. You say it wasn't the Secretary General's idea to begin with. Who first proposed it?'

'Pir Dato.'

'Oh.'

'But no idea which is seriously considered by the Political Bureau remains any one person's for long.' When he did not say anything, she added: 'Pir Dato has a very good opinion of you, you know.'

'I have the highest opinion of Pir Dato. I just *feel* that anyone as bright and clever and articulate as he is must always be careful about how his undoubted influence is used.'

'Clever or intelligent?'

'Well, both.' He thought for a moment. 'I wonder if Clare Wallace ought to see him while she's here. If he can manage it.'

'It might be a good idea,' she said quite naturally. 'I'll mention it to his personal assistant.'

'What is it, Leela?'

'I was wondering if it was Clare's being here that's made you start questioning things.'

'I don't know. Maybe she does bring out the investigative reporter in me.'

Eight days later at about ten o'clock in the morning, Clare Wallace was in Frere's office for a last visit before leaving for the airport. She had been entertained the night before by the Publications Department but there had been little chance for her to tell Frere what her impressions of her tour of Malia were. Now as soon as she was seated opposite him she began enthusiastically.

'It's quite fantastic, Colin! Those schools and clinics all over the country. And the factories which have sprung up everywhere. And the collectivised farms – well, it's, it's fantastic.'

He beamed like a parent hearing excellent reports about his children. 'It's what Lenin spoke about – releasing the vivid creativity of the masses, all that knowledge of production stored up over ages of social practice.'

'Look at this gorgeous shawl I got in Khangtu. I asked them if there was any outlet in the States for the beautiful things made by the handicraft co-operative. It's something I'll have to look into when I get back to New York.'

'You'll run head-on into the tightest boycott there's ever been!'

'Then I'll write about that. I'll ask American women if they realise what beautiful things at low cost they're being deprived of by our vicious attitude toward Vietnam and its closest ally.'

One of the young women in the department brought them coffee and rice cakes. Clare thanked her and, when she had gone, remarked to Frere: 'Since all the men and women I've been meeting are mostly dressed in boiler suits, I take it those lovely things I saw are for export only.'

'Yes. They're sent to the Soviet Union and the East European Peoples Democracies.'

'Everybody dressed so drably – is that policy or economic necessity?'

'A bit of both, I guess. Mainly it's essentials for everybody before frills for anybody.'

'As a man you can say that quite happily. You probably like wearing what you've got on for every possible occasion. And Leela, of course, Leela would look beautiful in anything. But I wonder how long most women are going to put up with it. I should have told Pir Dato that when he asked me if I had any criticisms to make of the new Malia.'

'What did you make of him?'

'He's very bright, isn't he?'

'Very.'

'I wondered if he wasn't almost – well, too bright. But he's cunning also, cunning enough not to let it show.'

'It's strange, you know. He's always struck me that way a bit, too, and yet he has the complete confidence of Secretary General Lee.'

'To say nothing of Leela,' Clare remarked shrewdly. 'He has the highest opinion of her, too. He has the highest opinion of you, Colin, for that matter.'

'Or is that his cunning?'

'No, I don't think so. He's remarkably intelligent. He was telling me how Malia got useful aid from the Soviet Union at first; but then when they were advocating peaceful co-existence with America, they stopped helping a country in America's bad books for its association with Vietnam. Then there was aid from China but it's being withdrawn because of that same association with Vietnam – which Deng Xiaoping seems to think ought to resume its place as part of the old Han empire. Pir Dato says the test of any country's genuine commitment to communism is its commitment to building socialism in one country on the basis of absolute self-sufficiency.'

'I'm afraid he's right.'

'Oh, he's very intelligent.'

'I know. I know. But still you and I have this slight reservation about him that people here, who know him far better than we ever could, don't have.'

'I think it's because he has a quality you and I are familiar with – we've lived with it all our lives, in ourselves and in those around us – personal ambition. We've learned to be on guard against it because, although it can make one do great things, it can also make one stoop to mean tricks against rivals. Having lived so many years in a socialist commune in the midst of a jungle, people like the Secretary General and your Leela, who don't have that characteristic at all themselves, aren't so likely to recognise it in others.'

'You're probably right. Maybe I've been doing him an injustice and forgetting what great achievements personal ambition, working in the right social harness, can accomplish.'

'Perhaps so; but it doesn't hurt to be a little on your guard, on behalf of those you love.'

Frere got up. 'There's a car down below which will take us to your hotel where we can pick up your luggage. Then it will take us to the airport.'

She got up too. 'Good. I'm all packed and ready to go.'

'But first there's a place I want to take you. I've been saving it for the last.'

The driver, Makhan, was waiting by the big black car when they came out. He shook hands warmly with Clare. Frere told him where to go and when the car stopped he helped Clare out.

There were a number of four-storey apartment blocks, each with its own garden of flowering shrubs and trees, divided by a broad avenue running through the middle, off of which paved foot and cycle paths branched out over the whole cleanly kept area.

'Do you recognise it?' Frere asked her.

Clare looked around to locate it in relation to recognisable landmarks. 'Why it's that horrible bustee!'

Just before them was a crowd of young people with children in front. Several of them had bouquets of flowers and they came forward and presented them to Clare.

She accepted the flowers and leaned down and kissed each child who had given them to her. When she looked at Frere, who was enjoying the scene enormously, there were tears in her eyes.

'Are those teenagers the tiny children we saw here with bloated bellies and staring eyes?'

'They are,' Frere assured her.

She looked down at the children again. 'They're beautiful. But then so were the babies and the young children I saw on my trip around the country – all with bright faces, glowing with health.'

'They're Malia's future, Clare. They have to be like that.'

Clare turned to the crowd and thanked them for receiving her this way and wished them well in their studies and in the work some of them would soon be taking up. A girl of about sixteen stepped forward and in correct if slightly stiff English welcomed her to the March Twentieth Housing Estate.

Frere took her arm and led her along one of the paved pathways. 'I want you to see a bit more of it. We've plenty of time.'

'Oh yes!' Clasping her hands in front of her. 'This says it all, Colin. I'm so glad you made this the last thing I'd see.'

'It was the model of similar estates in other parts of the country where there were such slums. The slum-dwellers themselves have been involved in the whole process of development.'

'All of them? There seemed to be thousands of them when you brought me here before.'

'Most of them. There's a general policy now of moving people out of crowded cities back into rural areas; but it couldn't be put into practice until facilities in the rural areas existed for them. So most of those you saw here then are living here today.'

'It's incredible!'

'The way it was done was to divide them up into accommodation units and then supply them with the materials and with the necessary advice of skilled technicians to build their homes themselves – with the assistance of voluntary labour supplied by older people who had retired and young people on holiday. Before they started they consulted architects about possible plans and each unit decided within certain cost limits what kind of place they wanted.'

Clare looked around her. 'They look nice. Simple but pleasant.'

'After the war,' Frere told her, 'Britain built a great number of housing estates; but the people who were to live in them were never consulted. Architects knew what was best and when the buildings, mostly high-rise blocks of flats, were completed, families were duly accommodated. Those habitations were a great improvement on what the people had lived in before but the process of housing them there was more like moving them into barracks than letting them choose homes to live in. *These* domiciles,' he took in the estate with a gesture, 'were decided upon and built by the people who live there. They're *their* homes – not official quarters to which they've been assigned. That's why they take such good care of them.'

They walked back to the car. Some of the children were still there.

Clare picked up a little boy of four or five and kissed him. The little boy laughed when she had put him down.

Frere was holding open the door of the car and she got inside. When he got in beside her, she turned and said: 'I don't know when I've ever seen such a marvellous transformation. Whatever happens you'll be able to remember that, Colin – the awful slum I couldn't get out of my mind for ages after you took me there and what it's now become. You'll be able to remember that and say; "I had a hand in it." That's wonderful!'

'Thank you, Clare. I needed to hear you say that.'

'You aren't beginning to have any doubts?'

'Not so much doubts. It's just – well, we went at everything in such a rush in that glorious time when we felt that clearing away imperialism gave us a clean slate on which to write the kind of society we'd dreamed of. Perhaps we have to pause a while to get our second wind.'

At the airport Frere checked her luggage onto her Aeroflot flight. They stood there waiting for the signal to board.

'Thank you so much, Colin, for organising this trip for me. I can't tell you how much it's meant to me.' She held out her hand.

He took it and kept hold of it. 'And I can't tell you how much it's meant to me to be able to see the kind of impression the new Malia has made on you. Be sure and send us copies of what you write. We don't always get American newspapers.'

'And you let me know what you think of what I write.'

'Oh I will. We must keep in touch, Clare. I need the sense of you out there as a kind of cool but sympathetic onlooker who helps me see where I'm getting to. Journalists probably shouldn't become as involved in their subject matter as I am here.'

'How I've been envying you that involvement, Colin. The lovely Leela and little Matt.'

'You must come back. Perhaps at the end of our next Five-Year Plan.'

'Perhaps.'

16

Frere could watch from his office in the Communications Centre the preparations for the People's Congress, the third since the founding of the People's Democratic Republic of Malia. Huge banners were strung over City Square extolling the Party or the Central Committee or the Secretary General – the latter always by office, never by name since Comrade Lee insisted that he had no right to praise except by virtue of the position he held. The dome of the People's Assembly was draped in red and yellow bunting and the crossed rifle and mattock flag flew from poles lining what had been renamed March Revolution Avenue. From the arrangement of loudspeakers all around the Square Frere took it that a large crowd was expected to gather outside the Assembly Hall and listen to a broadcast of the proceedings inside.

And there were other signs of preparation: Leela was much involved with the reports to the people which both the Marxist-Leninist Institute and the Women's Committee would be delivering on the first day of Congress; and in his own editorial department the *Das Vani* staff, writers, artists, printers and technicians were preparing a special issue of the paper covering the main events since the last Congress and getting ready to produce a handsome Congress '77 volume to be distributed all over the country as soon as possible.

At the first Congress in 1969 Frere had given a report to the people himself on *Workers' World* as the voice abroad of the Malian Revolution together with a summary of statements about that great event culled from progressive journals all over the world. It had been a moving experience and a photograph of him standing on the rostrum with Secretary General Lee and the members of the Government sitting on the stage behind him hung prominently on the wall of his office.

Indeed, that historical moment frozen in pictorial form, when an Englishman enjoyed a significant role in a southeast Asian revolution, struck him at the time as a high-water mark in the flow of his life. Ever since then, as if the problems of internal development *had* made the country more introspective and less concerned with what the rest of the world might think, the report on *Workers' World* had been dealt with as one part of a general statement on the printing and distribution of propaganda material in general – leaflets, pamphlets, reprints of the classics and so forth.

On the first day of the Congress, Frere went to the People's Assembly independently of Leela, since she had to be there early for preliminary meetings of delegates representing several of the organisations she belonged to. Although a place was reserved for him in what had been the press gallery of the old pre-revolutionary chamber, he was not involved in any of the last-minute preparations which were still agitating the members of the Publications department gathered there; and he simply drifted about the great hall, looking up at the elaborate painted ceiling now featuring stalwart workers and peasants, a good many of them bearing red flags, or he stared out of the huge plate-glass windows toward the pillared entrance-way before which coaches were beginning to draw up and disgorge their passengers; or he strolled about, hands in pockets and lips pursed as though whistling to himself, much as a journalist might hang about the edges of a meeting about to start in which his only interest was the assignment to write it up at the end.

That was how supernumerary and rather out of it all he felt right up to the time when the hall began to fill with an eager and expectant crowd. Then in nodding, waving and smiling at old friends and acquaintances from many parts of the country, some of whom he only saw on such national occasions, he began to be caught up himself in the collective excitement.

It had often occurred to him that open meetings of the working people in which one could actually observe that sociological phenomenon of ideas becoming a material force through taking hold of those people were the very essence of democratic centralism, of democracy in action, of democracy in which people collectively acting on one another moved themselves from where they were to where they wanted to be or where they thought they ought to be. Meanwhile a secret vote in which people as discrete individuals, cut off from any sense of their massed strength and less aware of their responsibility to their fellows for any choice they made, simply recorded statically where they happened to be at a particular time and, without mass meetings of some kind, were likely to stay for the convenience of their bosses or rulers.

Certainly, once the Congress was declared open and representatives from different regions and from various state farms, factories and public service departments like health and education came up to the rostrum, gave their reports and saluted the Party, the Government and their comrade delegates, Frere soon became aware of the way individuals, including himself in spite of an earlier sense of detachment, were transformed by the collective experience of belonging to such a body. Many of the delegates were completely unused to any form of public speaking and, for some of them, Indomalian was not their mother tongue and yet all of them, however hesitant the beginning of their short speeches, out of the sense of a common purpose which made nothing of idiosyncratic lapses, found a kind of rough public eloquence before they finished. He thought of them as each holding one end of a ribbon of material experience or spiritual aspiration brought here from different parts of the land, the other end attached to the high central point of leadership represented by the dignitaries on the platform, and, as they threaded their way in and out of the ranks of their comrade delegates, they were weaving their ribbons into the great intricate mantle of socialism which would slant down like a huge multicoloured tent to cover the entire land.

Such images tended to occur to him when he was telling Matt about the Congress where his mother was such an important personage that she was only at home for a few hours' sleep each night. Leela had been co-opted onto a special committee dealing with the consequences for the Party line of the speech the Secretary General was to make on the last day; and discussions in the committee on the exact form the accompanying statement ought to take kept her occupied late into the evening. Frere hurried back at the end of each session to spend time with Matt, having supper with him and then telling him stories about the country which once ruled over Malia.

'Where you grew up?' Matt would ask.

'That's right.'

'Weren't you scared, growing up in such a wicked place?'

'I didn't think of it as wicked then. And, besides, it isn't all wicked, you know. There are many good things about the country too. Some day, who knows, I may take you there to see it, to see the place where your father and your uncle were born.'

'But they steal from the workers.'

'Well, yes, they do; but the workers are organised. They fight back.'

'We can go there and help the workers,' Matt said.

'That's it,' Frere laughed. 'You and your mother and I will go there as an advance party. To scout out the land and see what help they need.'

'Yes!' Matt clapped his hands enthusiastically.

Remarks from Leela about divisions in the Party hierarchy, whispered references to some momentous development which was the real reason for the summoning of the Congress at this time and a general air of excited anticipation among some thousands of delegates which had finally reached its peak on the last day had all whetted Frere's own sense of expectancy in a way that surprised him.

He had been thinking of himself as rather out of things and thus feeling somewhat detached about whatever climax of the Congress had been devised; but when the Secretary General came forward to the rostrum and the whole hall was hushed, and when the silence continued like a held breath, and when the Secretary General still did not say anything but just went on looking around him in a vaguely benevolent way, Frere found the tension almost unbearable.

Perhaps there was to be no statement after all, Frere thought in a kind of panic. Perhaps there had been too much disagreement in the upper echelons of Party and State and the Secretary General was only going to congratulate all those assembled there on the success of the meeting and dismiss them to return to their various tasks in this or that part of the country. But it would *not* have been a successful meeting if the expectation that seemed to throb there in that huge chamber like the muffled sound of one's own heartbeat was to be cheated.

Lee stood there a few moments longer, still smiling benignly out over the vast assembly and then, as naturally as he might have greeted a close comrade he had not seen for some while, he said in a voice which sounded older than Frere remembered it:

'My dear comrades, gathered here from the four corners of Malia. You have given me great joy as you reported on the successes in socialist construction you have had a hand in, successes of so many kinds in so many places making a better life for all of us everywhere. Your faces speak to me so eloquently of the common purpose that unites us. I think the faces of the young among you, those in the bloom of life who are attending their first Congress, have filled this old heart with the greatest pleasure. The world is yours, as well as ours, but ultimately it is yours, all yours. You are Malia's future. You are Malia's hope.

'I could not but think, comrades, when you told us with such pride of the socialist achievements in your particular district, of how Malia was being transformed before our very eyes. It was like the fulfilment of a promise to all the comrades who fell in the long struggle for liberation waged over so many years. I could not but think, comrades, how here, in this capital city whose history goes back thousands of years, we servants of the people of Malia have sat and had reported to us, as once must have been reported to imperialist representatives the loot exacted from the people and the punishments visited on them, the great economic improvements brought about in our dear country by the unexploited labour of workers and peasants in factory and field.

'But then another thought came to me. Were we, the people's servants in Party and State, not being a bit too complacent? Wasn't it all a bit too easy for us, sitting here and commending the workers and peasants for their efforts? What were we ourselves but workers and peasants, even if our tasks took us into offices and institutions? Sometimes, in the evening, I have strolled through the residential section around the Great Pagoda, wondering if there was so much difference between the life being lived here now and that before the Liberation. Or I have looked in the offices of government buildings or the lecture rooms of the University to see if the work being done or the studies pursued were really in the interests of the people. And sometimes it has seemed to me that, relatively free of bribes and perks, we were only running the old system more efficiently, not creating an entirely new system with no purpose whatsoever but the people's good, all the people from one end of Malia to the other.

'You who have come from the poor districts of the high plateau or the jungle regions around Khangtu, or the recently cleared slums around the provincial towns, you haven't condemned us for the more comfortable life we enjoy here in the capital. You are at fault in that, comrades. Have we done anything to deserve such benefits? You do us a disservice not to remind us of the terrible discrepancies in the standard of living still to be found in our country. If nothing is said about these injustices, then we are conniving at them, aren't we?

'You will say that our Party line was never one of running before we could walk. It was never intended that we should attempt to implement full socialism from the moment of liberation. There was so much we had to do first to put power in the hands of the working people. We had to break up the big estates and religious holdings to give land to the tiller and then we had to achieve collectivisation by voluntary co-operatives and state farms. We had to confiscate all means of production and vest them, along with all natural resources, in our working people. We had to create public services, health, education, transport, to benefit our working people. All this we have been doing. But it's only a start. It isn't socialism: it's preparing the way for socialism. Aren't we treating a temporary camp on the slopes of the great mountain we have set ourselves to scale as if we were in sight of our final goal? Aren't we a little drunk with what we have achieved and swaggering boastfully instead of soberly preparing ourselves for the more difficult climb ahead?

'I think perhaps it is in the field of culture and the arts that I am most aware of the failure to press on, to carry the revolution forward to the next stage. In our life at base camp we had the inspiration of rousing poetry and revolutionary songs; we had dramatic performances of the resistance to tyranny and oppression and we had a level of writing about our everyday lives which enthralled us with a sense of political purpose. But when we came to power, instead of laying our hands on all the dance and music in the theatres and concert halls, on the stories and poetry which could now be distributed in thousands of copies, on the painting and sculpture all around us in a city of international standing like Rani Kalpur, it was as if we were overwhelmed by it. We seemed to forget that all culture, all literature and art belong to definite classes and serve definite political ends.

'Culture is a powerful weapon of the people. If they don't wield it, others will take it up and wield it against them.

'Where is the culture and art which should be mobilising us for the second and most important stage of our revolution here in Malia? We had our first Conference on Literature some years ago and we set up the Writers' Union. I've been listening ever since for new voices of popular upsurge; but what do I hear? – only the heroic strains of my old comrade Noor Fajan who rallied us back in the days of British rule. Where is the voice of youth, taking up the cry of progress and leading us on from where we are now? I remember all those revolutionary martyrs who have laid down their lives for the people in our long struggle and my heart is filled with pain, because we are not honouring them with our determination to carry on to the end the revolution for which they died. That is what our art has to be about.

'You all know our Party's line on a two-stage revolution – that in a country like Malia with little industrialisation and mainly feudal ownership of the land, with, therefore, a small urban proletariat and a large peasantry, we had first to establish a people's democratic dictatorship and then, when the ideology of the working masses had been more or less proletarianised, only *then* would it be possible to go forward to a Workers' State and the full development of socialism. The liberation struggle, which went on for many years and the revolutionary war which was soon over precisely because of that long preparation, both had the effect of speeding up the proletarianisation of the forces involved. Many of you will remember the lectures in Marxist-Leninist philosophy that were a feature of life at base camp. And the crash course of taking power in the people's name and beginning to lay the foundations of a socialist society – that all took us forward, too. We ought to be ready to push ahead with all our might now, comrades. We ought to see growing up around us the framework of our Workers' State – a pattern of steel girders against the sky to be filled in with bricks and stone and then to be beautifully ornamented so that it becomes a commodious habitation for us all.

'But it won't happen, comrades, if we don't make it happen. Now we have to give our hearts and minds to the task of thoroughly proletarianising ourselves in terms of the way we live and think and even of the incentives that move us to action. We can't expect the working people of Malia to be governed by collective socialist incentives if we at the centre, who are supposed to serve them, are driven by private ambition to score off others, to get ahead personally and make a better or more comfortable life for ourselves and those closest to us. It's to all of us in privileged positions here in the capital that I'm mainly addressing myself. What is that privilege we enjoy but the opportunity of being able to do even more for our comrades in factory and field than those not so fortunately placed? To all of us in responsible posts here I say with the utmost urgency: fight self-interest. Fight self-interest!

'You see, comrades, labour is value-creative. Working together people win food from the soil, make useful things, transform the world into a more habitable place. Associated labour is the basis of our language and culture. It gives us our common sense of time and purpose. Consumption, on the other hand, is private, acquisitive and selfish. We can work for each other; but no one else can do our eating and sleeping for us. Commodity production, making or growing things not for immediate use but for the market, has the effect of dividing a person in two – a social grower or maker of things and a private enjoyer of things. The gap between purposeful effort and its due reward has the effect of distinguishing reason, which looks ahead to future satisfaction, and the feelings, which make their demands in the present. With the assertion by one section of society of property rights in any surplus product, this distinction between the function of useful work and the gratification of selfish desires becomes more and more a class division between those who, on the whole, labour without enjoyment and those who enjoy without working. Socialism is putting sundered people back together again. Socialism is healing the split in sundered societies.

'We have dispossessed the class of exploiters to make sure that workers get their proper reward. We must make sure that the surplus is genuinely used for the common good, not just for this generation but for generations yet to come. Maintaining the proper harmony, both in the individual and in society, between selfless work and selfish rewards is a delicate matter which can only be achieved by those with a selfless dedication to socialism. That is what I am asking of the Party cadres gathered here today. A special effort to maintain for a whole people that delicate balance between work and satisfaction which our revolution has made possible, a special effort which will require of us that we put the satisfactions of others before our own. So I say to you, comrades, realise the full potential of the posts you have been called upon to fill. Fight self-interest!'

Lee paused and looked around him with that same benevolent smile. There was some applause, hesitant at first, as though they were not sure whether this was the end of the Secretary General's speech and, even more, not sure exactly what was being demanded of them. But as they became aware that those around them were possibly clapping a little louder than they were and, therefore, indicating a greater readiness to comply with whatever was being requested of them, they clapped louder themselves; and soon the applause resounded throughout the chamber and as the volume of sound rose so grew in them the feeling that this man standing there smiling at them could ask anything at all of them and they would do it.

Lee held up his hands with his palms outward and gradually the applause quietened. He stood there, tears glistening in his eyes and hands raised as in some kind of blessing. 'What I am calling for,' he took up the thread of his speech again, 'is some kind of ideological revolution. By proletarianising ourselves in thought and action we can speed up the whole process of transforming Malia into a socialist country. Some will say it can't be done like that. Ideas don't change material conditions. Material conditions shape and control our ideas. Greater industrialisation with more workers in power-plants and factories and mines, more state farms with workers organised in collectives will eventually proletarianise our ideology and to try to rush things could short-circuit that process. But there are countries which were industrialised a long time ago with large, skilled, well-organised working classes where proletarian ideology, which can only be the ideology of revolution, has yet to develop.

'I do not say that people are wrong who argue that we cannot bring about the social changes we want simply by strengthening our proletarian ideology. As materialists we believe that changes in material conditions are more fundamental than changes in ideas. But we are *dialectical* materialists and so we realise that the two things, changes in material conditions and ideological change, interact on and change each other. But I believe we are also, as a result of the liberation war we have successfully fought under the banner of Marxism-Leninism, radical enough in our understanding to realise that a revolutionary situation is precisely one in which the roles of material changes and ideological changes are reversed, when *ideology* takes command and dictates social changes in the *relations* of production in order to liberate the *forces* of production from their old constriction.

'When we set about some difficult task which has to be performed but there is as yet no clear guiding line, plan or policy as to just how it is to be done, then theory becomes more important than practice. It is like the situation Lenin describes when revolution has become necessary but there are no established principles for it: without revolutionary theory there can be no revolution. In liberated Malia where we have taken our economic destiny in our own hands we have embarked on a staggering adventure which only the clarity of our proletarian ideology can see us through. Think hard, very hard, comrades, and fight self-interest. Self-interest is the law of the world we are opting out of.'

He paused again; but there was no applause – rather a silence indicating a concerted effort to come to terms intellectually with what he had been saying. It was as if somewhat regretfully interrupting their reverie that he continued:

'But there is something else I want to say to you, something of a more personal nature. Moses never actually saw the promised land he had led the Israelites toward out of bondage. Lenin speaking to the youth of the Soviet Union after the October Revolution said that they would see a fully socialist society which those who had made the Revolution wouldn't live to experience. Well, comrades, I'm not so undemanding as Moses or Lenin. I want to see a socialist Malia with my own eyes. Only a glimpse, mind you. I'm too old to expect more. But while I'm still with you I want my glimpse of the future.

'So I say to our young people throughout the country, I say to you young people in this great hall looking up at me with your fresh morning faces; even if you aren't entirely persuaded by my arguments, humour an old man who loves you. Put just a little extra effort in the fine work you're doing so that this old man may get just a glimpse of the society he has dreamed of all his life.

'I say this to the young people because you are the most active and vital elements in society. You are the most eager to learn and the least conservative in your thinking. The new world we are creating is going to be *your* world. See if you can't make it possible for this old man to take a few tottering steps with you into that new world.'

He stopped speaking and brushed his eyes with the back of his hand and, as a breathless hush continued for a full minute, he looked around the great chamber smiling beatifically.

He was about to return to his place among the Political Bureau members and the Government ministers when suddenly the Young Pioneers contingent, seated at the front of the auditorium on the left, leapt to their feet and shouted: 'We will! We will! Comrade Lee, we will!' And their chief guide led them in raising their clenched fists in salute and added:

'On to Socialism, hand in hand with our Beloved Leader!' That cry was taken up by other young people in various parts of the hall who also got to their feet. And then many who were not so young stood up, too, and joined in the shouting of what was becoming a popular slogan – 'On to Socialism with our Beloved Leader!' An elderly man from the Mati region stood up as well, shouting in his cracked old voice: '*All* revolutionaries are young in heart!' At which the entire audience came to their feet and, keeping time with their upraised clenched fists, repeated in triumphant chorus over and over: 'On to Socialism Now! On to socialism now!'

Frere and others in the press box had stopped taking notes and were standing and shouting along with everybody else. With one tiny corner of his mind he was aware of a small surprise that Lee should have ended by exploiting his own personality in such an emotional appeal and he wondered for an instant in alarm if some quite dire situation might not have occasioned so uncharacteristic a conclusion. But a bigger surprise which quickly engulfed that flicker of unexpectedness at Lee's sentimental request was his own emotional reaction to it. Just when he had been feeling so apathetic had come this call to mobilise for socialism now. And he knew at once the sense of being caught up in the general enthusiasm animating that whole great chamber and of accepting without reservation the absolute rightness of any means which rekindled the burning purpose that united them all in selflessly seeking the same goal.

And just as the impulse which had first brought the Young Pioneers to their feet soon swept over everyone else at that historic Third People's Congress, so the 'Socialism Now!' slogan, shouted aloud by youthful marchers, borne aloft on red banners, painted in red on walls or picked out in white stones on hillsides soon covered the country with an urgent call to action. Soon the first companies of young people set forth to go by foot from province to province spreading the word of the rejuvenated revolutionary movement.

That first night, after the close of the Congress, Frere had waited impatiently for Leela to come back to the bungalow. The prospect of talking about it all with her had been part of his excitement during the exuberant clapping and chanting with which the Congress had ended. But when she did get back she was exhausted and Frere made her eat some hot soup and put her straight to bed. The next day they did manage to talk a little about what 'Socialism Now' might mean to them, not just in respect to her work at the Institute and in the Women's Movement or to his work at the Communications Centre, but, more important, to them as two human beings whose personal relationship had been intertwined from the start with Malia's struggle for independence, to such an extent that friends often referred to little Matt as the 'child of the Revolution'. What was it going to mean, what *ought* it to mean to two such committed people as they were?

'Should we think of living more simply than we do?' Frere wondered. 'This bungalow of ours is hardly palatial; but it would seem pretty luxurious to many people in this land.'

'We ought to avoid anything that's just a gesture, Colin. These bungalows exist: they might as well be used. And they can't really be used by the people who still need to be properly housed in other parts of the country.'

'Maybe *we* ought to live in another part of the country for a while – get right away from the easier life and the social attractions of the capital.'

'I've thought of that, too. I don't want Matt to grow up knowing only the children of the people of power and influence, going to the same schools and expecting to enjoy the same preferment.'

'We could go off to some poor district and throw in our lot with the people there – even if I can't think what use I'd be to them.' Suddenly he was quite excited by the idea. 'We could do that, Leela! Go off somewhere on our own. They're always urging young people to leave the capital and settle some place which has lost people to the towns. I'm not exactly young, but – '

'It wouldn't be for us to say whether we'd be as useful there as we are here. Perhaps we could go somewhere like that for part of each year. I'd like Matt to get to know the children of one of the ethnic minorities.'

'I wonder how friends of ours in similar circumstances are responding to the Secretary General's appeal.'

'Why don't you ask Tinoo the next time you see him if he and Moni have thought about it?'

Chin summoned a meeting of the Publication Section to point out that they had to take double notice of the Socialism Now Movement. They had to see that it got the fullest coverage pictorially and in print; and a little group of photographers and writers would be attached to the Movement as it developed and began to organise marches, demonstrations and campaigns – so that all of their publications would have a steady input of appropriate material. In *Malia Today* there would be theoretical articles on the political significance of the Movement, arranged in consultation with the Marxist-Leninist Institute. *Das Vani,* in addition to news coverage, would run regular features and open its correspondence columns for discussion. Considerable thought would have to be given to the question of how all this youthful thought and activity was to be explained to friends in other countries through *Workers' World*.

'You see the problem,' Chin said. 'We'll appear to be making a huge special effort to do what we've been saying all along we were already doing.'

'We'll just have to convince them that we're trying even harder,' Frere said. 'Which brings me to the other and more serious part of our responsibilities in relation to the Socialism Now Movement. We have to look at ourselves and our organisation constantly to see if we're really up to the challenge the youth of Malia are putting to us. In this big modern building with all its facilities for the rapid dissemination of news and views and ideals are we tending to become a bit bureaucratic in our attitudes? Are we behaving a little like wage slaves in a capitalist concern where we have to be on guard against an employer's cheating us over our paid labour time instead of like free socialist workers who can work as hard and as long as we like without any fear of being exploited?'

Chin looked at them quizzically. 'I take it that's the way all of you *do* feel.' They laughed. 'At regular intervals,' Chin continued, 'as work permits, we'll have criticism and self-criticism sessions to assess how well we're serving the people of Malia in supplying information and inspiration. No doubt you remember what Secretary General Lee says on the subject – that criticism is the democratic aspect of democratic centralism, the right of everyone to speak his or her mind: self-criticism represents the centralist aspect, the discipline of the individual in accepting the mass line once democratically established.' Several nodded, as much as to say: of course we remember. How could you doubt it for a moment?

Frere stayed behind after the meeting and congratulated Chin on how well he had managed it.

'Well, the meeting wasn't my idea,' Chin admitted. 'Comrade Hadar instructed me to call you together in that way.'

'And the criticism and self-criticism sessions?'

'Those as well.'

Frere thought for a moment. 'Perhaps the Socialism Now Movement itself is less spontaneous than I thought.'

'Oh, it was spontaneous enough when Comrade Lee spoke to us at Congress and when the youth reacted the way they did. But once the Party decided to take up the line officially, it all did tend to become just the least bit *organised* spontaneity.'

'You haven't heard any more about being released from your post as editor-in-chief?'

'Oh, they won't let me go now. What we're seeing at the start of the Socialism Now Movement is the positive, inspirational side. Soon it will turn into a bitterly critical phase and hold up to scorn those who have betrayed the people by not doing the right things for the right reasons. When that time comes, I'll make a very useful scapegoat. I can be blamed for any failure of our publications to mobilise the masses for even greater efforts. Then I can retire – in some degree of disgrace perhaps; but a disgraced man can grow as beautiful exotic flowers as an honoured one.'

'I don't think the comrades you've worked with all these years would allow such a thing to happen to you.'

'Well, I don't know. If the last service I can render the cause is to let myself be turned into an example of what must be avoided, thereby helping others to be better comrades – that would be something wouldn't it? And I have the advantage of having hardly any family. Only a son who I think doesn't approve of me anyway. Surely it's only just, therefore, that I should be made an example of. And you know, Comrade Colin, it's quite possible that whatever they decide to charge me with may, indeed, be something of which I'm guilty. If it's a question of changing society from top to bottom, no one can ever do enough and everyone must have failed to some extent. There's never the slightest room for complacency.'

'I don't know whether you're very loyal or just very cynical.'

'Both, I think. In so far as we're trying to create a paradise on earth, I'm very cynical. I know so many ways in which we're likely to fall short. But in so far as aiming for such a paradise, in which people don't exploit each other, is the only way we can improve on the societies the world has known so far, I'm a deeply committed communist.'

'I don't think I can be like that,' Frere said thoughtfully. 'With me the two attitudes would cancel each other out.'

'Ah, you lack my capacity to be contented with the cultivation of rare exotic blooms.'

'I couldn't stand to be publicly condemned for failing in my socialist duty, unless I was absolutely certain the charge was unjust.'

'Oh, it isn't likely to happen to you.'

Frere was not sure whether this was a compliment to the quality of his services or a reference to the support Leela was in a position to give him. 'If one aspect of the Socialism Now Movement is the complete rejection of the habits and prejudices inherited from the colonial past, well – won't it seem a little odd that someone called Colin Frere should be explaining to a world socialist readership how Malia has finally expunged the last faint traces of British influence?'

'Perhaps there will be no such witch-hunt as I've been suggesting. I hope not. Meanwhile all you can do is what I do – just keep going along the line you've been following until you come to a switch or a buffer while trying to watch the signals ahead to see if you can interpret what they're saying.'

Frere left the Communications Centre early and, since it would be some while before Leela would be home, he stopped off on the way at the Education Ministry, housed in the old British High Commission. Since Britain had not recognised the People's Democratic Republic of Malia, their public buildings, factories and various installations had all been confiscated, compensation to be paid out of the reparations bill Malia demanded for damage done by British-supplied arms during the revolutionary war of liberation!

He waved to the young woman at the enquiry desk and climbed the stairs to Tinoo's office on the first floor. Soon after Rani Kalpur was freed Frere had looked up Tinoo who, as soon as conditions made it possible, had been as eagerly looking for Matt's brother. They were both in their early forties and while quite different in temperament it was the kind of distinction which sparked off a lively dialectic instead of frustratingly cancelling out. The relationship they had both had with Matt made them feel like brothers to each other; and Tinoo's wife, Moni, who had been at school with Leela, became as close friends with her as the two men were.

Frere knocked on the door and was invited to enter.

'Colin,' Tinoo greeted with pleasure. He rose from his desk and held out his right hand. The empty left sleeve was tucked in a pocket in order not to get caught in doors or filing cabinets. Since not only the whole arm but a good part of the left shoulder, too, was gone, there was nothing doctors could do for Tinoo in the way of supplying an artificial limb. 'I'm used to it,' he always said – 'as long as people don't make jokes about my having a right bias.'

Frere, who did not smoke himself, put a carton of cigarettes on the desk top. 'My friend Clare Wallace sent them to me for you. She appreciated very much all the information you gave her about our schools and special training programmes. She was sorry that she didn't get a chance to see you again before she left. I told her to be sure and send you copies of anything she does on Malian education for the *New York Dispatch*.'

'Is there something special about the *New York Dispatch* that makes them willing to run articles on education in one of the socialist countries?'

'I think there's something special about Clare Wallace, who seems to be able to place such articles.' He watched Tinoo trying to make his lighter work and then, with a laugh, struck a match for his cigarette.

'That doesn't speak very well for our new consumer industries, Comrade.'

'Very healthful, these lighters. I think our designers must have seen reports from the West about how bad smoking is for you.'

'Speaking of education, what is the Ministry's line on all these young people cutting classes to travel about the country as cheerleaders for socialism?'

'We're supporting the Movement wholeheartedly. It's almost the end-of-year break anyway.'

'But won't it interrupt their courses?'

'They'll learn plenty travelling around the country. It's been arranged for Young Pioneer cadres to be with each group. Some of the younger teachers are going along as well – to look after those who are still only children really.'

'From what I've heard of some of the attacks on people for a lack of revolutionary zeal, it's the older citizens who may need looking after.'

'Oh, it won't hurt people to get shaken up a bit – as long as it doesn't get out of hand. How's little Matt?'

'Well, he hasn't started upbraiding me yet for my lukewarm attitude! Don't suppose you've heard anything about your being transferred to Publications?'

'No, and it won't happen now.'

'Chin is as keen on it as I am.'

'Good old Chin. Do you know he inspired my interest in English literature – oh, way back during my only year at the University. But I don't think anything can be done about my move. Heads of the Education Department are competing with each other like mad to show how keen they are to support Socialism Now; but they all seem pretty vague about what it means in terms of actual teaching programmes. Meanwhile the usual transfers and job swopping has all stopped until we have a clearer idea of where we're supposed to be going.'

'I don't see why...'

'It's like this, Colin. With this talk about the whole country becoming a vast school of socialism it could mean either that the Ministry of Education, suitably politicised for the purpose, would run all Malia as a huge comprehensive college in which the entire population was enrolled as students or it could mean that the role of the Ministry would be enormously reduced as *political* education, organised by other departments like Propaganda or the Marxist-Leninist Institute, took precedence over all ordinary classroom and workshop teaching. So there's a tendency for people at the top to talk big, hold tight and keep glancing over their shoulders.'

Frere wondered if Tinoo was surprised that he did not seem to have heard any of this from Leela; and only then did *his* surprise that she had never mentioned any of this strike him. 'But isn't that precisely what the Movement is all about – putting an end to thinking how something is going to affect you or your position and thinking instead how it might affect working people in general and advance the cause of socialism? You're suggesting, Tinoo, that the people high up in the Education Ministry are mainly concerned with how a movement to fight self-interest can best serve their own selfish interests!'

Tinoo laughed. 'But that's what always happens. You people who spent so long in base camp are such innocents! Those of us who had to opt secretly for the revolutionary cause while working for the old thoroughly corrupt puppet regime have a far clearer understanding of how things work.'

'I don't see what relevance a regime like that could have to our problem of establishing a *socialist* administration.'

'Those with organisational skills which can be used in the interest of the people are going to be promoted in whatever type of hierarchy you have. And once they've been promoted, are they going to have the same concern for people? I've seen what happens right here in my own Department. What begins with a passionate desire to see the benefits of education spread evenly over the whole land ends with the feeling that if there *are* any advantages to be gained in terms of particular schools or special entry to the higher educational establishments is there any reason why my children shouldn't have them?'

'That's what the Secretary General is trying to get at. And we're all guilty to some extent. I've been telling you about my doubts as to whether I'm still the best person to be editing *Workers' World* or not. But as soon as I begin thinking about how it might affect Leela or even Matt if I should step down, or, even worse, if I were dismissed, I get a panicky feeling. After all, what else am I qualified to do here? And then I have to face up to the ultimate question: why in a genuinely socialist country shouldn't I be pushing a wheelbarrow on the new dam site?'

'You might be pretty good at pushing a wheelbarrow, Colin; but the man presently pushing that wheelbarrow might not make even an averagely good editor of *Workers' World*.'

'But there might be some young person whose father pushed wheelbarrows and who's enjoyed the kind of education a worker's child can get now who would make a lot better job of editorship than I can. Perhaps that's what the Secretary General intended by his appeal to the nation's youth. He was calling on them to challenge the old-timers who may have performed services in the past but have lost any zeal for revolutionary reform.'

'That may have been what he intended but it would be easy enough for an ambitious man to gain influence among the youth and use them to blast away perfectly competent veterans who are blocking his way forward.'

'Someone like – ' Frere hesitated.

'Hadar, for example?'

'I was thinking of Pir Dato.'

Tinoo laughed. 'Well, Pir Dato is certainly ambitious. Remember, it was to Pir Dato that the Secretary General turned when he wanted help in damping down the personality cult that was growing up around him. Pir Dato made use of the appeal to fan the flames of popular admiration even higher.'

'That's true.' Frere laughed also. 'I remember just how he put it: "What other leader has ever made such a magnificent effort to moderate public idolatry?" Thus making a cult of the world's number-one anti-cultist!'

'But then, as far as anyone knows, Pir Dato's dead straight. Nothing tempts him but ambition. That's not true of some of those old veterans, you know.'

'Like Hadar?'

Tinoo did not answer.

Frere shook his head. 'I know some of them probably award themselves certain perks but – '

'I'm not talking about perks. I'm talking about corruption – draining off funds from the foreign trade account or accepting bribes in placing orders for English machine tools, which have to come to us by way of eastern Europe, of course.'

'Oh, I don't believe that.'

'You're such an innocent, Colin. It's happening. Oh, not on a large scale yet; but it's beginning to happen. And the Secretary General knows about it, too. Not precisely who's doing what; but enough has been whispered in his ear to alarm him. I'm told that his original intention was to expose the whole thing, or as much as he knew, at Congress. But then the Political Bureau argued that it would have a demoralising effect on the country and also provide enemies abroad with just the sort of anti-communist propaganda they want. So he was persuaded to deal with the problem by calling for the kind of campaign which would sweep the whole country clean.'

'You said those who are ambitious might use young people to get rid of those blocking their advance. Why shouldn't those who are involved in corruption use young people to help cover their trail and point the finger of accusation elsewhere?'

'Why not indeed?'

'You're such a cynic, Tinoo. I don't know whether to believe you or not. Back in base camp it all seemed so simple. Take power and then apply reasonable methods to real conditions in the people's best interest. That's all there was to it.'

'Nothing to do with people is ever that simple. You like to think in terms of once-for-all solutions, of final victories. But life isn't like that. The only solution of any problem is that another problem takes its place. The only victory is that we're still around to fight the next battle.'

'And there's no real progress at all?'

'Of course there's progress. Tremendous progress. Aren't the ordinary working people of this country better off in every way than before the March Revolution? Do you see starving, homeless children anywhere in Malia today? And all of us who have played a part in that are better people, too. But it doesn't represent any final conquest of poverty and suffering. The Secretary General is like you. He thinks in terms of a revolution so profound, going so deep down into the minds and hearts of people that the world will be an entirely different place for ever. But that's almost a religious idea – not just politics.'

'Maybe I am like that,' Frere admitted. 'Maybe it's because I came here originally, like my brother, to help right some terrible imperialist wrong in which we had shared. Only some final putting of the historical record straight could give us peace.'

'Yes, Matt *was* like that,' Tinoo said reflectively. 'Guerrilla struggle was never enough. If the cause was a just one then there ought to be a grand confrontational encounter on the field of battle where the issue would be settled for all time.'

'I often grieve over the fact that Matt didn't live to see that glorious tank victory in the City Square with his old comrade-in-arms in command.'

'I think of Matt's dying heroically in the darkest days of our struggle as providing all of us with the very pattern of how to hang on when things are desperate. I don't think of him as having missed anything by being killed when he was.'

'You're very wise, Tinoo.'

'Perhaps,' with a smile, 'as a result of being knocked out of the armed struggle, I've naturally taken a view of things which doesn't turn so much on decisive and conclusive successes. Do you and Leela talk much about all this?'

Frere hesitated before answering. 'We talk about the philosophical aspect of such questions. We don't – ' He was aware that he was actually trying to explain something to himself when he went on to say: 'We don't talk very much about what goes on behind the scenes at the Institute or in Central Committee meetings and I never discuss what's happening below the surface in Publications or in the Ministry of Information.

'I think it's because I never want to invoke in any way the kind of influence it might be possible for her to wield on my behalf and I don't want her to tell me anything which might affect her position if I accidentally made use of it. Certainly the tendency of wives or husbands to become influential simply because of the position their spouses enjoy is one of the practices the Socialist Now Movement ought to stop.' And then more positively, as though it was the answer he had known all along: 'Leela and I have always been determined to keep our areas of work absolutely separate.'

'That's a problem Moni and I don't have. Apart from serving as secretary of our housing commune and doing her stint in the local school canteen she doesn't have any responsibility but to do all the things I can't manage one-handed. I always say she's the cheapest nurse, handy-woman and general manager a man could ask for – to say nothing of the sweetest and most considerate comrade.'

'Ah well, you know how much of Leela there is to say nothing of!'

'Indeed I do.'

'Have you seen anything of Ahmed recently? We've rather lost touch with them.'

'As you know, he travels around the country a lot since becoming trade union representative of the whole textile industry.'

'He loves that,' Frere chuckled. 'The scion of one of the oldest feudal families becoming one of Malia's leading trade unionists!'

'He feels that the trade unions should be very much involved in the Socialism Now Movement. That it has to be class as well as youth. He's pushing that line in various quarters. That's probably why you haven't seen him lately.'

Walking to their bungalow Frere felt somewhat depressed. At first he thought it was because of the degree of corruption Tinoo had mentioned. He knew there were various privileges here in the capital that people of a certain rank enjoyed. Did he and Leela themselves not share in them? Had they not been discussing what they ought to do about it only a few nights ago? But actual speculation – if Tinoo was right and Frere was afraid he was – that was a different matter. Then he realised that what was really rather depressing him was the fact that Leela might also know and had not mentioned it to him for the same reasons that the Secretary General had not made it public at Congress.

17

In January, shortly after the New Year festival, there was the largest rally in the City Square that Rani Kalpur had ever seen. All the Pioneer groups which had been travelling about the remoter areas urging the final completion of the collectivisation of agriculture returned to the capital and thousands of young delegates from state farms and communes in various parts of the country had been arriving for several days and were temporarily accommodated in a vast tent encampment on the outskirts of town.

The day had been declared a public holiday and schools, offices, factories and shops were all emptied of their young people to swell the throng that had been gathering as early as dawn. Many children carried the flags and banners they had been making in their school workshops and there were stalls at which anyone could get Socialism Now badges or the big red pompoms to fix to a wide-brimmed Pioneer hat or to pin on a coat or blouse or simply to wave about.

In side streets leading off the March Revolution Avenue the floats representing various trades and services were receiving the last touches to get them ready for the parade. And beyond was the tank formation which was to rumble down the Avenue – just as Tuck's column had done on the day Rani Kalpur had been liberated, surrounded by contingents of old guerrilla fighters and detachments of the purged and completely re-organised army.

All of this could be seen quite clearly from the top of the Communications Building where Frere had taken Leela and Matt to have a good view of the day's proceedings and of the fireworks that were to be shot off that night. Frere looked over the balustrade at all that movement below. 'It isn't easy to say,' he remarked to Leela, 'whether it's a spontaneous demonstration of our youth which the Party has prepared the ground for or whether it's a Party function which the youth have been invited to liven up.'

"Does it matter?' Leela wondered.

'Only from the point of view of how it's to be described in *Workers' World.*'

'You can't really separate youth and Party, Colin. The Pioneers and the Youth League are junior Party organisations and the leaders of the Socialist Now Movement are all Party members.'

'I can't see a thing,' Matt complained.

Frere held him up so that he could look over the top of the balustrade. Matt waved the stick he carried with the red pompom on the end of it. Frere put Matt down and started to reply to what Leela had said. 'I know that's true but all the same – '

He was interrupted by the arrival on the roof of several other families of members of the Publications staff. He waved to them and Matt went over to be with some boys his own age. What Frere had been about to explain yet again was the responsibility he felt as a journalist to get as right as he possibly could any event important enough to write about at length. When they had been talking about whether he should make any reference at all to the possibility of some degree of corruption in the upper echelons, the same question had come up. She had felt that the important thing was to make sure that if there was any corruption it should be rooted out. Then he could write in a positive way about their getting rid of it. He could not make her see that, meanwhile, writing in glowing terms about the genuinely equitable society free of exploitation they were establishing here made him feel a bit of a fraud. He had not come all this way to do the kind of hack job any copy-writer back home did to sell flawed commodities. She quite properly accused him of getting things out of perspective. He agreed but pointed out that if his integrity as an honest journalist should become at all suspect he would be of less use to the new Malia. That happened occasionally when they discussed some important issue. They seemed to get further apart instead of coming together and would have to agree – sometimes at little Matt's insistence – to shut up, to hug and kiss and put the issue to one side.

'The Movement makes use of the Party and the Party makes use of the Movement,' Leela said. 'It's as simple as that.'

'As long as no one else is making use of the Movement,' he remarked and then wished he had not.

'Comrade Lee is making use of the Movement. He called it into being because young people are untouched by any sort of corruption and make an ideal force to correct us of any bad habits we may have acquired and help us keep our feet on the right path – just as you wrote in the last issue of *Workers' World.*'

'I know. They worship the Secretary General. But – well, isn't that making use of the very personality cult he himself has disapproved of?'

'I think it makes a difference who's the object of what you call a personality cult. History is full of people who exploited their charisma for their own selfish ends. Comrade Lee isn't like that. Remember what he says of leadership: "A true leader is simply the link between what a people are and what it's possible for them, progressively, to become." I think that's the way we must think of his mobilising the youth of Malia.'

'I'd forgotten that definition. Thank you, Leela. It will come in handy when I'm writing about today. And thank you, my dearest, for not letting me turn today into a stupid argument!'

Meanwhile the Square below had been filling up with young people and now the whole area between the great domed People's Assembly Hall, with its high gallery which was customarily used as the platform from which speeches were made, to the base of the Communications Building was one wide rippling lake of youth, still being fed by streams of the young pouring in from every side street.

The crowd in the Square was soon so large that it began to back up into March Revolution Avenue like a tidal river flowing up its estuary. The official parade with a single jeep at the head of the column began to move against this flow toward the Square; but when it got there the young people filling the Square parted just sufficiently to allow the jeep through and then closed ranks behind it, effectively blocking any further progress of the tanks and floats making up the parade. Stewards and soldiers tried to force a way through the crowd but were unable to make an opening.

The young people themselves took over the organisation of the rally. Self-appointed stewards made a way for the jeep to drive slowly through their dense midst; others acted as cheerleaders to co-ordinate the young people in a mighty cry of 'Lee for Us!' as the jeep passed them; while yet others directed the raising of red pompoms with each shout of 'Lee for Us!', so that during the twenty minutes or so it took the jeep to cross the Square to the Assembly Hall there was a steady beat of enormous sound as 'Lee for Us!', screamed from a hundred thousand throats, echoed among the buildings and the whole area turned bright red with every repetition of the call. There were two men standing in the open jeep which made its way across the Square – Secretary General Lee, of course, and a huge man beside him.

'Isn't that Comrade Kuan?' Frere asked Leela.

'Yes it is.'

Kuan, whom Frere always remembered as the important Liberation Army leader who had greeted him when he first 'went inside', held one hand around the frail old man to steady him.

'I hadn't realised how weak the Secretary General's become,' Frere said. But both Lee and Kuan were smiling and waving to the crowd and from time to time Lee said something which made the young people around them laugh.

The jeep moved no faster than an old man might stroll on a leisurely walk, the crowd opening just enough for the car to squeeze through and then closing behind it again. Frere held Matt up again to see what was going on below. Matt joined in the shouts of 'Lee for Us!' and waved his own red pompom.

Finally the jeep nudged its way through the clamorous throng to the steps leading up to the ornate pillars of the great Assembly Chamber. Kuan helped Lee down from the jeep and together they walked up the steps and disappeared inside the building. Back along the main Avenue another attempt was made to clear a way for the parade to enter the Square; but it was no more successful than before.

Frere said: 'I hope the fact that Matt's first great Party march-past didn't take place at all won't create any psychological problems for him.'

'Does it mean there won't be any fireworks?' the boy wondered.

'Ask your mother,' Frere advised light-heartedly.

'Will there be?'

'There will be fireworks,' she promised. And with a laugh: 'Since your father has put the whole thing in my hands, there may still even be a parade.'

Frere put Matt down. 'The only way they'll ever get through the Square is to come shooting – the way Tuck did on the great day.' He looked at the Square below again. 'It looks as though the youth of Malia are using the Secretary General. They've detached him from the rest of the parade and, indeed, the rest of us spectators and have made him their captive.'

'But these things always work both ways. To the very extent that we capture those we want to influence, we are captured by them as well.'

'That's dialectics for you.' He put his hand lovingly on her shoulder. 'With dialectics you need never lose an argument.'

Little Matt complained that he was beginning to get hungry. 'We'll have something soon,' Leela said, bending down to kiss him. 'Mother's brought some very special food which we'll have up here in the open air.'

Frere said a bit more seriously: 'Perhaps it's watching it all from this high roof, like superior beings looking down on mere mortals. It feels different from that first outburst of youthful enthusiasm on the last day of the People's Congress. I seemed to be caught up in it myself then; but now – '

'You feel detached from it?'

'Yes, and not just because they're so young. The Party youth on that first occasion were young but their response involved the rest of us of whatever age. There seems to me to be something exclusive now about the rapt way they're demonstrating. I feel a little the way I did once when I was covering a revivalist religious meeting.'

'Perhaps any collective response always seems a little strange to anyone who grew up in such a bourgeois individualistic society as you did, Colin.'

'That's probably true. But shouldn't there be more of a recognisable distinction between the collective response of socialist youth and that of – well, a bunch of football rowdies back home?'

'*I've* no difficulty distinguishing,' Leela answered quickly.

He wished he had not put it quite like that.

'For one thing,' she added, 'the symbols they wave about are so different. Signs of divisive chauvinism on the one hand, the red flags and banners of class unity on the other. I don't see – '

'Please, Leela.' He put his hand on her shoulder again. 'All I meant to say was that with all that crowding and shouting there was a superficial resemblance.'

'But there *is* something in you, Colin, something from your past which makes all collective feeling seem slightly suspect. I don't think you see the difference between *losing* yourself and *finding* yourself in a collective.'

He thought about it a moment. 'Will you say that again?'

'About the difference between losing and finding yourself in society you mean? But that's the difference between fascism and socialism.'

He hugged her in spite of the fact that married people in Malia did not normally express their emotions so openly in public. 'That's it, I think. That's the difference I was groping for.'

He released her and she stood there with a slight frown, still thinking about what they had been saying.

'It may be,' she said reflectively, 'that the distinction between losing and finding oneself in a collective doesn't arise so sharply for those who have never altogether lost their communal feelings, their sense of belonging to something of which they're an integral part. Perhaps it's a little like the difference between the folk art which still flourishes all over Malia and the extremely egoistic art of your part of the world. When you try to analyse what's happening down there, it may be like one of your contemporary Western critics trying to decide what sort of personal statement one of our traditional folk operas is trying to make.'

'I suppose so.' The good feeling of her offering him just the phrase he wanted to cover some aspect of revolutionary experience was lost a bit in the somewhat sad realisation that it was her understanding of what would always to some extent separate them which had suggested to her the very phrase he needed. He suddenly found himself wondering about his brother, Matt, and the woman who had shared his fate, Anna – had Matt, too, found that in spite of all that united two people enrolled in the same dramatic struggle something of their having been born half a world apart was always there? He was so sorry that after the liberation of Rani Kalpur, when he tried to look up Anna's mother, he found that she had died only a few months before.

'Am I getting preachy again?' she asked with a little smile.

'It's just that it didn't seem such a problem back in base camp. I knew less about this country then and couldn't even speak good idiomatic Indomalian and yet I seemed closer to the people I worked with there than I do now. But then,' suddenly brightening, 'when it's a case of *doing* something, whether it's editing a periodical or going on a jungle patrol, the nature of the task determines the relationship. When it's a case of *being* something, of having the right kind of attitude or of having the sort of motives one ought to have – like the call to fight self-interest – then everything gets more difficult and more complicated. Not just for me; but for all of us. Do you see what I mean?'

Little Matt was pulling at the end of Leela's scarf. 'I really am very hungry.'

'Of course, darling. We'll have something to eat now.'

Suddenly a hush fell on that crowd below where there had been a continuous susurrus of sound since Lee and Kuan had entered the People's Palace. Frere looked out toward the gallery high up above the pillared entrance of the City Palace and saw that Lee had appeared there with Kuan still beside him. He held up his hands and the hush was turned into absolute silence.

Frere found that he was listening intently, acutely anxious as to whether Lee would simply accept the highly emotional salute to him which the young people had offered up spontaneously or whether he would try to discipline them in some way for having frustrated the celebrations planned for that day. Indeed, he seemed to feel that the whole Square tensed with the same sort of suspense he felt and he reached out and took Leela's hand as they waited for his first words.

Lee had been smiling as he held his hands up for the quiet that would let him address them. Now he dropped his hands with a kind of finality which might have suggested that all of the words he still had to speak to them had become numbered. 'There is nothing like the enthusiasm of youth,' he said. 'All our hope for the future is in that enthusiasm. But remember, my dear young comrades, the ultimate source and also the object of that enthusiasm is the people, the working people of Malia.

'Just as all our knowledge comes from the productive process the working masses down the centuries have entered into in their co-operative intercourse with nature, so our best sentiments are those communal feelings of unity and strength which have made the greatest achievements possible. Our consciousness of that strength through unity is what you have so joyfully expressed here today.'

A great cheer went up and the whole Square turned red with the shaking of pompoms. And when at Lee's once more upraised hands it was quiet again: 'Your warm and generous greeting to me belongs also to Commander Kuan, my loyal comrade-in-arms who has led our armed forces from the period of the first small partisan bands against the Japanese invaders until now when we have a modern army capable of defending our frontiers and of serving the people in numerous ways.'

He paused and another but lesser cheer went up.

'Behind you, in March Revolution Avenue, are the floats representing various trades and industries, and lorries piled high with the produce from collective farms in various parts of our country. Never forget that Malia is a workers' republic. The working people rule Malia: it is a dictatorship of the proletariat. And who is the proletariat? All of us who live and fight for socialism. And against whom is the dictatorship directed? The enemies of socialism. It is as simple as that.'

Another cheer.

'Some of you young comrades have done your year's military service; some still have it to do. This practice helps to affirm the insoluble link between army and people. Now Comrade Commander Kuan will come down with me and we'll cross the Square to the partisan and army detachments and to the groups representing the working people of Malia and we will then lead the parade, which must be understood as Malia on the March to Socialism! Make way for the parade to enter the Square and as workers and soldiers pass by, join in behind them in a grand march through our capital city and back to the Square again.'

Lee and Kuan left the gallery. There was no response for some five minutes from the crowd and then a great shout of approval went up when Lee and Kuan appeared in the entrance way. They came down the steps and climbed up on the jeep and a way was quickly cleared for them.

Frere looking down saw that sea of red part down the middle and the two waves of youth roll back on each side leaving an open path all the way to the Avenue along which the jeep made its unhindered way. 'It *is* like Moses,' he said, remembering the reference in the Secretary

General's speech at Congress. And then he said sadly: 'Do you suppose that, like Moses, he's come to realise that he will not himself reach the Promised Land after all? Does what we've seen today mean that Kuan is his appointed successor?'

Leela did not answer. 'Come,' she said to Matt. 'We'll have something to eat and then come back to watch the parade go by.'

Something of the sadness he felt about the Secretary General's having to think in terms of what would come after him got into his realisation that yet again, whether because Leela was party to confidential matters at the highest level or whether because of him she was excluded from such knowledge, there were definite limits to what they could think about and discuss together in respect to immediate decisions which had to be taken about Malia's future. It was almost as if contradictions completely unbeknown to him which had opened up at those highest levels were beginning in as yet barely discernible ways to divide *them*.

But when they moved away from the balustrade around the edge of the roof and he spoke to writers and photographers and technicians he knew and when Siti, who was up there with her mother and father, picked up and made much of little Matt and when he was aware with pride that colleagues and friends were pleased that he should be in their company with his beautiful wife whom everybody knew to be someone important in the Party and the Marxist-Leninist Institute, he recovered his feeling of having made himself socially and politically at home in a country that was in every sense as distant from his native land as imaginable.

He wondered if he was remembered back there in England at all. There was quite a lot of publicity about his arrival in Malia and his apparent kidnapping by the guerrillas. But soon it was realised that he had, in fact, just like his brother, joined forces with his country's communist enemy and then he had been denounced in the press – all the more roundly for belonging to the fourth estate himself. And after that his name, like the news stories of Malia's post-revolutionary achievements which he sent regularly to his old agency, hardly ever appeared in the 'respectable' papers.

In the evening there was a magnificent display of fireworks supplied by China several years ago when the two countries enjoyed the friendliest relations.

Following on the great Socialism Now rally in the City Square came a wave of attacks on what were called 'bourgeois-feudal elements' which had to be purged. Some of the larger houses in the residential section belonging to those who were known to have been friendly with the British had painted on them in red huge pound sterling marks followed by exclamation points. During the night on the high gold-topped pagoda was splashed in the same red paint a huge hammer and sickle which could be seen from all over town. While concern was expressed about the possibility of damage to the intricate carving and delicate inlay work of the great monument, there was also admiration for the courage and ingenuity of the young people who had accomplished such a political defacement within a single night. A group of some fifty young people under a Socialism Now banner marched to the University and challenged those teaching in the English language and Literature Department as to why they were still trying to impose a reactionary alien culture on Malian youth. Some of the lecturers were pelted with flour and the head of the department was made to wear a hat with a Union Jack wrapped around it.

The head took this in good part, reminding the young people that what was taught at the University was a Party decision which he and the members of his staff merely carried out. He suggested that the young people should be calling for a proper discussion of the whole question of what was to be taught, how it ought to be taught and who had a right to be taught it, a discussion in which representatives of trade unions, of various industries, of the new rural communes, of the medical and other public services together with students, parents and teachers would all participate. The young people liked the idea and began shouting for Socialist Education Now.

Some of the criticism confrontations did not end so peacefully. There were rumours of violent assaults in certain of the provincial centres; and near Bandhal something of a pitched battle occurred between young people from the capital and team leaders of the local commune over whether there should continue to be any private plots at all or not.

Secretary General Lee never appeared in public without Commander Kuan at his side and the fact that Frere had been given no official instructions about how this was to be interpreted to Malia's friends abroad added to his sense of uneasiness about his job. How could he be an adequate interpreter of what was happening all around him when he was confused about it himself and when those who should have been able to help him seemed to speak in very different voices? He had been putting off a meeting of all those who were in any way involved in the production of *Workers' World* until he had decided whether the Socialism Now Movement should be dealt with on the basis of simply reporting it factually with appropriate photographs or whether there should be a series of articles by various Party officials, by lecturers at the Institute and by young leaders of the Movement to provide a philosophical explanation of its historical role.

The trouble with this last idea was that Leela and he found it almost impossible to draw up a list of those who could contribute to the clearest and most comprehensive understanding of how this youthful enterprise was going to advance the cause of socialism. Leela wondered if the very spontaneous nature of the Movement did not mean that he ought to call together the entire staff of *Workers' World* and let them thrash out in the frankest and most unfettered way how to deal with the Movement editorially by making themselves part of it in the fullest sense. But while he agreed that it would be the correct approach to any domestic task to encourage work mates to act with flair and initiative and run the risk of making mistakes for which they would have to be criticised, he was not at all sure that it would be the most sensible way to project abroad for a foreign readership a satisfactory account of this latest stage in Malia's development.

He finally decided that it was time he sought out his friend on the Secretariat, Comrade Ang, whom he had seen all too seldom over the last year or so. There was the relationship of Ang's having been one of the five on that last guerrilla action of his brother's; but Ang was never an entirely comfortable person to be with and the close friendship with Tinoo had provided in a more companionable way the sense of keeping in touch somehow with Matt. And yet of all the people Frere had met since coming to Malia Ang had impressed him as the surest guide to any questions to do with the role of a communist party and its relation to the class force it could never be separate from. What really was troubling him, Frere thought, was precisely how the Party fitted into Secretary General Lee's scheme of mobilising the youth of the country for a kind of ideological putsch. Until he understood that, he could not really approach the Party for advice on how to present the Socialism Now Movement in the pages of *Workers' World*, nor be certain of what to make of such advice as he got.

Meetings of the Central Committee were held in the small chamber at the rear of the People's Palace, behind the great Assembly Hall, and the offices of members of the Secretariat were along a corridor behind that. Frere was a frequent enough visitor to various parts of the People's Palace that it was rare for him to be challenged over his right to entry. He knocked on Ang's door and was invited to come in.

Ang got up from his desk and ushered Frere toward a table on which there was a pot of tea and a plate of cakes. They sat in chairs facing each other across the table and Ang poured tea for them.

'You've timed your visit well, Comrade Colin.'

'For the tea, you mean.'

Ang smiled. 'Not just the tea. Though you're very welcome to it. I was about to ask you to come and see me when you suddenly arrive.'

'It's amazing how much time can pass between visits to good friends who're just across the Square. I assure you it's mainly my appreciation of how much work you must have to get through.'

'The more work we have to do, the more important it is to break off sometimes for a friendly visit. We get back to work again in a better frame of mind.'

Frere took one of the saffron cakes and before biting into it inhaled a whiff of the pleasant odour. 'It's partly about my own work that I've come to see you.'

'Yes?' Ang encouraged with a lift of his eyebrows. Frere was thinking how old Ang looked, the same thought he remembered having when he had seen the Secretary General at the rally – as if all the country's great revolutionary leaders were running out of time together. 'A problem has come up for me about my editorship of *Workers' World*. I suddenly remembered, from something Tuck once told me, or perhaps it was Tinoo who mentioned it, that my brother sometimes found it difficult to reconcile the Party line with what he personally thought ought to be done. Indeed, I believe there were times when he was at odds with you; but in the end with your help he must have got it all sorted out.'

After a moment's thoughtful pause Ang said: 'I don't know how much help I was; but yes, in the end he got it right. They said he was killed when trying to escape. I've always known that Comrade Matt simply removed himself from any possible use our enemies might have made of him as a captive.'

'Yes, I've always known that too.'

'What is your problem, Comrade Colin?'

'My problem is knowing exactly what the relationship is between the Communist Party of Malia and the Socialism Now campaign.'

Again Ang was silent a moment before answering. 'Exact definitions of social relationships only exist in books.'

'Of course. But I do need to know how spontaneous an upsurge the youth movement is. Was it something the Party decided on as the best way to revolutionise the next generation's ideology in preparation for advancing to a new stage of socialism? Was it something the more radical wing of the Party devised as a way of outflanking those who were content with things as they are, who were even, possibly, making quite a good thing out of things as they are? Was it something the Party charged the Secretary General with launching or was it something the Secretary General, dissatisfied with the rate of progress toward true socialism, initiated on his own? Was it a rebellious upsurge against Party leadership as too conservative or too repressive which the Secretary

General's words just happened to touch off? Was it – ' Frere broke off and shrugged. 'Well, you see the difficulty of trying to explain Socialism Now to an overseas readership when I'm so confused about the real nature of it myself.'

'Yes I see. You've done a very good analysis of the different accounts of the Movement reflecting the conflicting interests and ideas which have gone into it.'

'But which account is right?'

'All of them and many others as well.'

'But some of them have to be more nearly right than others. Some must more nearly correspond to what's really happening.'

'In my opinion, Comrade Colin, you couldn't hope to explain something so complicated to our friends abroad. All you can do is to provide them with sample statements from various quarters about the nature of the Movement, to describe the criticism and self-criticism sessions that are taking place everywhere and, in due course, to try to sum up what ordinary working people make of it all and how they have been affected by it – which, finally, is the only measure of the Movement's essential meaning.'

'That's what I also decided should be done, given that I could carry the staff of *Workers' World* along with me. But even to provide a sound factual account of all that's going on I felt that I ought to be a little clearer myself on the actual sequence of events leading up to the launching of the Movement. That's when I decided to come to see you, Comrade Ang. And then I had to ask myself if the very fact that I had to seek your guidance didn't mean that I was no longer the right person to be editing *Workers' World*. Had we, perhaps, reached a point in Malia's socialist development when only a native Malian would be sufficiently in tune with cultural developments on such a vast scale as to be able to interpret them adequately for others.'

'I'm not sure I know of anyone else, native or not, who would have any particular advantage over you in dealing with contemporary events. Certainly it has never been suggested to me that a change in editorship was needed. I think the question of whether you're to continue in your present post or not is one you'll have to answer yourself. But the very reason I wanted to see you has a bearing on this question. I will come to that later.'

'I'm not sure I *can* answer it myself. I'm afraid that to the question of how to work properly in a collective or what contribution one can best make to it, no amount of private, individual rumination can supply much of an answer. That must have been Matt's difficulty too. We come from a society where egoistic considerations of personal interest govern every decision. Even our morality is simply a utilitarian generalisation of that selfish principle. You see what I mean?'

'Oh, I see what you mean all right. But,' with a smile for his little joke, 'you mustn't be so afflicted by an individualistic outlook that you think you're unique here in Malia in being afflicted with an individualistic outlook. You want to know what the Party's line is on the Socialism Now campaign?'

'I'd appreciate it very much.'

'Well, it hasn't one – yet. The Party is the main object of the campaign, not its subject. It remains to be seen whether the Party will seek to gain control of the campaign or whether, as you suggested, sections of the Party might co-operate with the campaign in purging other sections. You see, the process of infiltrating the whole puppet administration and military establishments before the Revolution by recruiting Party members wherever we could, together with the mass Party intake after Liberation in order to consolidate our gains, has inevitably meant a considerable dilution of Marxist ideology. That was why setting up a Marxist-Leninist Institute was so important. By the way, I see Comrade Leela of course from time to time. And how is your son?'

'Little Matt is fine.'

'We also,' Ang took up his explanation again, 'took over manufacturing industries and businesses which we allowed to function much as before as long as they were prepared to operate within our planning guidelines. That was the first stage of our two-stage revolution.'

'And the Socialism Now Movement is to take us into the second stage?'

'That's part of it. We couldn't simply issue a Party directive to the country at large stating that we were moving to a higher stage of socialism because the Party itself needed, if not purging, at least a good cleaning out. How could we purify the stream of socialism flowing through our society, watering the agricultural communes and turning the wheels of industry when all the wells were to some extent polluted? What force could we invoke to move our society more quickly in the right direction when many of those enjoying power were more or less corrupted? It was like the problem of finding an Archimedean fulcrum outside our world in order to lift it to that higher stage.'

'Yes, I see,' Frere nodded. 'Appeal to those who aren't corrupted yet. Let those who are the most idealistic and the least affected by selfishness, the youth, campaign for the next stage of socialism. Through them, through their "Red Front" as they've taken to calling themselves, we can get at the future. Yes, of course!'

'That was how Comrade Lee saw us transforming our country. The youth would activate with their enthusiasm the workers in factories and on the farms and the workers would share with the youth the knowledge they had gained from collective production; the proletariat would be strengthened in the process and the trade unions would begin to play a more dominant role in the Party which would have a much higher proportion of working-class members. So at last the sap drawn by the Party from its firm proletarian rootedness would flow through trunk and branches and burst out everywhere in the flowers and fruit of pure socialism.'

Frere raised his eyebrows interrogatively at the way Ang had expressed himself at the end. 'But you don't believe it?'

'I believe in it as a long-term process working itself out over many decades. I don't believe in it as a short-term measure for purifying the Party. There's a danger that it could weaken the Party.'

'And what about the People's Army?' Frere wondered. 'Comrade Commander Kuan's presence on the reviewing gallery must have some significance. I thought it was an indication of who was to succeed Secretary General Lee – an event which I'm sure we all hope is still some way off. But maybe it was meant to tell us that, while the process of proletarian ideological revolution paving the way for full socialism is working itself out, the People's Army will hold the ring.'

'"The Party commands the gun",' Ang quoted. '"The gun must never command the Party – nor even protect it from itself."'

'It all comes back to the Party then?'

'It has to. The Party is our mainspring. You can tinker with everything else; but – '

'But what if there *is* selfish individualism in the higher echelons?'

Ang's face hardened. His dark pupils struck Frere afresh with their grim opacity which could repel glances thrown in his direction like polished obsidian. 'Isolate it and cut it out – ruthlessly! Moral corruption or ideological corruption – it doesn't matter which – find it and destroy it!'

'Just like that?'

'Just like that.'

'None of this "killing the disease to save the patient" sort of thing?'

'That's for those we're winning over to communism, not for those who are supposed to be its leaders. Look, Comrade Colin. We talk about a dictatorship of the proletariat and about the democratic rule of the working masses. But in most of the countries in which there have been revolutions there was no tradition of democracy at all. The exploiters were overthrown but the exploited who were capable of liberating themselves weren't capable of ruling themselves. We the Party have had to rule in their name. And when members of the Party make mistakes or deviate from the Party line we have to get rid of them. That's the difference between us and the capitalist countries. When *their* leaders are crooked or make mistakes, the *people* suffer. When *our* leaders are crooked or make mistakes, *they* must suffer. A shot in the back of the head is probably the kindest punishment.'

Frere was appalled at what he was hearing. 'And suppose the maker of the mistake was you, Comrade Ang?'

'Then that's the way I ought to be dealt with too. Politics isn't a game. It's a question of life or death for millions of people. No one should join the Party who does not, as compared with the collective good of the people, count his own interests as nothing. Those of us who say we want to serve the people must accept the consequences of being shown to have done them a *disservice*.'

'But that's political elitism!' Frere objected. He almost welcomed these words of Ang's with which he so profoundly disagreed: they made him feel much closer to Matt. He realised that he may have been profoundly wrong in assuming that any differences between Matt and Ang must be the result of Matt's not being a thorough-going Marxist.

'It isn't democracy,' Ang admitted – 'not *your* kind of democracy. When through *our* kind of practical democracy, democratic centralism, the people of Malia have learned to rule themselves, they'll have, in a sense, absorbed the Communist Party. All power to them.'

'But by what right do you rule in the meanwhile?'

'By their need of us. When they revolted against their oppressors and exploiters they needed our leadership to win. We communists took them through the stages of guerrilla engagements and protracted struggle to victorious revolutionary war. Look around the world. Where have people been liberated from capitalist imperialism except through communist leadership? Will bourgeois democracy ever free the people from bourgeois imperialism? In building a planned socialist society they still need us. Only those who have renounced personal interest in favour of the people's welfare can lay the foundations of a society of co-operation rather than competition, of collective good rather than individual greed.'

Frere looked sceptical.

'I've spoken of their need of us. But we have just as great a need of them. It's only by working in the closest touch with them, only by recruiting constantly from their ranks new members and by going continuously among them that we maintain the right relationship. If we stand apart from them by living differently or if we become in any sense detached from them, we'll become corrupt and worse than useless. If we serve them as we should, we'll cease to be separate in any way. The Party from being an external guide will have become their internal conscience. It will take time, of course, and mistakes will be made. We're talking about ordinary workers and farmers everywhere getting to the point where they take into their hands their own destiny. We're talking about changing the whole world economic system from one based on profit to one based on human need. It won't happen tomorrow and, meanwhile, today Britain and the United States are still plotting to destroy us.'

'Just for the moment, I'd forgotten about them.'

'Don't ever. Not even for a moment. It's why you missed the real significance of Comrade Kuan's presence at the rally. Our Secretary General was mobilising the youth of the nation to deal with the enemy within – so that we can go forward to the next stage of building socialism. Comrade Kuan was reviewing our armed forces who will have to deal with the enemy without – so that we can defend the socialism we already have.'

'Yes, of course – the impetuous agitation of young people and the disciplined display of military power. Preparing to cope with internal and with external threats. But is there any reason to suppose that the external threat has grown greater?'

'There is. You know there have always been intermittent forays across the border – carried out by elements we expelled after the March Revolution who are settled along the southern boundary of our northern neighbour.'

'And who are supplied with British arms.'

'Well, it's no longer a case of the odd raid in which a school or hospital is destroyed and a few farmers are killed. We have every reason to believe that a large anti-communist mercenary force is being recruited to the north of us, armed with the most modern equipment. The raids are becoming more frequent and on the last three of them mines were left behind. Several people have been killed by them and a dozen or so, including children, have had their legs blown off.'

Frere's fists clenched. He would think he had distanced himself somewhat from that hatred of imperialist Britain which had played such a part in shaping his life and then something like this would happen. He wondered why he had been told nothing of these attacks. Once more he was feeling like some public-relations assistant who was expected to make a strong case for a firm which did not always choose to let him in on the true nature of its business and, worst of all, whose wife was on the board and seemed to be a party to this concealment!

Ang took this outburst of temper quite calmly. 'Come, Comrade Colin.

You know we don't alarm our people about a threat to their safety until we've taken steps to do something about it.'

'And have we?'

'All our northern forces have been put under the command of your old friend, Goh Tun.'

'Good!'

'They're being deployed all along the border. Our old base camp, you'll be pleased to hear, is their headquarters. We're rushing to them a company of soldiers skilled in the detection and destruction of mines. Furthermore, at the same time that news of these defensive arrangements is made public here, it will be announced to the world that our forces have been given permission to pursue invaders across the frontier and destroy their bases on foreign soil.'

'I see.'

'But that's not all, I'm afraid. For some time now arms have been smuggled into the Mei region. We've no way of knowing how many weapons may have eluded our searchers to be hidden away for future use. At the same time government-sponsored, so-called civil-rights groups in the United States have been raising the issue of our "suppression" of Buddhism on the Mei plateau. The issue is being raised in the United Nations and will inevitably result in the continuation of Malia's being boycotted and will also prepare the way for sympathetic action in support of any uprising of the Mei people.'

'And what are we doing about that?' Frere could only ask weakly.

'I'll come in a moment to one of the things we're doing about it. But first let's just think about the situation we're in. The arms being used against us on the northern border are better than those our own troops are supplied with. As you know, it's unlikely that we're going to get new weapons from the Soviet Union or even from China. Now, of all times, we're going to have to create our own armaments industry! But that's the way it works. Every socialist revolution is committed to peace and prosperity. War is never in the interest of the working class, only of the capitalists who exploit it. But, from the October Revolution on, the hostile aggression of capitalist imperialism, attacking from within and without, has forced us to waste so much of our energy and wealth on defence that socialism has been starved of funds at its time of greatest need. Even when we succeed in repelling the enemy, that enemy scores victories against us in postponing the world we're helping our working people to build. It's one of the main purposes of the imperialists to keep up a level of attack against us that can force us, in defending ourselves, to become more and more like them.'

'So what you're saying to me is that we're still at war.'

'The United States and Britain are flooding the world with arms. It makes profits for them and, with a bit of help from the CIA and MI6, turns every tribal, ethnic or national squabble into a civil war – particularly in any country where there's the danger of a progressive government serving the interests of the people. It's divide and rule on a worldwide scale and it numbers millions of dead and mutilated among its victims. Yes, we're still at war and our situation is still desperate. Let me tell you something about that trouble between your brother and me that I've only lately understood.'

He broke off to offer Frere another cup of tea, but Frere waved it aside impatiently and leaned forward to hear what Ang had to say.

'Things were very bad for us at that time and I realise now that your brother must have felt that it meant that perhaps we were wrong. If we were right, wouldn't the people have risen in their millions to throw out the imperialists? I tried to convince him that at such times all one could do was follow the Party line blindly and carry on whatever it cost. After all what *is* the Party line but the distillation of the experience of others who have fought against the most vicious exploitation and succeeded in emancipating themselves? Whatever doubts he'd had, your brother finally took hold of that line and followed it right through to a hero's death.'

Frere suddenly realised what Ang had been doing for him. Just as Matt had felt that if armed liberation struggle was right, then the people ought to rise up in a body to support it, so *he* had felt that if the right road to socialism had been indicated, then the people of Malia ought to take to it naturally and there should be no need for Socialism Now campaigns – or for Party purges for that matter. The future could be left to the democratic will of a people who had seen the light. And just as Ang had tried to explain to Matt then that changing society and changing ourselves in the process is not simple and sometimes requires us to obey the Party blindly in spite of personal doubts, so Ang was saying the same thing to him now that *he* was not sure about his course. He finally said: 'So I must listen to the Party's voice to decide what to do about carrying on with the editorship. But what if the Party speaks in several voices?'

Ang smiled. 'That's why we must have purges. The Party must speak with one voice. Particularly in difficult times like these.'

Frere obviously did not look too happy.

'For us,' Ang said, 'what other voice is there? Are we to listen to the random remarks of individual consciousness, ours or somebody else's?'

'No,' Frere answered doubtfully.

'You've been wondering about whether you're the best person to tell our friends abroad about all the complicated internal problems we're trying to solve. But that's your private conscience speaking to you. The Party didn't ask you to take on the job of editing *Workers' World* because you were thought to be the ideal person for sorting out our internal difficulties. The Party thought you'd be the ideal person to tell our friends abroad about the evil things their own governments were doing to keep us from building a socialist society here in Malia. I know because I can remember exactly how our Secretary General put it to the Central Committee when you arrived among us. Well, to your knowledge has the Party changed its mind about that?'

'No, I don't suppose it has.'

'Let me remind you of something, Comrade Colin. After your illustrated articles about the terrible toxic chemical and napalm attacks on us by the United States Air Force, what happened when the British launched their helicopter gun-ship raid?'

'There was a massive demonstration in Trafalgar Square.'

'And many people were waving copies of *Workers' World*, weren't they? And it was quoted from by speakers on the plinth.'

'Yes, but that was probably because so many of the helicopters were shot down.'

'Of course. Would so many Americans have been against the war in Vietnam if the valiant Vietnamese hadn't killed so many American soldiers? But you got the message of Vietnam across to the British people and they demonstrated against their own government. There were no more helicopter raids.'

'It would give me great satisfaction to believe I contributed to that.'

'Do believe it and do believe that you can go on doing that job for us.'

'Is that what you wanted to see me about?'

'Yes, it is.' Ang opened his desk drawer and took out a large folder. 'In here you'll find full accounts of the anti-communist force the British are mobilising to our north and the attempts by the Americans to foment an armed uprising on the Mei plateau. I know you'll make good use of the material.'

'Is this information to be made public here?'

'It will come out here at the same time that your readers are learning about it in Britain and the United States.'

Ang got up. Frere rose also and walked over to him. He reached down and took Ang's hand and clasped it firmly. 'Thank you for being my friend as you were Matt's.'

'You mean "comrade"?'

'Not just comrade, Ang.'

18

The front page story in *Das Vani* about the anti-communist force being recruited just north of the border and about the CIA plot to destabilise the Mei region had the effect of activating the whole country. In factories and fields, in offices and schools, in towns and in the countryside people threw themselves into their work with greater zeal as their answer to this renewed imperialist threat.

The Red Front, which is what the young activists in the Socialism Now Movement had begun to call themselves, added the capital crime of betrayal of the homeland to the other tags of opprobrium they used to designate the enemy within. The reappearance at the gate of the enemy without had changed all those the Red Front had called 'capitalist roaders' for trying to delay the advance to full socialism or 'bourgeois gluttons' for appearing to enjoy certain perks into out-and-out traitors. They felt justified by the urgency of the situation in carrying out the most frantic searches for those they accused of betraying the revolution by apathy or venality and reviled them mercilessly when found. They believed that because they had been originally sponsored by the Secretary General himself and could claim to be agents of his hopes for a more rapid development of a socialist Malia no one would dare criticise them for over-zealousness in carrying out his wishes.

But in spite of the wild enthusiasm with which they carried out this task they felt had been assigned to them they rarely resorted to physical violence. Humiliation was their main weapon. Those accused of crimes against socialism usually had sandwich boards describing their offence hung on them, a dunce cap pushed down over their ears and, forced to stand on the deck of an open lorry, were driven around the city so that others could learn a lesson from their mortification. Then in most cases they were simply released.

However the consequences of the Red Front's attacks on erring citizenry could sometimes be more lasting. They laid siege to the grander residences of the colonial period which had gradually, as the model of a simple lifestyle set by the Secretary General lost its force, been taken over by ministers and high-ranking officials. Activists of the Movement daubed the walls with red paint and screamed abuse at anyone going in or coming out. The guards who were posted outside these big houses usually ended up sympathising with the Red Front and joining them in denouncing the residents. Eventually life was made so unpleasant for the occupants that a resolution was passed in the Assembly to vacate the houses and turn them into hostels for the old and disabled.

Something similar happened in respect to the motor cars, supplied first by the Soviet Union and then by Czechoslovakia, which were practically considered as private property by senior Party and government personnel. Whenever the Red Front found such cars parked outside of dwelling places or in the shopping district they promptly slapped their 'Stolen from the People' labels on them. Sometimes they even threw rocks at them or stuck knives in the tyres.

Eventually a statement was issued by the Assembly to the effect that there were not now and would not in the future be any private motor cars in Malia. There would be motor-car pools in Rani Kalpur, in the towns and in regional centres from which cars could be drawn for Party or government purposes provided the user obtained the proper clearance. This was followed by a policy pronouncement by the Central Committee that there would be no manufacture in Malia of vehicles only suitable for personal use. There would be an excellent low-cost public transport system covering the entire country which everybody could make use of. The manufacturing industry would concentrate on farm tractors, coaches, trams for towns and freight and passenger trains for the Malian rail network with the intention of making the country self-sufficient in terms of transport as soon as possible.

Frere wrote a strong article for *Workers' World* pointing out that far from the lack of private motor cars indicating backwardness, it showed how far ahead of the highly industrialised countries Malia was. Humanity could not survive the selfish, ever-growing number of private cars in the capitalist West choking their own roads and poisoning the world's atmosphere. Malia was showing them the answer they must accept gratefully or have forced upon them!

The Red Front had already investigated the University and technical colleges. They had also attacked certain leading actors and musicians for introducing foreign influences into the cultural life of the capital. A few days before they had entered the Communications Building and harangued the broadcasting staff, using one of the television studios for the purpose.

Frere was not all that surprised, therefore, when he again heard shouting and the beating of a drum in the Square outside the Communications Building. He got up and went over to the window. Just as before there were several hundred young people looking up and calling out something he could not make out while frantically waving their Red Front flags.

Then in the corridor outside his office there was more shouting and the heavy beat of wooden staves thumping on the floor to enforce order. The shouting stopped and there was a pounding on his door before it was thrown open by a sturdy teenager. Behind him were a dozen more young men and women carrying lathis. These five-foot-long poles, which were traditional weapons and walking sticks in rural Malia, were the only arms the Red Front youth ever carried – more for the purpose of brandishing threateningly in the air or thudding on the floor for effect than for actually hitting anybody.

Frere and the youth gazed intently at each other for a few seconds as though the form their encounter would take waited on the dominance one or the other achieved in this visible clash of wills. Then the young man stepped aside and politely asked Frere to accompany them. He walked through the door and the young people lining the wall indicated that he was to go to the large television studio at the end of the corridor which they had used before.

They fell in behind him and there was a noisy beat as the lathis were raised and lowered to the floor in time with his steps, so that when he pushed through a door with a red warning light over it, he entered the studio accompanied by an ominous rumble of sound.

Others from the editorial department had already been herded onto the raised stage at one end of the huge compartment and strong rays from the ceiling battery of lights were focused on them. As Frere climbed up on the stage he saw Siti nervously twisting a small silk scarf in her fingers and he went over to stand beside her. A large Red Front banner had been propped against the wall at the rear of the platform on which those who were to be arraigned were standing. Frere smiled down comfortingly at Siti and turned to look out over the upturned young faces in shadow, holding his hand up to shield his eyes from the glare of the lamps.

What came to his mind was the people's trial many years ago in that little village of Teipur when a Puppet Government stooge had been condemned for his attempt to discredit the local Communist Party and had been executed – by a firing squad including him. It was almost as if, through carrying out a popular verdict which nothing he personally had ever suffered in this land entitled him to do, he must now appear before such a people's tribunal himself.

Then the drumming of lathis on the floor rose to a kind of climax and the doors swung violently open. Chin was pushed into the studio and stood there unsteadily. Another push sent him, reeling a bit, toward the raised platform. He lost his footing climbing the few steps and almost fell. He looked around apologetically with a vague little smile playing about his lips, nodded to members of his staff and turned to face the young people who were beginning to shout in unison: 'Reactionaries and Running Dogs Out! Reactionaries and Running Dogs Out!'

Many of those filling the vast studio were children really of fourteen or fifteen for whom it was like a holiday outing. Those in their late teens who made up the majority were self-conscious enough to take these occasions and themselves seriously – up to the point where they got swept up in mass emotion and lost all their still somewhat awkward self-awareness in an upsurge of revolutionary zeal or of indignation at what seemed to them a lack of such zeal in others. But some of the older young people, those in their early twenties, whether thrown up by the Movement itself or deputed as an unofficial leadership, maintained some kind of guidance during the most frenetic demonstrations. Three of these latter took control at this point, two young men and a woman stepping forward from the chanting ranks and climbing up onto the stage. They held up their hands to quieten the crowd. Then they turned to face those brilliantly lighted, uncomfortably shifting people standing there before them like suspects lined up for an identity parade.

One of the young men had a list which he squinted at in the glare and then called out a name. 'Come forward,' he ordered and a man on the staff of *Das Vani* took a few tentative steps out from the others and stood there looking very isolated. 'Tell us what you do,' the young man instructed him; 'and how it contributes to what our great leader has demanded of us,' the young woman added.

The man shuffled his feet unhappily and finally managed a description of his work as editor of *Das Vani's* correspondence column, in which arguments about the theory and practice of socialism were thrashed out. He said he tried to do his job as well as he could and always consulted his comrade colleagues about what letters to include and referred to the proper editorial authorities any issues he was not sure about. He hoped the young comrades of Red Front were not displeased with the selection of letters about the Socialism Now campaign which had been printed so far. They could always, he hastily added, write in any complaints themselves and he would see that their letters were published.

It rather took the wind of criticism out of the young interrogator's sails; but the woman wanted to know what he was doing to take Malia into a new age.

The man scratched his head. 'Well,' he said, frowning, 'I don't think it's for me to say. What I do is there in the pages of *Das Vani* for everyone to see. If anyone disapproves – '

The Red Front leader who had spoken first thought about this for a moment and then turned to those filling the studio. 'Is that not a satisfactory answer, Comrades? Modest and unassuming and trying, under the Secretary General's leadership, to do his duty to the people.'

There was a shout of approval from the crowd and the editor of the correspondence column suddenly beamed in relief, mopped his brow with a handkerchief and stepped back into the ranks.

Three or four more people who worked in various branches of Publications were dealt with similarly before the young Red Front woman walked over to the microphone and spoke the name 'Kalan'.

A plump man in his mid-forties stepped out from the others grouped on the platform and stood there in the blazing lights with a smile that was more of a smirk.

The young woman addressed him in a rather less strident tone. 'You are the editor of *Das Vani*?'

'I am.'

Frere could not but wonder if the young woman was about to challenge Kalan on the score of how he had got that appointment in the first place. What were his qualifications for the job compared with others who were being considered?

But what she asked was: 'Are you solely responsible for the political line of *Das Vani*?'

Kalan was about to answer in the affirmative when he suddenly thought better of it. 'I am responsible for seeing that the political line as relayed to me from the Central Committee of the Communist Party of Malia is strictly adhered to.'

'And are you in direct contact with the Central Committee for this purpose?'

Kalan considered the question carefully. 'No. Their decisions in so far as they affect the editorial policy of the national newspaper are passed on to me by the Editor-in-Chief of Publications.'

Frere was aware of what Kalan was up to. What surprised him was the young woman interrogator's easy acceptance of Kalan's ducking of responsibility.

'So you don't consider yourself solely responsible for the line *Das Vani* has taken on Secretary General Lee's Socialism Now campaign?'

'No, I have to say that I do not.'

'Did it occur to you that the calling into being of the Red Front to energise the Socialism Now Movement required a new approach to the coverage and dissemination of news about our country?'

'I'm not quite sure I – '

'I mean that if Secretary General Lee created the Red Front to drive the whole country forward to full communism, it would not be enough for *Das Vani* simply to write *about* the Red Front. *Das Vani* ought to become *part* of the Red Front, the *voice* of the Red Front.'

'I agree with that completely, Comrade.'

'But have you been in touch with the Red Front command about this?' She looked around those who were huddled together on the stage. 'I see none of the leading members of the Red Front on your staff.'

Frere caught his breath in anticipation of Kalan's answer to this.

'I see what you mean. I assure you that on several occasions I've urged that we should have some such relationship with the Red Front as you suggest.'

'And what happened?'

Kalan shrugged his shoulders. 'As I've said, I'm not solely responsible for such matters.'

The young woman's voice took on a sharper edge as she demanded, 'Who is? Who *is* responsible for *Das Vani*'s dissociating itself from us?'

'I, I don't like to say,' Kalan said quietly, as though determined to shield somebody else at whatever cost to himself.

'Is it the Editor-in-Chief of Publications?'

He hesitated, as though about to admit reluctantly that such was the case and then shook his head. 'I don't like to say.'

'Answer!' she shouted at him. 'Is it the Editor-in-Chief?'

There was a loud reaction from those in the back of the studio when he still did not answer. The young man in the leadership threesome who had not spoken yet pushed forward and said something quietly to the young woman. She nodded and stepped aside. The young man raised his hands, motioning those in the audience to silence, and then went over to the microphone and spoke into it the name of the Editor-in-Chief of Publications. Chin stepped forward into the limelight, blinking and raising one hand to protect his eyes from the glare. He managed a brief smile which came and went leaving his face blank but tense. Frere could not but note with a pang of anxiety how frail he looked. The hand he held to his forehead seemed almost transparent.

The young man addressed him coldly. 'You are Editor-in-Chief of Publications, are you not?'

'Well,' with another momentary smile, 'yes, I suppose I am.'

'You seem to have some doubts about it,' and a titter ran through the crowd.

'Only about my worthiness for such a post. Whenever that exalted title is spoken, I feel that it couldn't possibly fit me. It's like a boiler-suit you get at the Central Clothing Store which is three sizes too big for you.'

There was some appreciative laughter at this which the questioner stifled by challenging: 'Couldn't you have refused a post you weren't competent to hold?'

And as though this possibility simply hadn't occurred to him before, 'Yes, I suppose I could have.' And then: 'But I usually try to do whatever the Party asks of me.'

'Whatever your qualifications for such a job, or lack of them, you can't deny your responsibility for the general line of State publications.'

'I'm crushed by the sense of it,' Chin admitted.

'We of the Red Front have our heavy responsibility, too. We are directly responsible to Secretary General Lee for taking his command Socialism Now all over the country, into every commune, factory, school and office.' There were some shouts of 'Lee for Us!' which the young man quelled with a gesture. 'We scrutinise with the greatest concern the way our great leader's campaign to advance the cause of socialism is dealt with in the newspapers and magazines under your overall supervision. You understand?'

Chin nodded.

'We do not deny that *Das Vani*, the *Malia Monthly* and other publications provide adequate coverage of Red Front activities and deal sympathetically with the words and deeds of the nation's youth on the march. But as Comrade Mala has just said: more is required than that. Publications must speak for the Red Front. We say this is not happening because the wrong person sits in the Editor-in-Chief's chair. What do you say to that?' Stabbing at Chin with his pointed finger.

'You could be right,' Chin said reasonably. 'I've thought so myself for a considerable time.'

'Do you *know* why you're the wrong person?'

'I'm very old,' Chin suggested. 'Many, many years older than any of you.'

'It's not *years* that matter.'

'They do,' Chin told him, 'when it comes to that Editor-in-Chief's chair you were talking about. It's very hard and uncomfortable for stiff old limbs like mine.'

'At the University, just after the Anti-Fascist War, did you not teach English language and literature?'

'That is so.'

'The language and literature of the imperialist occupier of our country.'

'Well,' Chin said, 'the English could not learn Indomalian. We had to learn English even to tell them to "Get out!"'

'And you,' in the same hectoring tone, 'in a land where a great upsurge of indigenous literature about the lives and hopes of our own people was required, you taught the poetry of aliens.'

'Milton and Shelley,' Chin nodded. 'But Milton was a great progressive poet and the spokesman for the English Revolution. And Shelley was the poet of emancipation from capitalist tyranny.'

'And Shakespeare?'

'Yes and Shakespeare. They don't belong to the English, you know. They belong to the world. Just as Narmala belongs to the world.'

Frere admired Chin's courage in standing up for his literary favourites whatever their nationality; but this was hardly the time for it. He wished Chin would be more careful. And then it occurred to him. *Chin's* literary favourites! he exclaimed to himself. Just as if Shakespeare and Milton and Shelley did not belong to him, Colin Frere! He realised that such was his hatred of British imperialism and the crimes it had committed that, without thinking, he was disowning the British culture out of which that hatred of his had grown and forgetting the great names of the past who would have joined him in his condemnation. His gratitude to Chin for reminding him of who he was made him even more anxious about what was going to happen to him.

The young man turned and addressed those filling the studio. 'You see. Literary colonialism. He can only appreciate our own great literature if the imperialists accept it. That's why we need a cultural revolution to sweep away all feudal and bourgeois art and let our own native socialist art flourish.' There were some cheers at this. 'He taught our youth to bow down before the cultural values of our enemies. And today he thinks it's important for Malia to justify itself in Western eyes. He appoints a foreigner from the land of the imperialists to edit an English-language periodical. As if we cared what the English think of our Revolution!' And this brought forth a sustained burst of indignant protest.

Frere could not keep silent at that. He stepped forward, holding up his hand as though asking for permission to speak. When the angry shouting died down a bit, he called out in a loud voice: 'I was not appointed by Comrade Chin. Secretary General Lee appointed me.'

'Shut up!' the young man ordered. 'Your time for answering questions will come.'

But Frere did not give way at once. He spoke to the young people beyond the lights. 'Listen to me, Comrades. If a mistake has been made about my appointment, perhaps other charges being made against Comrade Chin are wrong, too.'

'You must wait your turn,' the young man told Frere in a somewhat politer voice and turned on Chin again. 'Before you were a professor at the University you taught English at the Khandev Academy, which only the sons of rich and influential Malians were allowed to attend. That school has another name now, but it's still the school for the sons of high-ranking Party officials – with only a few token sons of peasants and workers. Are you not on the Board of Governors?'

'I'm a *token* member of the Board of Governors. They never tell me when the meetings are because they don't like – '

He was silenced by a hard slap from the young man's open hand. 'Shut up! This isn't some student rag, you know.'

There were gasps of protest from those lined up on the stage which were overwhelmed by cries of support from the young people out there in the darkened part of the studio. The young man declared: 'We are working-class youth in deadly earnest. And we say that you're making light of the cause that's our life and the demands on us our leader has made.'

It was all Frere could do to keep from rushing forward and pushing the young man off the stage. It would not have helped Chin and, anyway, the young man was not the guilty party. All that about Chin's early teaching referred to a time before the young man was even born. Those accusations had been supplied by someone else, someone who was making use of these young people.

Chin stood very straight, head up and eyes closed against the bright light. The faint smile which had played about his lips for much of the interview was gone now. He spoke quite firmly. 'All my life I have tried to serve the youth of our country, in classrooms, in the Communications Hut at base camp and in the offices of this building we're in. I make no apologies.'

Frere wanted desperately to remind these young people of the fact that Chin had fled to the base camp originally because his life was under threat for supporting a student demonstration; but there was so much shouting and banging of staves on the floor that he could not possibly make himself heard.

The young man raised his hands and the shouting died down. 'Have you anything else to say?' he demanded of Chin.

Chin looked up and in a somewhat shaky voice said: 'Only this. On the question of attitudes to literature may I suggest that you read Secretary General Lee's "Advice to Writers" which, as I'm sure you all remember only too well, was a speech delivered at the first All Malian Conference on Literature in this very city.' The smile began to come back to tug playfully at the very corners of his mouth, just as if he were addressing a lecture room full of his students. 'Situations change,' he said, shaking his head sadly. 'Once I'd have given you lines for having construed so badly a standard text; but now – '

'Things *have* changed, old man. We don't have to listen to you any more.' Obviously the young man was afraid that if Chin were allowed to go on, he might begin to swing the crowd's sympathy toward him. He beckoned to a group of young people who rushed forward, climbed up on the platform and jammed on Chin's head the tall dunce cap they had been clutching.

There was no shout of approval. The place was very quiet. Chin stood there, the ridiculous dunce cap at an angle in such contrast to the kindly worried face beneath, that it was like a joke that had completely miscarried. Even then there was the ghost of a smile while a single tear coursed down each wrinkled cheek.

Aware that this was not going altogether as expected, the young man urged those clustering around Chin to escort him out of the studio. That is the way he put it – 'Escort the old man from here' and the crowd opened up so that Chin, having been helped down from the platform, could move through to the door at the back without any shoving or shouting. There were several flashes as cameramen at the back took pictures of Chin's ignominious departure.

Now the young man who had begun the interrogation took charge again and called out the name, 'Kaleen Frere'.

Frere was glad to be called next because he hoped that he could still do something to save Chin from further humiliation. 'Before you begin questioning me, Comrade,' he said at once, 'there's a statement I want to make. You challenged Comrade Chin about having, as the editor of *Workers' World*, a journalist from imperialist Britain. I explained to you that I was appointed to that post by Secretary General Lee. But let me tell you quite frankly that I, too, of late, have wondered if I was still the right person for the job. I put my doubts about this matter to the member of the Central Committee who's probably closest to our Secretary General and he assured me that it was felt that I should continue as editor. Now, Comrade, you may proceed.'

It not only anticipated the line of questioning the young man had in mind, it also set the tone of the interview as less inquisitional than before. 'We don't criticise you for the way you've run *Workers' World*. Everybody knows that you came to our country voluntarily and threw yourself into our revolutionary struggle. Everybody knows that you are the brother of one of the early heroes of that struggle. But we wondered if it wasn't a colonialist attitude, the idea that everything from the West is better than anything native, that was keeping you in a post which ought now to be occupied by one of our own people. But since you – '

'I don't think that attitude characterises anybody on the Central Committee,' Frere said reasonably. 'And it isn't a question of my doing the job better than – well, any one of you; but only of my having certain qualifications for convincing people in other parts of the world of the tremendous importance of what we're doing here in Malia.'

The young man did not know what to say but he obviously felt that it would be wrong simply to let Frere go.

Frere said: 'I'd like to add that I support wholeheartedly the Socialism Now Movement. And who better than I, who come from one of the lands governed by "the most violent, mean and malignant of passions, the furies of private interest", Britain, who better than I can appreciate the need for fighting self-interest?'

There was some surprise at these sentiments coming from such an unexpected quarter. Then there were a few cries of 'Lee for us!' and some applause.

The young man stood there frowning.

Frere spoke to the young people beyond the footlights. 'But my dear comrades, in your zeal to sweep away everything that hinders our march to socialism, be careful not to judge too hastily and not to be unduly influenced by interested advisers. Secretary General Lee always warns us "to know our enemy". The corollary of that is "to know our friends". Comrade Chin is a good friend of our nation's youth.'

He turned to the young man and shook his hand warmly. Then he stepped down from the stage and no one said anything to stop him. He walked toward the massed youth and was glad to see a way through their midst open up for him. He could only assume from the complaisance of his interrogator and from the lack of hostility on the part of the crowd that he had not been singled out for attack as Chin had been.

He hurried down to the main entrance and looked for Chin but there was no sign of him. There were a lot of young people about. He asked a young woman if she had seen Professor Chin.

'A poor old man with a dunce cap jammed on his head?'

'Yes.'

'They loaded him onto a Red Front lorry with half a dozen others. They've set off to drive around town. We cheered them on their way.'

Frere did not know when he had ever felt so utterly miserable. He supposed that any large movement to revitalise the revolution, to expose and punish backsliders and worse, was bound to make mistakes; he knew that the Red Front had been fed misinformation by some person or persons with ulterior motives; but that the righteous wrath of the youth should have fallen on the gentle, loyal, anxious Chin, the very man who had worked so patiently and considerately with the young all his life, was bound, nonetheless, to call the Socialist Now Movement into question. He was absolutely certain that Secretary

General Lee would be appalled if he knew what had happened. Or *was* he *absolutely* certain?

He walked slowly back toward the bungalow. 'What's become of the certainty and unity we had at base camp?' he cried aloud at one point and looked around to see if anyone had heard him.

When he got home he found that Leela had not returned from the Institute. Little Matt was with the village girl, Lara, who had brought him back from nursery school. Frere released her to study for the course she was taking in rural hygiene and joined in the game Matt had been playing. Since the game involved a small wooden railway engine, a largeish stuffed elephant and two green mangoes, the rules, which Matt explained to his father in English, were rather complicated but that did not seem to interfere with the liveliness of their play.

Having to appear light-hearted while playing with his son probably helped Frere get over the worst of his resentment at what had happened to Chin. After they had played a while he took the boy into the kitchen where he made tea for himself and laid out biscuits and milk for Matt. They were discussing the proposition of turning this light repast into something having more the nature of a high tea when Leela came in. Frere was aware that more than ever he depended on performing the daily magical feat of turning this beautiful woman who seemed to have no real contact with the everyday things around her into an ordinary enough wife and mother to deal with Matt's needs and, particularly on this day, to comfort and reassure him.

Leela took Matt on her lap and got him to tell them, in Indomalian now, what he had been doing in nursery school that day. Part of what he had been doing was learning a new patriotic song which he proceeded to sing for them letter perfect.

Later, after supper and after getting Matt off to bed, Frere placed the two large cane strip woven chairs facing each other and gestured for her to sit down. 'Would you like to know what I've been doing at the Communications Centre today?' he asked, frowning. 'In English. I'm too angry to say it adequately in Indomalian.'

She sat facing him. 'I heard that the Red Front guards had held one of their young people's courts there. I've been wondering ever since how you made out.'

'It's Chin we have to worry about. They treated him abominably. Shouted at him and slapped him; crammed a dunce cap on his head and drove him around town on the back of a lorry – as a lesson to others taking a counter-revolutionary attitude, they said. Chin of all people, the kindest, most thoughtful person I've ever known and the best friend the youth of Malia could have. Poor old Chin. If you could have seen the brave sad way he endured his humiliation!'

'Where is he now?'

'That's just it. Nobody knows, or will say. His son is scouring the town for him.'

'But that's terrible.'

'The young man who was making the charges referred to the time many, many years ago when Chin was a teacher of English at the Khandev Academy – which the young man could not possibly have known about. He'd obviously been briefed by somebody to make those accusations against Chin – somebody who wanted to get Chin out of the way or, at least, silence him.'

'Oh Colin, I can't believe anybody would do that – or that those young people would let themselves be used that way.'

'You have to believe it, Leela, because that's just what's happened.'

'I'm sure it was just a mistake. Have you, have you anything specific in mind?'

'Quite specific. Chin dropped a remark several days ago that he half expected something like this would happen. I know the problem he's always had – indeed a number of us have had – working under the Minister of Information.'

'Comrade Hadar?'

'Yes. Hadar. Even back at base camp I became aware of the way he held himself back from any line of development till it was obvious that it was going to succeed – and then criticised someone else for that initial lack of enthusiasm. Chin never got any real guidance. He worried his way through each problem of creating *Das Vani* out of nothing, helped by devoted young people like Siti and Swee Meng. When it went right, Hadar took the credit and when it went wrong, Chin took the blame. The policy of dealing objectively with the Socialism Now Movement, reporting its manifestations in news articles but keeping its revolutionary zeal out of editorials, was Hadar's. Chin's line was like what you told me the line of *Workers' World* ought to be. He has showed me instructions he sent to Kalan urging him to identify the paper more closely with the aims of the Red Front which Kalan had referred to Hadar and Hadar had told Kalan to ignore.'

'You're saying that when this policy of remaining somewhat detached from the Movement came under fire, Hadar simply put up Chin to be shot at?'

'Yes, I do. The precise charge made by the Red Front was that *Das Vani* talked *about* Socialism Now instead of being its proper voice – almost the very words Chin had used in his instructions to Kalan. And why did Hadar have reservations about the Movement? I think it's because there are those in the Political Bureau who didn't agree with the Secretary General's line on mobilising the nation's youth. Hadar doesn't want to fall out with anybody who's powerful, not at a time when a struggle for succession may be beginning.'

He looked at her to see what her reaction would be. She lowered her eyes and did not say anything. 'But you must know all this, Leela – far better than I do. The Secretary General's promotion of Commander Kuan as his dearest comrade-in-arms was prompted by the threat to our security on the northern frontier and by the instability in the Mei region – '

'It was terrible that the brothers should have been murdered!' she interrupted.

'Terrible,' he agreed. 'We seem to be losing, one by one, all those who were closest to us. But even if Comrade Kuan's sharing power with Comrade Lee was a recognition of external danger from Britain and the United States, it isn't unconnected with the question of succession, is it?'

He kept his eyes on her face, imploring her to answer, to say something anyway. But this had happened before when he suspected that some rift or contradiction at the highest Party level was affecting the work of Publications. She never argued, never took up any of the points he made. She simply lowered her eyes and was to all intents and purposes somewhere else. It raised again that old question of whether it was possible for her to be involved in things she could not share with him without its affecting their personal relationship.

'Don't you see, Leela, Hadar was using the very Movement he had kept Chin from dealing with adequately to blame Chin for not appreciating it properly. It's outrageous!'

Her lids fluttered and her beautiful eyes stared at him – beautiful, but it seemed to him at that moment that they had something of the opacity of Ang's. 'And Comrade Chin didn't say anything about that when accused?' she asked.

'Not a word. He just bowed his head submissively at the end, as though admitting that the ridiculous charges had some point to them. What worries me is that somebody was taking pictures as the dunce cap was put on him and he was bundled out of the building. I'm afraid that a photograph of Chin, dunce cap and all, will appear on the front page of tomorrow's *Das Vani* to prove that the Paper's on the right line now. I simply can't bear the thought of that. It's bad enough that someone who's worked all his life with young people and loves them so much should, by our finest youth, be held up to scorn. But that he should also suffer the gratuitous affront of being lampooned by the very newspaper he practically founded – it's, it's too much. Don't you see? We have to prevent that.'

'We?' she asked with a slight frown.

'You, Leela. I mean you. When it comes to putting a hold on anything about Chin in tomorrow's *Das Vani,* only you know anybody with the authority to do that.' He had thought of asking Ang to stop it; but if Ang was on bad terms with whoever Hadar was currying favour with – !

'I'd have thought that *you* could find someone to do it, Colin. You're one of the editors there.'

'So is Kalan. He'll just get Uncle Hadar to block anything I try to do about what goes into tomorrow's *Das Vani.*' He reached forward and took her hands in his. 'Please, Leela. Can't you think of someone who could keep Chin out of the paper till we can clear up the mistake about him?'

She withdrew one hand and looked at her watch.

'I know it's late,' he said, 'but – '

'Can't you think of anybody?' she asked desperately.

'I even thought of trying to get in touch with the Secretary General himself; but he isn't well and – Don't you see, there *isn't* anybody else.' He and Leela had got in the habit of referring to Pir Dato without actually mentioning him by name. He squeezed the hand he still held. 'Won't you try?'

'And there's no one else we can get to help poor Chin?'

She was pleading with him not to make her resort to Pir Dato and suddenly Frere realised why she was so reluctant. It was not that she felt she must keep from him certain things at the highest level or that she was reluctant to intercede at that level over something that mattered to him. She did not want to ask anything of Pir Dato because she did not want to be beholden to him. Frere was in the position of making his wife ask a favour of another man, of a very powerful and upcoming man, which would put her under an obligation to him when she knew it was a mistake.

Her gaze came up to meet his and her eyes were begging him to think of some other way. 'Must I?'

He thought intensely about everything involved and then at last he said: 'We must.' But at least he associated himself fully in what he was asking of her, meaning that any consequences, too, were as much his as hers.

He dropped her hand and she got up to go into the other room and telephone.

When she came back and sat down again, she did not have to tell him that she had got through and that it was done. Her face told him that. And now that it was done he felt angry. Angry with Hadar for getting at Chin in such a despicably underhand way; angry with the young people of the Red Front for being so idealistic they could not see through the simplest bit of all-too-human chicanery; angry even with Leela for being so beautiful that she had attracted long ago the attention of someone so dangerous; and most of all angry with himself for encouraging her to make use of a hold over Pir Dato she had never sought to have. But what was he to do? He did not think Chin would survive being treated as a traitor on the front page of what was in effect his own newspaper.

'There's much more to this business of humiliating Chin,' he told her abruptly. 'More, I mean, than just the business of making him responsible for a wrong line in *Das Vani*.'

She was surprised by his tone of voice, having obviously expected more consideration for what she had done at his insistence.

But he went on. 'While the Secretary General and Ang and some of the others have continued to live in the same Spartan way they got used to at base camp, look at the way the rest of them have been spreading themselves – summer houses on the shore of Lake Marik, trips to eastern Europe, special schools for their children, nepotism – '

She looked up. 'It's why the Socialism Now campaign was launched, Colin.'

'But suppose all that is just the frosting on top of the cake. Suppose the corruption goes much deeper. Suppose there are real crooks in the top ranks!'

Her face stiffened. 'That's not true.'

He wondered if she thought he was attacking Pir Dato. As if he did not know that Pir Dato was much too smart to get involved in anything crooked himself. But he might make use of crooks to strengthen his own position. Like Hadar? They were very close. That is why Pir Dato had been the right person to invoke on Chin's behalf. Was Hadar a crook then? Why else was such a vicious attack launched on Chin but to discredit him completely in case he knew anything about Hadar's double dealing? It made any charge Chin might make sound like vengeful whimpering.

'That's not true,' Leela said again, not angrily but pleadingly, not so much denying what he said as pleading with him not to say such things. 'Do you really think that's what our Revolution has come to?'

He did not know whether the hint of despair was for the Revolution or for him who must suddenly be sounding to her like an unsympathetic outsider. 'I think it's what the Revolution could come to if we're blind to some of the things that are going on.'

She put her hand to her mouth to stifle a gasp. 'You think *I'm* blind!' She got up and before she left the room she looked at him appealingly and her eyes were filled with tears.

19

When Frere went into the room where Leela was giving little Matt his breakfast the next morning, he fixed a smile on his face as though nothing untoward had happened to them the night before, but quickly removed it as completely inappropriate when he saw the look she gave him. If it had been reproachful or resentful, he could have apologised profusely whether he thought he was to that degree in the wrong or not; but there was nothing in that look at all. He had his last night's feeling that standing before her and looking into her eyes it was just as if there were no one at home and even though he wanted to throw himself at her feet and do or say anything at all that would restore things to the way they were, it would only be like knocking louder at the door of an empty house.

The fact that she had laid out his food for him in the usual way and was taking loving care of Matt's needs before he went off to school only made Frere's sense of the emptiness for him of that dear place more profound – like a house whose beautiful mistress is at home to everyone but the one person who cannot live without her. When they were ready to depart for their respective places of work, the completely impassive face she held up for him to kiss almost broke his heart.

As soon as Frere got to his office he began trying to get in touch with Chin's son. He found him at last and was told that Chin was in a hospital near the river. On the day before, toward the end of the lorry drive to expose Chin to public humiliation he had collapsed; and the young people, not knowing what to do with him, had taken him to the nearest hospital.

Frere took the bus down to the riverside hospital. He had a fleeting thought for how much worse equipped it seemed to be than the hospital they used near the Pagoda and then remembered that there had been no hospital at all for the people along here before the Revolution. Nearly at the end of a long row of beds he saw Chin, with his son sitting on a stool beside him.

Chin held out a frail hand for Frere to clasp and managed a rather wan smile.

'How are you, old Comrade?' Frere asked anxiously.

'I'm all right. But they won't let me go yet. I don't know whether they're still concerned about my health or whether they have to get somebody to agree to my being let loose.'

The son said: 'I keep telling him to let me take him home, whatever anybody says.'

'And I tell my boy that there's a right way and a wrong way to do things.'

The young man looked at Frere. 'I know who they are, two of those who questioned my father. One of them is called Razak and the young woman is called Mala. I remember her from technical school. I want to find them and tell them how wrong they are about my father.'

Frere thought with some satisfaction how wrong *Chin* had been about his son's attitude toward him.

'Explain to him,' Chin pleaded with Frere, 'that there's a right way and a wrong way of doing that, too.'

'Oh, it's all over as far as the Red Front is concerned,' Frere assured them. And to Chin, 'Whenever you feel like it, Comrade, you can leave here and go home. We still have to make it known how ridiculous those charges against you are.'

'Was, was there anything about it in *Das Vani* this morning?'

'Nothing at all.'

'I'm going to confront that Razak,' the son said.

'Don't do that,' Frere advised. 'Attacking your father wasn't their idea.'

'Did they attack *you*?' Chin asked him.

'Not really. It was *you* they were after. And you and I know why.'

'I know why but I don't know where I am now.' Chin turned his head from side to side on the pillow as though no position was comfortable. 'I don't know whether I keep my designation as Editor-in-Chief or what. I don't know what those I've worked with at the Communications Centre think of me – '

'You don't have to worry about that. When I spoke up for you after you'd been taken away, they cheered.'

'It's like,' Chin said, eyes wide as though no new experience was without interest, 'it's like suddenly waking up and finding yourself in limbo.'

Frere said to the son: 'Let's take him to your house. He can stay in mine if there isn't room.'

'No,' Chin said, 'I don't think I'd better try to move yet. I don't seem to hurt much anywhere, but I feel very weak.'

Frere told Chin's son to stay with him and look after him. 'If you need me for anything ring me at my office.'

Chin held out his hand and his eyes were glistening as he said in a voice that sounded very tired and old: 'Thank you so very, very much, my dear friend.'

Almost every day Frere looked in on Chin. Sometimes his son was with him. Once Frere found Tinoo there and he knew Siti had visited him too. Everybody else seemed to have been scared away by the reputation Chin had so unfairly acquired.

Chin always tried to appear in reasonably good spirits when Frere was with him, but it was obvious what a strain it was. Frere wondered if he might have suffered a stroke when he was being harassed that day; but the doctor did not know what was wrong. Poor Chin just seemed to go on getting weaker.

On one occasion Frere asked him if he would be satisfied simply to retire and let any question of his having failed in his duties as Editor-in-Chief be cleared up later.

But all Chin said to that was: 'They want to be rid of me. Just tell them to be patient a little longer.'

'But what about your cultivation of rare exotic blooms? Are your friends to be denied that glorious sight just because some over-eager youngsters shouted abuse at the wrong person?' Chin did not answer.

Frere explained to Leela that night that he did not believe anything but a complete withdrawal of charges by the Red Front, possibly accompanied by an exposure of who had put them up to it, would do Chin any good. It was only on such specific matters that he felt he could talk to her at this time.

'That won't be easy,' she said. 'But then so many people have been attacked by the Red Front now. Unless their accusations lead to action by the People's Court, they're just forgotten.'

'Chin won't forget.'

Several days later there was a message waiting for Frere when he got back to his office after lunch. Ahmed had left word that he needed to see him. He took a bus to the industrial section and walked the short distance to the Number One Textile Plant which the Soviet Union had installed as a gift to the new People's Republic of Malia. The trade union office was in a large room at the top of the building. A long window at the back of the room looked down on the main factory filled with interweaving looms and the muffled sound of flying shuttles.

Since the Number One Plant was something of a showpiece, it had frequently been featured in *Workers' World* and Frere had often consulted his old friend about the coverage of working conditions and productivity.

It had been some time, however, since he had visited the place.

Ahmed leapt up from his desk and came halfway across the floor to embrace Frere warmly. 'It's good to see you,' he said. 'How are Leela and little Matt?'

'Fine, fine,' Frere answered as much as to say 'what could be wrong?' 'And Narmala and the children?'

'They're fine, too. We must get together some evening – to talk about old times.'

'I was thinking about old times just the other day. Have you heard that the Mei brothers have been killed?'

'Yes. It would be both of them, of course. They were inseparable. That trouble on the Plateau seems to be getting worse.'

'And everything that happens gets blamed on Communist suppression of Buddhism instead of on the machinations of the CIA. I remember the way the Mei brothers and I practised our Indomalian together. That was when you and I first met. You were leading us from Kotal Bargh to the base camp.'

'I remember it well. I keep thinking we'll visit the Garden of the Asuras some time. Narmala's never been there; but you know how it is.'

'That's right. You keep thinking we're just about to get to a time when we can all slow down and relax – and it never comes.'

'Sit down, Colin. I'll tell you what this is all about.' Ahmed went to the door and called to a young man to fetch them some tea, then resumed his own chair again and lit a cigarette. 'Talking about old times, our old friend Goh Tun has taken command of the northern frontier forces.'

'I know. Things are very bad up there. And Goh Tun never took to life in Rani Kalpur.'

'It's our old June Tenth Commune,' Ahmed said, humorously reflective. 'They couldn't make the Revolution without us: they can't defend it without us either.'

Something came into Frere's mind that he had not thought about for a long time. 'Do you know those lines of Mao Zedong's? In a poem he wrote when he revisited his old home after a thirty-year absence: "Happy, I see wave upon wave of paddy and beans, And all around heroes homebound in the evening mist." I used to think of those of us who knew each other back in base camp one day relaxing together in the evening while former comrades-in-arms, in a now peaceful and prosperous country, returned home from field and factory, their long shadows stretching out before them.' He shook his head sadly. 'It may be like that in some of the rural areas: it's not much like that here, is it?'

'Oh, I don't know.' The tea was brought in and they helped themselves. 'Here we are now, chatting together about old times, and down below us several thousand workers in a factory that belongs to all of us are making the material out of which clothes will be fashioned for our compatriots – and without anybody being exploited in the process! That's not bad, you know.'

'Of course not,' Frere brightened. 'It's just that lately I've begun feeling a bit depressed. There was the excitement of the Secretary General's mobilising the youth for a great drive to socialism and then one of the results of it is that a fine old man – you remember Chin – is publicly humiliated. Everything used to be so clear. Now it's all so... muddled.'

'It's a bit complicated, I admit.' Ahmed took a drink of his tea. 'The farther you go along the road to socialism the more complicated it's bound to get. Because you're moving into uncharted territory. If people aren't going to be driven to work any more by the threat of starvation, what is going to make them give of their best for the community? How do we stop driving people with the individualistic incentives of stick and carrot and get them to act on their own for the collective good? It isn't easy, you know. It can't be done overnight.'

'No, you're right.' Was it simply that his difference with Leela, not all that great really, was making him feel depressed?

That brings me to what I want to talk to you about,' Ahmed said. 'I've received a letter from the Secretariat, from Comrade Ang himself. He questions whether the industrial working class is playing its proper role in the present push for socialism. He says that the youth movement was only intended to be a kind of spark-plug to get the organised working class firing on all cylinders as it were, because, of course, only the working class could carry us ahead to full socialism.'

'Under Party guidance?'

'The leadership in the trade unions and on the factory floor is in the hands of Party members. It's Party guidance but from within. Ang says that all facilities will be provided for me to call a conference of trade union representatives from all over the country as soon as possible. The purpose will be to mobilise industrial and social workers in the towns and cities to help spread proletarian ideology over the land.'

'Isn't that what the youth brigades of the Red Front are supposed to have been doing?'

'That was the first stage, a more or less spontaneous upsurge of indignation at failures to advance socialism and even attempts to deviate from it by would-be capitalist roaders. Now the working people led by the industrial proletariat take over from the youth and sweep the whole country forward. It's been suggested that teams of urban workers should be formed to go into the countryside and discuss proletarian theory and practice with workers in the communes.'

Frere was becoming interested in what Ahmed was telling him. Indeed, what was an ideological revolution but the realisation of socialism by a whole people in the most democratic way? But was that what Ang had been saying to him the other day? Had it not been Ang's point that for some time the Party had to rule in the working class's name which was why the Party had to be ruthlessly purged of all non-proletarian, non-socialist elements? And then suddenly he realised that this was the next stage in the social process. The purified and dedicated Party, instead of continuing to rule on behalf of the working class, would become, through just such a working-class movement as Ang was now suggesting, internalised as the conscience of the working class ruling itself. Was it not, in fact, the social equivalent of the experience of the individual who developed from being under the control of some Marxist-Leninist body into being a Marxist-Leninist in control of himself and able to act in the collective interest? But why, he wondered, had Ahmed summoned him to talk about this important directive that had come to him from the Secretariat? 'Is the Marxist-Leninist Institute to have some role in this?' he asked.

'I haven't heard anything about that. The reason I asked you to come here to see me, Colin, is because of something that's going to happen tomorrow. You know the manager of this factory.'

'Yes, Manjal. I don't really know him but I've met him on a couple of occasions.'

'The trade union has come to suspect him of, well, some pretty dubious transactions. But it's difficult to do anything about it because Manjal has very powerful backing. Also his is always one of the loudest voices in favour of more efficient industry resulting in greater profitability.'

'There's nothing wrong with profitability, as long as it's social profit not private profit.'

'Of course not. But we suspect he calls for the one while secretly pocketing a bit of the other. In a separate letter Comrade Ang tells me that the Red Front will be coming to the factory to challenge Manjal.'

'Isn't that a good thing?'

'No. It's apparently short-circuiting a high-level investigation of corruption which will not be complete for some while yet. It's a way of charging him publicly with some minor offence which he can swear he will rectify so that the real investigation can be called off. He wants me to hold them off Manjal for the time being by broaching the idea of industrial workers taking up the Red Front banner. He's also told me that the right person to report what happens here tomorrow is you.'

'Me?'

'Yes, you, Colin. Comrade Ang says that you understand the

importance of all this and that the piece you prepare to go out in *Workers' World* will also be the copy for the *Das Vani* account which will be circulated throughout the land.'

'A bit cart-before-the-horse, isn't it?'

'Comrade Ang says it has to be done like that because certain elements have been able to use the Red Front to get rid of Chin. That leaves Kalan with a free hand to deal with events like the Red Front confrontation here tomorrow and Kalan can't be trusted.'

'I see,' Frere said, almost gloatingly. There was no way he could explain to Ahmed just how much it meant to him to be involved in something like this at this particular time. 'And there will be no problem about my piece being used?'

'Comrades there at the Centre will be waiting for it, to use both in the national daily and in radio and television news bulletins.'

'But won't whoever's behind what happened at the Communications Centre censor my piece?'

'They can't. Because the Secretary General supports what Comrade Ang is backing me to do.'

Frere sat back, a pleased grin stretching his mouth agreeably. He was thinking about telling Leela of this. To someone like her, who had lost everything when her parents had been killed and the wartime promises of the imperialists were all broken, the anti-colonial struggle, the Liberation War had become everything. The revolutionary transformation of her country was mother and father to her; and when he had told her that he was not sure he still had such an important part to play in all that, it was like proposing that they should have a weaker relationship. It was not that she was angry with him or disagreed with anything he had said or done, it was just that, quite simply, anyone who felt that he had a less important part to play in what was the most real thing in her life also, to some extent, became less real. She had not been deliberately excluding him from her consciousness: in a sense he had absented himself. And now he had been brought back on the scene again to play a not inconsiderable part. He did not know whether to tell her all about it when he got home or to wait until after he had written an account of everything that happened tomorrow which he could then discuss with her. Some of his gratitude for this opportunity Ang had given him got into the warm hand clasp and slap on the shoulder with which he left Ahmed, having agreed to be there at the Number One Textile Plant early the following morning.

The question of whether to take Leela into his confidence at this time or not was taken out of his hands. She was not at their bungalow where Lara had been asked to stay on looking after Matt. Frere let the girl go and after a little rumpusing put Matt to bed. He was in bed himself, reading, when Leela returned. She looked in on Matt to make sure he was all right and then explained her lateness to Frere, saying that the Governing Board of the Institute had been summoned to an emergency meeting which had only ended about half an hour ago. She said that she was much too tired tonight to talk about all the things they had to discuss. It was certainly no time for him to say anything about his meeting with Ahmed and what he would be doing on the following day.

The next morning Frere was careful not to wake Leela when he got up early. He found that Matt was awake and gave him breakfast. By the time Leela was up and dressed he could only bid her a hurried goodbye before he was off.

When he got to the Number One Plant some young people with their Red Front banners were already gathering at the main gate. Frere was admitted by the guard and went straight up to the trade union office where Ahmed was busily making arrangements for the expected incursion.

Frere was provided with a cup of coffee and it was explained to him that the Socialism Now youth would be allowed into the largest of the spinning rooms where work would have stopped. They could then name anyone they wanted to question and workers would find that person and escort him into the young people's presence. It was not thought to be a good idea to let the young people roam about the factory on their own seeking those they wanted to harangue because of the damage they might do to the machinery and even to themselves.

When several hundred young militants had collected outside, the gates were opened and they marched into the main factory where they were funnelled through the only open doorway into the large spinning hall. There they were welcomed by a gathering of workers from all parts of the Plant who had been briefed by Ahmed and their shop stewards to be as comradely as possible, thus firmly establishing the principle that youth and workers were one.

At the far end of the huge room there were steps leading up to a raised platform on which one could reach the panel of wall switches controlling the machinery. Up these steps climbed Razak, one of the young people who had taken the lead in the criticism session at the Communications Centre. He beckoned Mala, the young woman who had shared the stage with him that day, to follow him; and together they stood on this narrow plinth above the crowd of workers and young people.

Razak may have felt somewhat disconcerted by the friendly way the workforce and the visiting youth had joined together. He was more used to whipping up his young cohorts to a frenzy of opposition against some group whom they felt to have been dragging their feet in the march to socialism.

'Thank you,' he said blandly, 'you textile workers of the Number One Plant, for the way you have received us this morning.' And then, changing his voice, he demanded harshly: 'But aren't you ashamed of yourselves? When there is at least one person in charge of this factory who is no friend of socialism, aren't you ashamed of yourselves that young people from outside have to come in to challenge him?'

Mala, taking her cue from Razak's tone, spoke up loudly: 'The man we're talking about says that Malian industry must be made profitable. Does he mean profitable for the people of Malia or for those with privileged jobs like him?'

Only the young people responded to this appeal, shouting: 'He means for him! It's profits for him!'

'This man says,' Mala went on, 'that a free market should play its part in the distribution of goods. Did we make a revolution so that comrades should compete with each other for the goods we ourselves have made?'

And again the young people alone shouted loudly: 'No! No!'

'You know the person we're talking about. We're talking about factory manager Manjal. Is Manjal here?' And when there was no answer: 'We want Manjal to answer us. Get Manjal.'

Frere was aware that the trade unionists, knowing that Manjal might try to drive away when he knew that the Red Front were paying them a visit, had arranged for him to be kept in a storeroom close to the spinning hall. Soon after Razak had named Manjal, two workers brought Manjal into the hall and made him climb the steps to stand beside the two Red Front interrogators.

Razak spoke to the workers. 'You aren't joining in the criticism of this man who's been exploiting you. Are you afraid of him? He can't sack you, you know.'

The hall was quiet. Then Mala spoke again, angrily: 'What shall we do with this Manjal? All of you? What shall we do with him?' She went to the edge of the platform and reached down to take from some young people near the front a sandwich board which had 'Capitalist Roader' printed in big letters on both sides. She held up the boards fastened together at the top with leather thongs so everybody could see. 'Shall we march him through the streets with this on his shoulders?'

And the young people called out: 'Ye-e-e-es!'

But then there was commotion among the young people close to the platform as someone politely but firmly pushed his way through them and mounted the steps. It was Ahmed. At the top he stood between the two members of the Red Front and a glowering Manjal, overtopping them all by several inches. He greeted Razak and Mala by name and asked permission to speak on behalf of the assembled workers. They agreed quickly and Ahmed turned to address a respectful audience, those who did not know him as a trade union leader recognising him as one of the heroes of the Revolution.

'We workers of the Number One Textile Plant,' he addressed them, 'welcome the comrades of the Red Front. We congratulate you on your vigilance in challenging the integrity of our plant manager. You are right in taking notice of the way Manjal's line on our industrial development keeps fluctuating according to what he thinks those who appointed him want to hear.'

He paused and Frere noted that he was holding the attention of the young people, who were listening quietly.

'I may tell you that we in the Number One Textile Plant, together with fellow workers in the Stalin Steel Works and rail workers in the Rani Kalpur marshalling yards, have been thinking seriously about the question of the appointment of the managers of industrial enterprises. You see, we feel that those who work daily under a particular manager get to know him far better than those who selected him for that post to begin with. Also we think that as long as he owes his job to whoever at the centre put in a good word for him, he will be more concerned about appearing to be following the right line than co-operating with the workforce to improve production and the quality of life of the producers. I'm sure our young comrades will appreciate the nature of the problem.'

There was a hush over the huge hall as they all thought about what he was saying.

'As I have said,' he went on, 'we appreciate your coming here today to warn us about Manjal; but when it comes to questions like raising productivity or the three-tier wages structure or the balance between central industrial planning and market considerations in the case of certain kinds of consumer goods – well, do you not feel, comrades, that these matters are better left to the trade unions?'

The young people were obviously not so sure about that and Mala spoke up for them: 'Does that mean that we only have the right to criticise what's going wrong in the tiny field we happen to live in or work in?'

'Did you hear that question?' Ahmed asked them. 'Comrade Mala wants to know if I'm saying that our criticism should be restricted to the narrow confines of a single workplace. If we did that, if we kept our noses pointed to our immediate task and didn't look around to see how that task fits in with the work of others doing similar jobs and ultimately with the whole pattern of production, our criticism of the Number One Textile Plant would be niggling and partial. We need to know, for example, whether the technical training you young people are getting at school is satisfactory and whether you are getting enough information about various industries to know what kind of work you want to opt for.'

That seemed to satisfy them on that score and Mala had nothing to say when he paused. He went on: 'But we must not forget that we have a daily responsibility for the effective running of that small part of the economic machine we operate ourselves. We know more about it than anyone else: we have to apply the Five-Year Plan to our own little corner and see if what's demanded of us is feasible. If we think some different method of work would achieve better results, we have to propose it so that our work mates and the section managers can test it to see if it ought not to be generally adopted. So, yes, we can and ought to look over the broad field of Malia's efforts to catch up with the rest of the world industrially in order to enhance the quality of our life under socialism. But we have a special responsibility for our own little section. If anything goes wrong we have to regard it as our fault. If some suggestion or criticism is made about our work which we know is ill-founded we have to reject it. But also if we achieve and, better, if we surpass the norms we have had a say in setting, then the credit is ours too.'

Frere had begun to realise early on that these were not off-the-cuff remarks Ahmed had thought up to deal with some fairly ordinary occurrence. This was a carefully thought-out speech into which had gone a good deal of briefing by Ang. From the first Frere had been taking it down in English shorthand to make sure of not losing anything. He had an idea that it was all leading up to something very important.

There were nods of agreement and murmurs of approval at Ahmed's common-sense generalisations about working-class responsibility and then he came to the real gist of what he had climbed up on the platform to say. 'Again, let me congratulate you young comrades on responding so magnificently to the call of our Secretary General. He asked the youth of our country to take the vanguard in our socialist pilgrimage and that's what you've so unsparingly done. Now it might seem strange that the lead in proletarianising our society should be taken by our youth, that you young people, like the sun at eight o'clock in the morning, should be called upon to light us on our way to our socialist goal. But that, as we all know, is a consequence of our country's past industrial backwardness. When we took over the country politically we did not inherit an organised section of industrial workers, steeled through generations of class struggle. But ever since Liberation we have been working hard to remedy that lack. And now today I am charged by my comrades of the Number One Textile Plant, and I'm sure the steel workers and the Malian rail workers would want to join with us, to thank you for the splendid job you've done and to say that we are ready, at last, to take from your young hands the torch you have borne so staunchly and carry it on to the great social triumph which must complete the victory won on the field in the March Revolution.'

There were shouts and applause from the workers and some of the young people a bit doubtfully joined in.

Ahmed turned to Mala and indicated that she should say something. She hesitated a moment, not quite knowing what to make of this change in the situation; but on thinking it over it seemed to her that Ahmed's words were very reasonable and had the sound of authority behind them. Indeed, once she began speaking she found she rather liked the view of the matter Ahmed had suggested. 'We thank our comrades here at the textile plant for their reception of us today,' she said. 'We are glad they recognise that the youth of Malia have been filling a gap until they could mobilise their own industrial strength to prevent any backsliding into capitalism.'

There was an enthusiastic response to this from workers and youth alike; and Razak added: 'Yes, we agree that a proletarian ideological revolution has to be the concern of the organised working class – of the trade unions. We will continue to travel about the country to inspire people in the rural areas to join them in the struggle against the capitalist roaders.'

More shouting and applause from all who were gathered there. And then Mala suddenly realised that something remained to be dealt with. 'But what about Manjal here? What's to be done with him?'

Manjal called out: 'Let me answer what these young people have said about me. Let me explain how wrong they are.'

Ahmed gave Manjal a pitying glance, almost as though he were not worth bothering about. 'You've had several years to convince us workers at the Number One Textile Plant that what these young people have said about you is wrong. We think they're right.'

'So what's to be done with him?' Razak asked.

'What we shall do about Manjal is something many of us have thought for some time ought to be done about *all* managerial appointments. We shall vote this very day whether Manjal is to continue to be manager here or not. In so doing we shall be establishing the principle that all such appointments must in the future be ratified after, say, six months' trial and that workers in any particular workplace have the right to suggest names from among those in their own ranks who they think should be considered for the post of manager.'

Frere was careful to get down these particulars exactly, fully aware of the political implications of such a practice. He knew that Ang had to be behind such a proposal for Ahmed to have dared make it; but he also knew that once it had been made, once it had been discussed and enthusiastically adopted by the joint trade union committees, it would be difficult for the Political Bureau of a workers' state to cancel it.

Manjal tried to speak but Ahmed warned him that he had better not. Ahmed turned him toward the steps and gave him a push in that direction. 'When we have voted Manjal out,' Ahmed said, 'and you can be sure that's what's going to happen, we'll leave it to those who appointed him to begin with to decide what to do with him now. I doubt if workers anywhere else will accept anyone as manager we've thrown out with good cause.'

And at this there was a great shout of satisfaction. Frere had to appreciate how neatly the scheme to keep a superficially contrite Manjal in place had been circumvented.

Ahmed smiled at Razak and at Mala on each side of him and then put his arms over their shoulders as a symbol of the unity of youth and workers and there was good-humoured rejoicing in the huge hall.

Frere wanted to get back to the Centre and start work at once on the news article he had to write. He had noted flashes at various points during Ahmed's address so one of the photographers had covered the event and there would be pictures to go with his account. He caught Ahmed's eye over the heads of the crowd and gestured that he was going. Ahmed smiled acknowledgement and waved farewell.

On his way back Frere was already working out some of the lines of argument he would be developing in telling the story of the day's events. For the readership of *Workers' World* he would be emphasising this extension of democracy into places of work. True socialism was not an alternative to democracy: it was democracy for the working people as opposed to democracy for those who exerted control over the working people through ownership of the means of production. Bourgeois revolution had established certain individual rights of freedom and justice – which had a restricted meaning for wage slaves and no meaning at all for the millions of starving poor that capitalism inevitably created in its economic colonies. Proletarian revolution disenfranchised the rich and powerful in order to realise those basic individual rights of freedom and justice for the whole mass of working people collectively. What had been seen today was an example of proletarian democracy and Frere felt considerable excitement at the prospect of writing about it, both for those in other lands following hopefully the course of the revolution in Malia and, even more, for those right here in the home of the March Revolution.

He realised that he did not know whether he would be describing something that now had the full weight of the Political Bureau behind it or something that with the support of at least some of its members, including, he was sure, the Secretary General, he was helping to establish; but he would certainly do the best job he possibly could of publicising it here and elsewhere – whatever the personal consequences for himself.

20

Frere had been looking forward to telling Leela all about what he had been up to, as much as to say: 'You thought I was trying to opt out of your revolution to some extent when I was only puzzled about what my part in it should continue to be. But see, others have found a use for me – and in connection with one of the most important political developments since liberation, too.'

But suppose she was influenced by other voices than the one which had summoned him to deal editorially with the democratisation of workplaces? All the writing he had done over the last three or four hours to get articles ready for *Das Vani* and *Workers' World* might seem to her nothing but deviationism from some correct political line.

And what *about* this business of democratising places of work he had been describing so enthusiastically? Was it really a demand of the organised working class to have a say in the management of factories, farms and offices? The trouble was, he knew that Ahmed was not really working class. He was the son of a wealthy Muslim businessman who had revolted in his teens from a privileged life to join the communist insurgents; and, though class was determined by one's relation to the means of production, one did not erase overnight the habits and attitudes of early home life. Sometimes Frere wondered if, for so many of those building the new society, including Leela and, of course, himself, it was not all just playing at proletarianisation – like Marie Antoinette and her courtiers pretending to be shepherds and shepherdesses in their little play village.

But that was ridiculous. What one committed oneself to altogether wholeheartedly and put one's very life on the line for was hardly to be compared with charades enjoyed in idleness. No, it was not so much doubts about the substance of the articles he had been writing which slowed his steps as he approached their bungalow as extreme reluctance to confront Leela in the way he had been imagining. He did not want to prove anything to her. He simply did not want to go on being in the position of feeling that he *needed* to prove anything to her.

He looked at his watch. It was late, well after ten. He let himself in, not quite knowing what face he ought to be wearing, and stared rather blankly at the little scene she had created – the two cane chairs, in one of which she was sitting, drawn up on opposite sides of a little table laid out for a late-night meal. So much the same setting as the last time they had spoken seriously that it might have been specially staged for a re-run. Did it mean that she had thought of some stronger arguments or that she had given more weight to his arguments which needed answering?

But her smile was so warmly welcoming when he had rather expected the not-at-home look of a few days before that it quite threw him for a time. Her laugh at his momentary discomfiture did not ignore its cause but made light of it and in response he could only grin, rather sheepishly, himself.

He went over and kissed her and then sat down and looked hungrily at the plate of cold fish salad she had prepared. 'It suddenly occurs to me that I've hardly eaten at all today.'

She did not begin eating at once herself but, elbows on table, cupped her face in her hands and gazed at him a few moments. Then she said: 'Thank you, Colin dear.'

'Thank you?' he asked, fork suspended.

'For making me see something about myself.'

'Oh.'

'Yes. I'd been letting them patronise me, without my realising it. I don't even think they realised it.'

'They?'

'My colleagues at the Institute and the comrades on the Central Committee. They accepted me as proof of their commitment to sexual equality. That's why they wanted me to become a full member of the Central Committee which hasn't a single woman on it. And I accepted being accepted by them. But they didn't take me seriously. I was excluded from the really vital disagreements that divided them. They all agreed with me and so I thought they all agreed with each other. With a little burst of bitterness she added: 'I was their token woman!'

'But, but – ' Exposing any such weakness in her political position had been the furthest thing from his mind. Was he to suppose, then, that what he had taken for shutting him out because a sense of his detachment from the revolutionary struggle had made him think of resigning from the editorship of *Workers' World* was really hiding herself away from him because she realised the justice of his charge that she had allowed *herself* to become detached? – Too detached to appreciate some of the things that were going on around her in the highest circles?

'I held my Marxist workshops,' she said; 'I served on my committees, and because everyone seemed satisfied with what I did, I assumed that everything was all right. That there were no problems racking the Central Committee.'

It occurred to him that the most natural way for her to find out what was really going on was to ask Pir Dato and that she would hesitate to avail herself of that source of information for the same reason that she had not wanted to ask for his help in keeping Chin's humiliation out of *Das Vani*.

'It was what happened to poor Chin that made me start thinking. That and what you said to me about it. I resented that because, deep down, I knew it was true.'

'But I thought you were being critical of *me*!' he exclaimed. 'I thought you thoroughly disapproved of my even thinking of resigning.'

'I thought of resigning, too, and then I decided "No, I won't", what I'll do is make them pay for needing me as much as they do. I *will* know what's going on up there – so that you and I can use it in doing what we think is politically correct.'

He shook his head in agreeable wonder that someone so dear to him, someone with whom he had lived intimately for so many years, could still surprise him completely by what she was really thinking or feeling. It sent a momentary shudder through him that the person one knew and loved best might, deep down inside, be someone else altogether; but this shaft of terror immediately became the penetrating thought that a relationship in which one could never take one's partner for granted was certainly never going to become, even in the slightest degree, boring.

He did not think this was just a very special and precious example of that loss and profit account of doubt and excitement which characterised one's life in a strange land among a different people: this was instead something quite unique about Leela, a quality of being so unconcerned about herself in a life lived so completely for others that she could make mistakes about who she was and the personal effect she had on other people – and then, with the most beautiful candour, apologise for the misunderstandings she inadvertently led other people into or share in the laughter at her own expense for the mistakes she made about herself.

He put down his fork and reached across the table to take one of her hands in his for a loving squeeze. He was smiling but his eyes glistened. Her eyes were so wide and open to him that he could not understand how he had ever thought for an instant that they were like the dark opaque eyes of Ang.

'But,' wondering if she might have talked with Pir Dato after all, 'was it, well, some particular encounter that made you see things differently?'

'It was Comrade Ang who helped me get straightened out. He stopped me in the corridor today behind the Central Committee Room to tell me something about what he had arranged with Ahmed at the Textile Plant. And the part you'd be playing in it, Colin. He had some time to spare so we went into one of the little offices which was empty and talked.'

'Just as he and I did a few days ago. When he made me see why I shouldn't resign.'

'I've always thought of Comrade Ang as such a Party man. He's a stickler for Party rules, you know; and he's constantly devising new means for making sure that we get the very best people as Party members and in the right proportions. But he was telling me that if the Party, which rules solely in the name of the working class, ever becomes at all detached from the working people of Malia it will begin to go bad. He didn't say it in so many words; but I realised he was talking about what you referred to the other day, Colin – not only a certain slackness among some of the senior cadres but actual corruption.'

'Which he doesn't think the Socialism Now Movement can do much about.'

'No. They can mobilise the next generation around the socialist ideal; but they can't purge the Party of bad elements. The Party has to renew itself by going back to the working people. Always back to the people. It's only to the extent that the Party is thoroughly involved with the people, intimately connected with them in everything they're doing and thinking, that it can pretend to be ruling in their name.'

'Yes. I got that idea from him too. Through Party members in the trade unions, in the rural co-operative committees, in the schools and medical centres and in local government the Party internalises itself in the people, takes its deliberations back into their midst to test their validity in popular practice. The way you said problems of planning and management ought to be taken back to the people they concern. Only thus can the Party pretend to speak with the people's voice. To speak with one proletarian voice, which is the justification of the one-party state.'

'It's like that Essential Saying of the Secretary General's: "We communists are the seeds and the people are the soil. Wherever we go, we must unite with the people, take root and blossom among them". It's made me reconsider the work of the Institute. To have people coming to us to learn how to use dialectical materialist methods to solve planning problems could become the way a chosen few solved the problem of getting to be planners themselves. We must go to the soil, to the people, find out what problems there are and, with the workers on the spot, using dialectical materialist methods, see if together we can't solve them

– just as we used to do in our base-camp workshops. The idea being, of course, to help workers become dialectical materialists themselves.'

'You may have to come to the Communications Centre and see what you can do with the soil there,' he laughed.

'Why not? It's my contention that even writers and journalists and intellectuals generally can, with a bit of encouragement and the right sort of prodding, learn to use dialectics.'

'As long as the prodding comes from horny-handed industrial workers like you, of course.'

'The difference isn't between mental and manual workers,' she reminded him. 'Only between those who realise they're workers and those who don't.'

'Do members of the Political Bureau think of themselves as workers?'

'If they don't, they've no right to high office in a dictatorship of the proletariat.'

He laughed. 'I see what you mean by making them pay for needing you.'

She leaned forward and kissed him. 'So neither of us resigns.'

'Well, it's occurred to me that in a country enjoying full employment, you can't resign from work. You can only change jobs – and I think I prefer the one I've got.'

'As the larger workplaces all over the country take up this proposal that appointments to managerial posts have to be ratified by a vote of the workers concerned, you're going to have plenty to write about.'

'What do you think will be the reaction to it in the Central Committee?'

'There will be some individual resentment at only being able to recommend, not actually to appoint, their favourites, but what they'll have to say is that it's a long-overdue reform. Comrade Ang has prepared the way for it.' She was thoughtful a moment. 'But what are we going to do about poor Chin?'

'I've been thinking about that. Even when we get his name cleared of that ridiculous charge, he can't go back to being Editor-in-Chief. He wouldn't want to. But one of the things he was charged with was teaching English literature. "Imperialist literature" it was called. And the other day some members of the Red Front destroyed some of the palm leaf manuscripts in the National Library because they represented the culture of feudalism.'

'That was very naughty of them. They were soundly ticked off for that.'

'But don't you think there's a danger of too narrow a national and class view of culture developing here? I like to think of the ordinary people of Malia, through the Revolution they've made, becoming the heirs not only of the rich cultural past of their own country but of the great cultural achievements of the world.'

'And you think Chin could help them claim their inheritance? Of course! I can remember how excited we who were students of his used to get when he talked about our own literature fed by so many different streams of which English is only the most recent.'

'Remember the Secretary General was complaining that there hadn't been the upsurge of creative writing he would have expected to accompany a great social event like liberation? Well, I think the spread of education all over the country has been too recent for us to be hearing many new voices yet; but perhaps also, culturally speaking, we've become a bit too closed in on ourselves.'

'And Chin could stimulate our youth with stories of epic struggles in other lands and – '

'And we could tell stories about our own epic struggles to those in other lands. I thought our own poet, Noor Fajan, could be associated with Chin in such a venture, not only deciding what great works of world literature we wanted to have available to our youth here but also what great works of our own Malian literature, past and present, we wanted to make available to the world.'

'Oh yes,' she said, 'Chin would love to be involved in something like that.'

'I can't think of anything that moves me so much as people who have been mere historical objects becoming subjects in their own right and learning something of the world and the other people they share it with. Remember that day on the Mei plateau when you burnt the debt rolls?'

'Yes!' the memory of that place where they had recognised their love for each other making her breath catch. 'Yes, always.'

'It was as if you had taken them by the hand and led them out of darkness toward the schools and colleges where they would come into their patrimony as citizens of Malia.'

She thought of something which pained her and she clenched her fists. 'And now,' she said bitterly, 'the Americans want to push them back into the darkness! They can't bear the thought of people anywhere freeing themselves to make better lives for their children than they themselves have ever had.'

'No. That's surrendering countries they think of as belonging to them to the menace of world communism. And Britain supports them wholeheartedly of course!'

She shook her head to free herself of such thoughts. 'But go ahead with what you were saying.'

'Well, that's it, really. I think Chin would make an excellent Minister of Culture.'

'I'll tell you someone who could help – Tinoo.'

'You're right,' he agreed at once. 'We've been trying without much success to bring Tinoo over to Publications. But it might be better to get him involved with Chin and Noor Fajan in this cultural project.'

'Why don't we have Tinoo and Moni here for dinner?' she suggested. 'So we can talk about it.'

'Yes, let's do that. I'm worried anyway about what Tinoo might do out of resentment over the attack on Chin. They've always been very close, you know.'

Tinoo and Moni came early a few nights later so that they could see little Matt before he went off to bed. Tinoo was a great favourite of the boy's and with the dexterity he had developed in his one hand he could perform tricks and feats of juggling which kept the boy gaping in wonder. To Matt's questions as to why his father had never learned such legerdemain Frere could only answer that he had been handicapped all his life by having two very ordinary hands.

Moni was small and exquisite. She and Leela had been friends at school and had managed to keep up with each other to some extent, even while Leela had been at base camp and Moni was helping to run one of the youth projects which served as an entry point for young people on their way 'inside' or back into the world again.

After dinner Frere explained his idea of making available to the people of Malia, even those speaking minority languages, the great treasures of world literature – on a carefully planned basis stretching over a number of years.

Tinoo thought it was a good idea but wondered if it should not be part of the work of the newly formed Writers' Union.

'But is the Secretary General all that happy about what's coming out of the Writers' Union?' Leela asked.

'That's because of the hack who was put in charge,' Tinoo said.

'And we can guess who was responsible for the appointment,' Frere remarked.

'What's happened,' Tinoo added, 'is that young writers have been set the task of producing poems and short stories setting forth the Party line in a most dogmatic way. Our Secretary General, being a poet himself, doesn't think much of them.'

'My idea,' Frere explained, 'was that Chin should be in charge of the work of deciding what foreign literature should be made available here and, perhaps, someone like Noor Fajan should be in charge of what Malian literature, in suitable translation, should be known to other countries – not just in the Soviet Union and China.'

'Chin's the very man!' Tinoo approved heartily. 'He and Noor Fajan would work well together. They could do a lot for the Writers' Union.'

'But making Chin Director of the Writers' Union brings us into head-on conflict with the same person who's probably responsible for the young people's attack on Chin,' Frere pointed out.

'The person who's *certainly* responsible,' Tinoo exclaimed angrily. 'Hadar!'

'And the Writers' Union comes under Hadar's ministry,' Frere shrugged. 'So, good as your idea is – we're stuck.'

'I don't know about that,' Tinoo demurred. 'The Secretary General takes a very active interest in literature. Indeed, he ought to have been made the official patron of the Writers' Union.'

'It was the Secretary General's remarks on foreign literature at the All Malian Conference,' Frere reminded them, 'which Chin quoted when he was being attacked as a former professor of English. But then the Secretary General isn't all that well, is he?'

'Well enough to put Chin in charge of the Writers' Union – and,' gleefully, 'make Hadar lump it!'

'There's something else Colin had in mind,' Leela said. 'He thinks you should be involved in this, Tinoo – as Chin's assistant. He'd need someone like you.'

Tinoo shook his head. 'I don't know about that. I seem to be imprisoned in the job I've got in the Education Ministry. They seem to think they've found the place where I can do the most useful work and create the least trouble. I don't think they intend to let me out. You remember what happened when you tried to get me into the Communications Department.'

'But if the Secretary General is backing the person who insists on your being his assistant – ' Frere began. 'Maybe it isn't just a question of the Secretary General's health. Maybe it's a question of whether he's still in full control.'

Frere shot a quick glance at his wife, knowing how she would once have responded to talk like this. But all she said was: 'Who do you think *is* in control then?'

'That's a good question,' Tinoo answered. 'I know Commander Kuan's supposed to be taking over as head of the same collective leadership we've had for some time now; but while Kuan has always been a great man on the field of battle, he's a bit lost, I think, in the corridors of power. Hadar certainly intends to be part of any leadership there's going to be. It's the only way he can keep his tracks covered.'

'I wonder if we're being too hard on Comrade Hadar,' Leela objected. 'There are those in the Political Bureau who have a high regard for his organisational ability.'

'Possibly those with such a high regard for his abilities are doing a bit of track-covering as well.'

'We shouldn't forget about the role he played during the most difficult period of struggle. When you and Colin's brother were fighting in the jungle with a pitifully small guerrilla army, Comrade Hadar organised the poor and unemployed in the shanty towns around the cities, and carried out acts of sabotage and assassination at the very heart of imperialist rule. He was captured several times and managed to escape. That crooked grin of his is the result of torture, you know.'

'I know.' Tinoo accepted her point. 'It's hard to understand how people can change like that; but some of them do. Sometimes I've wondered if it could be connected with the difference between the anger against the foreign exploiters which is enough to fuel the anti-imperialist struggle and the love of the exploited people of your own land which is necessary for building socialism. Hadar had the first; but he seems very short on the second. Of course, the investigation of Manjal may throw some light on what Hadar's been up to.'

'Is there a close connection between Manjal and Hadar?' Frere asked.

'It was Hadar who got him appointed as manager of the Number One Textile Plant. Ahmed told me that there was some kind of tie-up between Manjal and Sami Usman – '

'Who runs the handicraft emporia in Kotal Bargh?'

'The same. According to Ahmed they've been using the link between the Number One Textile Plant here and textile manufacturers in eastern Europe to smuggle some of the beautiful shawls and carpets made by our skilled craftspeople into western Europe and America.'

'At the very time when Britain and America are attacking us!' Moni exclaimed.

'There's no proof, Ahmed says.'

'Even if there's only a rumour of something like that,' Leela said, 'there would have to be investigations at the highest level.'

'But is there any high-level body Hadar himself doesn't sit on?' Tinoo wondered.

'If Comrade Ang had his way, I know what would happen to all three of them not much later than tomorrow,' Frere laughed.

'That's right,' Tinoo agreed.

'You be very careful,' Frere warned him. 'You mustn't mention any of this outside our circle. I want Chin to join you in running the Writers' Union. I don't want you to join Chin in purgatory.'

'It's no good trying to talk sense to him,' Moni said with good-natured hopelessness. 'Nothing will keep him from blurting out the truth as he sees it at the most inopportune times. He'd probably be deputy education minister now if he could curb his tongue.'

'High-ranking officials with curbed tongues are what we're beginning to have rather too many of.'

'All the same,' Leela remonstrated, 'you be careful, Tinoo. We seem to be moving into a difficult time.'

Tinoo laughed. 'To come out firing in all directions, that's my way. I suppose it's the frustration of being eliminated from the shooting war in my first engagement. And don't forget I spent years after that working under the Puppet Government where I could never express my real feelings at all.'

'Oh, you've got every right to blast away. Just make sure it's among friends.' And after a few moments Frere asked: 'Do you ever think about that last operation you were on, with Tuck and Ang and Kirin – '

'And your brother. Much too often. On my very first mission I was careless and got hit – almost by the first shot fired. From then on I was just a burden to my comrades – something your brother had to lug miles and miles through the jungle or argue with Ang about. Half the time I wasn't even conscious and the whole thing is like an endless nightmare.'

'He still dreams about it,' Moni said. 'I have to wake him up and get him a cup of tea and then he can go back to sleep again.'

'Each year at the Victory celebrations I find myself wishing I'd contributed more.'

'That's ridiculous,' Leela told him. 'I think it took a lot more courage to have been a secret member of the Party right under the enemy's nose than off there in base camp surrounded by good comrades.'

'I was only on one operation myself,' Frere reminded him.

'But you got a medal. And it wasn't even your fight.'

'It was my fight all right. It's what Matt left me.'

'That was the real war,' Tinoo went on with a distant look in his eye, 'out there in the jungles and hills. That was the real revolution – landless peasants taking up arms and joining the liberation fighters in driving out the British and then overthrowing the regime of collaborators they left behind. I just wish I'd had a larger part in it.'

'We'd never have won,' Leela told him, 'if it hadn't been for the information which comrades like you kept us supplied with.'

'Now,' Tinoo continued without heeding her, 'what I see is a lot of young people born too late to take part in the real struggle pretending to be tough revolutionaries; and hypocrites like Hadar strutting about like battle-hardened veterans.'

'Really,' Leela objected, 'that's not quite fair.'

'That's what I tell him,' Moni said. 'Young people can't help when they're born.'

'I know,' Tinoo agreed, 'but that's the way I feel.'

'I can understand it,' Frere said sympathetically. 'It's something I've been feeling, too – if not so strongly. How does one keep the kind of administrative tasks and off-stage comments so many of us are involved in here in Rani Kalpur from seeming just like what we might be doing in any bureaucratic establishment anywhere? And if what we're doing doesn't seem different to us, how can we be sure that things have really changed? But then that's always been my problem as writer and publicist – talking and writing *about* revolution instead of actually making it. That's why I kept badgering them to let me take part in some guerrilla foray.'

'Yes, it's like my wanting to get back into the fight.'

'I suspect that was partly because you wanted to get away from me,' Moni said jokingly. And to Leela: 'I think this masculine thing about wanting to go off where the fighting is may be just an excuse to get away from us for a while.'

'I'd have had to take you with me, Moni – to clean and load my gun for me and even to fire it when it comes to that. Do you know, I'm not even sure what kind of a shot Moni is. That's something we always knew about the young women who were inside with us.'

'Leela had ceased taking part in operations when I arrived at base camp,' Frere said, 'but I heard stories about her prowess.'

'She has a medal, too,' Moni pointed out proudly.

'They can always recognise the heroic in us,' Leela said dismissively, 'when it takes a form they have established themselves. It still remains for them to appreciate heroism in what we do every day of our lives.'

'That will come,' Frere assured her lightheartedly, 'now that we're sharing more in those daily tasks ourselves. I want to claim a medal for the very dangerous business of showering with a five-year-old boy who likes to play games with a slippery cake of soap.'

'I didn't mean just that,' Leela said. 'I meant heroism in those administrative, journalistic or educational jobs you were complaining about. I think now that women have a fairer share of such work they'll show you the kind of quiet courage they've always displayed in childbirth and rearing a young family.'

Frere, thinking of women he had worked with like Siti as well as of his own wife, nodded. But something he had discussed with Tinoo before came back to him. 'I think part of the problem with Tinoo and me is that our decision to become actively involved in the Revolution – Tinoo when he was at the University and I when I was a foreign correspondent floating around the world – seemed to us like an act of free will. Not like those who had no choice, those for whom it was revolution or nothing. And because there was that element of the arbitrary about our decision we go on having to justify it, both in terms of the righteousness and justice of the struggle we've adopted and of the value of our own contribution to it.'

'That's just like Matt,' Tinoo said fondly. 'He kept on having to be reassured that the Revolution had the same character which had involved him in it to begin with; and he constantly entertained doubts about his own efforts to serve it faithfully.'

'It's never been like that for me,' Leela said. 'My family was always identified with the liberation struggle. I grew up with those ideas. There was never a time when I stood apart and decided whether I would join the communists or not. I've always belonged to the Revolution. Everything about its underground seeding, its slow secret growth and its bursting forth in the ripeness of time has seemed to me as natural and as inevitable as – as childbirth.'

'I never had to make up my mind about it either,' Moni said, 'but it was different with me. A question of feeling, it's true, but not directly, only through Tinoo. During that long period when it was uncertain whether he was going to live or not and I nursed him continuously I got to the place where what was going on in *his* poor body, what *he* was feeling was primary and what was going on in my own was of only secondary importance. I guess it's still like that. Whatever he feels strongly about, I feel strongly about.'

'I tell her she has no right to put such a responsibility on me,' Tinoo said laughingly. 'I assure her that she hasn't got out of having to make choices herself simply by leaving everything to me, because, after all, she did herself choose me.'

'And I tell him that I *didn't* choose him. I had him wished on me when, as a young nurse, he was put in my care and I fell in love with him.'

The telephone rang and Frere went into the other room to answer it.

When he came back he looked quite desolate. 'That was Chin's son. About an hour ago Chin died in hospital.'

21

Conditions on the northern frontier were very bad. There were more and more hit and run raids by the Antis, as the Malian counter-revolutionary expatriates armed by the British were called. They used for cover the same thick jungle that had served the Liberation forces so well, avoiding those large, bare patches of poisoned earth where nothing would grow which were a legacy of the toxic chemical spraying of that part of Malia by the Americans.

They mainly attacked schools and medical centres and they left behind hundreds of the most up-to-date small land mines which were difficult to detect and hard to detonate safely. Hundreds of field workers and children were killed or mutilated. Furthermore all attempts to get artificial limbs through the United Nations were blocked by the Anglo-American boycott. Frere kept thinking that instead of the empty-eyed children with swollen bellies and skeletal limbs who were no more to be seen there were now the bright-eyed, healthy children with their legs blown off. If he could have pressed a button which would release tons of bombs on London and Washington, he felt that it would be almost impossible for him not to do so – except that the real villains would not be hurt. They would be off somewhere safe. Those who would suffer would be the most exploited people in *those* two countries!

The terrible increase of casualties was no reflection on the efforts of the northern military commander, Goh Tun. He planned and executed cunning traps into which bands of Antis blundered and were wiped out. He devised with the people of the area protective schemes for keeping children from going where the mines were likely to be and for equipping farm workers with electronic detectors so that they could clear fields and get on with sowing and harvesting.

But the Antis were paid big bonuses for invading the 'communist dictatorship' to the south and their supply of the most modern weapons was inexhaustible. While Commander Goh Tun was allowed to cross the border in hot pursuit, there was no question of his being able to seek out the main headquarters and arms dumps of the Antis and destroy them. That would be the excuse for Britain and the United States to mount massive air attacks all over Malia. Eventually a ten-mile zone along the border line was cleared and turned into a long defensive bulwark which it was impossible for the Antis to penetrate. But it meant moving thousands of people from their homes and villages and resettling them. It meant leaving many thousands of acres uncultivated. There was more trouble on the Mei Plateau, too, as subversive elements provoked demonstrations which had to be dealt with – thus creating resentment and deepening divisions.

Finally people's courts had to be set up to try to isolate and punish the bad elements causing the disturbances. The rough justice this involved soon became the subject of attacks on the lack of individual freedom in communist Malia by the World Civil Rights Union, itself an organisation sponsored by the CIA.

It was the attempt to use the Mei people to try to undermine socialist rule in Malia that was particularly upsetting for Leela and Frere. The charge that the liberation of the Mei people from feudal oppression was merely a despotic attempt to deprive the people of their religion in order to bring the Plateau under the rigid control of the communist dictatorship was bound, since it was the setting of their romantic recognition of their love for each other, to seem to them like an attack on the genuineness of their own intimate relationship.

In addition to all these externally imposed problems there was low rainfall that year and a bad grain harvest. 'That's a problem with communism,' Tinoo had remarked. 'The God of the Book and the other gods as well are all on the side of the enemy.'

While there was the circulation of rationalist tracts and information bulletins by the Information Ministry, there had not been much militant atheism in Malia. The two main religions, Islam and Christianity, were both associated with invading rulers who had used harsh means to force their beliefs on the people and there was not all that much resistance to depriving both religions of any political influence. And even in the northeast where native Buddhism was strong, the central government had been more concerned with breaking the feudal tie-up between lamaseries and big landholdings than with separating the people from their faith. But that did not save Malia from hostile criticism in which would-be capitalist exploiters were joined by religious fundamentalists of all kinds.

It was a time when Frere felt an uneasiness which had so many possible causes that it was difficult for him to imagine what particular changes might restore his equanimity. He could only think with regret of that beautiful simplicity of life at base camp when a couple of thousand people had been absolutely united in the kind of action that was needed to achieve a commonly idealised goal.

What he had been most aware of since that time were all the layers of contradictions, one after another, encircling Leela and him like so many concentric spheres. There were the contradictions between socialist Malia and the imperialist enemy without; between the communist government of Malia and the people it claimed to be serving; between the Political Bureau and the Party; between different wings of the Political Bureau itself; even, sometimes, between the two of them – but one could go on and on peeling away one set of contradictions after another and never getting to a peaceful core at the centre. There were instead simply those various levels of contradictoriness providing the dynamics of interconnected change; so that, understood, it was possible for human beings to intervene and, at least to some extent, make those changes serve humanity progressively.

But now the external war against imperialism, which was thought to have been won, was having to be fought all over again and the progressive resolution of so many internal social contradictions seemed to be in doubt. The whole complicated structure of interlocking globes of contradictoriness seemed to have jammed, so that they no longer had any understandable relationship with each other. He simply did not know what effect his public intercession on behalf of Chin or his championing of the cause of workplace democracy might have on his position as editor of *Workers' World*.

He had stood up to the Red Front and, by implication, to those powerful agents making use of it. He had yet to learn what they might do about it. He did not believe the fact that Chin had died was simply the end of the matter. Indeed he had no intention of letting it be. He was more determined than ever that Chin's name should be cleared and that his services to the March Revolution should be recognised.

But when some official reaction did come to all that he had been involved in recently, it took a quite overwhelming form. To express the gratitude felt by the Party and people of Malia for the founding and, during the nine most important years of the country's history, the editing of *Workers' World*, Secretary General Lee was honouring Comrade Colin Frere with a banquet at the People's Palace. It would be appreciated that the banquet would also be in memory of Comrade Matthew Frere, Hero of the Socialist Democratic Republic.

With the formal announcement came a letter from the Secretary General himself, in very shaky handwriting, thanking Frere personally for the excellent job he had done of keeping Malia's friends abroad informed of their revolutionary struggle and the building of socialism in their country. Since the idea of the occasion was to bring together as many of those whom Frere had known and worked with as possible, together with friends and associates of his brother who were still alive, any suggestions he might have to make about the list of guests would be welcome.

As he hurried back to the bungalow to tell Leela about it, his head was full of recollections of people he had known at this or that stage of his time in Malia whom he must not forget to have invited.

When he told her, she clasped her hands on her breast and uttered a little laugh of pleasure. 'Oh Colin, my dearest! It's wonderful, absolutely wonderful!'

'Had you heard anything about it?' he asked. In other words, had she had anything to do with it?

'Not a hint,' she answered at once. 'I'm as surprised as you are. And probably even more delighted.'

'I wonder if Ang had anything to do with it.'

'Why should it not be simply the Secretary General's idea? Which means that it wipes out for this special occasion all the splits and divisions we've begun to be aware of!'

He took her in his arms and kissed her and then he held her away from him and stared at her lovely face in which he seemed to see written in the most beautiful hand the happiness he felt and would never be able to express adequately. 'We'll sit down this very night and begin to think of names. Most of them, I'm sure, will be thought of by whoever's organising the banquet; but we don't want anybody important to *us* left out.'

'Yes,' gleefully, 'it will be like a sentimental journey back through our past.'

'One of the things that struck me first,' he told her, 'is that it will be a chance for me to speak about Chin. To say how much he helped me in everything I've done. It will be a way of putting the record straight and reminding everybody of how much we owe him.'

She paused for only a moment before saying: 'Yes, of course. My dear old Professor Chin!'

It occurred to Frere during the next few days that the recognition he was receiving through the banquet gave him just the purchase he needed for going ahead with the scheme for literary exchanges with other countries. He had thought of it to begin with as something Chin could take on with Tinoo's assistance; but he still thought the project worth backing, perhaps under Tinoo's direction. It would serve as a kind of memorial for Chin and it would get Tinoo out of the post in

Education he was presently trapped in.

He had already exchanged letters with Noor Fajan, who was secretary of the Writers' Union, about this idea of his and now he arranged to meet him at his house in the riverside village of Gongor. He set out several hours earlier than necessary to keep his appointment in order to have time to climb the curved mound beyond the village and enjoy his favourite view looking out over the river toward the foothills of the Lupang Range.

The last time he had trudged up to the top of this bald rounded summit had been just before the visit of Clare Wallace during the celebrations at the end of the first Five-Year Plan. It seemed a long time ago because so much had happened since then. There had been periods of late when he had doubted that things were going as well as he had in all good faith reported in the pages of *Workers' World*, periods when he would suddenly wonder if he was as convinced as he should be that the things said about the new Malia by its imperialist enemies were simply interested lies, when he would have the nightmare of waking up one fine day and finding that he had merely been party to a plot to *fool* people into thinking that there was a humane alternative to the dog-eat-dog world of capitalism where the greedy flourished and the rest went without. And at such periods the awful doubt about the possibility of ordering society in a kindly and equitable way would even seep into his relations with the one person in the world who meant everything to him.

But today he felt good and he assured himself that it was not simply the subjective glow of satisfaction at being appreciated himself but the very real sense that his views of what a society ought to be, or ought to be striving to become, were objectively validated by the celebration of his expression of them by the only people he could recognise as authorities on the subject. He stood there, looking up and down the river crowded with barges, and, with a laugh, looked across at the little button factory grunting rhythmically with the beat of the stamping machine within and emitting through its thin black chimney a steady succession of perfect smoke rings. He thought of it as a constant background to the surge and wane of crusades and campaigns, like a metronome keeping careful time while the contrapuntal movements of Malia's development filled the air with symphonic sound. Or, perhaps, like a man's heartbeat which goes on without very much change whether he is in struggle or in love or simply standing peacefully on a quiet hill top letting the past slide by in his mind like the silent barges drifting slowly downstream.

A widowed daughter who looked after Noor Fajan greeted Frere at the door of the little house and took him into a room where the old man was waiting. In spite of his age – he must have been in his late seventies

– Fajan got up and shook Frere's hand cordially. He had been too old to join the liberation fignters even when they first formed but he had visited the base camp from time to time and had supplied many of the poems they took inspiration from and the songs they marched to. He had often contributed articles on Malian literature to *Workers' World* and he and Frere had known each other a long time.

'You're very welcome, Comrade,' Noor Fajan said and, indicating a chair for Frere, sat down again himself. There was a table between them on which were prawn crisps and saffron cakes and soon the woman brought them tea and sliced limes and honey. Frere expressed his gratitude for such hospitality.

'I was so sorry to hear about Comrade Chin,' Noor Fajan said.

'I know. It's not unconnected with my wanting to talk to you.'

'I heard about the attack on him from some of the young writers who belong to the Red Front. I asked them why they'd been so hard on a man who had always been such a good friend of Malian youth. They couldn't say.'

'I think we've got an idea of who put them up to it. But what they charged him with was having been a teacher of English language and literature. It made him a running dog of British imperialism.'

'Some of these young people forget how much we were inspired in our ideas of liberation by Shelley. They ought to know how often Marx quotes Shakespeare. Indeed, the first copies of *Capital* we read were printed in English and smuggled to us by comrades in London.'

'I'm afraid they weren't thinking of anything like that. They were just repeating charges against Chin which had been put into their mouths by others.'

Noor Fajan burst out indignantly: 'When he had to go inside for refusing to name students who demonstrated against British rule! When he practically founded our national daily *Das Vani*!'

'It was the period when they were denouncing all culture in any way connected with feudal or colonial times as anti-working class. I think they've moved away from such dogmatism now.'

'When it's too late to help Comrade Chin! I was faced with something like that in the Writers' Union. As you know, it grew out of the Conference on Literature organised by Secretary General Lee. The Political Bureau, in setting out the reasons for instituting the Union, stated in a dogmatic way that it was to encourage socialist realist writing as opposed to bourgeois modernism. Some of the younger writers immediately complained that socialist realism was what was insisted on in the Soviet Union; they were in favour of revolutionary romanticism instead, as advocated by Chairman Mao.'

Frere laughed. 'What did you do about it?'

'Referred the matter to the Secretary General who promptly took a correct dialectical line. "Socialist realism is the materialist base on which our literary endeavours have to be grounded, revolutionary romanticism is our aspiration to change the world, not just to understand it." That ended the theoretical argument so that we could get on with the practice of actually producing something for our people to read.'

'And are they?'

'They're beginning to. It's very important.' Noor Fajan took a sip of his tea. 'In this, like any country, there's plenty to divide us. We've got Buddhists and Muslims, some Hindus and Christians and, among old-time communists like me and a lot of the young people, too, we've got atheists. There's a large community of Chinese merchants and a small community of British ex-soldiers and minor officials left over from colonial rule. We've got two major ethnic-minority languages in addition to the Indomalian which all people speak and most now can read and write and we've got English which is the second language of most of the important people. *But,* we all live in Malia which has a rich cultural tradition going back a long way and which, through the spread of education, more and more of us are becoming familiar with; and, just as important, we all work in Malia and that unites us against any foreign capitalists or any local compradors who want to exploit us. That's the reason why, in spite of such cultural differences, we can all live together peacefully and out of such rich diversity begin to create a common proletarian culture which is thoroughly Malian. You see what I mean?'

'Perfectly!' Frere said approvingly. 'It's why literature here really can belong to the people. Not like Britain where the gulf between literature and ordinary working people gets wider and wider. As those ordinary British working people become increasingly involved in struggle against exploitation and oppression they're going to identify with our liberation struggle and appreciate the cultural reflection of the efforts of the people of Malia to build a socialist society.'

'That's proletarian internationalism, Comrade Colin.'

'It's what unites us, in spite of national, cultural and linguistic differences, with people all over the world. Anywhere there's struggle against exploitation. That's really the basis of my idea. We should be receiving novels, short stories and poems from our comrades in other lands and supplying them in turn with the works of our own writers here. It's the way we can end the isolation the imperialists are trying to impose on us.'

'And just as there's a kind of commonwealth of struggle against imperialist exploitation stretching across the contemporary world,' Fajan took it up, 'so the struggle to create civilised societies stretches back into the past. Great works of ancient times in other literatures, like the Greek and Indian epics, could be exchanged for our *Arjen Nemastabadh*, of which we're making a new English translation, incidentally.'

'Oh there's plenty to think about in connection with such traffic in literature.'

'I believe something like that was intended to be part of the work of the Writers' Union. But we've been too busy organising the selection of poetry and prose for publication here to do much about it.'

'It's what I hoped Chin might help out with.'

'And now poor Chin's not with us any more.'

'But I've someone else I think might do the same sort of job. My friend in the Education Ministry – Tinoo. You know him?'

'Very well. He's made new and better English versions of some of my earlier poems, you know.'

'English is very important for us, even if it is the "second language of important people".'

'Oh I wouldn't deny that,' Noor Fajan hastened to say. 'It's a kind of pipeline connecting us with the literature of the world. Through good translations we can pump the best of our writing to other countries everywhere.'

'And we can also suck back the literature of the world *we* want for our people, instead of having pumped on us what the imperialists want us to have.' Frere paused for a moment and then added thoughtfully: 'Is that arrogant, Comrade? To choose for the ordinary people of Malia the literature of other lands which we think appropriate for them?'

'It is. It is,' Noor Fajan chuckled. 'What arrogance! But it's not *our* arrogance, Comrade Colin. Not yours and mine. It's the fantastic arrogance of those ordinary people, landless labourers and industrial wage slaves, taking hold of their own fate and saying what kind of a world they want to live in. We dare take on a task like this because we speak for them. And, anyway, those ordinary readers of Malia in their growing numbers will, in the fullness of time, sort out our decisions on their behalf and decide themselves what's really right for them.'

'That's true.'

'For us *not* to act on your proposal would be a kind of censorship.'

After a pause Frere remarked wistfully: 'If only I'd talked to Chin earlier about this role he was ideally suited for. It might have rallied him.'

'We'll dedicate the project to Comrade Chin,' Noor Fajan said.

For the most part, Secretary General Lee's insistence on a frugal lifestyle for Party and State officials meant that the great banqueting hall in the People's Palace was only used for entertaining the dignitaries of friendly countries or the trade union delegations of not-so-friendly ones. The staff of cooks, waiters, actors, folk dancers and a large company of musicians, a few of whom had been in attendance in the old days before Government House became the People's Assembly Hall, were delighted when some domestic occasion gave them the opportunity of displaying their various skills before those most likely to appreciate them.

Frere sometimes wondered in the days preceding the event in his honour if it did not have the effect of changing him from the native Malian he felt himself now as practically being, back into the sympathetic foreigner from Britain. He almost wished that his services to the March Revolution were not being distinguished in such an extraordinary way. But then he would think of the honour also being accorded to Matt, who deserved it so much more, and be glad to be taking a prominent part in such a celebration.

At one time dress for such functions would be the same boiler suits for both men and women as they wore at work; but gradually this had begun to seem too ostentatious a claim of being 'simple manual workers' whatever social duties upper-rank people might be called upon to perform. Plain cloth suits for men and some form of *salwar-kamiz* for women had become the more usual wear for an evening at the Palace.

Little Matt insisted on reviewing his parents on the night of the banquet to make sure they passed muster. He turned to Lara, who would be staying with him, to see if she agreed that they both looked all right. Frere stepped forward and threaded the stem of a white hibiscus bloom he had picked for the occasion in Leela's dark lustrous hair. She laughed and started to remove it as unlicensed adornment in socialist Malia.

'No, keep it! I like it!' the boy said.

'I'm afraid you'll just have to put up with it,' Frere said, looking at her admiringly.

'Well,' she shrugged, 'since it's your affair – '

'Wear it for *me*,' Matt insisted.

'I'll wear it for both Matts,' Leela concluded the discussion.

'I only wish Clare Wallace could see you now. She doubted that our socialist regime could last if it insisted on putting all women in such an unattractive uniform.'

'I'll consider myself a martyr to the clothes revolution Clare demands!' Leela held up her clenched fist. 'Come. I hear the car outside.'

The driver was the young man who customarily attended Frere when his duties required the use of a car. As the two of them came out of the bungalow, this young man, grinning broadly, came up to them, said good evening to Leela and shook Frere's hand warmly, congratulating him on the happy occasion.

'Thank you, Makhan.' And in an aside to Leela: 'I forgot to mention Makhan as one of the people who ought to be invited.'

'I *am* invited,' Makhan said. 'I'll be at one of the tables and will know exactly when to get the car to drive you back.'

'Not too many toasts,' Leela warned gaily. When they arrived at the People's Palace, the uniformed guards and a number of the cleaning and maintenance staff were lined up to greet them; and they shook Frere's hand and wished him well on this special night.

Frere and Leela had only dined three or four times in the large chamber with its three enormous chandeliers and its murals lit by elaborate lamps glowing at intervals all around the room – usually when the visit of some cultural group from abroad made the presence of the editor of Malia's international journal appropriate. The replacing of scenes of imperial splendour by a leading British painter of the time with the depiction by contemporary young Malian artists of people plying old crafts and skills against typical Malian landscapes had been the subject of a special coloured supplement in *Workers' World*.

Instead of a few long tables with the inevitable suggestion of gradations in rank from top to bottom there were a number of round tables, each seating ten people, scattered all around the chamber. The form of such dinners as this was that in the time between courses, which might be as many as a dozen or more over several hours, people would circulate among the tables, greeting various friends and joining in mutual toasts.

The table designated for Frere and Leela was at the very centre of the vast hall. Already there were Ang and a number of colleagues Frere had worked with during his time in Propaganda and Publications like Siti and Swee Meng. As he had requested there was an empty chair where Chin would have sat and beside it was a place for Chin's son.

Frere had wondered if Hadar would be at his table; but looking around the other tables he did not see Hadar anywhere. He did see a great number of others though to whom he gave a brief wave as a promise of an interval meeting – Tinoo and Moni at a nearby table where the Minister of Education and the Director of the Marxist-Leninist Institute were sitting, Noor Fajan presiding over a table of writers and artists, Ahmed and his wife, Narmala, at another table with Mala, the Red Front leader, and so many more. He caught a glimpse of his old friend, Goh Tun, on the other side of the room and waved to him energetically.

'I hope it means things in the north are a bit better,' he said to Leela.

They took their designated places at the table. Frere sat there with a pleased, dazed expression on his face, looking around him, right hand raised in a little salute ever so often as he caught the eye of some comrade, and turning ever so often with a slightly incredulous smile to Leela who smiled back and put her hand in his as much as to say: 'Oh yes, it really is all happening to you, my dear, and it's no more than you deserve'.

On every table there was a candelabra and these soft flickering lights filled the space between the brighter shine of wall lamps all around the sides of the huge room, while in the middle there were the three great galactic glows of the chandeliers, like a scale model of the universe – a universe inhabited solely by his friends! He peered about him trying to take it all in, this overwhelming courtesy paid to him in this land not of his birth. He shook his head again in a kind of wonder and looked lovingly at Leela in the depths of whose eyes were two tiny orreries reflecting infinitesimally those myriad lights; and his own eyes moistened.

On a dais at one side of the great hall a party of musicians with their string, horn and percussion instruments were playing the classical music of Malia. Later they would be joined by vocalists, several of whom Frere had suggested by name. Ang leaned toward him and said: 'Yesterday the Secretary General asked me to give you his warmest greeting and to tell you that he would be arriving later. The doctors didn't think he should try to be present for the whole affair.'

'I'm distressed that he should have to make any effort at all on my behalf.'

'Nothing would keep him away – even if he can't stay long.'

Frere wanted to talk to Ang about the project he had been discussing with Noor Fajan but felt that this was hardly the place or time for it. He arranged a meeting with him at the Secretariat offices for the following week. He was glad to note that Siti was looking after Chin's son, whom she seemed to know quite well, and seeing that he was included in the conversation among the publication comrades. That empty chair was the only sad touch to a joyous celebration.

Heaped trays of the indigenous foods that made such delicious hors-d'oeuvres were brought in and placed on the tables. Soon after the end of the Liberation War every part of the country had been circulated with a request that lists of all native remedies with any reputation at all for curative properties should be sent to the centre where tests could be carried out to ascertain which of them ought to be included in an inexpensive pharmacopoeia for general use: a by-product of this exercise had been the popularising throughout the land of tasty fruits, nuts and vegetables which grew in particular areas, together with traditional recipes for their preparation. Visitors to Malia often commented on the wide variety of exotic comestibles they had to choose from. In the intervals between courses Frere and Leela would either remain at their table while associates, colleagues and dear friends came by to greet them or else they would set forth to wander among the other tables, constantly encountering faces out of the recent and distant past, some of whom Frere had not seen since he first came to Malia.

At Ahmed's table they were pleased to see how well he was getting on with Mala, who seemed to entertain no resentment at all at the way the trade unions of industrial workers had taken over the direction of the Socialism Now campaign. Frere wondered what she felt about Chin's death, if she knew about it. While Leela was chatting with Narmala, Ahmed told Frere that he had been given an office and staff here in the People's Palace.

'It's to supervise nationwide workplace elections,' Ahmed explained – 'to approve present managers or select new ones where those appointed from the nomenklatura are considered unsuitable.'

'Congratulations. That sounds like real progress.'

'We'll see,' Ahmed laughed. 'I don't know whether it means the trade unions have penetrated the state machine or the state machine has swallowed up the trade unions.'

Frere laughed too. 'Of course it could mean that your name was drawn from the nomenklatura as the ideal person to handle any democratic rebelliousness on the part of the industrial unions.'

'It might,' Ahmed agreed. 'But perhaps they've made a mistake. Perhaps they've picked the wrong person.'

'That's the way it will appear in *Workers' World*, anyway,' Frere assured him good humouredly.

He was keen to see Goh Tun and, with Leela in tow, made his way during an intermission between courses across the room to a table occupied by senior military officers, some of whom Frere only knew by name.

'Are you here for a few days?' he asked Goh Tun.

'Only tonight. I'm flying back first thing in the morning. I couldn't miss an occasion in honour of my old bunk mate, could I?'

Frere looked around the room. 'I'd expected Comrade Field Commander Kuan would be here.'

'He's with the Secretary General,' Army Chief Sulman explained. 'He'll probably be coming later.' Sulman had been one of the highest-ranking officers in the puppet army who was a secret communist all along.

On the way back to their own table they were suddenly confronted by a large man who leapt to his feet and, filling glasses for Frere and Leela, insisted that they join him in a toast. Although the face was familiar, Frere could not at once place him until the man's very assurance that no one could possibly forget him gave Frere a clue. It was Sami Usman, the manager of the carpet factory who had showed him around Kotal Bargh just before he made contact with the liberation forces.

'You look as successful as ever,' Frere said. He was thinking of what he had heard about Usman's connection with Hadar in some highly questionable deals.

'Of course! This government tried to get along without me for a time; but they soon realised they couldn't dispense with Sami Usman. I'm a director of the handicraft industries now.' He said 'now' as though no such moderately important post could detain him for long. 'And this is your charming wife of whom I've heard so much.'

On the way back to their table Leela said: 'I'm sure you didn't put *his* name down.'

'I didn't, but a little thing like that wouldn't stop Sami Usman.'

'He acts as though you're his dearest friend.'

'I suspect Sami Usman doesn't have friends, only people he can use from time to time.'

They were sitting at their table agreeing that, even with the walking about between courses to work up a bit more of an appetite, they could not eat another mouthful when Tinoo and Moni came over and joined them, sitting in chairs temporarily vacated by those also making the rounds.

'It's just as well Hadar isn't here,' Tinoo said. 'I don't think I could have kept from hitting him, or at least from saying something – not after poor old Chin's dying like that.'

Frere told him about his conversation with Noor Fajan. 'He likes the idea of working with you. It's even more important now that we should get on with something Chin would have found pleasure in doing.'

'Of course. But it won't change my mind about Hadar. I suppose you realise that old crook, Sami Usman, is here.'

'No more please, Tinoo,' Moni urged. 'We're here tonight to enjoy ourselves and to pay tribute to our good friend Colin.'

'Yes, of course!' Tinoo said, looking for a glass he could fill with wine and then holding it up in a toast: 'To you, Colin.' He took a sip and holding up the glass again: 'And to Matt.'

'To Matt,' Frere said and then, turning to the young man beside Siti, added: 'And to Chin.'

Chin's son stood up and drank to his father. A little later Frere and Leela decided that for the moment they had done enough exchanging of greetings and toasts and slipped away from the banqueting hall. They walked through dark corridors, climbed deserted stairways and stepped out onto that balcony which served as a reviewing stand at public ceremonies.

There was a full moon and the whole square basked in the dim heatless rays that bounced off its surface, as though night were only a kind of lesser day in which all the features of that part of town were plainly if more softly revealed – the Communications Centre opposite, the broad, tree-lined, lamp-lit March Revolution Avenue stretching away beyond it and, immediately below, the wide steps of the People's Palace leading down to the expanse of pavement dotted with motionless shrubs in boxes arranged in a geometric pattern.

Frere put one arm over Leela's shoulder as they leaned against the parapet and with the other he pointed down. 'That's just where Tuck was standing on the top of his tank when a shot from about here killed him. It was very odd. I seemed to know before it happened that the shot was coming and that Tuck would be hit; but I knew it as in a dream when one is powerless to do anything.'

'Comrade Tuck was one of the greatest of military irregulars,' she said.

He thought about it a moment. 'Do you mean that it was fitting in a way that he should have died at the moment of victory in the kind of warfare he understood so well?'

'No. I simply mean that we'll never be able to think of our revolutionary victory without thinking of Comrade Tuck.'

'I often wonder what various of those who died in the course of the struggle would make of Malia today. It's part of the feeling I have that when things are going right and we seem to be realising, if slowly, the great ideals we all shared about a society in which people don't exploit each other, then I can think with equanimity of those who fell along the way; but when things are going wrong, as they sometimes seem to these days, when we seem to be making grave mistakes for which the people will have to pay, then I think of all those who sacrificed their lives with the greatest pain.'

'And what are you feeling now, Colin?'

'Now, at this moment in time, standing here with you,' he squeezed her shoulder, 'and looking down on that peaceful moonlit scene of past triumph, my mind's at rest. It's strange. Quite a considerable portion of my life was lived before I made contact with Kuan and his men that day in the hills above Kotal Bargh; but I remember no more of it than one usually recalls of early childhood – just vague glimpses and momentary snatches. I can't even imagine any more a life lived apart from all this,' with a wave of his hand for the bit of Malia they could see, 'and you, Leela, and all those wonderful people down there in the banqueting chamber.'

She rose up on tiptoes and kissed him. 'We'd better go back to them,' she said with a little laugh.

When they got back everything seemed to be the same except that Ang was not there. 'He said to tell you,' Siti explained, 'that something unexpected had come up. He might not be here for the little ceremony that was planned but you'd understand that he associated himself fully in the tribute to you and to your brother.'

'I wonder what it could be,' Frere said. And looking at his watch: 'It's really quite late. Do you suppose the Secretary General is really coming?'

The banquet went on with courses of fruits and various sweets which many of the guests who had dropped out of several courses previously were now able to partake of gingerly. There was still considerable circulation and the drinking of toasts; but all rather subdued and occasionally there were glances at watches and looks all about as if to ask 'what is to happen next?'

Frere was wondering if there might simply be some kind of announcement that the occasion was over when the music stopped and there was a hush and a craning of necks toward the main entrance way. And then, entering the room alone, looking very fit and handsome in a white achkhan cut to suit his slim figure, appeared none other than Pir Dato!

He walked straight to Frere's table, shook hands with Frere, who had risen, and urged the others to remain seated. He led Frere to the dais where the musicians had put aside their instruments and the two of them stepped up on the platform where they were in full view of all the guests.

Was the evening going to end with his being congratulated on his services to the Socialist Republic of Malia by Pir Dato? Frere wondered – the man who of all those enjoying great political power was possibly most suspicious of him? What a supreme irony!

And then a bleaker thought occurred to him. What if Pir Dato had arranged the whole affair and had merely made use of the Secretary General's name! What if Leela had persuaded him to do it, as she had persuaded him to protect Chin's reputation, by using to the full and more whatever influence she had with him! Perhaps she felt it was the only way she could keep him from resigning from the post on which their position here depended! He shook his head to dislodge such thoughts as one of the musicians struck a gong to reinforce the call for quiet.

Pir Dato said: 'I bring you greetings from our Secretary General who regrets that he cannot be with you in person. There is no reason to be alarmed about his health; he is recovering from his recent illness. But his doctor has decided that undergoing the strain of coming here and joining with us in this celebration might put his recovery at some risk.' There was an audible sigh of disappointment and sympathy.

Pir Dato unfolded a single sheet of paper. 'The Secretary General wishes me to read out exactly what he has written for the occasion. These are his words: "I don't have to tell people anywhere in Malia, let alone this gathering here tonight, about Comrade Colin Frere and what we owe him. He came here voluntarily to take up the cause his brother died for so heroically. He has shared with us all the adventures of life in our jungle fortress; he has endured with us the dangers and hardships of the revolutionary war of liberation; and he has set forth with us on the road to socialism. He has interpreted our struggles, our difficulties and our successes, for working-class leaders in other lands and he has won friends for our Party and people all over the world. But, more important than that, he has proved himself our brave and generous comrade who has won a place in all our hearts." That is what Comrade Lee has said about Comrade Frere.'

There was loud applause at this point and Frere felt his eyes prickling with the emotion he felt. Pir Dato held up his hand again. When it was quiet he read further: '"I know that our Comrade would wish me to mention his gratitude to the comrades he has worked with most closely in the Publications Department and especially to Comrade Chin who, unfortunately, is no longer with us; but who will always be remembered for his great work in founding and developing our paper, *Das Vani*, and for his training of our young people to carry on the tradition of revolutionary journalism." That is what our Secretary General has written and I can assure you that there will be an appropriate memorial for Comrade Professor Chin.'

And Frere led the applause himself at this point. It was precisely what he had asked to be said about Chin in a note he had sent to the Secretary General and the sharp doubts about this ceremony in his honour which had momentarily stabbed him were withdrawn.

When it was quiet again, Pir Dato continued: 'It is the wish of Secretary General Lee and of the Secretariat and of the Central Committee and, I'm sure it will be the wish of all here, that Comrade Colin Frere's contribution to Malia's achievements and his recording of those achievements for people in other lands to read about should be commemorated in some way. I hereby bestow,' reaching into his pocket and withdrawing a beautifully worked gold medal suspended from a red silk ribbon, 'on our Comrade this token of our gratitude.' He placed the ribbon around Frere's neck as he bowed his head to receive it; and as he straightened there was more applause.

When the clapping had died down, Pir Dato added:

'That medal, fashioned by the goldsmiths of the Central Bazaar, is the insignia of the Order of Friendship. I can't tell you a lot about this Order because we've only just created it. We may have to wait for the only member so far to tell us more about its rules, prerogatives and responsibilities in due course.'

There was some chuckling at this and Frere was able to express some of the feeling which had been choking him in a burst of laughter. Pir Dato asked Frere if he wanted to say anything. Frere merely mumbled his thanks to those who had organised the celebration and to all who had come. 'That is often the way with writers,' Pir Dato said. 'They would rather go home and put their reflections down on paper than try to recount them in public. I'm sure we'll read a glowing account of tonight's affair in tomorrow's *Das Vani*.'

22

On a Wednesday night a few weeks later Frere and Leela were listening to a programme of classical Malian music on the radio. Suddenly the music stopped. There were two or three minutes of absolute silence. Then the announcement was made that Secretary General Lee was dead. He had died quietly an hour before. Nothing more was said. After another minute or so of silence the announcement was repeated, followed by a recording of solemn music. They stayed tuned to the same capital city station but there was nothing more.

'But I thought he was slowly getting better,' Frere said almost resentfully. As if to all the other disasters Malia had recently been subjected to was now added this gratuitous one of the Fates themselves playing tricks on them. 'That's what we all thought,' Leela wailed.

The next morning *Das Vani* came out with a black border around the edges of the front page. The paper was full of encomia on the great leader and all that he had done for the people of Malia. But there were no details about the cause of death and nothing at all about any question of succession or how the business of government was to be carried on.

There were frequent announcements over the radio that at noon there would be a funeral speech from the gallery of the People's Palace which would be broadcast to the country at large. There was no school that day and Frere and Leela took Matt with them when they joined many thousands of people in the Square.

At precisely twelve o'clock Pir Dato appeared on the gallery and expressed on behalf of the whole country the great sense of loss everyone was feeling.

'But let us remember,' the loudly amplified voice rang out over the city, 'that death has never brought to an end a greater or more successful life. We must not be bowed down by our grief. We must express our joy at the privilege of having had such splendid leadership by throwing ourselves, heart and mind, into the struggle he led for a socialist Malia. Remember what he always told us: "It is people, not things, that are decisive. The contest of strength is not only a contest of military and economic power, but also a contest of human power and morale." Morale is most important for us at this time. I call on the Ministry of Information to help us turn what could have been the despondency at our tragic bereavement into the determination to realise our great leader's dream of a prosperous Malia from which exploitation has been eliminated.'

He went on to speak of the Secretary General's most recent efforts to mobilise the working people of Malia in the towns and on the land to take the lead in the march forward and of his wish to increase trade union representation in the Party to bring the country closer to the ideal of a true dictatorship of the proletariat. He ended with pledging that this campaign for direct working-class involvement, which was the logical continuation of the Socialist Now Movement, would be carried through to the end.

The silence of that vast crowd listening carefully to Pir Dato's memorial speech continued for some time after he had finished speaking. Only gradually did people begin to move and to comment on what they had heard in hushed voices.

Frere leaned down and spoke in Leela's ear. 'But why was such a speech not delivered by Kuan?'

'I don't know,' she said.

'Wasn't it generally understood that Commander Kuan was to be the Secretary General's successor?'

'You don't suppose – ' she began in some alarm.

'That things are so bad in the north that Kuan has had to go there,' he finished for her. 'Yes, that might be it.'

'The Antis might think we'd be thrown into confusion by the Secretary General's death. This could seem to them the time for an all-out attack.'

'And Commander Kuan has rushed up there to anticipate such a move. Yes,' Frere agreed, 'that seems the most likely explanation.'

'Not,' Leela said, 'that Comrade Pir Dato didn't speak well.'

'He always does. One has to give him that.'

Matt, who was holding Leela's hand, called up to them. 'Are we going home now?'

Leela thought for a moment and said to Frere: 'I'd like to go to the Central Committee rooms. I'm bound to find somebody who can tell me what's going on.'

Frere started to say something and hesitated. Then he said: 'I must go to the Communications Centre. I want to get them started on the special issue of *Workers' World* we've already planned. I'll take Matt with me and meet you back at the house.'

He took Matt to the canteen which was beginning to fill up with people who were coming back to the Centre from the Square. He bought two boxed lunches and with Matt in tow went up to the top floor. On the way to his office they passed an open door and Matt looked inside.

'There's Aunt Siti,' he said.

Siti invited them into her own small office. She had been rather side-lined since Kalan took over *Das Vani* and spent most of her time here writing the special articles she was assigned.

Frere could see that she had been crying. 'I can't help it,' she said. 'He was so close to us there at base camp. Ever since we've been here I've felt that they were keeping him away from us. When I listened to the speech, it was almost as though it were about someone else.'

'I know what you mean.' He lifted Matt onto a chair high enough for him to eat off the desk and opened the two boxes. He asked Siti if she wanted anything, but she shook her head. She got up and heated water for tea on a gas ring and set a cup before each of them. 'Thank you, Siti. Could I leave Matt with you while I deal with a few things? I won't be long.'

'Please do. Matt will cheer me up.'

'Well, I'll try,' the boy said.

Frere went to his office and took out the file he had been keeping against this very event. There were biographical articles dealing with the Secretary General's life up to World War Two, during the period of the liberation struggle and since the March Revolution. There were several more articles on his Thought which Leela had prepared at the Institute, well illustrated with excerpts from his own writings. The best-known sayings from the 'Essential Quotations' would be used throughout this issue as headings for articles or features or in the spaces between. He had also got Tinoo to work out some new and improved translations of a half dozen of Secretary General Lee's finest poems.

After going over all this material, Frere simply sat there staring at it – as if only now was he allowing himself to realise the tremendous loss this death represented to Malia and, indeed, to the whole world of the oppressed and exploited.

It had a very sobering effect on him. And then came the shock of his personal loss. Somehow, by some historical means that seemed quite mysterious to him now, this great, internationally known figure had been his friend, had chatted with him familiarly, had actually expressed a wish for his help which had changed his whole life and given it meaning.

He knew that this was only the beginning of his appreciating what Secretary General Lee had meant to the world and to him, which was and for long would continue to be beyond expression – just as the night before, when they first heard the news, he and Leela could only hold each other tightly, not saying a word, for a long time. He shook his head and rang the buzzer on his desk to summon the members of *Workers' World* staff who would be getting on with the tasks of setting up the special issue.

One of the most important articles, that dealing with measures taken to ensure that there would be no break in the political line of establishing a socialist Malia free of exploitation, would have to be dealt with when he had more information himself. Or, better, he would get Ang to write it.

When he got back to the bungalow with Matt, Leela was already there. She gave Matt his supper and put him to bed after what had been a big day for such a small child. She came back and sat beside Frere on the sofa and he put his arm around her shoulders. She looked solemn but she did not say anything about her visit to the offices of the Central Committee – rather as though she still had more thinking to do about it.

He told her what he had been doing at the Communications Centre. 'Most of the people I talked to were puzzled about the memorial address. They all thought of Kuan as a kind of heir designate and were surprised when he wasn't the one to speak.'

He left the question of 'why Pir Dato?' in her lap as it were, but she did not answer at once. When she did speak it was to say: 'When I arrived at the Central Committee council chamber, I was practically met by a delegation – just as if they knew I'd be coming. They put it to me that under the circumstances I ought to agree to become a full CC member.'

He did not ask if this request came from anyone in particular. 'What did you say?'

'I told them I would let them know as soon as possible. You remember what we were saying the other day about their making use of me, about their wanting me for their token woman.'

'But we decided that we'd make them pay for that, Leela. That they'd have to make you a party to everything they were thinking about, that you'd have to know about any splits or divisions. It seems to me more important than ever, now, that you should agree to what they're proposing.'

'Not for them. For us.'

'"Us" being all those in and out of power whom Comrade Lee taught to care only for liberating the people.'

'Yes, I'll tell them tomorrow.'

'It's important for me. I was thinking today that in the special issue I must include assurances that there will be no change in the policy of building socialism. You'll be able to advise me on what those assurances are.'

'That's very important. People will be thinking about what happened in the Soviet Union when Stalin died.'

'And what happened in China after Mao's death.'

'Only in Vietnam did a great leader leave behind a collective leadership that carried on without a break.'

'And that was partly,' Frere recalled, 'because Ho Chi Minh died when the war against the American aggressors was still raging. Remember how united we were during our liberation war!'

'If only – ' there was a catch of breath – 'if only we didn't have to think of all that. If only we could just, just give ourselves over for a while to our grief!'

She lowered her head in her hands and sobbed a few times. He tightened his arm around her. 'Unfortunately it can't be like that. He wouldn't want it to be like that.'

'No, he wouldn't.' She lifted her head and dabbed at her eyes.

'And what about Commander Kuan? Did anybody say where he was?'

'All anybody said was that as far as they knew he was right here. They certainly hadn't heard that he'd been sent anywhere.'

'But Pir Dato giving the memorial address?'

'Well, he *is* a good speaker, they said. They didn't think I ought to read any more than that into the situation.'

'What do you think, Leela, after being there and talking to them?'

'I know what I'm supposed to think – that it's a bit presumptuous of me to believe anything but that Kuan's quietly getting on with running things while others relieve him of certain distracting public duties.'

'But that's not Kuan's way,' Frere objected. 'You know that, Leela. He always leads from the front. He likes to be out there where everybody can see him – his comrades so that they can be encouraged by his example, the enemy so that he takes the same risk his men do. He's hardly one of your back-room boys. I'm worried about him.'

'I know. He was on that last guerrilla operation your brother was involved in, wasn't he?'

'And he was the first member of the Liberation Command I met. In fact he organised the foray which covered my slipping away from the puppet police and getting to base camp to begin with.'

'Perhaps we're unduly alarmed.'

'I don't know. He's such a big, amiable, noisy man, it seems unnatural not to be hearing him in the present stillness. One expected that strong voice to be helping us get over this sad time.' He shook his head reminiscently. That bravery and that tremendous zest for life. That deep laugh of his which started as a rumble far down inside him, like the first signs of a volcanic eruption, and then burst forth in a great explosion of sound! 'It seems eerie not to hear the sound of Kuan. It makes one feel that something's wrong.'

Frere had been right in supposing that the banquet in his honour would help him get approval for the scheme he had discussed with Noor Fajan. Funds were provided for the Writers' Union to acquire the space and appoint the scholars, translators and clerks needed to organise exchanges of literature with other countries. Noor Fajan would keep an eye on the project and Frere would see to the publications side until such time as Tinoo could be brought over from Education to take overall charge.

A paper was issued by the Writers' Union which demonstrated that the points Chin had been trying to make to the young people who attacked him were not in conflict with what the Secretary General had said when launching the Socialist Now Movement. When he said that 'all culture, all literature and art belong to definite classes and serve definite political ends' he did not mean that the culture of one class has to destroy the culture of another, as some of the young people had thought when burning beautiful old palm-leaf scriptures in the Square or defacing paintings by European artists. He meant that one class might use culture for purposes of elitist exclusivity while another class might use culture for the revolutionary emancipation of all, and further develop existing culture in the process. Culture, like language, belonged by right to a whole people. Even the Western cultural stream which, as a result of British occupation, had flowed into the lives of the Malian people, mainly the upper class to begin with, was, with the revolutionary spread of education, becoming a strand in the native culture belonging to all. This was the understanding of culture on which the exchange of literature was to be organised – a cultural exchange among countries which was in the interest of the people of Malia as they built their socialist society. In so far as it was an application of the ideas of the Secretary General, the setting up of the Department of Cultural Exchange could be seen as a way of 'raising our morale for the revolutionary contest of human power' as had been urged by Pir Dato in his memorial address.

Only a few nights later the same thing happened as when the Secretary General's death had been announced. There was a completely arbitrary break in the programme Frere and Leela had been listening to on the radio, followed by several minutes of absolute silence – a silence that became more ominous the longer it lasted. And then a voice stated emotionlessly: 'Commander Kuan is dead. He died by his own hand.' Just that. Nothing more.

They were silent themselves for a time and could hear each other's heavier breathing. Then Frere burst out: 'That's a lie! Oh, not his death. I think we've known that all along. But suicide! Kuan would never do that.'

'No, he wouldn't,' was all Leela could say. 'Unless – '

'Nothing would make Kuan kill himself – not the worst torture imaginable, whether of his own sick body or inflicted by others.'

'No, I think you're right.'

'I wonder if I ought to try to get in touch with Ang.'

'I wouldn't,' she advised. 'Wait till I've heard what's said at tomorrow's meeting of the Central Committee.'

In the next day's *Das Vani* there was nothing but a black box on the front page with the news of Commander Kuan's death and, again, the statement: 'He died by his own hand.' As if it was something that no one else would or *could* do to him.

No one Frere saw at the Communications Centre knew anything more than he did and he could not bring himself to ask Kalan whether there was any information the paper was holding back for some reason. Certainly those who had been at base camp were as sceptical about Kuan's having committed suicide as he was.

He returned home early, eager to know what Leela might have found out; but she did not get back till much later.

'Wait a minute,' she begged. 'Let me get my breath,' as he began questioning her straight away.

'Have you eaten?' he asked. 'Come into the kitchen. I can heat up what I left of supper while you tell me what's been happening.'

She sat down at the table and began telling him about the meeting of the Central Committee. 'Most of the time was taken up with a very full account of the desperate situation the country's in. It's much worse than we imagined, Colin.'

'Yes, one suspected that they were keeping things back for the sake of public morale.'

'We knew about the bad grain harvest but we didn't know that the Soviet Union isn't supplying us with grain any more. They've also cut off our supply of oil. Petrol is about to be rationed.'

'Maybe that will enforce the decision taken some time ago about the private use of motor cars.'

'But what about oil-fired power stations? What about our diesel trains?'

'Yes, of course.'

'Medical supplies came to us from the West by way of Czechoslovakia or Poland and that seems to have stopped too. Our hospitals and medical centres are running out of medicine.'

'But there must still be an abundance of local remedies.'

'Yes, but what about antibiotics and insulin and things like that? Our intensive-care units are equipped almost entirely from the West and already there's concern about premature births.'

'The attack on our children never ends, does it?' Frere said bitterly.

'The worst of it is that, because we've been so close to Vietnam, China includes us in its boycott of Vietnam.'

'During the Cultural Revolution they hung a capitalist roader sign on Deng Xiaoping and marched him through the streets of Beijing. A bullet in the back of the head is what Ang would have prescribed!'

'So what we're facing,' Leela summed up, 'isn't just some shortages and rationing of non-essential goods. We're facing very tough times indeed.'

'And who reported all this? Was it – '

'No,' she answered quickly. 'Hadar delivered the report – as Minister of Information and Communications.'

'But what about Kuan?'

'The desperate plight of the country is very relevant to what's happened to Commander Kuan. Apparently he only became aware of how bad the situation is when he took his place alongside the Secretary General.'

'As his successor, we assumed.'

'Be that as it may, when he found out the true state of affairs, he felt that something had to be done about it. And here I must tell you that some implied criticism of the Secretary General crept into Hadar's report. Without any specific charge it was hinted that the Secretary General toward the end just couldn't face giving the people such bad news when they'd rallied so splendidly to his call for a greater effort.'

'It wasn't like the Secretary General to keep anything back from the people; but then he was very ill during the last months.'

'Anyway, when Kuan found out, he decided that something must be done immediately to relieve the situation. So – and this is what it's so difficult to believe – so he thought of approaching the British Government to see what political concessions they would demand before releasing Malia's blocked reserves.'

'Approached them on his own, without consultation with the Secretary General? No, I don't believe that. Not for a minute.'

'What was said was that he didn't want to put the Secretary General in the position of having to consider such a reversal of policy before finding out just how punitive the terms for releasing the blocked currency would be. Of course if he *could* get the use of those funds which really belong to Malia then a lot of our immediate problems could be solved.'

'So he approached Britain on his own.'

'Yes. And it was found out by our Security. Even though it was understood why Commander Kuan had taken such a step, it *did* amount, in strict terms, to dealing with a hostile government with which Malia has no diplomatic relations.'

'In other words, a traitorous act.'

'Kuan was told that there must be a public trial.'

'I see,' Frere said doubtfully.

'Commander Kuan wrote out a statement explaining his reasons for what he'd done and then shot himself.'

Frere sat down opposite her and they looked at each other for some time. 'When things start going wrong, there's no end of it, is there?'

And then she said something very much like what he had thought himself a few weeks ago. 'There seems to be no connection any more between what we all do to advance the cause of socialism and what happens to our country. Or if there is a connection, it's made by others, not ourselves.'

He reached across the table and took her hand in his. 'And do you believe that's just how it all happened?'

'No. They've worked it out very cunningly. There's little discredit on Kuan who, after all, was acting from the best of motives and there's considerable credit for those in absolute power who allowed him to make his exit in such a dignified way.'

'And they've been able to launch the idea of coming to terms with Britain in order to see what public response there is.'

'Exactly so.'

'What really happened was that when the question of surrendering to Britain was raised, Kuan was adamant in opposition. So he had to be got rid of.' He tightened his grip on her hand while he waited for her response to his blunt way of putting it.

'Yes,' she simply said.

'And what did Ang say to all this?'

'Comrade Ang wasn't there. I asked about him and was told that he's ill.'

'There's another amazing coincidence!' Frere burst out and banged on the table with his other hand. 'What it means is that they've decided to pay the price Britain demands to get our own money back and be able to trade with the West.'

'Perhaps they won't take the decision on their own. Perhaps they'll put it to the public for their response.'

'And who's to tell us what that response is? Hadar?'

'Anyway, everything I've told you will be in tomorrow's *Das Vani*; but naturally we on the Central Committee had to be told first. I'm surprised none of your colleagues on *Das Vani* said anything to you about that arrangement.'

'My relations with the *Das Vani* editorial board practically ended when Kalan took over the editorship. And then when I wrote the workplace democracy articles which they were forced to use – '

When Frere went into the Communications Centre the next day, he talked with various people about the Kuan revelations which had come out that morning. Most of them seemed willing to accept the account of the matter as set forth in *Das Vani*. There was hardly anybody left he could discuss such matters with freely any more.

He did raise with Siti the question of whether he ought not to go ahead and bring out the special edition of *Workers' World* celebrating the life and thought of Secretary General Lee and leave to a subsequent issue the question of how the political and economic advance to socialism was to be continued.

'I think you better had,' Siti told him. 'It could be some while before we're clear about what's to follow. I just wish Chin was here to guide us.'

'Yes.'

He tried several times to get through to Ang; but he was not at the secretariat office and he was not at his flat. He had no relatives whom Frere could ask about him.

That evening Leela was able to tell him what the Political Bureau had decided about the arrangements to carry on the Government during the present crisis. 'It's been decided,' she explained, 'that the best way to ensure continuity is that those who were primarily concerned with the Socialism Now Movement which Secretary General Lee started should take over the collective leadership of the country.'

'Let me guess,' Frere said. 'Pir Dato and Hadar for a start. They don't mean those who were concerned with the Socialism Now Movement, but those who used it! Who else?'

'You'll never guess who the third person in the triumvirate is to be.'

'It won't be the person who ought to be there – Ang. I've been trying to get hold of him all day. Was he at your meeting?'

'No. Nobody could tell me where Ang was. Do you give up on who the third person's to be?'

'I give up.'

'Our good friend, Comrade Ahmed.'

'No!'

'Yes. Because he helped workers take over the Socialism Now Movement. It's the way the triumvirate demonstrates that the Government is still a dictatorship of the proletariat.'

'I see,' Frere said. 'Pir Dato becomes Secretary General – '

'It's been decided that the title, Secretary General, has become so identified with Comrade Lee that it won't be used any more.'

'Hadar, of course, has absolute control of everything that gets printed or published, which is very useful for any government. And Ahmed

– Ahmed provides them with cover. I wonder if Ahmed realises he's being cut off from his base and rendered harmless.'

Leela paused for a considerable time and then she said: 'I wonder if we ought to be completely negative about this, Colin.'

'But you don't think – '

She put her hand on his arm to stop him. 'I have the same doubts that you have. But what can we do? Don't we have to work in any way we can to have *some* say in what they're doing? Don't we have to be willing to go along with what they say they're doing in order to try to make sure that what they actually do is in accord with the ideas of our great Secretary General? Shouldn't you, Colin, be thinking that Ahmed's inclusion in the ruling collective might give you something of a voice there?'

Did she mean, Frere wondered, that Pir Dato's position did the same for her? He did not answer at once. He could not help but think that his own dear Leela was being taken in again. Was it because being so passionately concerned with the success of the socialist experiment in her country she simply could not bear the thought of its failing, could not bear to think of people who had suffered so much and fought so hard being let down by those pledged to serve them – including herself? He said: 'It seems to me that this is something Pir Dato planned decades ago, back in base camp. And now at last he's brought it off. And the two men associated with him he knows he can dominate completely, Hadar because he's a crook who can be threatened with exposure and Ahmed because he's too high-minded and inexperienced to be able to cope with such practised cunning.'

'But over those decades,' she reminded him, 'didn't the Secretary General himself put his trust in Pir Dato? Isn't your reaction due in part to the fact that no one, no one at all, could have taken over from our beloved Comrade Lee without our feeling a terrible sense of letdown?'

'Well yes, but – '

'While he was still among us, with his modest, unassuming manner and his quiet poet's voice, so compassionate where his comrades were concerned and so precisely relentless with those who exploited us, we couldn't altogether appreciate what a magnificent leader he was. Not until he was laid low did we fully realise how he towered over us.'

'That's true.'

'Think of succeeding someone like that! Don't we have to try to support those who assume the tremendous task of trying to follow in his footsteps – particularly if it's the only way we can have any influence at all in what happens?'

'That support might be more forthcoming if there wasn't any question of deceit in the way those assuming such a task were appointed.'

'The Political Bureau proposed them. The Central Committee approved – unanimously.'

'But we know how Pir Dato won control of the Political Bureau.'

She thought about that for a few moments. 'What if someone is so sure that he's the right person to carry on the great work of building socialism that he's prepared to cut corners to get the chance of proving it? What if he's willing to do questionable things to gain control because he's so certain he's the person to achieve what all of us want? Perhaps leadership always has to begin with a more or less illegitimate assumption of power which can only be vindicated eventually by those he's supposed to be serving?'

'Is that what you think of Pir Dato?'

'I don't know. We'll have to see. But who else is there?'

'Comrade Ang.'

'Yes, perhaps Comrade Ang; but he's taken no steps to put himself in such a position.'

Frere shook his head and said ruefully: 'Maybe I think those who have a right to lead would never have the arrogance to assume such a responsibility.'

But Tinoo, when Frere looked in on him the next day to talk about the cultural-exchange project, was practically shaking with anger at what he had read in that morning's paper. 'To think that so many good comrades down the years should have died so that a rogue like Hadar could rule over us!'

Frere glanced significantly around the office.

'Of course it's bugged!' Tinoo exclaimed. 'Otherwise it wouldn't be worthwhile shooting my mouth off about what a villain he is. I should have spoken out when he was responsible for the attack on poor old Chin. I let you and Leela talk me out of it – partly on the grounds that Hadar was bound to get his just deserts in due course; and what happens? He's promoted to one of the most powerful positions in the land!'

'You know *he* isn't powerful, Tinoo. He's just being made use of.'

'Like your friend, Ahmed?'

'So he's become *my* friend now!'

'I don't see how he can be mine – if he's part of the Red Triumvirate. I call it the Bloody Triumvirate. Look at what's happened to Kuan. You don't believe what they said about Kuan, do you?'

'No, I don't.'

'And maybe Hadar is only being used; but while that's the case he can still do a lot of damage.'

'I wonder. I suspect he's being kept well under control. Perhaps you oughtn't to attack the whole threesome, Tinoo.'

'Why not? It isn't some Holy Trinity. I'm sorry about Ahmed; but if he allows himself to get sucked into – '

'Just think about Pir Dato. He's the one who matters. It's too late to do anything about his taking over. We have to see if, by supporting him, we can help him hew to the Secretary General's line. That's what Ahmed must have decided. I think perhaps it's right.'

'You think so, or is it Leela who thinks so?'

Frere looked at him and pursed his lips; but he did not answer.

'I'm sorry,' Tinoo apologised. 'But you know what it's all about, don't you. It was obvious after the lies they told about Kuan's death. We're going to see reforms adopted. Only minor reforms, of course, little changes like switching over to a market economy and allowing Britain to start exploiting the hell out of us all over again.'

'Nothing like that,' Frere protested. 'There may be some compromises to get us out of the economic crisis we're in but – '

'You'll see!'

'What I mainly see,' Frere insisted, 'is that we must press on with anything we're doing which had the blessing of the Secretary General. If we can prove that it had his backing, I don't think any effort will be made to stop it. And that includes our cultural-exchange programme. Noor Fajan has set up a headquarters in the Writers' Union and is just waiting for you to come and take over. Have you heard anything about your release from the Education Section?'

'I understand it's going through – if the scheme survives the new regime.'

'It will survive.'

'I wonder. Has it occurred to you, Colin, that what the Secretary General intended as a celebration of your continuing to edit *Workers' World* may have been turned by Pir Dato into your pensioning-off ceremony?'

'Nothing about my going has been said to me yet.'

'There's never any warning, you know. You only know when it's already happened and it's too late to do anything about it.'

'*You'd* better be careful, Tinoo. Until we get this cultural-exchange programme going. Then if they decide they don't want me to go on editing *Workers' World*, I can come and work with you and Noor Fajan. I wish I could talk with Ang about all this.'

'You haven't been able to reach him, have you?'

'No.'

'The same thing's happened to Ang that happened to Kuan.'

'I don't believe that.'

As Frere left the Education Building he was thinking that Tinoo, always so outspoken, might be in serious danger. He must think about how he might protect Tinoo from the consequences of expressing himself too openly about the changes. Perhaps Leela could help. It was almost like finding himself in his brother's position all those years ago with a wounded Tinoo on his hands.

He walked toward the People's Palace determined to find out about Ang. He had hardly noticed before that it was a very pleasant day. He looked around him as he made his way across the Square. Everything looked the same – the same boxed oleanders set out in geometric order, the same people walking to and fro about their business, some of whom nodded and waved to him as he passed them, the same statue to the heroes of the Revolutionary War. Beyond that, just opposite the entrance to the Assembly Chamber, was where it was intended to raise a great marble mausoleum as a memorial to the Secretary General, though there had been a certain amount of comment about the irony of someone with such simple tastes having imposed on him such a grandiose monument.

Everything looked the same. But it did not feel the same. It was almost as if he were seeing the same general scene but through different eyes, as though he were getting disconcerting flashes of how Malia might look to others, the way it might appear, for instance, to a journalist with little knowledge of the country's history seeing it for the first time or a returned imperialist taking a jaundiced view of a country he knew from an entirely different point of view. It was like a *trompe-l'oeil*, a cube, perhaps, which, looked at one way, was a contained space stretching away from a free observer outside of it, but, looked at another way, reached backward to imprison that same observer in a cramped cell.

He shook his head. Was he not, as Leela had said, giving too much importance to the jockeying for political position that was bound to occur after the demise of a leader like Lee? While it was perfectly possible to work out an orderly succession for replacing ordinary office-holders, when it was a question of finding a substitute for the man who had formed the Party, inspired the struggle, led them to victory and presided over all their peacetime efforts – well, there was bound to be a certain amount of turmoil created by the vacuum left. Ang would help him sort it out.

But when he presented himself at the side entrance of the People's Palace, he got again that sensation of things looking the same but being somehow different. He went in and out of the building two or three times a week and thought nothing of it at all. He usually exchanged salutations with the soldiers on guard but these two stood rigidly at attention looking straight ahead. And the officer on duty at the desk inside the door was no one Frere had ever seen before. This officer seemed to take a long time examining Frere's identity card instead of simply waving him through as usually happened.

'Do you have an appointment with anyone?' the officer wanted to know.

'I don't have an appointment but there is someone I want to see.'

'Who's that?'

Frere had a sudden thought that it might not be a good idea to mention Ang's name. 'Look here,' he said, 'I'm the editor of *Workers' World* and I often come here to see various people in connection with my work.'

The officer merely shook his head and started to hand back the identity card. 'Ring Comrade Pir Dato's office,' Frere told him. 'Ask them if I'm not to be allowed to enter.' The result of the call was to make the officer a bit more friendly. 'We have to be careful,' he said, standing aside so that Frere could pass.

Frere walked up a flight of marble stairs and down a long corridor toward the small chamber behind which were the offices of the Secretariat. It had never struck him before just how long this corridor was, with so many offices along it in which people seemed to be perpetually shut up. He could not remember whether in the past he had ever seen anybody coming out or going into any of them. And there were several intersections with other corridors stretching away to the right or the left with numerous other offices as firmly closed. He had an inclination to knock on one of the doors, just to see if there was anybody inside. Better not. He walked through the small chamber which seemed not just empty of the delegates who occasionally met there but actually deserted by them – as though some alarm had put them all to flight.

When he got to the door of the office of Ang's personal assistant, he did knock. There was no answer and he knocked again. He tried the door, which was unlocked, and opened it. There was no one there, making him wonder in an instant panic if the whole building had been evacuated. The inner door to Ang's adjoining office was ajar and he went in. Ang was not there and the top of his desk was as clear of papers or writing gear as if the office were quite unoccupied. There was a large filing case against the wall which was locked and nothing else in the room at all.

He wandered around the labyrinth of passages and offices making up the Secretariat section trying to find someone he could ask about Ang. He found several junior officials looking rather like zombies behind their cleared desks but they could not tell him anything about the man who was supposed to be their chief. It was all beginning to seem very eerie to Frere and then, at the end of one of the corridors where there was a flight of stairs leading upwards, he could hear sounds of activity.

He climbed the stairs and came to a large room which was a scene of the most frantic activity. There were some thirty or more people banging at electric typewriters, running off pages of print on a couple of mimeograph machines, looking up details in card indices, sketching cover designs on lay-out sheets, speaking into tape recorders and all shouting at each other and frequently laughing at a joke one of them had made as they dashed about the room. It was as if all the animation which seemed to have been drained from the rest of the Assembly Building had been concentrated here in this chaos of frenzied movement that was as unnerving in its way as the deathly hush that had fallen on the Secretariat.

Frere found someone who seemed to be in charge, if anybody really was, and learned that this lot had been pulled together from all over the building to get out a statement of government intent which had to be in the hands of the managers of factories and state farms all over the country, within the next two days.

'But what is it?' Frere asked.

'It's the final stage of the Socialism Now Movement as it's to be implemented by the entire working class. Here. Have a copy.'

Frere took the pamphlet and thrust it in his pocket. 'Whose idea is it?'

'Our new chief, Comrade Ahmed, I think. But it's going out in the names of all three of the joint Heads of State.'

'The Red Triumvirate.'

'Yes, the Red Triumvirate.'

'But why is it all being done here? Why not in the Communications Building?'

'Security.'

'I see,' doubtfully. 'Do you know anything about Comrade Ang downstairs? I can't find anybody in the Secretariat who has any idea of what's become of him.'

'Come to think of it, I haven't seen Comrade Ang recently.' He called out to the others. 'Anybody know anything about Comrade Ang?'

No one did. Frere thought of trying to see Ahmed but decided that under the circumstances it would be better if he made an appointment. He did not know whom to ask about Ang. Those most likely to be able to help him, Chin, Kuan or Lee himself, were all dead. It shocked him to realise it like that.

Although he had been unable to get Ang by telephone at his home, he decided to go to his flat anyway and see if he could find any evidence of where he might be. Ang lived very simply in one of the new residential blocks not far from the People's Assembly. His flat was on the ground floor at the very end and had its own entrance. There was a carefully cultivated flowerbed with exotic blooms in front.

Frere rang the bell and could hear no sound inside. He knocked on the door and then, stepping carefully to avoid the flowers, peered through one of the windows. There was a shout and he turned around and saw two policemen who had just come out of the main entrance. 'What do you want?' one of them demanded

Frere stepped back on to the pavement and explained that he was looking for Secretariat Member Ang who lived there.

And when they asked him why, he shrugged and said he was a friend who was concerned about whether Ang was all right.

'He's not here.'

'Do you know where he is?' Frere asked.

Now an officer had come up and was asking the two policemen what the trouble was.

'We saw him,' pointing at Frere, 'trying the door and then going over and trying to look through the window.'

'Have you any business here?' the officer asked him brusquely.

'Look. Comrade Ang is my good friend. I haven't seen him or heard from him recently and I'm worried about him. If you can help me find out –'

'He's not here. This flat is under guard and no one is to be allowed in.'

'Can you just tell me something about Comrade Ang? Has he been taken to hospital?'

'I know nothing – except my orders, which are to keep anybody from going inside that flat and take the name of anyone who comes prying around. Show me your identification.'

Frere produced it and the officer took down his name. 'Is that all?' Frere asked.

'That's all for now.'

Walking back to the bungalow, Frere kept thinking about how things had changed. He could not remember ever having had a run-in with police or security guards before. Was that because he had never in the time before ever had the slightest difference with those who ultimately commanded such forces or was it because this was a Rani Kalpur in which such forces were going to be much more in evidence?

One of the first things he said to Leela when she got back was not to pursue openly the question of what had become of Ang. 'If you hear anything or if you can steer a conversation around to some mention of Ang without committing yourself, that's good. But don't, please, Leela, ask about him directly.'

'No, I won't. But it seems so strange to me to have to take that kind of care among my own comrades.'

'Things have changed.'

'Yes, I know', she said quietly.

'You know what I was thinking as I was walking back? Ang seems to have gone; Tuck's dead and Kuan's dead. Tinoo's under threat. All of those who were with Matt on that last action, those I could talk to about Matt and felt closest to, are gone now – or going. It's almost as if there were a spell on them.'

'It's more likely,' she said, 'that particularly staunch defenders of the line of our Secretary General would prove to be obstacles to any change of line that might be thought necessary.'

He did not ask: 'Shouldn't *I* be thought of in those terms, shouldn't *we* be?' but she was aware of his not asking it and took his hand in hers.

'We must be very careful,' she said.

He told her about the frantic work on a new pamphlet he had seen in the People's Palace when he was looking for Ang. 'I don't know why that work wasn't being done at the Communications Centre. That's where most Party publications are printed. They had collected all the gear they needed and were running off copies right there in the Secretariat.' He gave her a copy.

She looked at it curiously. 'Have you studied it?'

'I just glanced through it. I got the impression that it's a way of getting people in the factories and on the farms to work harder by means of some kind of bonus scheme. It all seemed to be connected with Ahmed's having been made one of the Red Triumvirate.'

'You know what this is!' she exclaimed after reading a few paragraphs. 'It's a major policy statement which is being rushed out without having been seen by the Central Committee.'

'Perhaps it was considered to be a matter of such urgency – '

'Not urgency, Colin. Secrecy. The Institute has been working on a draught document along these lines that's about to be presented to the Central Committee. A little while ago those of us who have been most closely associated with the use of dialectical materialism in workplaces to solve practical problems of production were asked to deal with the question of incentives. Some thought was needed on the question of how the initial enthusiasm of the Socialism Now Movement could be best utilised for the long haul of creating a well-founded socialist society.'

'Yes, I remember your telling me about it. Something to do with working out some of the theoretical and practical implications of organised workers taking over the main thrust of the Movement from the youth.'

'That's right. Well, this seems to me to be a rush job which ignores the work of the Institute and bypasses the Central Committee. It seems to be intended to short-circuit any further consideration of a vital subject by a top-level ukase.'

'You read it, Leela. I'll get us some tea and biscuits or something and then we can talk about it. Or rather, you can tell me about it.'

When he came back to the room with two cups of tea and some biscuits, she had finished reading the pamphlet and was sitting there with her hands folded in her lap, brows drawn together in a frown.

'It starts just where we did at the Institute,' she said. 'It was felt that, as the Socialism Now campaign reached its final phase in places of work all over the country, something more was needed than the flat "Fight Self-Interest" slogan of the earlier phase when the Secretary General first launched the Movement.'

'Yes, we talked about that.' He had put the tray on the table and now he sat down beside her.

'We started off, you remember, with the Secretary General's remarks about the harmful effects of giving exaggerated importance to personal interests. Because it means giving priority to the individual over the collective; to the interests of the moment over those of the future; to material not to moral incentives. Hence the slogan "Fight Self-Interest"!' She paused and took a sip of tea. 'Have one of these biscuits. But then we went on to say that self-interest was nonetheless an objective fact, quite rational and legitimate. Society is not something abstract but is composed of people, with all their individual needs, just as general interest is not something abstract but is made up of all the vital interests of workers. Therefore the fight is not against the very existence of self-interest but against placing it above general interest. We are for combining and harmonising them by subjecting personal interests to the interests of the working class, of the people, of socialism. That's roughly the line we were developing, taking the revolutionary slogan of "fighting self-interest" in order to change society and then turning it into the socialist slogan "subject personal interests to the interests of the working class." But there's no reference to any of that in this pamphlet.'

'I thought that's what it was saying.' He took the pamphlet from her and thumbed through several pages. 'Here. It says: "Replacing all individualistic competition with pure socialist emulation was something a great leader like Comrade Lee, enjoying the devotion of the whole people, could demand. We" – meaning the three signatories to the pamphlet, of course – "don't feel that we're in a position to demand so much. We believe that the natural desire for material rewards must be harnessed to the wagon of socialism" and so forth and so forth. Isn't that what you were saying?'

'No, it isn't. It's one thing to *subject* self-interest to the collective interest in building socialism. It's quite another to say that naked self-interest can be made to *work* for socialism, that purely materialist incentives can actually *build* socialism.'

'Yes, I see. That's like the line of the philosophers of individual liberalism, like Adam Smith. In a capitalist market economy all the competing individual interests simply modify each other for the general good.'

'That's right.'

'You understand these things better than I do.'

'Only at the level of abstractions, Colin. If this system of bribing people for good work were put into practice, you would see the difference clearly enough. It's also, by implication, a way of depriving those who *don't* do such good work. And who's to decide? It could easily become an attack on fair wages for a day's work and even the right to work at all. I simply don't know what's happening any more. The Institute is given a job to do and then something like this is dashed off behind its back.'

Frere looked at her seriously. 'I don't believe this pamphlet represents Ahmed's views. It certainly isn't what he was talking about the day he relieved the young people of their responsibility at the Number One Textile Plant.'

'No, I don't either. It's what we said before. Ahmed is being used to make a change in the Socialism Now line look like a further development of it.'

'Red Triumvirate!' Frere shook his head solemnly.

'It's almost waving the red flag to defeat the red flag,' Leela quoted. She shook her head too. 'I just don't know what to think any more. We never thought it was going to be easy; but we seemed, all of us united together, to be embarking on a great adventure. History having made us, we were beginning to make history – our own history! Not like the old explorers and conquerors who opened up new territories for exploitation. We weren't driven by greed, nor by the desire for fame, but simply by our concern for the collective good of our people, the people of Malia and our understanding that in the long run nothing could be good for the people of Malia that wasn't good for working people everywhere. How could we fail when what we wanted was so right!'

'I know, my darling.'

'And this,' she picked up the pamphlet distastefully. 'Is it betrayal? Or is it that with the whole capitalist world determined to destroy us, desperate measures to mollify them are necessary?' She turned to him and placed her cheek on his chest. 'Oh, my dearest Colin, what are we to do?'

23

Several times when he was walking around the streets near the old bazaar area Frere was aware of boys and young men hanging about in groups with, apparently, nothing to do. On one occasion one of them stopped Frere and asked for money. Frere put his hand in his pocket for his coin purse and then stopped. What had suddenly come back to him was the memory of this part of Rani Kalpur when he had first arrived, full of beggars of all ages, mothers with hungry babies in their arms, children whining as they held out their hands, old men with twisted, misshapen limbs. He shook his head as if to rid himself of that awful recollection. The young man took the gesture as a denial of his request and started to turn away.

'Wait a minute,' Frere held him there. 'Do you and those others live here? Don't you have work to do?'

The young man explained that when thousands of families had been moved out of the northern border strip under threat from the Antis, no proper provision had been made for them in neighbouring provinces and many of them had drifted to the towns, mainly Rani Kalpur, looking for work. They had been joined by others from those parts of Malia worst hit by drought, where there was unemployment on the land. When Frere gave the young man some coins, other youths gathered around them hoping to get something for themselves.

'And there's no work for any of you?' Frere asked. They shook their heads.

This was the worst thing of all, Frere thought dejectedly. The one great principle of the Socialist Republic of Malia was that of absolutely full employment. No one who wanted to work should ever be out of a job. He took out of purse and wallet all the money he had on him and gave it to the young man who had first spoken to him to divide among the rest.

'Don't you get any relief at all?' he asked.

'They give us a pittance. It isn't enough to live on.'

'Not even to survive on,' someone else said.

'What about the families who have come to the city?' Frere wanted to know.

'There's an encampment near the river about five miles out of town. They've been given army tents and, at least, there's water to drink.'

'And food?' Frere wondered.

'Barely enough for the women and the little children.'

That night Frere complained to Leela. 'And there's been nothing about all this in *Das Vani*.'

'Of course not,' she said bitterly. 'That's why Hadar is a member of the Triumvirate.'

'But has nothing been said about these poor people in the Central Committee?'

'We've had a report that the best possible care has been taken of those driven from their homes by the attacks of the Antis. Some of them no doubt *have* been accommodated in various parts of the country. We've heard little about the actual conditions in that settlement outside of town.'

'I remember taking Clare Wallace around the rehabilitated area where the old bustee had been and showing her the fine residential blocks the people had built for themselves. I remember showing her the bright-faced children clustering around us where there had once been beggars and undernourished starvelings. Is that all going to come back?'

'No, Colin. It won't. We won't let it. I'll bring up the question of the way people who have been forced to come to the towns are being treated.'

'I don't know what the Central Committee can do if the Triumvirate has made up its mind to ignore the issue.'

She placed her hand on his forearm. 'We mustn't oversimplify things. There's no way of knowing whether the bad things that are happening began some while ago and only now have reached a point where the reform policies of the new government have to be taken or whether the reform policies being taken are the cause of the bad things that are happening. There's no way of knowing how much our problems are due to the imperialist enemy's renewing attacks on us in different ways and how much to our own people's tiring under the enormous strain put on them to build socialism entirely by their own efforts in the shortest possible time.'

'Or to the supreme Party functionaries and high-ranking bureaucrats here in Rani Kalpur thinking they have to solve those problems themselves on *behalf* of the working people of Malia instead of in *association* with them. Who, therefore, keep the problems and their proposed solutions to themselves.'

'Yes,' Leela agreed, 'that, too. We have to do what we can and that means being careful not to cut ourselves off from any possibility of discussion or action.'

'Of course.' He put his arm around her.

'And you must see Ahmed.'

'I will.'

But Tinoo did not observe any such discretion. After a visit to the river settlement, he used the weekly publication of the Education Department to describe how bad conditions were and to point out that there were no facilities for the education of children nor for literacy classes for adults. And then he went on to condemn the editorial policy of *Das Vani* in concealing the facts about the way people driven out of the northern border areas and off the land were being forced to live on the outskirts of the towns they had fled to. Then he ended by making it quite clear, though without actually naming him, that the main responsibility for hiding the truth from the people must be laid at the door of the former Information Minister.

The immediate result was that Tinoo was banished to the little town of Baidan on the edge of the jungle as the local education officer. Frere did not have to wait long to find out what effect Tinoo's banishment might have on the World Literature Project Tinoo and Noor Fajan were to manage jointly. Noor Fajan came to the Communications Centre to talk to Frere about it and they went down to the canteen together. Frere collected tea and cakes for them and found a relatively isolated table where they could talk freely.

'I suppose you know why I'm here,' Noor Fajan said.

'I can guess.'

'Have you seen Tinoo?'

'Yes, I saw him yesterday,' Frere answered. 'He told me that instead of being seconded to the Writers' Union to work with you on the project we talked about he was being exiled to a little town up north.'

'About the same time as he was being posted I received notice that the grant for establishing the Department of Cultural Exchanges had been withdrawn.'

Frere had expected it but all the same he felt a pang of disappointment at the end of something in which he had begun to take an excited interest. 'Just like that?'

'Just like that. We're out of business.'

'It's Hadar, of course. Is there any explanation?'

'Mainly that it costs too much. When the plan was approved in principle, the economy wasn't in such a parlous state as now. A way is being considered of achieving similar aims without its costing anything.'

'I can guess what that other way is,' Frere said bitterly. 'Letting the publishers in some capitalist country decide what literature's best for backward people and dumping it on us.'

'While Hadar probably gets a cut on the deal,' Noor Fajan said quietly.

'Exactly.'

Noor Fajan took a folded-up memo out of his pocket. 'There's a bit more if you want to hear it.'

'Go ahead.'

'It says that for a tiny committee which could hardly be called representative of this country to make a selection of world literature smacks too much of an elitist approach separated from the people.'

'Let me read that.' He took the sheet of paper and read the whole memo. 'Hadar, the great champion of the people against alienated intellectuals like you and Tinoo and me! Could I keep this? I want to show it to someone.'

'You're going to fight it?'

'I doubt it; but I'd like to think about it.'

'If you decide to fight against this decision, I'll try to help. But I don't know what use I'll be – now.'

'What do you mean, Comrade?'

'It's been suggested to me that I should resign from the secretaryship of the Writers' Union.'

'Oh, I'm so sorry.'

'I'm not. I can retire to my little cottage on the bank of the Andor and do nothing but write poetry – when I feel like it.'

'You're not just saying that.'

'No, I'm serious. You come and see me there, Comrade Colin. You'll find a contented old man to welcome you.'

'I will. And you can read me your latest poems.'

After Noor Fajan had gone, Frere got to thinking gloomily about how all the people he had known best and worked most closely with were disappearing from the active political scene. He recalled what someone had said about his ceremonial evening at the Palace being more of a golden handshake than a confirmation of continuing service. Would it be possible, he wondered, to live in a country trying desperately to establish socialism without being an integral part of that vital struggle? If he were not caught up in some active work contributing practically to the general ideological battle of class forces, if he found himself in the position of simply watching the political process going on all around him as a detached observer instead of as an involved partisan, how was it going to affect his understanding of the history this country was making?

It could be argued, and usually was in the West, that detachment enabled one to observe something more objectively, more as it really was; but that was only true of something dead and static which could be laid out on an operating table and carved up and analysed. To see and understand something in dramatic movement one had to be a part of it because the interaction between that lively, throbbing ever-changing active world of the new Malia and his own individual consciousness simply *was* the dialectic of understanding. To see something like this from the outside was to begin, however slightly at first, to see it in terms other than those it was formulating itself to describe its own progressive development and, therefore, to run the risk in the end of becoming indistinguishable from those who could *only* see it from the outside because of a biased rejection from the start of everything it really stood for.

He was terrified of finding himself becoming more and more a carping destructive critic of something vital and real simply because it had no need of him. He could see himself, politically speaking, clinging desperately to Leela like a non-swimmer in a shipwreck and perhaps – he shook his head violently to dislodge the dreadful thought – pulling her down too. It was fear of that which made him, when Leela asked if she ought to try to intervene on behalf of the cancelled literary project, almost shout his opposition. 'No! Don't! Don't do anything at all. There's nothing that *can* be done!'

She was somewhat taken aback, no doubt assigning his outburst to that old deep-seated jealousy of his which, for all that both of them knew there were no grounds for whatsoever, never entirely disappeared. 'There are *other* comrades I can discuss it with, Colin.'

'Oh, I'm sorry,' he said quickly. 'That's not what I meant at all. Look at this memo which was sent to Noor Fajan. That "unrepresentative member of the committee" who has no right to exercise an "elitist censorship" on what people are to read – that's me, Leela. I'm a foreigner and, not only that, I'm from the very country Malia has had to fight all these years in order to win its independence. What business has such a person holding any responsible post here?'

'Hadar's behind this.' She handed back the memo. 'It has more to do with Tinoo's involvement in the scheme than yours. And as for your having once been British, Hadar has a lot more to do with our former rulers than anyone else I can think of – and very likely for his own good rather than that of the country.'

'Is there any more talk of seeking a change of relationship with Britain, of trying to get the boycott lifted? I mean, that phoney story about Kuan's suicide – that was just kite flying.'

'Oh, there's plenty of talk but nothing at all official. Again, who can say whether our serious economic difficulties are the reason why there's rethinking about our diplomatic relations with Britain or whether our economic problems are being exaggerated and possibly even to some extent caused by those who would gain from improved relations with the capitalist world?'

Frere laughed ironically. 'Here's you a member of the Central Committee and a principal of the Marxist-Leninist Institute and me who's supposed to be informing the world of Malia's advance to socialism and we don't really know what's going on. Could you ever have imagined this happening, Leela, when we were back in base camp?'

'No. I couldn't. Of course, there's one person who might give us a clearer idea of what's really going on.' And quickly: 'I mean Ahmed.'

'Yes, I've been thinking of seeing him; but I suppose he has his hands full these days.'

'Don't forget, Colin. He called on you when he needed help. And you played a part in his being where he is now.'

'That's true. I wonder if he thanks me for it now.' And then, 'Yes,' he said, eyes brightening and a smile beginning, 'Ahmed, one whole third of the great Red Triumvirate! Of course, I'll see Ahmed.'

And a few days later, on his way to see the first friend he had made in Malia, a very junior guerrilla leader then, one of the three most important people in the country now, Frere was feeling better. If Hadar did not like him, he had never received other than the most courteous treatment from the most powerful of their number, even if he had a private reason for never asking him for the slightest favour.

The offices of the Collective Leadership of Three were at the very top of the People's Palace in a suite at the front of the building. Indeed, Pir Dato's huge high office, well-lit by numerous skylights, opened out onto the gallery from which important announcements and speeches were made and, on ceremonial occasions, the armed services were reviewed.

Frere hoped that he would be able to reach Ahmed's own office without encountering Hadar. This was no problem since each of the three of them could only be approached through a graded succession of personnel from secretary receptionist to personal assistant by way of several different smaller rooms like the chambers enabling divers to accustom themselves gradually to a more rarefied atmosphere.

When Frere finally entered the large office, Ahmed got up from behind an enormous desk and came around to shake his hand cordially and invite him to take a chair placed before the desk whereupon he went back and sat down again. 'A bit different from my office at the Textile Works,' he said with a laugh.

But the laugh did not sound quite as Frere remembered it and the words, though what might have been expected, did not ring exactly the same either. He supposed that being a member of the welcoming committee for every important delegation that arrived, entering into important political discussions with groups from inside the country or with various representatives of the socialist world, to say nothing of the opening of new factories, awarding of sports trophies, speaking at training colleges and all the other things one saw the Three constantly engaged in on television could not but change a person subtly – particularly someone like Ahmed who had suddenly been thrown into the midst of it all. It was as if the self-possessed, diplomatic manner he had to don so often never altogether came off, rather like professional actors Frere had known in England whose most casual greeting or deepest expression of feeling came across as an act.

Certainly the brief account Ahmed, at Frere's request, gave of his life now sounded like a setpiece.

Frere said: 'Another member of the old June Tenth Commune, my comrade wife, wishes me to pass on her warmest greetings in this new life of yours.'

'Tell Leela that I've often thought recently how nice it would be if my comrade wife and I slipped off from this new life and spent the evening quietly with two old friends.'

'Yes, I will.' Frere did not add to that.

Ahmed raised his eyebrows. 'Is this just a friendly meeting or did you have something you wanted to take up with me, Comrade Colin?'

'I wonder if "just friendly meetings" are possible in our country today, Comrade Ahmed.'

Ahmed thought about it a few moments. 'Probably not.' And it was as if the official mask he unconsciously wore these days had dropped away. 'Probably not. I'd been waiting for you to ask for an appointment. And when you did, I said to myself: "At last, someone I can really talk to!" Is it the cancellation of the Literary Exchange scheme you worked out with Noor Fajan you want to ask about?'

'Only in so far as it seems to be typical of a lot else that's happening now.'

'You're right, Colin. It's tied up with other things. But before we start on that, let me say that I did manage to get your good friend, Tinoo, posted to a place where he'll be safe instead of being locked up here.'

'Thanks for that. I thought he was your friend, too.'

'Yes, but there's always been a special relationship between you two. Because of your brother, I suppose.'

'That's true.'

'I mention this because I want you to be careful, Colin. Things are happening that have to be kept secret – for the time being anyway. And anybody who challenges what's going on has to be dealt with.'

'Like Ang.'

'Yes. Like Ang.'

'Has he been killed?'

'No. He isn't dead. That's all I know.'

'I don't suppose you can talk about "what's going on" as you put it.'

'I have to talk to someone about it. That's why I was so relieved when you asked to see me. You're about the only person I can talk to about it.'

'What is it, Ahmed?'

'Let me just give you one example. As you probably know there are thousands of deformed and premature births as a result of the toxic chemicals the Americans rained down on us before liberation. We're running out of the technical equipment and medicines to deal with something like that. We can't get them from the West because of the boycott and now we can't get them from eastern Europe or the Soviet Union or China either. We can't yet make the artificial limbs we need for all the victims of the mines laid by the Antis.'

'I don't suppose the increase in natural remedies supplied to all the medical centres helps much.'

'Natural remedies are no answer to what highly industrialised countries can inflict on us.'

'Things in the north are as bad as that then?'

'It's the murderous rearguard action imperialism wages all over the world where progressive governments are trying to liberate their people. Modern weapons are poured into the ex-colonial territories, turning tribal and national differences, exacerbated by an arbitrarily drawn map, into the most terrible civil wars and cross-border invasions stirred up, of course, by the CIA and MI6 in Angola, Mozambique, Guatemala, Chile. We're better organised against it than most – thanks to another member of our old June Tenth Commune.'

'Yes. Good old Goh Tun.'

'But that's not the worst of it. Our industry was established on the basis of our being able to get coal from Poland and oil from the Soviet Union. But we're already being supplied with less than we need and who knows when those sources may dry up altogether? We've laid a good foundation of heavy industry but we've reached the point when technological advance is needed which we can't manage on our own. We could buy the improvements we need with our gold reserves but Britain will continue to deny them to us. None of the advanced countries are prepared to ignore the boycott anyway.'

'But why hasn't all this been made public?'

'Why depress our people with the awful problems we face until we have some idea of what to do about them?'

'And that is –'

'We have to increase production in field and factory so we've issued what we call "The Final Appeal of the Socialism Now Movement".'

'I've seen it,' Frere said curtly.

Ahmed ignored his tone and continued: 'We offer material incentives to get people to produce more. But if you give bonuses to people to make them work harder, then you have to have the kind of consumer goods they'll want to buy with the extra money they've made. Those in the towns already know what they want to spend their money on – the sort of glossy indulgent things capitalism advertises internationally.'

'So what are you saying? That we have to surrender?'

'No. I don't say that. But I admit that we have to compromise for a time. The way Lenin had to take a step back and adopt the New Economic Policy. It isn't possible for Malia, as an isolated island in a worldwide capitalist-market sea, to build socialism all on its own. So why shouldn't we pretend to accept as much of a market economy as we have to in order to get what we want from them? We have no illusions about free markets. They are dominated completely by the great capitalist powers. But as the Soviet Union weakens, the great capitalist powers will be at each other's throats again, enabling us to play one off against another. Let them invest in our industry and in our natural resources and when the time comes, we'll confiscate the lot!'

'Do you believe that, Ahmed?'

'I wouldn't be where I am now if I didn't. I'm here to see that in this difficult time of compromise we have to go through the workers I represent don't suffer.'

'And do you really think that "Final Appeal" sent to all the managers of factories and state farms isn't going to hurt workers in the long run?'

'That document was prepared to impress the British and Americans with our reformist intentions. It isn't going to have a long run.' Ahmed took a pamphlet out of his desk drawer. 'Here's a complementary document to that "Final Appeal" you object to which is being sent to every trade union secretary in the country. It tells them exactly how to deal with any infringements of decent wages and conditions which management might try to inflict in misinterpretation of the real intentions of "The Final Appeal". And don't forget – the managers are elected by the workers now. Take it, Colin. Show it to Leela.'

Frere folded it and put it in his pocket to read later. 'And what about the other members of the Triumvirate? Do they feel about all this the way you do? Does Hadar?'

Ahmed paused. 'I don't know. Sami Usman is in London now beginning to work out the kind of deals which will become possible once Malia has agreed to the economic reforms the British Government demands as the price of ending the boycott. Sami Usman is Hadar's man and Sami Usman doesn't care whether Malia is communist or capitalist so long as he owns a big share of it – which is why he makes a good negotiator for us at this time. One of the deals he's working on is the supply by British and American publishers of books – textbooks as well as fiction.'

'So that was what ruled out Noor Fajan's and my plan for a Literary Exchange Programme controlled by the Writers' Union.'

'Yes, it did.'

'I can't bear to think of our children having to learn history from British textbooks.'

'Who says they will? We'll make use of their books on science and technology and ignore their books on history and economics. We have to deal with them; but we don't have to play straight with them. They never played straight with us for two hundred years.'

'But can we do it?' Frere wondered. 'Can we preserve some kind of socialist base we can build on when all of this apparent capitulation is no longer necessary?'

'As I said before, Colin. I wouldn't be sitting here at this desk if I didn't think so.'

Frere was thoughtful a moment. 'So, on the one hand, there were Kuan and Ang who refused to consider any compromise.'

'And had to be got rid of,' Ahmed said sadly. 'You'll have to make sure that Tinoo doesn't suffer the same fate.'

'And, on the other hand, there are you, Ahmed, and Leela and I who go along with the new policy hoping to save as much of the socialism that's been established here as we can.'

'There are a lot more than just us. But it's going to be difficult for a long time to get to know each other. Indeed, we'll only be sure of each other through practice.'

'And there's Hadar, who probably welcomes the end of socialism and will embrace a restored capitalism with both arms.'

'That's his value in our efforts to convince Britain that we have every intention of becoming what they call a free-market democracy.'

Frere waited a while, drumming his fingers on the desk top. He looked around Ahmed's handsome office. Ahmed laughed. 'You think I wouldn't have had the services of the best electronics experts we've got?

To fit out this room with the best technical equipment and, incidentally, to keep it clear of any such devices as you're thinking about.'

Frere drummed his fingers a few moments more and then finally put it to Ahmed. 'And Pir Dato?'

'Ah, Pir Dato. Who can possibly say? The moment anybody *can* say Pir Dato has failed. He has to convince Britain that he's going to dismantle socialism. That means he has to take the severest action against anyone who opposes the economic reforms he'll be putting in place. At the same time, without arousing any suspicions on the part of the British, he'll have to be thought of as the one person under whose leadership we might save our socialist base for a fresh start when the time's right.'

'But what do you really think?'

'I don't dare think of it like that. To think of it like that runs too great a risk of compromising him or of compromising myself. What I think instead is that if there are enough people like us who go along with the political charade because there's no alternative at this time, then we'll be able to determine the line to be taken when the possibility of resuming the advance to socialism returns.'

'But how do we know that the British won't be able to restore themselves as our rulers and exploiters?'

'No. We've driven them out of Malia and nothing can change that. It's just that they and the other big capitalist countries still control the world Malia's a part of. But I don't know for how much longer.'

'Aren't you in a very dangerous position, Ahmed? Particularly since you've given up your working-class base.'

'I would be. Remember how we always said that we guerrilla fighters were the fish and the peasants were the water we swam in? Well, the industrial workers have become the water I swim in.'

'And aren't you a fish out of water here?'

'That may be what was intended. They told me I wasn't losing my base in giving up the job of trade union organiser of the Number One Textile Plant but was gaining the far more substantial base of representing the whole working class in the Triumvirate. Good, I told them, but I'll keep my position as elected chair of the Malian Trade Union Council as a proof of that representation. So I still swim about in that water of workers. That's my protection.'

'Thank you, Ahmed. You've been a great help to me. But – '

'But what, Colin?'

'But I'm wondering how I can go on editing *Workers' World*. I can't tell our readers in other lands that we're not really betraying socialism, of course; we're just playing a very cunning trick on our former exploiters.'

'No, you can't. It's the kind of problem all of us who still believe passionately in socialism have to learn how to live with over this next period.'

Frere got up. 'You've given Leela and me a lot to think about.'

Ahmed got up too. 'We'll have to go on helping each other. But we'd better not meet. Not for some time anyway. We'll find means of keeping in touch.'

'Goodbye, Comrade.' He shook Ahmed's hand warmly and left.

When Frere and Leela talked about it that night, they realised that what Ahmed had said came as no shock to them. The desperate situation of the country and what it was intended to do about it were pretty much what they had supposed.

'I don't know why I was so slow in realising it,' she said ruefully. 'You seemed to see it before I did.'

'That's probably because you were so caught up in it all. Socialism meant so much to you that you couldn't bear to think it could ever fail or falter or be betrayed.'

'But you've always cared about socialism too, Colin.'

'I've not been so much a part of it, though – seeing it more from the outside in order to tell people in the non-socialist world about it.'

'I was wrong about Pir Dato,' she said simply.

'So was I,' he assured her quickly. 'I thought he was merely hungry for power. But he's more complicated than that. He really does feel that he's the only one who can get Malia through this difficult period.'

'Doesn't that make him more dangerous?'

'It's a dangerous time, for so many different reasons. Not since I began editing *Workers' World* have I had such doubts about the line I'm supposed to take in the next issue. I kept expecting that someone would summon me and give me some pointers on how to deal with current problems and policies. But they haven't. And then I tried to think of what Pir Dato himself would tell me to write and whether I would be willing to comply completely with his instructions or not. But then I realised that it was just as Ahmed said. If Pir Dato really is appearing to the British to put an end to socialism as the only way we can get the kind of help that in the long run will enable socialism to survive, then there is nothing he could say to me about what I'm to put in *Workers' World*. I have to work it out myself, knowing what the risks are if I get it wrong in terms of saying either too much or too little.'

'That's what all of us have to do, all of us who still believe in socialism. Unless – '

'Unless?' he prompted when she hesitated.

'Unless the right thing is to refuse to compromise, as Kuan probably did. As Ang certainly did.'

'Ahmed says Ang's still alive. He couldn't tell me more than that.' And in answer to her reservation: 'Yes, I've wondered about that too. Isn't it the right thing always to say exactly what one believes is just and true and never compromise at all? But then I realise that Ang wouldn't have been believed for a moment if he had come out in support of the new line. He had no alternative course, which has simply got him removed from the scene.'

'But in getting himself removed from the scene,' she pointed out, 'he's added to Pir Dato's credibility in adopting, for ulterior motives, the new line. He's, in a sense, a martyr to the duplicity of which he thoroughly disapproves. Oh, it's too complicated!'

'It is indeed. You'll have to help me, Leela.'

'We'll have to help each other.'

'And protect each other.'

'And Matt,' she added almost tearfully. 'You remember how we congratulated ourselves on his having the chance of growing up in a wholesome socialist society.'

'We'll never stop fighting for that, my darling.' He kissed her.

A few evenings later they were sitting in front of the television set with Matt on a cushion between them when Pir Dato addressed the nation on the subject of the new pragmatic approach to the problems of the day.

'We were right,' he began, 'under the inspired leadership of Secretary General Lee to make our Revolution when the people of Malia needed it, not when the material development of Malia was ripe for the transition to socialism. We inherited a poverty-stricken country and an undeveloped economy which by great collective effort we have at last got moving in the right direction. We quickly achieved the tremendous success of being able to feed, clothe and house our entire population. Let no one underestimate the importance for all of us of knowing that whenever we sit down to a meal, or dress ourselves for the day or give thanks for a roof over our heads, we need not worry that anywhere in Malia is there anyone hungry, or naked or lacking shelter. That's a great victory, Comrades, and we'll defend it always. That's the very basis of socialism.'

'That's not altogether true any more,' Frere interjected.

'I'll tell you later what the Central Committee's done about that.'

'But we can't expect our people,' Pir Dato continued on a different tack, 'to go on working so hard for so little. We aren't bonzes, you know, who have taken vows of poverty. We're ordinary people who want a more enjoyable life for ourselves and our children. We know that with so much that was good in the great Socialism Now Movement on which we embarked under our great leader's direction there was some bad, also. There was envy of those who might seem a little better off, quite forgetting that under socialism there isn't supposed to be any flat equalisation of conditions for all.

'Some work harder and contribute more and they must get more. And in working harder and getting more they are making a better life for all. In towns some have the capacity to run a business and add to the variety of goods available to all in a market where all enjoy the right of buying and selling. In rural areas some make such good use of their private plots that they have a surplus they can sell to others and deserve to have even larger private plots assigned to them. It was good that in the beginning we should accept no limitation on our efforts to build socialism but there were bad consequences of trying to run before we could walk. That is why we must be a bit more pragmatic now. It's not a question of abandoning any of the principles of our great leader – ' and he held up a copy of the *Quotations*. 'No, it's a question of applying those principles to the time we're living in now.'

'We must not forget that things change,' he began to bring his address to a close. 'Our circumstances are different – not only inside our country but outside as well. Other countries have changed in their attitude toward Malia. Some who were the enemies of our Revolution, realising that the Socialist Republic of Malia is here to stay, are willing now to enter into mutually beneficial trading relations with us. Some, whom we thought of and still think of as our friends, are not finding it possible to help us as they did in the past and they sometimes seem unwilling to accept that we have our own foreign policy based on the interests of our people – not theirs. These new relationships with other countries mean that Malia can now trade with the whole world, giving our people access to the enormous variety of goods on the world market. What this means is that on the socialist basis established by ending class exploitation we are now in a position to raise – '

Leela leaned forward and switched off. 'That's all I can take of that. Do you suppose anyone could be taken in by it?'

'It will please those who have been black marketeering in smuggled articles and the fruits and vegetables from private plots. They've become respectable businesspeople.'

'I meant anyone who fought for and cares about socialism.'

Frere shrugged. 'Maybe it wasn't supposed to take them in. Maybe the whole idea was to present a statement of intent that would impress the British and Americans and not fool our own dedicated people for a minute. What did you think of it, Matt?'

'He talked a very long time. I'm glad Mother turned him off.'

Hearing Matt describe what Leela had done gave Frere a momentary feeling of exultation. Switching off Pir Dato that way finally buried him completely and wiped out any significance he had ever had as an influence on her and any suspicion in Frere's mind that some hint of that old influence on her might still remain. And then as quickly he dismissed this selfish jubilation as hardly appropriate to the seriousness of the situation in which they found themselves.

After Matt had been put to bed, Leela came back into the room looking very solemn.

'What is it, darling?'

'I was just thinking of what's going to happen to our country.' As she spoke Frere remembered the look on her face when he had first got to know her in base camp and, eyes looking upward and hands clenched at her sides, she had spoken of her most cherished beliefs. 'Marxism taught me how the individual will can function with moral force in a society whose laws of development are realised in human action. It's a method for analysing the world with a view to changing it, of producing the ideas which can grip the minds of oppressed people and become a material force for liberating them. It shows us a world in which human aspirations can be meaningful and moral action possible. The struggle to end the exploitation of class by class, whatever form it may take in the place where you are, is the ultimate expression of humanism. And we have won battles in that struggle, Colin, and were continuing to fight it.'

He was listening to her raptly. 'You've put it so beautifully,' he said with a catch in his voice.

'And now,' bitterly, 'we have to go back to that selfish jungle of material incentives with people all out for themselves. We have to listen again to all the lies about how a so-called free market is a clearing house of individual needs, bringing about, quite incidentally, a just and equitable society – all the ruling-class rubbish we thought we'd thrown out with imperialism.'

'We're told that it's only until we can strengthen our position economically, until we can get on our feet again. That the socialist basis we've established – is still there.'

'How much of it will be left?'

He made her sit down beside him on the sofa. 'Are you saying that we ought not to go along with the Triumvirate's line to try to save what we can? Are you saying that we ought to stand up like Ang and oppose it absolutely – even though we know that at this time there's no alternative? Is that what you're saying, Leela?'

'No, I'm not saying that. But I'm wondering if it isn't what we ought to be saying.' She thought for a moment. 'You know what's the most tragic irony of all?'

'Yes. Little Matt.'

'We were going to build a socialist society for Matt to grow up in, free from all the perverted ideas and feelings of class prejudice – and because of our concern for what might happen to Matt we're going along with the indefinite postponement of that good society.'

'I know.' He put his arm around her.

'It only makes sense,' she said, turning to look at him beseechingly, 'if we really do join with others in doing everything we can to see that what your brother and so many others have died for is not finally betrayed.'

'Yes, my dearest, we must.'

24

Frere was wholly engaged in the complicated task of working out the line of the next issue of *Workers' World*. It had to explain what was bound to look like an abandonment of socialism in such a way as to suggest that it was only a necessary postponement. It had to place the responsibility for the apparent change in policy at the door of the capitalist powers which still enjoyed ascendancy on the world scene without alienating them from providing Malia with the kind of economic aid they had formerly denied. It had to demonstrate that Britain was resuming relations with Malia on an entirely different footing – not as imperialist conqueror but as chastened ex-colonial power dealing with a newly independent country on equal terms. In short, it had to demonstrate that Malia still deserved the concern and interest of exploited peoples all over the world without invalidating the contention of the governing Triumvirate that the country was now prepared to take its place among the nations of the free world subject to the advice and control of the International Monetary Fund, which was the form capitalist imperialism increasingly took.

And, furthermore, he had to work all this out with no help from anyone in the higher reaches of Party or State, knowing that the only indication there would be that he had got it wrong would be his sudden removal from editorship with every possibility of being locked up. He had never longed more for Chin's shrewd and kindly guidance.

He found that his relations with colleagues and those he had to consult in other departments were subtly altered. No one was actually hostile but everyone seemed to be very careful about any statement made or any proposal offered. There was little of the cordial friendliness that had existed before. He could not tell whether this was a change in them as a result of some word about him which was going the rounds or as a result of their own appreciation of the need for caution in the expression of attributable opinions. Or perhaps it was a change in himself and the way he saw things as a result of his awareness of the changes in the country.

They were all the same people doing the same things and yet somehow everything was different. It was like a change of trumps at bridge: one might hold the same cards in one's hand but their values were different; and his own particular hand, which had seemed so strong at that banquet in his honour not all that long ago, was of dubious worth now and he was not at all sure how to play it.

There were changes to be noted on the streets of Rani Kalpur too. There seemed to be a greater variety of consumer goods in the state stores – much of it attractive junk for which there was no real need. Stalls began to appear in the old bazaar area, some of them offering expensive articles which could only be bought with foreign currency. Some of the unemployed youth who had taken to hanging around street corners smoking cigarettes and trying to cadge pocket money were now seen going about with trays of various objects for sale.

On several occasions there were marches and demonstrations for opening up the country completely to foreign merchandise, staged by the homeless, out-of-work people who had settled on the river bank outside of town. Since they would not have had the money to buy such exotic goods themselves, Frere wondered if they were not organised by the Government to give an appearance of popularity to what it was planning to do anyway. He could not but shake his head sadly at the sight of this tatterdemalion gathering plodding along under banners they had obviously not made themselves, contrasting it with the lively parades of the young people with their red flags who had filled the streets during the Socialism Now campaign. The Great Ideological Revolution launched by Secretary General Lee was turning into the Great Pragmatic Restoration which these shabby people were celebrating in exchange for food and shelter.

That this was the case became obvious when an opposition group of young people calling for a return to socialist values suddenly appeared in the Square and confronted the bedraggled upholders of a free-market economy. The police arrived on the scene at once and attacked the young socialists! The police tore up their banners, confiscated their red flags and marched the leaders off to gaol. That evening there was an announcement over the radio that there would be no more impromptu demonstrations in the capital.

The following day there was a much larger demonstration which obviously did have government approval. There was a huge crowd made up of representatives of all the various departments of state, a number of Party members who could be known by their red buttonhole badges and many women who were there as wives and mothers of those active in the civil service as well as those who were there as officials in their own right. There were also delegations of young people from all the schools and technical colleges. Only missing from the ranks of these protesters and agitators were workers from local factories. Not one trade union banner was to be seen anywhere.

The banners and placards, which must have been prepared in advance days ago, called outright for 'democracy' and a 'free market'. The slogans that were chanted sounded like the rehearsed performance of a local choir rather than the spontaneous outburst of an agitated citizenry.

More show! was Frere's pronouncement on the display; but who was to say how many of the people in the demonstration were there because they had been told to turn out and how many really were voting against socialism with their feet? Who was to say how much it represented Pir Dato's efforts merely to impress the British and Americans and how much it might represent some real change in Pir Dato's political line for Malia?

He remembered reading a short story about a daemonic attack against a cathedral on the marches of the Christian world which took the form of the facial expressions of the statues and paintings being subtly changed from blissful to obscene and all the offices and rites gradually being diabolically perverted without the congregation's being aware of the change that was taking place – or, at least, being prepared to admit that they were aware of it. That was the way what was happening in Malia struck him. He had the feeling that if he called out: 'The cathedral's being taken over! We're losing to the forces of evil everything we fought for!' he would simply be regarded as mad and in all probability locked up.

But Leela said to him that night: 'There are many of us who feel that way. Look at those young people who came out on the streets the other day. It's just that we have to find ways of making ourselves known to each other, of organising ourselves and staying in touch – without provoking the authorities. No opposition to the new line of "socialist pragmatism" must ever be revealed, of course.'

'Or we'll simply disappear – like Ang.'

'Yes, security has been tightened at this time because the British have been expressing doubts that Malia is sincere about economic reforms. Several people at the Institute have vanished.'

'From the Communications Centre too. One explanation is that there's some kind of an epidemic striking people down; but no one believes it.'

'I just wish Tinoo hadn't picked this time to make a speech in Baidan.'

'When?' Frere asked her in alarm.

'In the last few days. We only got to know about it today. He was opposing any idea of cutting communal land up into private plots.'

'Is Hadar here?'

'No, he's in London for the final negotiations on restoring diplomatic relations and releasing our reserves.'

'When Hadar knows, he'll act against Tinoo at once.'

'Arresting Tinoo would serve as another proof of Malia's fulfilling the conditions for ending the boycott.'

'I must get word to him immediately.'

'But how can you, Colin? Neither the phones nor the post can be trusted at a time like this.'

'I must go to him.'

'That's too dangerous for you, my dearest. There must be another way.'

'No, I have to go. I can't just leave Tinoo to their mercies. I must try to save him.'

She sighed. 'Just like your brother.'

'I hadn't thought of that.' And then with a faint smile: 'Yes, of course. It's just what Matt did for Tinoo all those years ago.'

'Promise me that you'll be careful.'

The next morning Frere took little Matt with him to stand on his mound at the river's edge and look out, over the river traffic going up and down the Andor, to the terraced hills beyond. It was a kind of goodbye he hoped would not last long to his favourite scene in his son's company before setting off on a journey that might be dangerous.

The boy laughed at the factory blowing smoke rings which his father had told him about and which he had wanted to see for himself. He watched some more, head thrust forward, mouth open, eyes sparkling, and then he laughed again, throwing his head back.

'Tethered down there,' Frere said, pointing to a jetty sticking crazily out into the water, 'on the day Rani Kalpur was liberated, was a barge half full of rice. Twenty of our fighters buried themselves in the rice – '

'How did they breathe?' Matt wanted to know.

'They had bamboo tubes.'

'Like the flute Uncle Matsu made for me out of bamboo?'

'Like that. They floated downstream, past the river patrol boats and when they got to the main city docks, they sprang out of the barge and captured the whole dock area.'

'Could I breathe through my bamboo flute?'

'I suppose so.'

'I could stay under water, playing my bamboo flute.'

'I'm not sure about that, but I'll make a couple of air tubes for us to take swimming with us when I get back.'

'Will you be gone long?'

'I shouldn't think so. Shall we go home? I have to catch a coach this afternoon.'

'Let me look at the factory again.' He stared at it for a few moments, face bereft of any expression, then, once more, throwing his head back, he laughed loud and long. Then he put his hand in his father's and they walked down the little hill.

Before he set out with as little luggage as possible Leela looked at him and there were tears in her eyes. 'I don't want you to go. I desperately want you to stay with Matt and me – particularly at this time. But you feel you have to go, don't you?'

'Yes, I do.'

'I'll tell you something you may not have guessed. Back in base camp when I heard that you wanted to take part in an actual guerrilla operation, I thought I ought to try to stop you. I was going to say that you had joined us to do an important editorial job and had no right to risk your life in some minor jungle battle. But I knew it wouldn't do any good.'

'But I thought you'd hardly noticed me at that time.'

'That was the impression I thought it was right to give.'

He laughed and embraced her. 'You know why I was so keen to go on at least one operation? I wanted to impress you – or at least to convince you that I was in some measure worthy to associate with brave comrades like yourself. I was like a small boy in my part of the world showing off before the prettiest girl in school. And ever since then I've brought my little trophies, like praise from the Secretary General for a particularly good issue of *Workers' World* or the gold medal awarded to me at the banquet to lay at your feet.'

'You're not still doing it, are you? Going off to warn Tinoo isn't part of that, is it?'

'A little, maybe.'

'Surely, Colin, we've got beyond that stage now,' she pleaded.

'We don't ever get beyond that stage with someone we love. It just takes subtler and more sophisticated forms.'

'Can't I go with you?' Matt wanted to know.

Frere picked the boy up and held him aloft, then kissed him and put him down again. 'Who would look after Leela?'

'I'll look after her,' Matt stuck out his chest.

Frere took Leela in his arms again. 'My dearest one. Please, please be careful.'

'I'll be all right. Don't worry about Matt and me. It's you, my love. You must be careful. Remember what it would do to me if anything happened to you!'

Carrying only the one bag, Frere walked away from the official residential section around the Pagoda Gardens and made his way by side streets through the market area to a coach station on the outskirts of town.

He put his bag down and wiped his forehead. It was hot already and he had been walking briskly. Against the clear blue sky there was the purple haze of jacaranda blossom. There was something – some memory had flitted across his mind. Oh yes. That coach trip he had made when he had first arrived in Malia. Then, too, his journey up into the hills toward Vimla had been politically motivated, lured deeper into the country by a slip of paper promising him a rendezvous with representatives of the Liberation Army.

He looked around him comparing that time with this.

There were some people waiting for the next coach, most of them dressed as inconspicuously as he was, though, as one saw recently on the streets, there were a few women in bright sarongs. Clare Wallace would be pleased. She had argued that there was no reason for socialism to be drab. But was this to go on being socialism?

At least, he thought with a smile of quiet satisfaction, there were not the dozens of pot-bellied children staring at them out of empty eyes there had been then. And when the coach started, there was not that appalling wasteland of crumbling mud huts and shabby tents of sacking stretching away on both sides of the road.

Even before all the present doubts about Malia's future, he had been, for the most part, so immersed in immediate problems that he often forgot what had been achieved. What remained to be done always loomed so much larger than what had already been accomplished that every victory was robbed of its significance almost as soon as it was celebrated.

The people in the coach paid no attention to him, the years he had spent among them having made him practically indistinguishable. He glanced around him, noting by little touches of one kind or another that some were probably Muslims, others possibly Buddhists and a few perhaps Christians. Because the population was so divided in terms of religions, with no one faith enjoying any political power through predominance, it had not been necessary to wage a campaign of militant atheism against any of them. Strict secularism as far as the State was concerned and sound communist training of the young in the overriding unity of class had prevented any violent forms of communalism from breaking out. That was another achievement.

There were so many achievements. But were they not precisely what had brought down on their heads the hostility of the capitalist world?

But that demonstration a few days before calling for 'democracy', not working-class democracy, not socialist democracy but just democracy – the bourgeois democracy that gave the most vicious capitalist exploitation its look of political respectability – did that not represent some fundamental human weakness which made it all too easy for Pir Dato to stage his show? Whether to fool the British or to fool his own people...

Following the country's revolutionary emancipation there had been that great outburst of creative energy which had got all the factory wheels spinning and had made the collective farms flourish; but then, after that, was there possibly something about the very nature of socialism which made it impossible to sustain that explosion of economic growth? Were people too basically selfish for anything to work in the long run but the crassest material incentives? He could not bear to think that was so. Too much of his life had been dedicated to the liberation struggle his brother had died for, to the socialist cause so many comrades had served so faithfully. And not only his life – Leela's too. Their life together was so inextricably intermixed with Malia's Revolution that the socialist movement was like a contrapuntal bass to the gay arpeggios of their love. Fundamental doubts about the one could not leave belief in the other unaffected. Finding himself wondering if he could have been wrong about the utter rightness of people's liberating themselves to build a socialist society prompted once again the most terrible thought it is possible to entertain: what if the dearest person in the world, whom he knew better than he knew himself and cherished infinitely more, what if she quite suddenly should do or say or feel something that brought collapsing about his ears his assurance of understanding her! What if he should have to look at that beautiful adored face and admit, after years and years of the most intimate life together, that he was not really sure what was going on behind it!

Perhaps that particular nightmare lurks below the waking consciousness of every loving relationship, a subliminal sense of its precariousness that gives it a deeper value; but what if the nightmare should begin to spread its black wings in broad daylight and darken one's whole private world! That is the way any doubts about socialism could affect every single aspect of his intellectual and emotional life.

He shook his head to clear away such thoughts and looked out of the window. They were travelling through fertile fields flourishing in the fresh new green of spring, making their way toward the edge of the great north jungle; and his spirits lifted somewhat with the sense of embarking on an adventure. The road curved among low hills and he watched tamarind and jackfruit trees change to pines as it climbed upward. In the afternoon the coach stopped at a little town and, as they sat at tables outside a small restaurant drinking tea, Frere watched a queue of happy children winding their way back from school. The farther he got from Rani Kalpur the more he felt as though he were waking up from a nightmare. Indeed he almost began to doubt the cogency of his trip and began to think of it simply as a break he needed from the intensive work of planning and bringing out the last edition of *Workers' World*.

At Dohar Junction he spent the night and took another coach the next morning, a rather less comfortable one, which would take him to Baidan. It was quite late at night when he got out of the coach and walked along what seemed to be the main street, the shops on it all closed. Only a single row of street lamps rather doubtfully held back the pitch blackness on either side of the thoroughfare. Coming from Rani Kalpur he was struck by the darkness, and by the quiet. Instead of the ground bass of big city hum from which individual sounds stood out briefly and were then swallowed up, there was an utter stillness which gave what few sounds there were – a dog barking somewhere outside of town, the voices of two people invisible to him bidding each other good night – a peculiar poignancy.

This neat, silent little town had been completely reconstructed since the March Revolution. He remembered when he and Salmi had visited the blackened shell which was all that was left of it after the napalm bomb raids all those years ago – Salmi who was to be killed only a few days later.

At the end of the street was a new large structure which must be the administration building. That would have been the place to find out where Tinoo lived but it was completely dark. There was hardly anyone around to ask. He had forgotten how early people retire in rural communities. But farther on, beyond a little park where he could smell queen-of-the-night, he did find a small bar and restaurant which was open. He went inside and walked up to the counter behind which stood a middle-aged man who looked him up and down but, surprisingly, offered no greeting. Frere asked if it was possible to have a cup of tea and in due course, without saying a word, the man placed a cup before him.

Frere asked the man if he knew where the district education officer lived. The man merely shook his head. Frere walked over to a table where three elderly men with small glasses of toddy in front of them were sitting. They had been talking among themselves but fell silent when he came in. He greeted them formally and asked if they knew where he could find the district education officer.

One of the men asked him: 'Are you from Rani Kalpur?'

'Yes,' Frere answered and the man simply looked away from him. It occurred to Frere then that these men might think he was some kind of official pursuing an investigation of some sort. He told them that Tinoo who had taken up the post here a month or so ago was his very good friend and he would like to see him, and his wife, Moni, too.

'You know them personally then?'

'Very well. Tinoo's one of my best friends.'

Their manner changed at once. They made room for him to sit down and offered him a drink.

'Two policemen from the capital were making enquiries about our education officer the other day. That's why we have to be careful.'

'Is Baidan always so quiet?' Frere asked.

'Yes, as late as this. Remember we're a farming community. We start work early and turn in early – except on weekends. Those you see here are old people like me who have retired from active work. We like to meet here at night and gossip about the past.' He introduced the other people at the table.

Frere shook hands and explained that he was editor of *Workers' World*.

'Have you come here to do an article about the Baidan area?'

'I might.'

Then Frere was introduced to the other men there and the barman, apologising for his original coolness, insisted on giving him a drink on the house. One of the men who lived near where Tinoo and Moni were staying offered to take Frere there.

On the outskirts of town they came to a substantial bungalow which must have been the living quarters of a district officer in the old colonial days. Frere's guide knocked on the door and it was soon opened by Moni.

'I've brought someone who claims to be a friend of yours.'

'Colin!' Moni exclaimed when she saw him. 'However did you find us?'

'I helped,' the old man said.

'Come in,' she urged Frere, holding the door open. And to the old man: 'Won't you come in, too?'

'No, I must go home. But I'll see you at the celebration tomorrow.'

'Oh, right.'

As Frere stepped inside, Moni called to Tinoo: 'Look who's here!'

Tinoo threw his arm around Frere delightedly. 'This is wonderful, Colin. I've been wanting desperately to see you.'

'I'll get you something to eat,' Moni said. 'You must be starving. I know that coach trip from Dohar Junction.'

Tinoo led Frere into the study and indicated a cane chair while he straddled a straight-backed chair he turned away from the desk. 'I can't tell you how glad I am to see you.'

'I thought it was better not to let you know in advance.'

'Very wise. They're watching us, I'm sure.'

'And listening,' Frere said with an admonitory laugh. 'In Rani Kalpur I heard about your speech against dividing up communal land into private plots.'

'Oh, that. They'll be hearing from me again tomorrow.'

'What's happening tomorrow?'

'You've arrived just in time for our memorial to the guerrilla fighters from this area who died in battle. I've been asked to speak.'

Frere started to say something about Tinoo's being so outspoken in these dangerous times and then decided to wait until later. 'And how are things in this part of Malia?'

'Good. I can't tell you how glad I am that they exiled us from Rani Kalpur. It's here in the countryside that real changes have taken place. But it's also here that these changes are an organic development out of the past. The village panchayats, for example, have developed into a real rural democracy. They elect the representatives who form the assemblies in regional centres like Baidan which provide a very effective local government.'

'Like what Ahmed has been doing in using the trade unions for the democratic management of workplaces.'

'Yes, but trade unions are a much more recent development in Malia than panchayats. What's really enabled these changes to take place is the spread of literacy. There was eighty per cent illiteracy all over this part of Malia. Now those figures have been reversed. They're eighty per cent literate. And what a difference it's made!'

'A great difference indeed,' Moni said, coming in with some food for Frere and tea for them all. 'It's helped women achieve greater equality, for one thing. No women could read or write before. Now there are family-planning clinics everywhere and women can understand the explanations and instructions handed out to them.'

'And everybody can read newspapers about what the Government is doing in Rani Kalpur,' Tinoo added, 'and then write and distribute pamphlets commenting on how such government policies will affect us here.'

'And what are the reactions to the latest pronouncements of the Triumvirate?'

'The new pragmatic line, you mean. I always say the change from the Marxist principle that what's theoretically correct can be tested by social practice to the line that what works must be theoretically correct may sound insignificant but it's not.'

'Tinoo's been lecturing about the difference,' Moni said. 'Starting with that argument of Pir Dato's that "I don't care whether a cat is black or white as long as it catches mice".'

'Leela says the trouble with that kind of pragmatism,' Frere remarked, 'is that it leads to the sort of intellectual twilight in which all cats are grey.'

'That's nice,' Tinoo approved. 'I'll use that.'

'But we've heard in Rani Kalpur that there's been a very positive response in the countryside to the new line.'

'There's been some discontent here in the past that they probably hoped to take advantage of. For one thing, young members of the Red Front who came to the rural areas in the early stages of the Socialist Now Movement sometimes behaved with too little regard for local sensibilities. For another, the state farms in which confiscated land was treated like a government-built factory with peasants simply working there for their wages weren't popular. They didn't satisfy the peculiar relationship peasants have with the land. So when there was talk of restoring private ownership and allowing people to make money by growing what they liked on their own plots – cash crops, for instance, instead of food grain – some people were won over at first.

'But it wasn't collective ownership they were objecting to. On the agricultural communes where the land belonged to particular communes and the members of the commune had a say in what was to be grown and the methods for growing it there was great satisfaction with the new order. They've now organised themselves to fight against any scheme for extending private plots and introducing a free market in agriculture. You don't have to tell peasants about what will happen to the land they cherish if private profit is allowed to rule.'

'What do you think now,' Frere suddenly asked him, 'about whether the new policies represent a real restoration of capitalism or just a show of complying with British demands in order to end Malia's boycott?'

'I don't care what Pir Dato really intends. We have to be pragmatic too and take our stand on what we see actually happening. There's no doubt that Hadar and Usman and those associated with them really are acting as though there's been a complete restoration of capitalism and they're getting rich out of it.'

'That's perfectly true,' Frere agreed. 'There's no doubt either that those who disagree openly with the new line really do die or disappear. That's why I've come to see you at this time. To warn you, Tinoo.'

'Thank heavens!' Moni exclaimed. 'I've been warning him but he won't listen to me.'

'But I keep telling you they've already acted against me. Why else do you think we're stuck away up here in Baidan?'

'You owe the lightness of your sentence so far to Ahmed, you know. But do you think that's going to satisfy Hadar, knowing as much about what he's up to as you do?'

'I'm not exactly alone here, you know. I've made friends. I'm a member of the Assembly. Even more important, I'm in touch with Goh Tun. He feels about things just the way we do. He was furious about what happened to Kuan. And remember Goh Tun is in charge now of the whole northern force. You know yourself that Ahmed supports me.'

'You're right, Tinoo. This puts you in a very important position. But that just makes it all the more likely that they'll feel they have to deal with you. You must be able to go on working with the people the way you are now. And that means going underground, living among those people like a fish in water. Just like the old days.'

When Tinoo did not answer, Frere pleaded with Moni. 'Tell him I'm right. Tell him he has to go into hiding.'

'You know Colin's right, my dearest. He's come all the way here just to warn you. Please say you'll do it.'

'When do you say I should go?' Tinoo asked.

'Now. The first thing in the morning. I can't be sure that no one knows I've come here. I had to take that chance to warn you but – '

'Not in the morning. I have to be here for our victory celebration tomorrow. Perhaps the following day – '

'Not perhaps,' Moni remonstrated. 'Definitely you'll go the day after tomorrow.'

'Do you know where you'll go? How you'll live?' Frere asked.

'We've thought about this possibility. There are places not too far from the old base camp. That's territory cleared of most of its inhabitants because of the raids of the Antis. Up there I have a whole jungle to hide in and Goh Tun to look after me.'

'And what about you, Moni?'

'I'd like to go with him but he won't let me. And I might slow him down or give him away. I'll go to my brother who runs a school in Vimla.'

Frere shook his head sadly. 'Who'd have thought it would come to this – that in the new Socialist Republic of Malia the most loyal defenders of the Revolution would have to go into hiding!'

'Once the Party and State officials, and all the central planners and administrators, begin to rule on behalf of the working class we're on the way to a new bourgeois ruling class. As our Secretary General knew. That's why he launched Socialism Now. And for all the mistakes that were made it did a lot of good – particularly after it passed from the hands of disorganised youth into the hands of organised workers. Ways have to be found of institutionalising that direct involvement of factory workers in the towns and agricultural workers in the countryside. We don't simply get rid of individualistic bourgeois democracy: we develop it into collective socialist democracy – '

'As Ahmed's doing in Rani Kalpur and you're doing here!' Moni finished for him. 'I believe Colin knows all that, darling.'

Tinoo laughed. 'But he has to pay something for coming up here to get me on the run.'

Moni reminded them of what a big day they had ahead of them and cleared them off to bed.

The next morning Tinoo took Frere around to the tractor station so that he could see what industrialisation had done for Malia's agricultural community. There were many tractors, a number of them being worked on by the skilled mechanics attached to the station. There were also the various mechanical devices, harvesters, ploughs, seeders and chemical sprayers which the tractors pulled.

'Aren't certain types of implements wanted all at once by everybody according to the season?' Frere wondered.

'It takes a lot of planning and a lot of co-operation but we manage.'

'What about all the new types of seeds and fertilisers we hear about in connection with what they call the "green revolution"?'

'There's a technical college in Baidan with its own well-equipped laboratory and glassed-over plots of earth for experimenting with new techniques and plant forms,' Tinoo explained. 'They can weed out whatever isn't really suitable for us. Of course, the work of the college has been slowed down by our not being able to import anything these days from East or West.'

Just before noon in a grove of acacia trees outside of town there was a gathering of hundreds of people from Baidan and the surrounding villages. Banners with revolutionary slogans or the names of famous guerrilla actions were hung from branch to branch. Tables were being set with a wide variety of food. The people met and talked and formed ever-changing groups and the children played and chased each other.

Soon there was the sound of chanting and a rhapsode was to be seen walking among the trees improvising a song about a major battle of the Liberation War which had been fought nearby. As he sang the lyrics in a high-pitched voice he emphasised the rhythm by accompanying himself on a single-stringed instrument. Tinoo explained that this sort of folk orature had been given a new lease of life by the March Revolution and was to be heard at all such celebratory events in the area.

'Some of the old praise poems,' he said, 'have been written down and published so that they can be studied in school. And, of course, a copy of Narmala's great epic is to be found in every household. It's led to an interest in the epics of other cultures.'

'It's almost as though our scheme for literary exchanges on an international scale which they banned is taking root right here in Malia's heartland – in spite of them!'

'Isn't it, though!'

In the middle of an opening among the trees there was a platform equipped with microphones and large horn-shaped amplifiers pointing in all directions. An old man with a rather tattered volume under his arm climbed up onto the platform and thumped one of the microphones to make sure it was live. A group of ten children, boys and girls all about eight or nine years old, trooped up on the platform and lined up behind the old man, who looked around to see that they were in place. Then he took the volume from under his arm and opened it to a particular place. He looked out to see if the people were properly attentive.

'He's our local historian,' Tinoo explained to Frere.

The old man read from the book a short account of one of the first young men from that region who had joined Secretary General Lee's guerrilla forces and who had been killed by the British. When he had finished reading, he looked over his shoulder at the line of children.

'He died that Malia might live!' they intoned together.

The old man next read about a young woman who had led one of the early demonstrations in the area and had been arrested and locked up by the British and had died in gaol.

'She died that Malia might live!' the children sang out.

And so the old man continued, giving name after name of those from this region around Baidan who had given their lives for an independent socialist Malia. And as the list grew and the children repeated their choral salute and the crowd listened intently, the emotional impact increased until it seemed that just one more name would be bound to interrupt the proceedings with some kind of a pathetic outburst – a catch in the old man's voice or choking sobs drowning the children's antiphony or a loud collective moan going up from the crowd.

But all that happened was that yet another paragraph was read out about yet one more of the beautiful people and yet once again was heard the childish proclamation – 'dead that Malia might live!'

Frere could not but tell over, in time with the old man's recitation of the brief biographies and the children's moving repetition of the simple response, his own dead: his brother Matt who had brought him to Malia to begin with; and Salmi who had been killed not many miles from here; and Tuck who had been murdered at the moment of victory; and Chin who need not have died; and all the wonderful people he had known in base camp and in Rani Kalpur whose lives had been given for the Revolution – a revolution which might possibly be on the point of betrayal.

And then, just when the tension seemed to have become unbearable, the old man closed the book and the children trailed down from the platform. The old man simply said: 'We'll never forget them.'

And the crowd, in a great sigh of relief that the ordeal of recounting the cost of the good life they now enjoyed was over, called out 'Never! Never!'

The old man said: 'We're now going to hear a few words from the newest member of our community – the District Education Officer.'

Tinoo climbed up on the platform and shook the old man's hand. He turned and faced the crowd. 'Let us think for a few moments about what these heroes and heroines of our country have won for us.' He made a sweeping gesture of his arm which took in all the wide fields and low hills surrounding the town of Baidan and this grove where they had met to celebrate their liberation. 'This land where you were born, where you have your families, where you work to support yourselves and to feed the people of Malia – whom does it belong to? It's not private land. All the rich landlords who used to own it have been expropriated, thanks to the glorious efforts of its sons and daughters you've been hearing about. Is it state land then? Does it belong to the Government? That's not what Secretary General Lee said when he summoned those courageous people we've been honouring into battle. What he said was "Land to the tiller". That's our answer. Land belongs to the tiller – not individually but collectively. It belongs to the members of the communes into which the rural areas are divided.'

He continued: 'Individual families may have small private plots for their own use but that's not the basic form of land ownership nor will it be. When someone like that representative of the Ministry of Agriculture who was here a few days ago talks about the possibility of privatising the land and promises that some of you might get to be very rich at the expense of others, what is he saying? He's saying that we can go back to the situation where rich private landowners lord it over the rest, back to the very situation from which the heroic people we've been hearing about have liberated us. Do we want that?'

A great shout of 'No!' went up from the crowd. 'I don't know how long I'll be with you, my new comrades of the land; but wherever I am I'll be helping you defend your collective ownership of the fields you work, the fields you preserve for your children to work and your children's children. Because your ownership and care of the land that feeds us all is one of the basic conditions of a socialist Malia.'

There was loud applause. The old man thanked Tinoo and then he called out to the crowd. 'Food is on the tables. Let all eat their fill! And while we're eating and drinking, our own poet will sing us songs about the old days.' The rhapsode climbed up on the platform and began strumming his instrument and preparing to recite.

'It's all right,' the old man said. 'He's already eaten.'

That evening Frere sat over a light supper with Tinoo and Moni. He told them how moved he had been by the ceremony of remembrance.

'I wish I'd come here just for that, Tinoo, and to congratulate you and Moni on having settled down so quickly to life in this very pleasant place – instead of having to drive you into exile.'

'No, you're right. I have to go. I saw several people in the crowd today who I'm sure have come from the capital to check up on me.'

'And after that speech!' Moni said crossly.

'Was it so bad?' Tinoo asked innocently,.

'You know what I mean.' And to Frere: 'All our lives together I've been trying to make him be more careful. Not simply to blurt out what he feels without thinking of the consequences. And now it's led to this – ' with a little sob, 'we're not going to be together any more.'

Tinoo put his arm around her. 'I'll find ways of seeing you in Vimla or wherever you are.'

'I don't think this bad phase is going to last all that long,' Frere said. 'I've been enormously encouraged by my visit. In Rani Kalpur we see too much of the temptations of consumerism on people whom city life tends to turn into rootless individuals. We see a potential bourgeoisie beginning to want the kind of things they're told the bourgeoisie enjoy in the West. Trade union leaders like Ahmed are going to have to fight to maintain the collective strength of the working class against the individualism of the so-called free market. But here in Baidan when we were watching people coming back from the fields at sunset you know what I was recalling – '

'Yes, because I've heard you recite it often enough. That poem of Mao's.'

And Frere did intone softly: 'Happy, I see wave upon wave of paddy and beans, and all around heroes homebound in the evening mist.'

'Perhaps we can arrange for you to stay on as a local rhapsode,' Tinoo suggested. 'Leela can join you – if Leela could ever tear herself away from the centre of power.'

'While my hero,' Moni complained, 'is being driven into hiding.'

'I'm not going off to cower in a hole somewhere, you know. I'm carrying on the war. It's just that I must have maximum mobility to be able to do so.'

'When are you going?' Frere asked.

'Tonight. Before dawn. I'll be gone when you wake up.'

Moni got up. 'I'd better start getting some things together for you.'

Frere and Tinoo stood up too. Frere took his friend's hand in his two hands and held it tightly. He looked deep into his friend's eyes, his own eyes brimming slightly. 'You know, Tinoo. It may well turn out that when my brother saved your life, he performed an act of service to Malia's liberation from the clutch of capitalism so great that rhapsodes will sing songs about it for a thousand years!'

The next morning a tearful Moni told Frere that Tinoo indeed was gone. 'Just like that – gone.'

'Don't worry. If I know Tinoo he'll devise dozens of cunning schemes for keeping in touch.' And he added gravely: 'He's a great man, Moni.'

'Yes, I know.'

'And you're great too. You deserve him.'

'I hope so.'

'Don't forget. You've always got us. Leela's still in a position to be able to help a lot. Come to us whenever you want to, Moni.'

After a light breakfast he walked to the centre of town and took the coach south. When he got down from the coach that evening at Dohar Junction, he saw four soldiers who seemed to be under the orders of a man in civilian clothes waiting outside the station. He was about to pass them on his way to the lodging house where he would spend the night when the man stepped in front of him and held up his hand.

'You're under arrest,' the man said.

25

Frere was more surprised than alarmed at being stopped by the man in civilian clothes and told that he was under arrest. 'Do you know who I am?' he asked, not indignantly but simply to enable the man to realise that he must have made a mistake.

'You're better known than you seem to realise. You're Colin Frere and I'm arresting you on the orders of Internal Security.'

'Not Comrade Frere?'

'We don't arrest comrades.'

'And those men there?' Frere pointed to the four soldiers.

'They're your guard, to see that you don't escape.'

'I'm flattered.'

The man led Frere, with the soldiers following after, to an army van parked a little way down the street and opened the door at the back.

'What are you doing with me?' Frere asked. 'Where am I being taken?'

'To the Army Recuperation Centre.'

'But I feel fine!' Frere said with a slightly nervous laugh. 'Why am I being taken there? Why have I been arrested?'

'I'm not allowed to speak to you about that.'

'Can I send word to my wife from here that I've been arrested?'

'No.'

The man climbed into the front seat with the driver; Frere and the soldiers got into the back. The benches along the side were not very comfortable for what was going to be a long ride. He had heard of the Army Recuperation Centre as a place somewhere in the high hills west of Rani Kalpur where political prisoners used to be held in the days of the Puppet Government. Before that it had been a resort hotel for British officials and the wealthier citizenry of the capital to escape to in the summer. He asked the soldiers if they knew anything about what it was used for now; but they had obviously been instructed not to speak to him at all.

The first thing he had thought about when he was arrested was whether Tinoo had got clear away or not. Was his own arrest a result of their having caught Tinoo that morning? He did not think so. His crime seemed to be making the trip across country to see someone under surveillance, not helping that person to escape. They must have followed him as far as Dohar Junction and, on finding that he had bought a return ticket, simply waited to pick him up on his way back to Rani Kalpur. Feeling somewhat relieved, he settled himself for the long tiresome journey.

When they finally reached the Army Recuperation Centre he could see that the main part of the building and grounds were used as some sort of rest home and vacation centre for senior army officers. But he was marched right around to the back and up many flights of stairs to a tiny room where he was locked in. At least there was a window which gave him a splendid view of the Lupang Mountains rising mistily in the distance.

Somewhere off there was the hill station Kotal Bargh where he had first made contact with the liberation forces under Secretary General Lee. He had glimpses of the Andor flowing rather skittishly through the hills to become, many miles farther down, the stately waterway which bore barges to and fro past the comic little button factory. In the midst of such a spectacular landscape to be shut up in such a tiny room seemed grimly ironic.

After a while he thought about the possibility of escape; but it seemed quite impossible. The drop from the window to the rocks below was a good seventy or eighty feet. There was a paliasse filled with straw but no bedclothes of which he could make a rope. He doubted that he could make his way through the building unobserved even if he managed to elude somehow the guard who brought him his food. He supposed there would be food, food and water. And then he remembered the way certain people of late had simply disappeared, including some as powerful as Ang. 'If you're simply going to be made to disappear,' he thought, 'why should they feed you? Or do anything for you at all? Or let anyone know where you are for that matter?'

He was, in fact, given food at intervals and there was a bottle of water left just inside the door. He supposed it was drinkable. Not that it made much difference if one was about to disappear anyway. Sometimes it seemed to him that this bad dreamlike place of incarceration might simply have been called up through his finding himself, because there was no role for him to play in a differently conceived Malia, a man on the outside, a dissident. You fell out with the crowd that was in and you condemned yourself to be locked up. It was as simple as that; and all the arguments about which side was right or wrong were nothing but endless rounds of special pleading.

At other times he took the treatment he was presently receiving as the proof of just how right he had been in his suspicions of the Secretary General's successors. He could see himself in some public trial marshalling his arguments against the ideological enemy in the most telling way and he resented the fact that only very junior soldiers and guards attended him and there was no one of any authority on whom he could practise his polemics.

As he had noticed from other times when he had been for any length of time absolutely on his own, there was a tendency for passing moods of the moment to become enormously exaggerated. The pain of being separated from Leela and little Matt and the frustration of being suddenly cut off from playing any part in the cultural and political life of the nation could produce in him a feeling of absolute despair. And on the other hand the mere fact that he was considered important enough to have been meted out the same fate as Ang himself, that no less a person than Hadar, a member of the Triumvirate, should consider him an enemy, gave him the sense of being a revolutionary hero of tragic stature – like Matt, perhaps.

This dialectic of the emotions no doubt reflected the ups and downs of his personal fortune over the last few years, from the peak of the state banquet in his honour to the depths of this isolated cell nobody knew about. It occurred to him that he might simply be one of those people who was always out of step, who in any kind of society at all would sooner or later find himself in a minority committed to changing it. He had rejected the society he was born in and had come halfway around the world to dedicate himself to a new one, only to find himself once more in the position of the radical outsider. What he had taken to be his passionate advocacy of socialism might only be his reaction to the society he happened to have grown up in – which just happened to be capitalist! And that forced him to come to terms with the greatest irony of all: that this idiosyncratic, non-conforming individual, destined always to end up in a negative camp of one, should have affected as his life's major dedication socialist collectivism!

But that was all nonsense. He *was* a socialist. He had learned about socialism from some of the greatest theoreticians and practitioners living and dead. It was because he did understand socialism and could spot deviations from it that he was here. And yet, shaking his head, how could anyone who had seriously devoted so much of his life to a cause like socialism, have to admit at the end, even for a moment, that his devotion might have been misplaced, his whole life utterly wasted?

He could only take refuge in an area of life which was not subject to the vagaries of belief – his deep constant feeling for Leela and their son. He had never stopped trying to get word to her somehow of what had happened to him and he knew that she would be trying as hard to get word to him. And suddenly a terrible thought occurred to him, a thought he believed had been put out of his mind for good that night when Leela had switched Pir Dato off as having nothing to say worth listening to. He had believed that the last ghost of any hint of jealousy had been laid for good. But now the most awful possibility he could imagine rose before him. What if Leela had to choose between using Pir Dato's feeling for her to do something about her husband even if she knew her husband would hate it or by acceding to what she imagined her husband's feelings in the matter would be to do absolutely nothing about him at all! He remembered how he had hesitated before asking her to intercede with Pir Dato for Chin. He could never have asked her to intercede for him! He did not even think he could walk out of his prison if she did. And then it occurred to him that it might have been solely to create such a dilemma for *her* that *he* had been arrested! All that big talk in his mind about his political importance having consigned him to this prison and it turned out instead that it was simply the way a man of real political importance got rid of a tiresome fellow who had got in the way of his desire for a lovely woman!

It so infuriated Frere that he swung his fist hard against the wall of his room, cracking the plaster – and injuring his knuckles too. He looked at his damaged hand and smiled ruefully. He must not let himself react like that to vagrant thoughts. He was letting them defeat him when he reacted like that.

Weeks passed. Even his request for something to read – old copies of *Das Vani*, the Writers' Union *Journal*, anything – was ignored. He wondered who was editing *Workers' World* now. It would be very strange in this bare cell to be given to read a copy of the periodical he had founded himself! He thought it was most likely that *Workers' World* would simply have been discontinued.

He spent most of his time staring out of the window at that magnificent view. It was a kind of relief that neither the crumpled hills nor the river's incised gorge showed any signs of the efforts of human beings. But then sometimes the Malian revolutionary movement itself would seem to him like a natural force, like the rock-shredded waters of the Andor, rising in high places and finding its own course to the sea, sweeping away all attempts to guide it into particular channels or to harness it to special needs, even by so great a social engineer as the Secretary General himself. How then did he dare come into this country from the outside world thinking that he could make the slightest contribution to raising any restraining dam or designing any practical canal which was supposed to modify in human terms the course of that wayward stream? He was simply a detached leaf which had been carried along by the flood for a time and at last deposited on this lonely bank. But that was only the awful depression of absolute isolation speaking to him again.

One morning between meagre breakfast and lunch the door of his room was opened to admit a very senior police officer from Rani Kalpur. Frere did not actually know him but they had seen each other at official functions. The man did not offer to shake hands but he did not look unfriendly either. He looked around the little room, saw that there was no place for them to sit and beckoned Frere to follow him. There were two soldiers on guard outside the door and they marched on each side of Frere as the officer walked along the corridor toward the front of the building and down many flights of stairs to a kind of reception hall on the first floor where there were comfortable chairs.

The officer pointed to one of the chairs. 'Sit down,' he said politely enough. And with an irritable wave of the hand dismissed the two soldiers.

'Am I at last to be told why I've been arrested?' Frere asked.

'I must tell you that I know very little about your case. I've been given very specific instructions which I shall carry out as faithfully as possible.'

'You've been given instructions by whom?'

'That, I'm afraid, I'm not at liberty to say.'

'What *can* you say?' Frere asked irritably.

'I can say that your case is not entirely unconnected with that of the Education Officer of Baidan District. Do you know where he is?'

Frere tried to conceal the jubilation he felt at knowing Tinoo had got away, safely. 'I can honestly say that I've no idea where he is.'

'It was thought that he would be careful not to tell you and, therefore, I'm not to bring any pressure to bear. It was simply wondered if on reflection you might not have changed your mind about associating yourself with such a troublemaker.'

'I'm proud to be associated with him.'

The officer shrugged.

'Am I to be tried?' Frere asked.

'You *have* been.'

'What was I charged with?'

'I don't know.'

'But I *was* found guilty.'

'I don't know that either. As I told you, I know nothing about your case. I only know what it's been decided to do with you.'

Frere felt an icy stab of fear, all the colder for the bland way the officer had dealt with him – as though his fate was a matter of the slightest importance. Was that the way one disappeared?

'I think the idea of employing someone like me who knows nothing about your case is that it forestalls any arguments or protests on your part. It isn't that I refuse to discuss your case with you: I quite simply can't.'

Frere did not want to ask what had been decided. He wanted to put off as long as possible hearing anything but that he was to be released – and that was ruled out by the whole nature of the interview. He sat there looking at the officer in a way he hoped had no element of pleading in it. Gradually he began to feel that the waiting was less tolerable than knowing the worst. 'What, what *is* going to happen to me?'

The officer was relieved too at being able to get it over with. 'It's not as bad as you might have been expecting. You're to be expelled from the country.'

'I have to leave Malia?'

'Yes.'

'That's ridiculous. Do you realise that the Secretary General himself asked me to stay here? – To do a job he'd picked me out for.'

'But the Secretary General isn't with us any more, is he?'

'And the whole country's suffering for it, too.'

The officer started to say something and then checked himself. 'That may well be true. And what do you say to your order of expulsion?'

'With my wife and son, of course.'

'No. You're to go by yourself.'

Frere's eyes narrowed as he looked hard at the officer. 'I won't go without them. There's nothing you can do to *make* me go without them. I'd rather die here.'

The officer was affected by Frere's grim stare. 'I'm merely the messenger, remember. I have nothing to do with the decision except to deliver it.'

'You can go back and say that you *did* deliver it and the answer was a categorical "no" – not without my wife and son.'

'I was told that you'd probably take that line.' He reached inside his tunic and brought out a folded paper which he handed to Frere. 'That's an application for you to be allowed to leave Malia. You see, it's signed by your wife, Leela.'

Frere took the paper without looking at it. Everything, all reserves of energy or resistance, went out of him, draining his face of any expression and pulling down the corners of his mouth like a pilot undergoing strong negative 'g'. He slumped in his chair. His eyes fluttered and he said without hope: 'It's, it's a forgery.'

The officer shook his head. 'No, it's her signature. You can confirm that she signed it. You're to see her.'

'When? When am I to see her?'

'Today. In a few minutes in fact. Your wife is here. I brought her with me from Rani Kalpur.'

They both got up and Frere followed the officer out of the room to a broad stairway leading down to the main reception area where a number of army personnel were variously engaged. They watched the police officer and Frere as they crossed to a smaller room with two guards on the door. The officer stood aside to let Frere pass within.

He took several steps inside and stopped, his mind like a jammed switchboard – questions about her signature and little Matt's wellbeing and why he had been arrested and what the future held all interfering with each other in a frantic jumble. And then he saw her turn and look at him with those dark engulfing eyes and there were no questions any more, only the love he felt for her surging through him with such force that he saw that beautiful face and graceful form as through a mist. He took the five more steps separating them and enfolded her in his arms, his cheek resting on her lustrous dark hair as he breathed in the faint smell of champak blossom. Then he held her away from him to look deep into her eyes. He glanced over his shoulder and found that the officer had stayed outside and that he and Leela were, indeed, alone.

He led her to a settee with threadbare upholstery and they sat down. Again, holding her hand in his, he simply looked at her, not saying anything.

She spoke at last. 'You're all right? They haven't hurt you?'

He shrugged the question aside as of no importance now.

She spoke again: 'That expulsion order I signed – '

'I understand. They made you do it. It's all right. I've told them I'd never leave without you and Matt.'

'They'll never let me go.'

'I won't go without you,' he simply repeated.

'But don't you see, you can't stay with us. You'd disappear too. Like Ang.'

'Has anything been heard about Ang?'

'He's here somewhere.'

'In this very building?'

'Yes, but no one can see him. He's supposed to have headed a deviationist faction. Tinoo is said to have belonged to it. He's disappeared too. Were you able to warn him?'

'Yes. He got away. He's off in the northern jungle somewhere. He's in touch with Goh Tun.'

'And Moni?'

'She's gone to relations in Vimla. I told her she could always get help from you. And I'm supposed to have belonged to Ang's faction as well?'

'Yes. When you didn't come back from your trip to Baidan, I knew what you'd be charged with. I knew what they'd do to you. I couldn't let it happen. I'd do anything to *keep* it from happening. I saw everybody I knew, pleaded desperately with everybody.'

'Thank you for trying to save my life but it's useless to me without you and Matt. I won't go.'

She squeezed his hand tightly. 'For me and Matt you must go. We couldn't bear it if you were executed. And what good would it do?'

'What good would it do for me to live if I'm to be separated from you, Leela?'

'Things here will change,' she said fiercely. 'We have to *make* them change. Wherever you are, you will still be part of that struggle. You will be making things change, too.'

He did not say anything.

'I was a long time in seeing it. I did not *want* to see it. You *helped* me see it, Colin. And we both have to live to do something about it.'

'You'll disappear too.'

'No,' she said evenly. 'I won't disappear.'

He frowned. 'Is that for the same reason that it was possible for you to get permission for me to leave?'

'Yes. But there's something you have to believe, something you *do* believe. I have never surrendered the least part of what belongs intimately to us both, and *only* to us. I will never, on my life, my dearest, let go of the tiniest fraction of it – for anything! It is ours and only ours for ever!'

'Deep down I know that.'

'And you must think of what it would mean, not just to me but to Matt, having you disappear and not knowing what's become of you but fearing the worst.'

He did not say anything.

'And there's something else. Whatever's happening here now, I belong to Malia. Matt belongs to Malia. Even if they'd let me, I can't leave, least of all now. I belong to the March Revolution; and what the people of this country have won in struggle must not be given back to the imperialist exploiters. The people will not allow that to happen and I must be here with them. And I won't just be fighting for the Malia which our Secretary General and all the brave people who fought with him have striven for. I will be fighting also for the Malia you can come back to, my dearest, to be reunited with Matt and me. That's why you have to live.'

And when he still did not say anything, she continued passionately: 'It will happen. Don't be misled by what we've seen all too much of in the upper ranks of the leadership at the centre. All over Malia there are heroes like those in that poem of Mao's you often recite.'

'Yes, I know. I saw some of them when I was in Baidan. One could believe that "the sun and moon were shining in new skies" there. Tinoo helped me see how socialism in the rural areas has rooted itself organically in the lives of the people and soaks up nourishment from the past. It's burgeoning. It won't be destroyed so easily in the countryside. I kept thinking if only we were there, the three of us, on some commune in the middle plains.' He broke off to ask about Ahmed. 'Is he all right? Nothing's happened to him?'

'No,' slightly surprised. 'Ahmed's in a strong position with his trade union backing.'

'They're all working together, you know – Ahmed, Tinoo and Goh Tun. Goh Tun represents the army, Tinoo the peasants and Ahmed the organised industrial workers. There's your triumvirate that will save socialism!'

'And the Institute has been flooding the country with new editions of the works of the Secretary General. They can't stop it since they still pretend that the new pragmatism is simply a particular reading of Comrade Lee's line best designed to meet the needs of the moment.'

'The British won't be very pleased about that.'

She quoted one of the best-known sayings: 'Imperialism is ferocious, its nature will never change. The imperialists will never lay down their butcher knives, will never become Buddhas, not until their doom.'

He was silent for a while and then he groaned. 'How can I part with you, Leela!'

'Hush!' She kissed him. 'It's the only way all three of us can stay alive. You must think of *me* as homebound in the evening mist, back home to look after our son and to tell him stories about his father and his uncle, and about Tuck and Kuan and Ang.'

'It puts me pretty firmly in the company of the dead,' he said wryly.

'In the company of heroes. Little Matt is our pledge that you and I will be united again and in the kind of Malia we've dreamed of.'

'You promise that you'll stay alive for that reunion. That you won't get involved in anything heroic but foolish.'

She said very solemnly: 'I promise that for you and Matt I'll stay alive.'

He took her in his arms and kissed her. They were determined to use every minute of the time allowed them. He told her about his stay with

Tinoo and Moni, about the Remembrance Day celebration in the acacia grove. She told him what Matt had said when she explained to him that his father had to go away for a while.

'He wanted to know if you'd be editing something there like *Workers' World* here.'

'I don't know what I'm going to do. It doesn't matter much. It will simply be a chunk of dreary prose to get through. The poetry will have been left behind.'

'You're not to brood, you hear.'

'I won't brood. I'll dream – of you two.'

The time inevitably came when the police officer rapped on the door and entered the room. They got up from the settee and Frere held her as though he was never going to let her go and she murmured so low his ear alone could hear her say 'I'll love you always and always'; and it had been seldom enough that she had put her deepest feelings for him into speech that her words thrilled him and would go on echoing in his mind over and over again through the years to come.

The officer beckoned to Leela and she walked away from Frere, turning in the doorway to give him a last beatific smile that went perfectly with those last words of hers. And she was gone. Frere was taken back up to the tiny room on the top floor and told that on the following morning he would be driven to the Rani Kalpur airport and put on a plane for England.

When he got down from the van the next day and was escorted to the Viscount waiting on the main runway, he was bound to be thinking of his first arrival at this same airport, could it really be only some fifteen or sixteen years ago? So much had been crowded into that historically brief span of time! In the air the plane swung in a wide climbing turn over the city and Frere had his last sight of the huge domed People's Palace, the sweep of the broad Andor through the town and the Great Pagoda and its surrounding gardens where their little bungalow was. He dropped his head forward in his hands to conceal the tears that welled up.

26

It was a little over a year after Frere's return before an assignment brought Clare Wallace to London. He had been looking forward to seeing her as the one person he could talk to freely about what was happening in Malia, the one person who knew Leela and his son and could be made to look at photographs of them and listen to his fond reminiscences.

He had renewed his membership of a slightly seedy but respectable enough club in John Adams Street to which quite a few foreign correspondents belonged; and he arranged for her to meet him there for lunch. When she arrived, he took her to one of the alcoves just off the main dining room where it was possible to dine in detached quiet.

Clare had admired the dim Edwardian monument as they walked through it. 'I like this place. Could a woman correspondent become an associate member, do you think?'

'I'm sure it can be arranged. Now tell me about yourself, Clare.'

'There's very little to say about *myself*. If you've seen the articles I've written from various parts of the world – well, that's me. Oh, last year I won a Pulitzer Prize.'

'I like that,' he laughed. 'Oh, last year I won a Pulitzer Prize! Congratulations. I hadn't heard about it.'

'I'm not surprised with all that's been going on in Malia – and in your own life, Colin. Couldn't you really bring that beautiful wife and that darling child with you?'

'No,' he said simply, 'I couldn't.' And then raising his glass: 'To your Pulitzer!'

She smiled and drank and then frowned. 'I'm sorry that so much you believed in and fought for seems to be collapsing out there in Malia.'

With thumb and forefinger on the stem of his glass he turned it clockwise and counterclockwise, while his brow wrinkled reflectively. 'I wouldn't say that. It's what I felt at first. That everything so many brave, good people had struggled for was being swept away.'

'Was it Pir Dato? We talked about him when I was there quite a few years ago, remember? We both had doubts about him others there didn't seem to share.'

'He's part of it.' He turned the glass one way and then another and finally he said: 'Nothing could be more freely democratic than the way a revolutionary leader like Lee is selected. He starts with no influence over the people at all, with no control over them whatsoever; he is appointed by the people listening to him and believing him; he is confirmed in office by their following him into struggle; he holds his position solely by serving them. It was the same with Lenin and Mao. But their successors – '

'Yes,' she nodded. 'Those successors!'

'Leaders, real leaders like Secretary General Lee are simply the link between what the people are and what it's possible for them, progressively, to become. That's the real change. Not changes in personnel at the top, not the who's in and who's out of politics.'

'But don't the people require the democratic means of electing those successors at the top, of voting for the government they want?'

'Real democracy has to be the empowerment of people at their workplaces – factory, farm, office or shop. When people have a say in the way their workplaces are managed and controlled – which is what they know most about – then they have laid the foundation for a democratic society in which they have a voice in their own destiny. That was beginning in Malia; but it takes time – time and peace from the bloody attacks of vindictive imperialism.'

An ancient waiter came, took their order and then walked slowly away, not too steadily. 'I hope he makes it,' Clare said.

'It's what I like about this place – operating at about a quarter of the pace of life outside. It's ideal for someone who's been driven willy-nilly out of the only place he wants to be and can't really hope to return to and is having some difficulty in adjusting to life in the place where he is.' He looked around him. 'This is a kind of civilised refugee camp.'

'It would do nicely as a quiet resting place for someone always on the go, too. You must put my name down for associate membership.' She reached in her bag and brought out a news clipping from a New York paper and handed it to him.

He read the headline aloud. 'SANITY PREVAILS IN MALIA. Yes, the papers here, too, have been cock-a-hoop over the restoration of "democracy" in Malia. They think it means the country's once more open for Western free enterprise to loot and exploit to their hearts' content.'

'And it doesn't?'

'No.'

'You must tell me about what's actually happening in Malia, Colin. Ever since I knew you were back, I've been looking for your reports on the real situation there. I can't tell you how I've missed *Workers' World*.'

'I haven't written anything which goes very deeply into what's happening in Malia – not under my own by-line. And no paper's going to print anything I won't sign. I don't dare. Not with Leela and little Matt held there practically as hostages.'

'I see.'

'There's plenty of material I can give you – to make what use of it you like. As long as you don't mention me as your source.'

The waiter did arrive with their food which he served with a quivery elegance. Then he poured two glasses of the wine Frere had ordered with Clare's approval.

She looked at him with some concern. 'And how are you making out, Colin?'

'Oh, I get by working freelance. The news agency I was working for when I pretended to be kidnapped all those years ago wouldn't touch me with a bargepole. And none of the newspapers would take me on as a regular correspondent. But I know enough about what's really going on in certain parts of the world to write some marketable stories.'

'If you wanted to sell them to papers in the States, I could probably help.'

'Thanks, Clare. But wouldn't I be remembered as the journalist who wrote such vicious attacks on America's toxic chemical bombing of Malia?'

'Malia's joining the "Free World" has probably wiped all that out.'

Frere gave a rueful shake of his head. 'Yes, I suppose so – wiped out all my journalistic endeavours over the past fifteen years.'

'I didn't mean that. Tell me what really has been happening in Malia.'

'What's been happening in Malia is that a small country which by revolutionary means has liberated itself and begun to establish socialism has found further progress blocked. On its own, in the midst of a hostile world market completely dominated by the imperialist powers, Malia is apparently capitulating to the enemy in exchange for an ending of embargoes and boycotts and political isolation. That stalled revolution in Malia was the gloomy view of the future I brought back with me. But the Britain I'd come back to was in a much worse plight than Malia. Britain had a huge trade deficit with the very world of which it had once been the workshop. It could no longer produce the goods it needed for itself. In Malia there's been a check to progress: in Britain there's no check to decline.'

'And you think the two things are linked?'

'Oh, they're linked. I remember a conversation I had with Secretary General Lee when I'd just arrived at the jungle base camp. He explained to me how in a country like Malia the people are exploited both by an imperialist power which still dominates the economy and by compradors and corrupt officials who rule locally. The working masses can only liberate themselves from that double exploitation by revolutionary means.'

Frere continued: 'Then he went on to explain how, stripped of its colonies, the uncompetitiveness of British industry plus all the economic deformations at home of imperialist domination of overseas trade would have to be paid for – by the British working class, of course. The extra exploitation exported to the colonies would flow back to be added to the normal exploitation workers under capitalism always suffer. They would only be able to liberate themselves from *their* double exploitation by revolutionary means too. There's the connection. It wasn't till I came back to Britain that I realised how far that linked process had gone.'

'A lot of what you have been saying about Britain is true of the United States too,' Clare said.

'It's worse in Britain because imperialistic capitalism began here, partly financed by the slave trade which can only be compared with the Nazi "final solution" as a crime against humanity. And who pays? The British working class whom foreign capitalists are being invited to come and exploit as the cheapest, least protected workers in Europe! So the people of Malia offer to the British working class as an end to its vicious exploitation the Marxist weapon they used to liberate themselves from the same capitalist enemy. There's the link.'

'Socialism.'

'Yes. What Britain desperately needs is the co-operative effort of its entire workforce to rebuild its industry and realise its full productive potential in order to meet the needs of all. What Britain needs is socialism. So you see, the next major battle for socialism which a country like Malia started by liberating itself from imperialism will be fought in the imperialist country itself.'

'And what happens to the individual rights people in a country like Britain still enjoy, for all its difficulties? Remember, Colin, I'm a liberal, not a communist.'

'Individual rights were established by anti-feudal revolutions and they're very important; but individual rights in an exploitative society simply become the privileges of the relatively few at the expense of the relatively many. And in a Britain in decline that transformation of universal rights into individual privileges is speeded up. Socialism changes those individual privileges at the expense of the many back into the collective right of all to share in the material and spiritual goods all have created. The October Revolution was complementary to the French Revolution. The March Revolution in Malia was complementary to the First English Revolution and is a signpost to the Second.'

'After the War we seemed to be living in a revolutionary period,' Clare said reflectively. 'The Soviet Union victorious over Nazi Germany, Socialist China liberating itself from foreign influence, the United States and Britain defeated by the countries they would colonise, but now – well, you could hardly argue that we don't seem to be moving into a counter-revolutionary period now.'

'Human progress is like that – two steps forward and one step back. The change from exploitative society where the law of the jungle rules even if it *is* worked out on the most modern computers to a society in which there is no exploitation of human beings by human beings, that is to say *civilised* society at peace with itself and with the environment, is a tremendous transformation which will take centuries to complete. But the twentieth century has seen tremendous advances as well as considerable retreats. It has seen the beginning of the end of imperialistic capitalism as the poor exploited people of Russia, of China, of Vietnam and, yes, of Malia applied Marxist methods to their problems, liberated themselves from domestic and foreign exploiters and began to build socialism. The workers of Britain owe them much for helping to create the conditions which have put socialist revolution on the agenda here and proved the efficacy of Marxist methods of emancipation.'

He suddenly thought of something. 'Just a few nights ago I was asked to address a radical group about recent events in Malia. When I'd finished, a professor of philosophy in the audience who calls himself a Marxist got up and said that he wasn't surprised by the collapse of socialism in Malia. Socialism was inconceivable without a high level of development of the productive forces and a high standard of culture developed by urban civilisation. Marxism, he told us, was never intended to be the way desperately backward societies could leap into the twentieth century and the consequences of such an attempt he called Stalinism.'

'He must be some kind of a Trotskyist.'

'I restrained myself from hitting him and managed to explain that the desperately backward society of Malia had prepared the way for theoreticians in Britain to stop treating Marxism as a kind of game intellectuals could play and begin to use it, as Marx intended, for expropriating the exploiters of the British working class – if they had the guts!'

Clare laughed.

'I left them copies of the *Essential Sayings* and several of the *Works* of Secretary General Lee.'

After a few moments Clare asked: 'Do you feel great bitterness about what's happened in Malia recently, Colin? Pir Dato's reforms and all that. You and your brother were so caught up in that historic struggle.'

'History is the form in this place or that, now or in the past that the struggle between exploiters and the exploited takes.' He could not but think of those very words on Leela's lips. 'Matt, and I, too, thanks to him, chose to be in the front line of the most crucial form of that struggle in our times. No, we don't feel let down. We were privileged to participate in one of the great victories of our era. We were able to purge ourselves of the guilt we felt at being born in a privileged part of the world, privileged at the expense of the millions upon millions of people who have yet to emancipate themselves from the cruel economic tyranny of imperialistic capitalism. We were never promised – ' his voice caught an instant – 'we were never promised long life or lasting happiness.'

'You feel you've helped put an end to imperialism.'

'As direct colonialism, yes. Now it it takes the form of global capitalism, called "neoliberalism", with the G7 nations headed by the United States ruling through the World Bank and the International Monetary Fund. Governments of the developing countries, corrupted by the bribes of aid funds, are ordered to privatise and deregulate industries and public services so that they can be taken over by multinational companies and run for the benefit of shareholders back in the metropolitan country. The exploitation of cheap unorganised labour and the looting of natural resources goes on unchecked. Any attempts by the developing countries to protect themselves from the flood of tobacco, fast food and ersatz culture are prohibited by the GATT agreement. Those collaborating with this exploitation get rich but the majority of the population suffer the most appalling conditions.'

'As much as they did under direct colonialism?'

'Very nearly. But in a country like Malia the people have won by their collective effort the rights of education, healthcare and full employment. They will not be willing to see such rights sacrificed. And, of course, neoliberal imperialism – which has nothing to do with *your* liberalism, Clare – is much more vulnerable than the old direct rule by military force. At any time a country like Malia can simply declare all debts invalid and take over all the various foreign-owned enterprises to run in the interests of their own people. And there's not a thing the G7 nations could do about it. Perhaps that's what Pir Dato has in mind – once extensive investment and a lot of relief funds have poured into the country.'

'Do you think so?'

'He's kept that possibility open. Perhaps Malia will join with Vietnam and other southeast Asian countries in cancelling all debts and taking over all foreign property for their own national use. Perhaps Cuba, Nicaragua, Guatemala and the countries of the Caribbean will do the same.'

'And Zimbabwe and the other countries of Southern Africa?'

'Why not? The global financial market would be destroyed and the multinationals deprived of all their overseas holdings. What a signal to the working class in the G7 nations that it's time for them to take over and expropriate their capitalists so that their industry, too, can serve their national interests.'

'So that's how Malia's March Revolution will be linked to the Second English Revolution.'

Frere spread his hands as if to say that he believed it anyway.

After a pause Clare asked: 'Do you hear from Leela?'

'Oh yes, she writes often, but I can tell how careful she has to be about what she says. Usually there's a scribbled note from little Matt on the bottom.'

The waiter brought them coffee.

'You know,' she said quite light-heartedly, 'there was once a time when I halfway thought I was in love with you.'

'Yes,' he smiled, 'I think I kind of thought you maybe thought you were. But it's the sort of mishap it wouldn't have been polite to draw attention to.'

'Well, it turned out to be something better. I *like* you, Colin. We haven't seen all that much of each other; but I've always thought of you as a true friend. And there aren't many of those about.'

'I've always thought of you the same way. And I'm rather badly in need of one.'

'Sorry I can't be a comrade.'

'It's a friend I need here now.'

'You know how I know I've got over my, my "mishap" as you call it? I'm not the slightest bit jealous of Leela. To me she's like a beautiful younger sister. And your brother, Matt, whose story first interested me in Malia, has always seemed like my older brother. And little Matt my nephew. You've made me part of your family, Colin. Or else this lone acquisitive female has taken over the lot of you for her own.'

He reached across the table and grasped her hand. 'When you first met me in Malia I thought I was incapable of ever feeling anything deeply for another human being and ought to warn the people I met accordingly. Then life in that base-camp commune where all were such good comrades – all, as it were, marching to the same drumbeat – so softened me up that Leela, when she appeared, went straight to my heart. And now that I'm back here – well, in terms of personal relationships I still feel a bit quiveringly open in a place where one probably can't afford to be vulnerable.'

She laughed. 'That's all right. I'm tough enough to look out for you – until you've grown a new carapace.'

'Thank you, Clare.' He squeezed her hand and released it.

'Well, Colin, I've had a delightful meal in a club I think I'm going to enjoy being an associate member of. But you, you've hardly eaten anything at all. I don't think at this rate you're going to build up the strength to make any more revolutions.'

'For all my socialist pretensions I've exploited *you* outrageously. But what I've been hungry for is just someone who'd listen sympathetically to what I've been working out in my mind since coming back – whether she agreed with all of it or not. In other words, Clare – you.'

'I agree with a lot of it.' She picked up her glass. 'Here's to your revolution.'

'Which one?'

'The Malian one, I think. Your second English Revolution sounds to me a bit like the Second Coming.'

'I have to convince Leela that the next phase of what began in Malia is to take place here. I want her and my son here with me. I must find a way to get them here. Perhaps when Malia and this country have re-established diplomatic relations it will be easier.'

'I hope so, Colin. And I hope a good deal of what you showed me had been achieved in Malia isn't going to be changed for the worse.'

'It won't be,' he said firmly. 'There are the people there and the leadership who will never allow the time to return when selfish greed is paid for by starving babies. There are heroes enough in that land of new skies to put aside their tools and hoes if they have to and take up their guns again.'

He felt better after his talk with Clare. He really believed that he would find the way to become involved in the appropriate form of the struggle between exploited and exploiters here in Britain.

But, oh, that ghost of the scent of champak blossoms that would haunt him forever and, oh, the memory of the form of his dear beloved, ever before him as he must be before her, and, oh, the quick glimpsed sight of her moving gracefully through the cane bowers, ruffled by fragrant breezes, on the banks of the storied Andor. Would he ever hold her and their dear son in his arms again? Ever?

William Ash's last novel

A reading by Doug Nicholls

Heroes in the Evening Mist, written in 1995, can be read perfectly well as a free-standing novel. But it is, in fact, a sequel to an earlier novel, published in 1962, called *Choice of Arms*. Together with that work and with several other novels relating to national liberation struggles and the creation of a new, post-colonial world order, this book marks William Ash as one of the most significant novelists of twentieth-century imperialism. He is one of its most devastating critics and one of its most active opponents. His scope is as wide as the social and economic developments of the unfolding class politics in the latter half of the last century.

As a result of his penetrating insights, Ash's works have been ignored by analysts of 'post-colonial' and progressive literature and the novel form generally. I believe his novels are amongst the most significant of our times and provide some of the deepest insights into the political interplay between class struggles within imperialist countries and the struggles against imperialist domination by nationalist and socialist forces. He is one of the very few British-based novelists who transcends parochial interests and is able to tackle truly international themes and to consider the real meaning of internationalism in a neoliberal world. His regular deliberation in his work upon the contribution that progressive nationalist struggles make to internationalism provides readers with a highly relevant and unique account of the balance of world forces in the post-Second World War period.

Ash has written fourteen novels. These form a body of work that deserves a much wider readership, as they address very forthrightly some of the central ethical and political concerns of our epoch. He speaks directly in novels of the choices for humankind in an authoritative way born out of a lifetime of struggle against fascism, imperialism, de-industrialisation and for union organisation. He does so in a manner unlikely to appeal to the liberal, fragmenting and consumerist affectations of postmodernist fads. He writes novels of explicit social relevance in a plain style that echoes the early English Protestant revolutionaries.

Ash's own personal journey provided him with a unique experience from which to examine the main trends of our times. He was born in

Texas but volunteered to join the Canadian Royal Air Force to fight fascism. He became a Spitfire pilot and was captured by the Germans on several occasions, only to become a notorious escapee from concentration camps who evaded a firing squad thanks to the Red Army. After the War he worked for the BBC and visited India, where his awareness of Marxism grew amidst the colonial arrogance and the domestic destitution. Still working for the BBC on his return to London, Ash became a lifelong trade unionist, an inveterate campaigner against racism and a proponent of a new working-class politics. His novel *But My Fist is Free* is a modern-day equivalent of *The Ragged Trousered Philanthropist,* and far superior to it – giving a unique account of the early struggles to save British manufacturing industry, even before the Thatcherite blitz. His journalism, editorship and stewardship of a new publication, *The Worker,* combined to make a real impact on the thought and struggle of a generation of the most class-conscious workers in Britain in the 1970s and 1980s. His wide international connections and support for national liberation struggles, not to mention his close study of countries seeking a socialist path, imbued his work with a forceful and generous internationalism. Throughout this period, he adapted his core philosophical text to conditions of the new world order: it was originally published as *Marxism and Moral Concepts* in 1964 and, following five editions, is now *Workers' Politics, the Ethics of Socialism.*

In recognition of this exceptional background for a novelist, a contemporary reader approaches *Heroes in the Evening Mist* with huge reverence and some trepidation. It is going to be a read like none other we have recently experienced. Its historical resonance and its moral imperatives are exactly those that culture seeks to deny and deride, yet they are exactly the ones that in our hearts and backs of our minds are vital, and expressive of the future we still demand and create. After three decades of neoliberalism we do not return to a past epoch, but we revisit the enduring perceptions and ethics that have underpinned progressive politics throughout the ages.

Revisiting is a metaphor in Ash's novels. In an earlier novel he returned to the United States, the land of his birth, to reflect on what might have been. In *Heroes in the Evening Mist* he refracts the metaphor of return in a more complicated way. Colin Frere is a journalist visiting Malia, the country where his brother Matt died while fighting against British imperialist forces in the earlier novel *Choice of Arms.* Having adopted Malia as his home, Colin then returns at the end like a visitor to the country of his birth – a Britain transformed by Malia's liberation and changed by his own consciousness of the connection between the struggles in the two countries.

The novel is initially set in 1969 during the bombing of Vietnam and then, in Part Two, in 1977, after its revolution. Colin Frere ostensibly goes to Malia as a foreign correspondent to cover the progress of the country since independence. He comes both as the brother of a liberation fighter and as a professional journalist. The tension between the two functions, echoing the theme of insider and outsider, is a revealing motif throughout the book. Malia and Britain become quite swiftly established as imaginary maps on which to chart not just the progress of former colonies, but the strengths and weaknesses of socialist and capitalist ideas generally. Put another way: the debate between neoliberalism and the alternative to it is profoundly prefigured in this novel.

Frere quickly teams up with American journalist Clare Wallace, herself motivated as a foreign correspondent partly by having experienced various forms of chauvinism. Her rebelliousness on the feminist front compares initially with the self-confessed political quietism of Frere, who has never really 'wanted anything enough to rebel'. Yet, despite this self-perception, he has a semi-cynical, semi-concerned understanding that the system his brother died fighting for has now, in an independent Malia, become betrayed by stooges and compradors. When observing the evidence of street poverty before them, Wallace and Frere are both depressed to witness the difficulties of the country and the role which their homelands continue to play in its oppression, having created a system in which the conquest of cheap labour has cheapened humanity and held back the advance of liberated post-colonial endeavour.

Malia is not a land of milk and honey. It is in turmoil. Socialist revolutionaries are fighting to liberate the country from the puppet capitalists put in place after decolonisation. Frere is captured in a stage-managed kidnap by the People's Liberation Army, something he has arranged in advance. The reader then experiences the rebel camp through Frere's eyes, in what must be a unique fictional depiction in Western literature. The revolutionaries live literally within the soil and caves of the heart of the country and the book affords one of Ash's few inspired descriptions of natural phenomena, as if it is only the presence of the revolutionaries that imbues bleak nature with beauty.

Frere decides to join the hardened revolutionaries. His eyes are opened to the socialism within the commune where people live with primitive, ingenious technology but have a sophisticated, political and philosophical understanding of the world.

Frere's kidnap into this world is not without self-interest. He has uses for the revolution. His skills mean he can provide sympathetic and modern propaganda about the People's Liberation Army via a newspaper known as *Workers' World*, which is distributed widely abroad.

His family ties to the country, professional role and curiosity and partly formed sympathy, put him in the ideal position to be kidnapped and subsequently persuaded by the revolution. This is the perfect literary trope for the philosophical theme underlying many of Ash's novels: that the involuntary social conditions which provide us both with conformity and insight into rebellion, determine and are changed by our elective and inevitable roles. The ancient paradox of destiny and will are depicted in a new way.

Frere comes to believe passionately in the struggle. Having debated the politics of the revolutionary position with some impressive revolutionaries, he finds he is changing: 'I want to live exactly as if I myself were a Malian who'd come inside out of conviction in the justice of the liberation movement.' The play on 'inside out' is significant. The inside is the secret base camp of the guerrillas. But Frere is frequently turned from insider to outsider and vice versa and this is one of the main organisational themes related to his development. The pulse of being inside and outside gives the book its philosophical and organisational rhythm.

The Malian communists, seeing their revolution as the applied internationalism of the world working-class movement, do not doubt Frere's sincerity, but question his ability to change and really be one of them: 'If you live just as we do, won't it, rather, emphasise the fact that you're not a Malian who's taken up our cause in the most natural way. Surely it's better for you and for us to accept your separateness... Practice validates our theory for achieving some goal – for us the liberation of Malia. Your goal is to edit a periodical explaining that revolution to the outside world.'

To this Frere replies: 'You mean that the liberation of Malia can't be a goal for me because I'm not Malian? Neither was my brother.' The response to this is equally significant: 'Your brother came to know Comrade Lee during a war in which they shared the same limited goal – driving the Japanese out of our country. It was on that basis that he was able to rejoin Comrade Lee for a greater goal when Britain subsequently broke its wartime promises to us.' Frere's job is, to be specific, to amplify the message, and not to pretend to be a Malian revolutionary. He should deploy his Western journalistic skills from the position of sympathy to inform workers throughout the world of the national and international significance of this struggle. His contribution is to be the comradely observer, distinguished precisely by his difference. This fictional representation makes its own comment about the nature of internationalism. The naturalness of the position is reflected in Frere's quizzical comment: 'I seem to have been struggling frantically for the last hour or so to achieve what was going to happen anyway.'

His only distraction from his duties is his developing romantic relationship with one of the leading revolutionaries, Leela, whom he eventually marries and with whom he has a son. It is this relationship that provokes his most profound questioning. He can probe the question of foreignness more directly as if in an inverted mirror by asking her: '... what made you cut yourself off from that world out there to fight it from in here?' Leela is ferociously committed: 'Living a meaningful life is simply a question of understanding the particular form of class struggle which characterises one's own time and place and committing oneself to it with all one's heart and all one's mind.' Her deep commitment causes him to reflect: 'Was it the profession he had followed so long, writing about movements and the people caught up in them from the outside, that always made him seem somewhat detached from the passion and devotion and commitment of others? Or was it something in himself, something in himself that would always separate him from – well, from Matt.' This is significant, for it casts doubt upon the meaningfulness and validity of Matt's actions. Is international solidarity taken to such extremes valid and worthwhile?

Moreover, Leela questions the authenticity of Frere's growing affection for her, asking whether it is really a displacement of his romanticised feeling of empathy with exotic people. Frere uses this trepidation on her part in fact as a ploy in seduction, making a virtue out of their differences. Against this interplay of emotional love interest, the question of legitimate conviction and commitment is set. Against it too, is a constant reflection, dramatised by the depiction of several characters of the dialectic between social conditions and moral choice – choice forced by circumstances, but made by independent minds. The relationship with Leela touches more convincingly than any other love affair in Ash's novels, the subtle connections between a personal relationship and wider caring and concern for fellow humanity. Love as the basis for social thought is delicately hinted at. The feeling of unity and intimacy between two individuals is foregrounded symbolically as the basis for improved social organisation. It is a prose equivalent perhaps of the poetry of Paul Eluard.

To come closer to his cause and his love, Frere must accordingly push himself to the point of being involved in killing for the revolution. In order to establish his authenticity and ability to speak convincingly on the revolution to a wider world he must experience and willingly carry out its most necessary and brutal actions. But in the act of shooting, or patrolling with arms, at a moment of danger and exertion, he always feels outside of himself, too reflective for his own good in a way, as if another person is in command of him – most likely his brother. But being commanded by the latter is not exactly being commanded by the revolution of which he is part. He goes much further than John Reed did in revolutionary Russia yet expresses a greater sense of distance. John Reed was a part of the Russian revolution and conveyed it. The dilemma for Frere is more complex.

In his close identity with the struggle, its opposite, a sense of alienation, emerges. His sympathy with an overseas revolution is a source of discomfort. Though welcomed into their trusting hearts by those who fight with him, Frere immediately recoils: '...there is a sense in which I'm pretending to be one of you, trying to convince you and even myself that this is where I belong. There's something individualistically willed and, therefore arbitrary about my being here – so that I feel the need to justify myself and prove my right to be treated like any of you.'

His commitment lacks the organic root of his peers and the imagined passion of his brother before him. But even his brother's most trusted comrades reveal to Colin that they considered him really more a humanist than a Marxist. In speaking of the imperialists Matt Frere fought to expel from Malia, his brother reflects: 'He hated them enough to kill and in killing them he possibly felt that he was killing that in himself which he felt was like them.' In what must rank as a unique insight into a revolutionary movement, the novel records in vivid terms the victory of the People's Liberation Army. This revolution affords Frere with a rare moment of complete fulfilment:

> 'All this time he had been looking for his life's meaning and suddenly, here on this high plateau, he had found it, among people he could never have imagined encountering and with whom he could only exchange facial expressions of joy and friendliness. Found it for himself and found it for Matt, too. They had both been driven by the same sense that they were the unintentional heirs of wealth robbed from people all over the earth and, once that realisation had dawned, it would let them settle nowhere and nowhere be at peace. So much had been taken out: something had to be put back. Something had to be repaid: some lesson had to be learned.'

Yet, of course, Frere's moment of optimum reconciliation and ecstasy is thrown into ironic relief as well as becoming heroic. While Matt and Colin can be read in this section as embodying a positive spirit of international revolution, it is their real position as itinerant mercenaries that determines the conscience-laden constraint of their transcendent, almost religious moment. As always they are outside and in. This curious emotional effect relates directly to the author's personal position over a lifetime of struggle, and the new concept of workers' nationalism he was forging in the post-War, post-colonial period within the heart of imperialist Britain. The recurrence of these related themes is almost psychosomatic but also deeply political. At the beginning of Part Two Frere again reflects:

> 'He could not but think again of that absolute dichotomy between those who lived out their lives somewhere in the land of their birth among the utterly familiar which, like comfortable, perfectly fitting old clothes, become as unremarkable as one's own skin and those who planted themselves exotically among strangers with different customs and never, no matter how long they stayed nor how fluent they became in the tongue, never ceased altogether to be alien.'

The high point at the end of the revolutionary seizure of power in Part One is followed by Part Two, eight years later, a profound contemplation on the politics of maintaining revolutionary power in a largely hostile capitalist world. Initially there are real benefits: the starving children have gone; literacy has spread in inverse proportion to the decline of corruption. But Part Two goes beyond revolutionary optimism to explore the problems that arise in the internal politics and approach of the ruling Communist Party and the difficulty of sustaining a self-reliant socialist economy in an underdeveloped small nation. To my knowledge, no other Western novelist has approached such questions, which were highly relevant to the people of Russia, China, Cuba, Vietnam, South Africa and many other post-colonial countries as well as, by analogy, to the daily struggle for progress in the industrialised capitalist countries.

He also looks at the moral questions surrounding the concept of cultural revolution following a seizure of power. He considers the difficulties that the actual withdrawal of aid by the Soviet Union and China caused to newly liberated countries. He examines how political and personal differences as well as the transfer of leadership power within a communist party have played out in history. The presentation of the dynamics of these issues in literary form is genuinely remarkable. Ash's novel engages with issues that affected a large proportion of the world's population in the twentieth century.

In an irony only Ash could provide, the novel that most sensitively meditates upon the outsider status of imported revolutionaries in struggles overseas acts itself on the Western reader as an outsider. The novel strikes us as being odd. It reminds us in the industrialised nations of the immense transformations that have taken place elsewhere. It conveys a sense of the alien to the reader in a way reminiscent to some extent of Brecht. The value system of the reader, as it seeks to dismiss this material, is thrown into such sharp and new perspective. What interest do we have in a fairly detailed rendition of a colonial revolution? Very little, it makes us uncomfortable.

It becomes increasingly apparent in this book that the fiction of writing about identification with a far-off former colony, and our alienation from it become, through attention to the political questions of power that the new rulers raise, throw up issues that can face any workplace in any advanced industrial nation. The alienation effect is that what seems foreign one minute is on our own doorstep the next. The link is in the realm of ideas. The workers and peasants who eject the imperialists, bring down the puppet government and then prepare to eject a flagging and potentially corrupt communist party, are emblems of the ethics of revolution that lurk within everyone's mind and within every country. Strangely, it is as if the very distance of these concerns from a conventional British novel readership is a point in itself, challenging us either not to care and to be bored, or to become enraptured in the striking relevance of the issues for so many of the world's population.

The future, and the 'other' come to haunt us in this novel. They are the heroes, they are always within the mist, and they are always there. But those heroes are never romanticised. This novel has another unique feature in that it provides an insight into the excesses of cultural revolution and what might be termed ultra-leftism. The liberation of the country makes its people heirs not only to the best of their own cultural heritage, but those of the whole world. A radical rejection of the past and external influences, particularly in the cultural sphere, brings its own problems. As well as these more sophisticated political issues, the country faces, as so many have done, war clouds of intervention, interference and natural disaster. It has to debate in these circumstances the pace and realism of certain socialist aspirations, as all post-revolutionary regimes have done. The debate on these matters in philosophical terms in Part Two is as riveting as was the narrative of the revolution at the end of Part One. It pulses in the way few novels appear to do with the beat of a really lived national history.

The external enemy has been vanquished at the end of Part One and this creates a problem for Frere. 'It's just that when my brother came back to Malia after the War it was to take up arms against imperialism – his own country in fact. To a lesser extent that was true for me, too. That same imperialism still ruled through its puppets and hangers on. But now when the external enemy has been banished and all the problems are purely domestic ones – well, I'm not so sure I'm the person to write about them.'

As is often the case in Ash's work, this uncertainty is followed by a dialectical opposite. Paradoxically, as the editor of a newspaper about the revolution that is read all over the world, outsiders identify Frere as the person 'from whom they've learnt most about' the situation in Malia. His identity with the struggle appears to those outside to be complete.

Yet one more step towards complete unity with the country is possible. Alienated from the problems of sustaining a revolution, Frere is the one character, because he has lived under the forces of a dominant capitalist and consumer-led culture, who can penetrate most quickly the seeds of capitalist restoration and its language and manners, its nuances of regrowth. Ironically, this causes him to recognise the acutest signs of the real decline and betrayal that begin to unfold in the country. Consequently he is able to undertake a dangerous mission to help prevent a corrupt new party leader from completely destroying the gains of the revolution. His ultimate action is to leave Leela and their son in order to save the revolution.

On Frere's mission he is arrested. Again it is opportune and pressing for him to reflect upon his predicament:

> 'He had rejected the society he was born in and had come halfway around the world to dedicate himself to a new one, only to find himself once more in the position of the radical outsider. What he had taken to be his passionate advocacy of socialism might only be his reaction to the society he happened to have grown up in – which just happened to be capitalist! And that forced him to come to terms with the greatest irony of all: that this idiosyncratic, non-conforming individual, destined always to end up in the negative camp of one, should have affected as his life's major dedication socialist collectivism!'

Following imprisonment, Frere is forced to leave Malia and, in another of the many painfully ironic twists, finds his expulsion papers have been signed by his high-ranking wife Leela, who had been pressed to do so by the corrupt regime. His migration home is enforced. But it holds a further transformation of conviction for him. The ecstasy of liberation in Malia filled him obviously with great satisfaction and a sense of troubled belonging. Now he makes a prosaic connection:

> '...stripped of her colonies, the uncompetitiveness of British industry plus all the economic deformations at home of imperialist combination of overseas trade would have to be paid for – by the British working

> class of course. The extra exploitation exported to the colonies would flow back to be added to the normal exploitation workers under capitalism always suffer. They would only be able to liberate themselves from their double exploitation by revolutionary means too. There's the connection. It wasn't till I came back to Britain that I realised how far that linked process had gone.'

He is able in this perception to purge himself of the guilt of being born in a capitalist nation. He longs, unrealistically we sense, to be able to bring Leela and his son to Britain to participate in the revolution in that country. He believes that he will 'find a way to become involved in the appropriate form of the struggle between exploited and exploiters here in Britain.' And the novel ends with a luscious evocation of the Malian 'scent of champak blossoms' and the thought of reunification with his Malian wife – a symbolic expression of the need for the energy of the people of Malia and Britain, former colony and imperialist power, to be united in a new social system. Only on Frere's return can he hope to find a relevant way to continue the one long revolution that connects the disparate circumstances of Malia with every workplace in Britain.